MW00509313

THE ENIGMA DIRECTIVE SERIES

PRIMAL THIRST

J. KENT HOLLOWAY

1

Why do I keep letting Randy talk me into these stupid goose chases? I thought, brushing the sweat from my burning eyes as I hacked through the underbrush with my machete.

The sweltering jungle heat rose from the ground, strangling the air around us as the sun crept slowly below the tree line. The darkness wouldn't cool us off and I knew our hike was about to become infinitely more dangerous in the nightscape of the jungle.

I slammed another mosquito that landed on my bare arm. I'd finally gotten used to the bird-size pests doing fly-by's past my head, gorging on the only fluid still available in my body. Unfortunately, they weren't the only insects that we had to contend with at that moment. A virtual army of red ants marched up my leg from underneath my pants.

"Ow!" I yelled, smacking furiously against my trousers. "For crying out loud!"

Ants. No matter where I went, I seemed to always walk directly into a nest of ginormous ants hungry for a bit of cryptozoologist flesh.

"How much further, Dr. Jackson?" asked Nelson Daniels. "I'm getting eaten alive here."

"Join the club," I said wincing at the name he'd used and dropping a medium size rubber tree with the machete. "And how many times have I told you, Nelson? Call me Jack."

My given name was an abomination—Obadiah Jackson. It's one of a zillion reasons I've never gotten along well with my folks. They are a bit religious, to say the least, and thought giving me a wholesome biblical name sounded like a good idea at the time. The joke, of course, had been on me.

Most of my life, people have just called me Jack.

The title "doctor" was just as bad. My dad was a doctor. So was my mom. Both highly respected in their fields, but a bit on the fringe due to their beliefs. Of course, my chosen avenue of research was an embarrassment to them. Serves them right for naming me Obadiah.

"I'd say we still have another three or four miles to go before we make it back to camp," I continued.

My team and I had been trekking through a putrid swampy parcel of land along the Amazonian border of Brazil for nearly two weeks now and had found absolutely zilch for all our pain. A pin cushion's worth of festering mosquito bites and a couple of debilitating blisters on my feet, but that was it.

"So what do you think the natives have been seeing around here, Doctor, er, Jack?" asked Nelson, who was our current expedition sponsor and a former professor of tribal folklore and anthropology at the University of South Florida. "Do you really think it's the Pombero? A real gnome?"

The thing I've learned to despise the most about going into the field with inexperienced partners was their incessant questions, especially the inane ones. But Nelson was footing the bill for this particular excursion and I had no choice but to put up with the motor-mouth for a little while longer.

"I've really no idea what they're seeing," I said, hoping it would placate him.

"I mean, in the past twenty-three years there have been nearly four hundred accounts of a miniature man-like creature rummaging through these jungles. Extremely hairy. Wearing clothing of some type," Nelson had a real knack for regurgitating things we already knew. "And even more spectacular, he's been known to actually build rather primitive structures and erect a type of tribal totem in the various regions he's been known to go."

I was seriously getting annoyed. We'd discussed this very topic at least ten times since breaking away from the rest of the team the day before. I even knew what he was going to say next.

"Uxmal," I said under my breath.

"Think about the implications," Nelson continued his rambling. "The pyramid Uxmal, the largest of its kind in the west, was said to be built by a similar creature in only one night. Add to that the fact that almost every culture in the world bearing a 'gnome' or 'dwarf' myth depicts them as industrious builders. It's simply amazing!"

Without warning, I stopped, causing the little four-eyed, bald headed chatterbox behind me to slam head first into my back. We'd come to a steep gorge, the result of an Amazonian tributary carving its way through the earth for millions of years. Others, including my fundamentalist parents, would have been a little more conservative on the number of years, but then, they were firm believers in Intelligent Design.

"How are we going to cross that?" Nelson asked, guzzling the remains of our last canteen.

How well can you swim?

I didn't ask the question. I wanted to, but I decided to play nice for now.

"If I remember right, there's a bridge just a few yards south of us," I said, turning to my right and ducking a low hanging vine. Nelson didn't see it in time.

"Aaiiyyy!"

I turned to find the professor on the ground, dangerously near the edge, wrestling furiously with the vine.

"Snake! Get it off me! Get it off me!"

Shaking my head, I reached down and grabbed the feeble piece of vegetation, held it up so the little guy could get a good look at it, and chunked it down the gorge. He took my hand, averting his eyes from me, but didn't say a word. His cheeks turned a hundred shades of red.

Finally, I might have a few minutes of quiet for a change, I thought, as I turned back around and headed towards the bridge.

I use the term "bridge" loosely—about as loose as the few strands of thread the natives called "ropes" held to the two trees on opposite sides of the ravine. In reality, the bridge was little more than one thick rope with two parallel lines about three feet above the first, linked precariously from one side to the next. I was beginning to have second thoughts about crossing. Maybe it would be better to just climb down. It'd certainly be safer. Then again, nothing in the Amazon—especially at night—was exactly safe.

A soft purring erupted from the tree tops several yards to the east of us. *Oh great,* I thought. *Just what we need.*

Nelson heard it too. His head darted around spastically as he tried in vain to pin point the origin of the sound.

"What is that?" he whispered, his knees bending into a crouching position as he rifled through his satchel for a flashlight.

"Leave the light alone," I scolded. "That would be a big mistake. Right now, there's nothing to worry about. Just a little kitty out for its evening stroll. No big deal."

I wished I believed it myself. But jaguars in the night time jungle were nothing to throw a ball of twine at. The fact was, we didn't have much time. I hadn't wanted to admit it to myself, but the cat had probably been tracking us now for several miles. I'd seen the signs, heard the clues, and had chosen to ignore them for the sake of optimism. Guess, that would teach me to be a "glass half full" kind of guy when traipsing through an uncharted rain forest.

"Now, Nelson, I need you to do something for me. Well, actually two somethings."

"What's that?" he asked, wiping condensation away from his glasses with his shirt.

I stilled myself. I had to remain cool and collected. I had to say my next few sentences with the utmost care. The last thing either of us needed was for the professor to become unglued. Taking a breath, I told him what I needed.

"Number one, until I tell you otherwise, keep your mouth shut."

His eyes went wide, mouth opening to protest until I clamped my calloused hand over it. For emphasis, I placed an index finger up to my lips. The meaning was crystal: "Shush."

He relaxed a bit, so I removed my hand.

"Now," I continued, "the second thing I need you to do...very very quietly, mind you, is to climb out onto that rope bridge there and ease yourself across."

Nelson stared at the bridge for several seconds and turned back to me shaking his head emphatically.

"Nelson," I whispered. My voice was beginning to strain from, I'll admit it, panic. "Would you rather be tonight's version of 'Meow Mix'?"

He looked back towards the sound of the purring jaguar and back at the bridge. Like a trooper, the little weasel scampered up onto it with no further protest. While Nelson inched his way to the other side, I peered warily into the jungle darkness, scanning for any signs of movement. So far, the cat hadn't seemed to move at all. Its purring continued rhythmically in the trees above at approximately the same distance it had first sounded.

I unsnapped my holster, fastened by a nylon strap around my shoulders. Its weight had always given me a sense of security at times like these. Drawing my .40 caliber Glock, I slowly pulled the slide back to chamber a round.

There's nothing wrong with being prepared, I thought to myself.

I peered back over my shoulder at Nelson. *Sheesh! Could this guy be any slower?* "Hurry up!" I whispered harshly across the gorge.

Nelson hurried his pace; pushing his legs, hands, and ropes to their limit as he shimmied across the bridge.

Snap. Snap.

Two sounds, even more paralyzing than that of a purring jaguar, shattered the stillness of the night.

"Oh crap," I said out loud, just as the rope bridge gave way with Nelson still clinging to a frayed end. I couldn't help but feel a bit guilty for the little guy's present situation. In hindsight, maybe he should have kept his original pace.

"Help!" Nelson screamed out into the night, holding desperately to the thin rope on the other side of the ravine. "Help me!" I guess he'd forgotten there was a rather large, and presumably hungry cat skulking around nearby, but then, he was safe and sound on the other side.

To make matters worse for me, the purring sounds had stopped.

Things just keep getting better and better, I thought. But maybe his screams helped scare it away. Yeah, right. And I may already be the million-dollar winner of Ed McMahon's sweepstakes.

Scanning the jungle one more time, I turned my attention to Nelson, his short, pudgy legs flailing widely roughly thirty-three feet in the air. I had no idea how I was going to get across to help him before his grip gave out. It was times like this that I wished I'd learned to use a bull whip like that other globetrotting adventurer I'd heard of.

"All right, Nelson," I said. "Don't worry. I'll figure something out." I refused to tell him to "hold on." Redundancy always did irritate me.

Getting down on my stomach, I peered one more time over the edge of the ravine. It was deep. Too deep to climb down and back up before the professor lost his grip. I had a rope in my backpack, but without a way to secure it on the other side, it was pretty useless. I could have thrown him the rope, and let him swing back over but there was no way to be certain he wouldn't let go mid-swing and crash to stream below. Plus, we'd be back in the same position we were in before the mess started. One step forward, two steps back. Just another way of saying "redundancy."

The radio on my belt crackled to life, causing me to jerk.

"Jack. Jack. Can you copy?"

My heart raced at the sound, a glimmer of hope welled from deep inside my chest. It was Randall Cunningham, my best friend and current Tech manager of my expedition team. Nelson and I had left Randy and the others at base camp yesterday. If I was getting a radio signal in this dense jungle, then camp couldn't be as far off as I'd first supposed.

"Randy!" I whispered into the mike. "Randy, get over here…now."

"Er…where exactly is 'here?'" his electronically hollow voice asked over the radio.

Right. Where was here anyway? I mean I had a pretty good idea of our position, but how was I supposed to describe it effectively enough for them to locate us and, in effect, save poor Nelson? Then, I got an idea.

"Randy, listen to me. We're in a hurry here," I said in a hushed, but adamant tone. The purring had returned, only it was quite a bit closer now. "I don't have time to explain. But I've just activated Tag 23. Use it to track us."

I flipped the switch on the small tracking device used to tag various animals we encounter on our travels. For the life of me, I couldn't figure out why I hadn't thought of it sooner.

"And Randall," I used his formal name to let him know just

how serious I was, "get here quick, but quiet...if you know what I mean."

"Roger."

I belted the radio and looked back at Nelson, still hanging helplessly on the rope.

"Jack, I'm slipping."

"Well don't," I said with a reassuring grin and looking down into the dark gorge once more. "You don't know what's been in that water."

I'd hoped my joke would ease his mind. It didn't.

"Are you serious? I'm hanging on for dear life and you're making jokes?"

"Only bad ones," I said, whirling around as the sound of purring changed abruptly to a low growl. I extended my gun, aiming into the gloom of the jungle.

This is definitely not good.

A crashing of limbs and debris on the other side of the ravine caught my already frayed attention.

"Jack?" someone yelled from the darkness.

For crying out loud! What part of 'quiet' did these people not understand?

"Jack? Where are you?" A female voice. Vera Pietrova. Definitely easy on the eyes, she was our team medical officer. We'd met in St. Petersburg. Russia twelve years before and had been close friends ever since. At least I had always considered her a friend until she started shouting my name from the mountain tops loud enough to bring every big cat in the vicinity stalking up my backside.

"Shhhhh!" I waved to their shadowy forms as they approached the steep gorge. "Be quiet."

A rustle of padded feet tread through the soft turf of the rain forest about fifty feet away. At least the growling had stopped. Of course, anyone who'd ever been hunted by a three-hundred-pound cat knows that that isn't a good thing.

My team finally appeared through the vegetation on the other side, carrying lanterns and flashlights to blind even Ray Charles.

"Help Nelson," I said as I pointed at his dangling form, legs still kicking frantically against the embankment.

They pulled him up without incident and then turned their attention to me. Waves of ice tiptoed up my spine as I edged to the precipice and threw my rope across. Another set of paw sounds crept through the underbrush to my right. I was being hunted by two of them.

Randy and Vera set to work tying my rope to a large rubber tree as I finished the super, industrial strength "Obadiah Jackson" knot I developed back when I was a twelve years old Eagle Scout. It was a knot to beat all knots and could easily be released by a simple flick of the wrist. You never know when retrieving one's rope is a matter of life and death.

"All right! Rope's tied," Randy said in hushed tones from across the gorge. Nelson must have filled them in on what was currently stalking me and now they were finally taking my insistence on silence seriously.

Holstering my gun, I grabbed the rope and tested the tension of the line. It seemed secure, but I'd learned a long time ago that very little ever measures up...especially something like security. I wasn't exactly happy about what I was about to do, but it had to be done. Grabbing the rope with both hands, I hauled my legs up and began inch-worming my way across—upside down. Just before my head crossed the line of the embankment, Garfield decided to make me his next lasagna dinner.

The cat plunged down from a nearby tree, hurtling through the air directly at my hovering form. Thankfully, I hadn't moved out past the embankment yet. With a thud, I dropped to the earth, its claws shredding through my bowling shirt, leaving thick red welts bubbling up across my chest. The second jaguar jumped into the clearing and pounced on my leg.

Suppressing an urge to scream, my feet wailed against the big cat, pounding against its snout with a flurry of sturdy kicks. I struggled to retrieve my gun from its holster once again, but it was swiftly batted from my grip by a thick paw as soon as I pulled it out. I watched helplessly as the weapon plummeted into the ravine below.

A great explosion rang out through the night air. Screeching birds ejected from their perches into the sky in a mass exodus. Nearby colonies of monkeys howled at the sudden sound. And the two jaguars jerked away and ran swiftly into the darkened jungle, the hairs on their backs standing up on end.

Sheesh. Why the heck didn't I think of that earlier? Next time you're attacked by large hungry cats, shoot your stupid gun!

I lay on the cool, wet earth for several seconds catching my breath and patting my body up and down to make sure all necessary limbs, organs, and other vital parts were still intact.

"Well, don't just lay there gawking at the stars all night," cried Randy from across the gorge, resting his trusty Remington .30-06 across his shoulder. He was completely unconcerned with my condition, the jerk. "Get over here. We've got some big news for you."

2

Randy didn't have to tell me twice to get a move on. I knew the two famished felines hadn't gone far. They were probably already stalking their way back to me even as I stood there. I inched my way over the newly constructed rope bridge and dusted myself off.

"Jack, we need to get back to camp," Randy said. The fuzzy soul patch under his bottom lip twitched excitedly. "Something big..."

I held up a hand, silencing my over-zealous friend. To emphasize my need for quiet, I glared at him, raised one eyebrow, and sat down on a nearby stump. I needed to unwind. I needed a bit of a breather. I needed to throw up. My legs were still throbbing from the claws of the big cat that had mistaken it for a ball of yarn.

Vera, seeing the scratches, let out a sigh. "At least they're not too deep," she said, pulling a med-kit from her backpack and setting to work on the wounds. "And I don't see any bite marks. Looks like you'll live."

She was extraordinarily gifted with soft healing hands and a topnotch bedside manner. Her ethereal light blue eyes revealed a blend of deep sensitivity mixed with a strong, analytical mind. Her high cheekbones and full, pouty lips betrayed her Slavic roots. And her silky fine chestnut hair was cropped short revealing a long, sensuous neckline. In other words, she was the kind of doctor just about every guy on the planet had fantasized about.

Finished with the patch-up work, she bent down on lean, muscular legs and smiled at me.

"You okay?" she asked.

"Like you said, I'll live. How's the chatterbox?"

"About as good as can be expected, I suppose," she winked and finished wrapping my injuries before turning her attention to Nelson.

Randy fidgeted as I sat back, crossed my legs, and looked up into the thick foliage of the jungle above me. I gulped in a huge breath and retrieved a rather fat cigar from the side pocket on my cargo pants. Biting the end off, I flicked my Zippo lighter to life and lit the stogy in one fluid motion.

Because my job is so dangerous, I decided years ago that if anything was going to kill me, it wouldn't be the hazards of the job. I was determined to die a very slow, quiet and dignified death. No. The day I kick the bucket would be from smoking, not from being mauled by a pack of ferocious aquatic ferret-creatures from Zimbabwe. This is why I only smoked after any near-death experience such as the one I'd most recently had. I was in no hurry, after all.

After several minutes of relaxing with my stogy, I nodded my head at Randy and looked back up at the sky. He needed no more encouragement.

"We have a visitor in camp," he said, his shaggy mane of dark brown hair hung down low, partially hiding his wide brown eyes. I could swear he was salivating as he rambled on. "A very important visitor actually and he's come specifically to see you."

I looked around for Nelson, who was now all mended up by

Vera and nestled down on the ground, rocking back and forth with a blanket draped over his shoulders. He didn't look good, but then I couldn't really blame him. For such a bookworm, he'd handled himself better than I would have imagined. Despite his annoying habit of flapping his gums constantly, the little guy had started to wear on me. I actually kind of like him.

"Are you listening?" Vera asked, sliding a canteen in my hand and urging me to drink. Though she'd held it together while nursing Nelson and me back to health, Vera's own excitement was about to go critical mass. "He's a United States senator...from Texas. He wants to hire us for something amazing."

"Where's Arnold?" I asked, ignoring the enthusiasm my friends were currently enjoying. "I was hoping Arnold would be here."

Randy and Vera glanced at each other, irritation etched on both their faces. This, of course, is exactly the reaction I was trying to elicit. I'd always been somewhat of an instigator and enjoyed riling my friends up for no other reason than the entertainment of it.

"Arnold's fine. He's watching the senator," snapped Randy.

"Have you fed him lately?"

"The senator?"

"No, not the senator. Arnold," I said. "He's not been eating well lately."

"Arnold's fine, Jack," Vera said, a half-smile forming on her face. Smart girl, that Vera. She was catching on.

"Well, what about Witz? He hasn't bailed on us has he?" I asked. "That jerk owes me a lot of money."

I was only half joking now. Anthony Kowskowitz was a two bit mercenary and occasional partner who was absolutely horrendous at poker. We'd hooked up on the expedition when I learned of a possible drug cartel problem in the area and he'd lost his shirt in what I thought was a low stakes game two nights before. I definitely didn't want him skinning out before he paid me what he owed.

"Jack, will you give it a rest for a few minutes? We have more pressing matters to discuss," Randy growled.

I looked up at Randy from my stump and grinned, tossing the stub of the cigar on the ground and grinding it out with my foot.

"All right, all right," I said, standing up and tossing my backpack over my shoulder. "Let's go see this senator of yours and find out what all the fuss is about. Besides, it's time to feed my dog."

AS WE ENTERED THE CAMP, I instantly regretted it. Sitting in one of our folding chairs was a monster of a man with a round paunch, sucking on one of my expensive Cubans. Arnold, my ever so loyal Jack Russell terrier, was lounging quietly in his lap. The big man, who I presumed to be the senator, was dressed in khaki shorts, a flower print shirt, and a large straw cowboy hat that didn't quite fit his head. A thick, bushy mustache curled slightly up around his bulbous nose on which small wire rimmed glasses rested. In many ways, the man reminded me of Teddy Roosevelt.

The sight of four black-clad men standing guard at the four points of the camp with rather formidable looking bull-pup style machine guns draped over their arms caused me a little discomfort. When I'm surrounded by gun toting soldiers, it usually means trouble. For some reason, I didn't think today would be any different.

Of course, there was no sign at all of Witz. His tent was gone; as was the gear he'd brought with him.

"Ah, crap. I knew it," I cursed, stomping a foot down before striding into the camp. "Wait until I get my hands on that greedy little weasel."

One of the men, the soldier closest to our entry point, leveled the barrel of a super slick Belgian-made assault rifle, a P-90, directly at my head. I'd rarely seen the real thing outside of Stargate episodes. Under other circumstances, I would have loved to get a better look at the magnificent weapon. At that point, however, all I wanted to do was get away from it. Having an ultra-futuristic gun pointed at you is something that no one enjoys. And no matter what the good guys do in the movies, in reality, you never exactly know how to handle it.

"Whoa, whoa!" I said, holding up my hands. "Let's not get carried away now, okay?"

"Ah, Dr. Jackson," the robust man in my chair said, craning his double chins around to look at me. He shooed Arnold away and lumbered cautiously up from the nylon chair. He stretched out his hand for a shake as he sauntered towards me in a way that can only be described as very "Texan." He glared at the soldier. "Put that thing away, boy. There's no need for that."

The soldier quickly lowered his weapon and resumed his sentry around the camp.

"I'm glad your friends found you safe and sound," he said, looking back to me with a wide smile. "Now, we need to get down to business."

"I'm sorry," I said, taking his hand and reciprocating the shake. His grip was like a steel trap. "Do I know you?"

"Oh, yes, yes…I'm truly sorry. I'd just assumed your people had already explained to you why I was here."

I looked over at Randy, who looked sheepishly down at the ground as he kicked a small pebble into the nearby campfire. He'd refused to give me even the slightest hint of what the "big news" was during the short trek back to camp. He hadn't wanted to spoil the surprise, he'd said.

"It must have slipped their mind," I said, giving both Randy and Vera the evil eye. Nelson scurried into his tent without a word. I figured his thirst for adventure had run its course.

"Well, we really have very little time. My daughter is in great danger and I need your help."

"You still haven't told me who you are."

"Oh, forgive me. I'm just rather preoccupied at the moment," he said, dabbing the sweat away from his forehead with a handkerchief. "My name is Stromwell. John Chesterton Stromwell. I am actually a good friend your dad's. He's the one who suggested I come see you about Nikki."

A friend of my dad's? I wasn't sure Stromwell realized it, but throwing my dad's name into the conversation wasn't the quickest way to pique my interest. Still, Randy was excited about the whole prospect and he wasn't someone prone to exaggerated enthusiasm. I decided to hear him out.

"Nikki?" I asked, getting back to the subject. I motioned the senator to take his seat as Randy, Vera, and I plopped down Indian style on the ground. The soldiers continued staring stoically into the jungle.

"Yes, that's right. She's my daughter."

"Well, I'm not sure what your daughter has do with me."

"She's in trouble," the senator said, edging himself forward on his rickety chair. "I tried to stop her. I did everything I could, but she just wouldn't listen to reason. No reasonable, college educated young lady has any business traipsing off to Malaysia. But no one could convince her of that. 'It is God's work,' she would say. There simply was no reasoning with her."

The senator's ramblings were causing my head to spin. I found it hard to get my bearings around him. Although his dialect and demeanor were quite eloquent, his delivery could definitely use some work.

"Okay, senator. You need to start from the beginning." Arnold skipped up to my side and nuzzled his nose against my leg, settling down on the ground beside me. His hind quarters jerked spastically as I scratched his underside absently with my fingernails. Reaching in my backpack, I pulled out a raw hide bone, which kept him busy gnawing for several minutes.

Stromwell opened my humidor on the table near his chair,

grabbed another cigar without asking, bit the end off, and started explaining his dilemma in slow, deliberate sentences.

Doesn't he know how expensive those things are?

"I'm sorry. I tend to get carried away when I talk about this. So many people simply don't believe me," he said, blowing a stream of smoke through the corners of his mouth. "But I believe my Nikki is in serious trouble. You see, a year and a half ago, my daughter signed up to be a missionary in Malaysia. Her mother and I tried to talk her out of it, but she just wouldn't listen.

"Some friends of hers had convinced her to start going to a little Baptist church in our home town. We didn't think it was that big of deal at the time, but then she came home spouting all this nonsense about being 'called' to the mission field..."

"Senator, forgive me. I get the point," I said. Have I mentioned how much redundancy annoys me? "I understand that you and your wife didn't particularly care for your daughter's vocational choice. But I'm still waiting to hear what all this has to do with me."

Stromwell glared at me for several seconds. He was clearly not used to being interrupted.

"You're right, of course," he finally said. "Anyway, she's been in a tiny village about ninety-six miles south of the capital city of Kuala Lumpur. The village is extremely isolated by jungle and there is virtually no law enforcement in the area at all.

Three weeks ago, Nikki emailed me a very strange message. She talked about how the villagers were being terrified by some superstitious nonsense. She was concerned because at least three people had died already from whatever was happening there."

I perked up. I had a feeling I knew where Stromwell was heading and I practically salivated at the thought. Malaysia is notorious for their superstitious myths and legends, but rarely do people die as a result of them. I knew several of the legends by heart and the possibilities of any one of them being true would shatter the scientific community's concepts of zoology, biology, and even evolutionary theory itself.

"Tell me about the superstition," I probed. Randy continued fidgeting. He'd already heard the story and knew exactly what was coming. He was acting like a kid at Christmas.

My friend was a lot of things. He was a wizard at technology, a comic book collector, a video game junkie, and a number of other things one usually does in the basement of their parent's house. But he was also level headed and not one to get easily excited. Whatever was going on, I knew it would be good.

"Well, I'm not saying any of its true, mind you," he said, taking another draw on the cigar. "It's just what the locals are saying."

"I understand. Now, please, tell me what they say is going on over there."

"The locals got a name for it...they call it the jingo...jingle... jin...well, in my area of the country they'd call it a Chupacabra. At least that's what it sounds like to me."

"The jenglot? They're talking about the jenglot?"

"Yeah, that's it. The jenglot. They say it's some kind of vampire doll like thing. Preys on people in their sleep or some such."

"The jenglot?" came the rasping voice of Nelson from inside his tent. He unzipped it and poked his head out for a better vantage point. "Are you serious? Jenglot? Actually, they're nothing like chupacabra...not at all." It appeared that his taste for adventure had just been reborn.

The jenglot. I can understand the professor's excitement. I've tracked them before. About five years before, Randy, my college buddy Stephen, and I traveled to Borneo looking for the enigmatic creatures. They are said to be tiny, only about six or seven inches in height with long, straw-like hair. Even weirder, they're said to look kind of like voodoo dolls, but with flat, white faces and long, needle-like teeth. And yes, they were known to feast on the blood of humans, but no one ever knew how. According to legend, there were never any puncture wounds or injuries to any of their victims. Just severe blood loss.

We'd gotten close in Borneo. Or at least, I think we had. I even caught of glimpse of one of them darting away into some underbrush. And it was more like one and a half to two feet tall... not inches.

If this guy's daughter was being plagued by an actual, honest to goodness jenglot infestation...well, the implications were enormous. Oh, and of course, she was in quite a bit of danger too. But in all honesty, her safety was really the last thing on my mind at that moment. I've never been real big on playing the shining knight to anyone's distressed damsel. Call me calloused, but it's true.

"Dr. Jackson? Are you okay?" Stromwell asked, staring at me with some concern in his eyes. "You look a bit distracted."

"Oh, yeah. Sorry about that," I said, standing up and pacing the camp to think. "And what exactly are you hoping we can do for you, Senator?"

"Well, I guess I'm asking you to go over there and bring my daughter home," he said as matter a fact as he could muster. "But you're not going to be able to. She won't leave. There'll be no convincing her."

I stopped mid-stride and looked at Randy and Vera's enthusiastic faces. I then turned to Stromwell, waiting for him to continue.

"I want you to get to the bottom of all this craziness and put a stop to it if you can. But above all, I want you to protect my little girl."

"I'm not a body-guard, Senator," I said, walking over to a cooler in mid-camp and made a bologna sandwich. It had just occurred to me that I hadn't eaten in about thirty-six hours and I was famished. I stuffed the sandwich into mouth and took a bite.

"I'm aware of that, son," he said. "But I'm willing to pay you a quarter of a million to try."

I nearly choked on bologna. Pieces flew out of my mouth as I spat to clear my air way.

"Two hundred and fifty thousand? Dollars?"

"That's right. And all you've got to do for it is go to Pingitti village in Malaysia and protect my daughter from whatever is going on there."

I mouthed "two hundred and fifty thousand" to Randy, who nodded his head and jumped quietly up and down from behind the senator. There was just one problem and it went back to the fact that I wasn't a body guard. After all, I could hardly guard my own body, much less someone else's. I had to be honest and tell the guy the truth.

"And if you're worried about not being able to protect her," he said, anticipating my next sentence. "Don't worry at all. I'm sending Landers over there with you."

Landers? I looked around and saw the same soldier who'd pointed the Stargate gun at me earlier. He stopped just short of the senator, came to attention, and saluted us with expert precision.

Just one look at the guy and I already found myself disliking him. He stood at just over six-foot-tall with thick, well-toned pecks jutting out from his overly tight black T-shirt. His short, brown hair was gelled into spikes along his head that just screamed hedgehog. Perfectly white teeth gleamed underneath thin lips pulled back in a casual, good natured smile.

"Lance Corporal David S. Landers, sir," the soldier said to me in perfect military fashion. "United States Marine Corp."

Swell.

As much as the money he offered would help further expeditions, I knew bringing the Boy Scout with us would be a huge mistake. Military types and I don't always get along. I'm not sure why, but it's a fact of life. Maybe because they're just too stuffy. Too disciplined. Too clean and organized. Who knows?

But what I did know was that I did not like the thought of Captain America going with us on even a trip to Disney World. I mean the guy pointed a gun at me for crying out loud.

I lifted my index finger at Stromwell. "Just a second. My partners and I need to confer for a bit," I said as we gathered into a loose huddle on the other side of the camp. It took us a mere thirty-seven seconds to come to our conclusion after I'd scarfed down one more sandwich.

"All right, Senator," I said. "Make it three hundred thousand and you've got yourself a deal."

Randy nudged my arm. I'd forgotten one little detail.

"Oh yeah, and Landers there doesn't get a cut," I said with a great big grin growing across my face as I nodded at our newest team member. The corporal didn't budge as he stared at me with indifference. *What a jerk, I thought. I can't even goad him. He's just not going to be any fun at all...I can already tell.*

"I want to go too," Nelson said, poking his head once more out his tent.

"Go back to bed, Professor."

"But..."

"Now," I said a little harsher than I should have. Then, looking at the quiet form of our newest benefactor...Stromwell, "Do we have a deal?"

"We have a deal," the senator said, standing up and walking to the durable Land Rover parked on the northeast corner of camp. "Your plane leaves in twelve hours at a small air strip just ten miles north of us. Don't be late."

3

We said goodbye to Nelson and left Brazil the day after our meeting with Stromwell. Taking his private jet, we flew directly to Hong Kong with only one stop for refueling. Once there, we hooked up with Marc Leeds, an anthropologist and expert on Asian folklore.

I'd worked with Marc a few times before, but we'd never been what you'd call close. He was a bookworm of a guy, rail thin, narrow face with a very weak chin and large, black glasses hanging over a hook nose. But he was quiet and knew more about the Malaysian culture than anyone around. I had no worries as far as he was concerned, if we could learn to deal with his annoying habit of employing a thesaurus in every sentence he spoke.

His arrival brought our number to five, including the rather dull Lance Corporal that Stromwell insisted we bring.

After plotting out a tentative plan of action, we gathered the necessary gear for the expedition and chartered the only plane and pilot willing to take us to a rarely used landing strip just south of Malaysia's capital city. The local customs agents in Kuala Lumpur were nosey and always itching to make a quick buck, so flying in under the radar was essential to our mission. We just didn't have time for the games we'd have to play if we traveled through normal channels.

"Sturges wasn't very happy," I said to Randy as I cradled my satellite phone in its pouch and sank back in the duct-taped passenger seat of the old C-54 transport plane we'd chartered. Arnold jumped into my lap, attacking my ear with his tongue.

"So what?" asked Randy, sipping a cap of whiskey from his flask. He was never the greatest flier, but when traveling in giant rust-encrusted death traps with wings, he became a complete wreck. Alcohol was his only comfort during such times. "Who cares what that tightwad says?"

"That 'tightwad' just happens to be the Academic Dean and my boss."

Randy coughed out a laugh, nearly spitting out his mouthful of Jack Daniels. "Come on, Jack, your job is a joke. You teach Biology at an insignificant little community college. It's like teaching the thirteenth grade."

"It's a great job. I like my job," I said curtly, miffed that we were having this discussion again. "And I'd appreciate it if you stopped criticizing what I do and lend a sympathetic ear once in a while. Like I said, Sturges is not happy with me extending my leave of absence."

Arnold whined as he hopped down from the seat and trotted to the back of the plane for peace and quiet. It always irritated him when we talked about work.

Randy rolled his eyes. He had never understood my decision to keep my teaching position at Saddleton Community College over the infinitely more prestigious Ivy League schools that had been wooing me for a teaching gig. But then, he had never been ridiculed mercilessly by those very same schools for years as I had during my early days in the field. It wasn't until my discovery ten years before of mummified remains of a creature that could only be described as an honest to goodness fire-breathing dragon in a isolated region of the Andes.

Such carcasses were commonplace in dragon warped cultures like China, where every charlatan with a few bucks and a little ingenuity could whip themselves up a convincing facsimile of the scaled fire breathers. But they had all been proven fake.

My discovery, however, was not. Needless to say, it helped bolster my credibility and soon, colleges and universities from Harvard to Berkley were beating on my door with offers that would make any academic's head spin.

But pride has a way of rooting a man to what's really important. I was truly satisfied with the life of a community college teacher…just as long as they allowed me the freedom to take the occasional expedition when I needed to. The way Sturges had spoken to me, I was beginning to think I'd pressed my luck one too many times.

"All right. I'm sorry," Randy said. "It sucks and everything that your boss yelled at you." He tossed a tissue into my lap and smiled with a wink.

The jerk. I couldn't help but return his smile.

Randy had never been what you might call sympathetic to anyone. Well, with the exception of Randy. He was spectacular at sympathizing with himself. But his own head was just too big to concern himself with other's problems.

We'd been friends since high school. I'd been the average underachieving football lineman barely scraping by with my grades. He'd played the part of nerdy, if not overly confident, hacker in need of a little muscle. We'd fit well together and helped each other out more times than I can remember. Even more so after I recruited him for my expeditions.

Still smiling at my friend, I leaned back in the seat, closed my eyes, and willed myself to get a few winks before we arrived at our destination. But I guess sleep just wasn't in the cards for me.

Landers, in full military fatigues, shuffled forward from the cockpit of the plane and sat down next to Randy.

"The pilot says we're about a half hour out. ETA is 0630," he said looking at me. "I suggest we gear up. We have no SITREP for the area down there and we need to be ready for anything."

I stared at GI Joe for several seconds without blinking and then looked at the bemused face of Randy, leaning back in his seat with his hands behind his head. He was loving this. He knew how much I despised army talk and his amusement over the corporal's gung-ho demeanor was plastered all over his smug expression.

"SITREP?" I asked, turning back to the soldier.

"Yes sir," Landers nodded. "Situation Report, sir."

"I know what the word means. I just can't believe you actually used it."

Vera, who had been sitting quietly behind us, leaned forward—her grin taking up the entire space between the seats. Darn her. She was enjoying it too. Marc sat next to Vera, oblivious, his nose buried deep in some book about aboriginal mating customs or something along those lines.

All right, I thought. Now is as good a time as ever to set this guy straight about some things.

"Look, er...what was your name again?"

"Lance Corporal David S. Landers."

"No, no, no," I said, shaking my head. "Your real name...the name your friends call you."

"My first name is David," he said, a bit of a frown coloring his face. "Most people just call me Scott though."

"Okay Scott, listen. You and I need to talk about some things."

The lance corporal stared silently at me, waiting for me to continue. Don't speak until spoken to, I guessed. Randy took another pull from his flask and then set to work examining his nails in feigned disinterest.

"We're all friends here. I don't see any sirs and I sure as heck don't see any ma'ams," I paused, glancing around at Vera with a wry grin. "The point is that we're all partners here. This isn't a military operation. You're the only one here even remotely military caliber. In fact, the whole military thing just makes me a bit..."

I struggled to come up with just the right word. I wanted to make my point, but I didn't want to offend either. From the looks of things, Scott was a seasoned vet, more than capable of taking care of himself. But this trip could get real complicated and I wanted to keep the peace between the entire team for as long as I could. Besides, I knew he was only acting the way he'd been trained.

"It just makes me a bit creeped out." *Great*, I thought. *I have such a way with words. I knew I should have continued memorizing that thesaurus when my mom urged me to.*

Landers only stared in silence.

"I mean, not 'creeped out', really...just...look, just go casual for the rest of the trip, okay?" I screwed on the sincerest smile I could at him.

Landers smiled back.

"No problem, sir...I mean, no problem, Jack. I completely understand. We'll keep this casual."

My smile broadened. *Good, maybe this trip wasn't going to be as bad as I first thought.*

A loud pop from outside the plane ripped us from our conversation as five pairs of eyes flew immediately to the tiny windows that were currently clouded with smoke. The plane lurched forward, then suddenly dropped altitude before the pilot regained control of the craft. A gust of wind blew the smoke back, revealing the burning wreckage of what was once our left wing.

"Oh, this is so not good," whispered Randy who downed the remainder of his flask.

The pilot threw open the cockpit's curtain and peered back at us. His appearance was not encouraging to say the least.

"We've been hit. It looked like a STA missile as it approached," he said. "I've already sent out an S.O.S., but our antenna was damaged by the blast. I'm not sure it got through. That's the good news."

We glared at him, no one willing to ask for the bad. We didn't have to.

"The bad news, ladies and gentlemen, is that we are most definitely going down."

On cue, the plane pitched in a downward arc, propelling us backwards into our seats. I struggled frantically to find the seat belt. My heart crashed into my stomach with the pilot's next report.

"Er, you guys might want to hold onto something," he said, absently flicking a row of switches on the panel in front of him. "I removed the safety harnesses last summer when I re-wired the plane. Long story. Don't ask. Needless to say, grab hold of anything you can find that's bolted down and pray to high heaven."

The jungle canopy below barreled towards us. I scanned the cabin for anything that might offer protection from being smushed like a bug from a crash landing, but nothing came to mind.

I glanced over at Randy, his eyes clinched tight, hands gripping the armrest so tight I could swear it crushed a little.

"This is why I hate flying," he growled, pulling his hands away from the armrest to remove his belt from around his waist. He opened his eyes only slightly and tied the belt furiously to the seat. "Fly the friendly skies...my right ear."

Not a bad idea, I thought, ignoring my friend's panicked diatribe.

I had only freed my own belt from the first loop before reeling forward as the aircraft's fuselage scraped against the spiny trees nestled against the jungle floor.

Ah, man, I thought, agreeing with Randy's earlier outburst. *This is so not going to be good.*

A crunch of metal and breaking glass filled my ears as we plowed down through the mass of trees and vines. Vera lunged forward, striking the back of my chair and would have flipped end over end through the cabin if I hadn't caught hold of her wrist and hauled her into my arms.

Then, chaos. Thankfully, the plane struck the ground on a muddy slope and skidded down a steep embankment. Crashing through the foliage, we careened out of control for more than three hundred yards before splashing into a bog at the base of the hill.

None of us moved. Not a word was spoken as we waited for the inevitable...a fiery end to an otherwise unremarkable day. It would have been par the course. But the fireball we all had expected never came. One by one, the breaths that were collectively held were released in a symphony of relief.

I bolted from my seat and released Vera from my grip. "Arnold!" I said. "Where are you, boy?"

The little scamp, shaken and dazed, waddled up to me, his tail wagging. I knelt down beside him, reached into my pocket, and gave him a Milkbone before standing to survey the situation.

Checking the cabin, it looked as though everyone on the team had survived with only minor abrasions to show for their experience. Which was deadly enough. Any cut or open wound, no matter how serious, could prove fatal in the tepid climate of the jungle. Vera set to work, mending the injuries as I strode over to the cargo area and surveyed for any damaged equipment.

"Crap," I muttered, kicking a shattered crate containing the debris of some very expensive computer equipment. Fortunately, the others appeared more or less in tact.

"All right," I said, opening the crate marked "Medical Supplies," pulling out my holster belt, and looping it over my shoulder.

I'd learned a long time ago never to carry weapons out in the open or labeled when traveling to possibly hostile countries. The run of the mill customs agent or police officer becomes mighty skittish when he catches you bringing weapons into his country. But they rarely ever give medical supplies a second glance, so it was one of the best places to hide our hardware.

I dug into a neon orange first aid kit and retrieved my new Glock. Checking the clip, I pulled the ejector slide to chamber a round.

Hopefully, I'll hold onto this a bit longer than the last one, I thought as I holstered the weapon.

Suddenly, Landers' suggestion of being ready for anything was starting to make a lot of sense. "That wasn't so bad."

"Um, Jack," Randy said, peeking into the cockpit. "You need to come see this."

I trudged up to the front of the plane and looked past the cockpit curtain. The pilot's head leaned back against his chair, eyes staring blankly at the ceiling. The windshield was shattered and a very large branch had hurled through the opening and pinned him to his seat.

"Oh. Crap," I said. A wave of dizziness swept through my head, my stomach retching at the sight. "I didn't even know the guy's name."

It was really the only words my addled brain could muster. A proper eulogy would have to wait for someone much more eloquent than me.

Truth be told, I was a lot like Randy. It's why we got along so well. Like him I've never been able to see past my own swelled head to really care about anyone but my closest friends. Strangers rarely ever rate the slightest concern. But when I'm directly responsible for another man's death...well, that just blows to put it bluntly.

"Jack, I hate to bring this up," Landers said cautiously, looking over at the impaled pilot before turning to me.

"What?" I shouted. I knew I shouldn't have snapped, but I really was in no mood for another round of Super-Soldier Tactics 101.

"Sir, the pilot mentioned a STA."

"A surface to air missile?" asked Marc, rummaging through the crates for the gear packs and handing them to each member of the team.

"That's right. Surface to air," Landers said. "That's pretty serious ordinance. It also means that someone knows we're here and they probably don't want us alive."

He looked over at me as he cocked his P-90 rifle. "We need to get moving sir."

As much as I hated to admit it, the big guy was right. He'd been right all along and I was kicking myself for not listening to him from the beginning. Perhaps if we'd used a little more caution, we wouldn't have been in this situation.

"All right, people," I said. "You heard the man. We'll follow his lead until we get to the airstrip."

The plan had been to meet Stromwell's daughter, Nikki, and some guides at the strip. Without her, we had no way of knowing where the Pingitti village would be since it wasn't found on any map. I looked over at the corporal with an apologetic smile. "Um, where exactly is the airstrip?"

"Don't worry, sir," he said as he pried open the hatch to the plane with a crow bar. A gust of hot, tepid air and the screeching sounds of the jungle pummeled us as soon as the door opened. "I'll get us there. Trust me."

He jumped down into the muck, held up a closed fist to keep us from following, and scanned the terrain. Reaching in his pouch, he pulled out a long cylindrical object and screwed it on the barrel of his weapon. A silencer. If he had to discharge his firearm, he didn't want it to be heard for miles around.

I was beginning to like the big Boy Scout.

The sun peeked over the jungle roof as it ascended into the

sky. Vaporous moisture billowed under Lander's feet like ethereal balls of cotton.

It's going to be a hot day, I thought as I watched the soldier begin his reconnaissance.

Tiny swamp mice scampered from the wreckage, seeking refuge from the newcomers that had invaded their domain. The sing song croaking of frogs wafted through the air around us. A long, thick mass of scales and muscle slithered under the boggy water just below the plane's hatch. Not sure what kind it was, but the snake had been huge.

I half expected to see the squat form of Yoda waddling over to our downed aircraft to greet us.

Landers circled the perimeter once as we waited patiently inside the cabin. I gripped the Glock, peering around the corner for any advancing interlopers that had managed to track the plane's descent. Once again, I knew the corporal was right. The presence of an STA missile suggested we were not welcome in these parts and it was a sure bet they'd be wanting to check the wreckage for any survivors. We'd have company soon.

"All's clear," Landers said as he made his way into view. He reached his hand up and helped Vera climb down from the aircraft. Randy, Marc, and I, after checking to make sure we had as much salvageable equipment as we could carry, hopped down into the bog, squishing up to our shins. Arnold jumped boldly into my arms and lapped excitedly at my face.

"Great," Randy grimaced as he pulled one foot free from the mud. "I just bought these boots."

"From the size of that snake we saw a few minutes ago, I'm sure we can make you a new pair," I said, setting Arnold down on a dry patch of earth. I pulled a Cuban from my shirt pocket and, lit it up. "These things are going to be the death of me.

I turned to Landers. "Okay, Scott, it's your show now. Lead on."

Taking one last check of the terrain, the Marine flipped open a super high tech style compass, scrutinizing its readings. His head turned left, then right. Then back down at the instrument's display. Without a word, he closed the compass, stuffed it into a pouch on his belt, and darted into the thick webbing of the jungle.

"Well, people, let's go," I said, gripping the cigar tight with my teeth and trotted after our guide.

WE'D HIKED for two hours before we were forced to stop and rest. The heat was unbearable and it was like swallowing fire every time we took a breath. Thorny vines dug deep into our skin, as we hacked our way from the merciless jungle.

Coming to a clearing, the corporal stopped and swept the area for any signs of pursuit. None was evident, so we laid our gear down, dropped to the ground, and took a short break.

Vera pulled a small bowl from her pack, filled it with the bottled water she'd salvaged from the plane, and laid it on the ground for Arnold. His tail blurred as he savored the cool liquid with his tongue.

"So how are we doing?" I asked Landers who sidled up next to me and sat down Indian style.

"Not bad. I'd guess we're only about four hours west of the landing strip."

He didn't look optimistic. His spiky brown hair drooped, sopping with sweat and woodland debris. His hard, square jaw set tight as he ground his teeth together. I looked around our makeshift camp. Marc and Vera were busying themselves with the ration packs while Randy fired up the radio to listen for any chatter about our downed bird.

"But you're not telling me something, are you, Scott?"

His dark green eyes glanced down at the ruddy soil for several seconds before looking back up at me.

"Yeah," he said. "We've got a problem."

I glanced over at the team to make sure no one was listening in.

"And what's that?"

"We're being followed. I heard the sound of footsteps flanking our position about five miles back," he took a gulp from his canteen and wiped his mouth with his sleeve. "At first, I thought it was probably an animal, but then I heard it again...twice... within the last mile and a half. Then I caught a glimpse of one of them just as he dove for cover. I think they're guerilla fighters, sir."

It wasn't something I wanted to hear. The Malaysian government had been stable for years with five Sultans taking turns leading the country at different intervals. The country had always been 'Muslim', but had enjoyed a rather loose democratic policy. Only the Muslims were subject to Islamic law. The rest had been free to live pretty much however they wanted within reason.

But recently, a group of "Freedom Fighters" had cropped up wanting to wrest control of the nation—their agenda still unknown to the general public. In the last three months, there had been a rise in insurgencies and a fouled up coup attempt against Sultan Mohammed Samir, the nation's newest leader, just last week.

I figured it was the guerilla fighters that had shot our plane down and that they figured us for government relief workers. If that was the case, they'd be none to happy about our presence. I'd been under the impression we'd managed to give them the slip. But then, that's never the way my luck works. I should have known better. My heart thumped against my chest as I prepared my next question.

"How many do you think there are?"

"It's hard to say, sir. My guess, it's a scouting party. They've probably already called in our location, so more are undoubtedly on the way."

"And you decided now was a good time for us to take a breather? We need to get moving."

"It won't help," he said as he globbed a chunk of green and black camouflage paint across his forehead and blended it in. "They'll be on us before we reach the next ridge."

I sat motionless, flipping through our options. But apparently, options had decided to take a vacation, along with logic and reason. By the determination in which Landers was greasing his face up and double checking his rifle, I had a feeling that a shortage of ideas wasn't as much a problem for him..

"Any suggestions?" I asked, trying to swallow the enormous lump in my throat.

"Yes, but you're not going to like it."

"Try me."

And with that, the corporal laid out his game plan. He was right. I didn't like it. Not one bit.

4

We pushed on for an hour and a half before we stopped for another rest. The team sat quietly in a circle on the ground wolfing down the tasteless rations probably packaged in 1949. Landers was no where to be seen, which suited me just fine after he'd laid out his crazy plan for getting us out of this mess.

Reluctantly, I'd agreed to it and filled the team in on our current situation. They were about as enthusiastic as me. But we all realized that there was nothing that could be done about it. Our only hope rested in the training, instincts, and skill of the United States Marine that now led our team.

"So how much farther did he say we had to walk?" Randy asked, munching down a brownie that crunched beneath his teeth.

"About another three hours."

"And he doesn't think we can make a run for it?"

"Randy, they probably have vehicles," said Vera after finishing off a bottle of water. "They know the terrain better than us. I think Scott is right."

Marc said something in Russian to Vera over her last comment that neither Randy nor myself could understand. I'd only managed a few words of Vera's native tongue and none of them could be repeated in front of anyone's mother. Whatever he said, she wasn't too happy about it and spat out a series of Russian obscenities that even I'd never heard before. Marc just grinned back at her.

"Okay, okay. Speak English, will you? You know how much I hate it when I don't know what's being said," Randy scowled. "Look. All I'm saying is that I just don't see how sitting here, waiting for them to come is going to do us any good." He pulled out his flask and shook it only to remember he was fresh out of booze. "Great. Just great."

Arnold stiffened and coughed out a single bark, turned and darted into the bank of trees.

"Arnold?" I called after him. "Stupid dog."

A snapping twig about twenty yards in the opposite direction wrenched our attention away from the fleeing mutt. I stiffened, craning my head for a better listen and absently drew my pistol and held it against my chest. Something was moving, circling around us in a slow even gait.

With no further warning the entire clearing erupted in a cacophony of gunshots and screaming as a contingent of twelve guerilla fighters burst through the trees and leveled their weapons at our heads. One of the fighters marched towards me and spouted a string of words that I couldn't understand.

"I'm sorry. My Malay is kind of rusty," I said to the mean looking man with the gun.

"He said for you to lower your weapon," Marc said quietly. "He also said that we are all now captives of the People's Liberation Army and that to resist means death."

"Oh, well...isn't that nice," I said, smiling at the scowling figure who was pointing his AK-47 directly at my head. What is it about guns and my noggin? Without further comment, I gently laid the Glock on the ground, pushed it towards the guerilla, and brought my hands up to show I was no threat.

"Randy, Vera, do as the nice man says."

Wisely, they complied—Randy's Remington .30-06 and Vera's .357 were both thrown over to our captors. Marc never carried weapons. Which was good. The nervous little guy would probably shoot one of us instead of the bad guys.

The guerilla spoke again.

"He says there was another person with our group. He wants to know where he is," Marc translated.

"Tell him that he went to get help," I said. "He's trying to make his way back to civilization or at least a village to bring aid."

Marc repeated what I had said which spurred the insurgent to bark commands into his radio. Six of his men bolted off to the west, presumably searching for Landers. The leader gestured to the remainder of the guerillas, who pulled us to our feet and bound our wrists tight with leather straps. With a shove from the butt of a rifle, we were prodded forward into the thick vegetation of the jungle.

Arnold was no where to be seen. Neither was Landers.

Come on, Scott, I thought. Don't let us down.

I WASN'T sure how long we'd marched. The sun was all but obliterated by the foliage that formed the forest roof. My tongue was swollen and clung to the roof of my mouth, as the heat sapped all the moisture from my body.

A quick glance at my companions revealed they weren't faring any better. Randy stumbled on a stone and would have fallen head first to the ground if his personal guard hadn't grabbed him by the shirt collar and righted him.

"This is ridiculous," I said, skidding to a halt to the chagrin of my own escort who began shouting what I could only imagine as obscenities at me. I wheeled around at him and growled, "We need to rest! We need water."

Marc, clearly shaken by my sudden outburst, translated my demands. The guerilla leader scowled at me, raised his rifle, and took aim. For several long seconds, I stared the man down. I was standing my ground. I had to. There was no way any of us could continue at the pace we were traveling in the sauna-like terrain. Besides, I knew I had to give Scott time to catch.

"Please," I added with a warm smile.

The rebel's face softened a bit, as he lowered his AK-47 and spat out several commands.

"He says we can rest here for five minutes only," Marc said. "He's going to send one of his men with a canteen to fill it for us."

"Thank you." Placing both hands to my chin, I bowed slightly to the leader. He nodded back and turned to offer a report over his radio.

The four of us huddled together and discussed our situation in hushed tones.

"This is crazy," Randy said. "I never signed up for this. Searching for little vampiric dolls from hell is one thing. Tussling with armed insurgents is something entirely different."

"I don't like it either," I said. "But we're pretty much committed. Now we've just got to figure out how to get out of it."

The guard returned with two canteens and handed them to us. We passed the water around and savored the cool wetness. I tried to forget about the type of organisms that polluted the fresh waters of Malaysia as I washed my parched throat. I was more than willing to deal with dysentery later. At that moment, the water just tasted too good.

Getting my fill, I wiped my mouth off with my sleeve, passed it to Randy, and continued our conversation.

"We just need to be patient. Scott will figure out how to get us out of this," I whispered.

"Are you sure?" Vera asked irritably. Water, even clean water, was never one of her preferred beverages. The longer she went without coffee, the worse I knew her attitude was going to get. I just hope she didn't get us killed in the process. "Now that we're here, it really doesn't sound like much of a plan to me."

"That's because it isn't. I've said it all along," Randy chimed in. "It was a lame-brained scheme at best. Let the Marine leave the team and hide out in the jungle. Wait until we were overtaken and follow us until we get to a vulnerable position that Rambo can take advantage of."

I had to admit, it wasn't the best plan in the world. But it was the only one we'd been able to come up with. Landers had seemed like someone more than capable of handling whatever these guys could throw at him.

Sounds of shouting erupted from the jungle, followed by gunfire and more shouting. Something was happening, but for the life of me, I couldn't figure out what was going on. Surely it was too soon for Scott to have sprung his trap. I'd only wanted to give him a chance to catch his breath, not storm the rest site.

The muffled sounds of a silenced assault rifle dashed all my hopes. Landers was engaging the enemy. This wasn't good at all. The other insurgents leapt into the jungle, cocking their weapons as they prepared to join the battle that was moving closer to our campsite. The rebel leader once again leveled his rifle at my team and we could only raise our hands in submission.

A short five minutes later, the guerillas marched into camp with Landers, bound and bleeding, limping among them. He grumbled under his breath, never looking us in the eyes as he stumbled into the group.

"Not a word," he growled, glaring at Randy and sitting down on the ground with his back against a tree. Arnold trotted cheerfully behind them, his tongue hanging to one side of his face and tail wagging furiously as he nipped at the heel of one of the insurgents.

The freedom fighter turned on my dog and brought down the

butt of his rifle, but Arnold skipped out of the way and plowed towards me and safety.

The rebel leader and the others conversed wildly over the Marine's assault as Marc filled me in.

"It seems that Scott had been tracking us quite adeptly and none of their scouting party had a clue to his presence," he whispered. "It wasn't until the blind, stinking bad luck of spooking a colony of nearby monkeys that his location was compromised. Landers had no choice but to engage the enemy, but was simply out numbered. He'd decided discretion was the better part of valor in his situation and surrendered to fight another day."

After several more minutes of apparent debate on what to do next, our captors snatched us away and we found ourselves plodding through the jungle once again.

THE SUN WAS SETTING against the horizon as we marched into the rebel camp nestled against a cliff face of a small mountain range. The home-base of the group sported twelve wooden huts used as barracks, an open air pagoda used as a mess hall, and a large tent-like building designed to be dismantled quickly and reassembled again should the necessity arise.

The lead insurgent gestured towards the larger structure and we were shoved through two canvass flaps into the dark interior. My eyes were forced to adjust to the dim light. When they finally focused, my mouth dropped in awe of the state of the art technology that hummed throughout the building.

Top of the line computer terminals mixed with GPS, radar, and some unidentifiable high-tech equipment lined the various tables set in parallel rows. Weather readouts and satellite feeds flashed across flat screen panels. One large monitor mounted on the far wall displayed a map of Malaysia and Indonesia with tiny red and blue dots flickering in various locations.

It was an impressive display given the primitive setup. *Whoever is funding this operation had money to burn, I thought.*

We were ushered towards the back of the building and forced into folding chairs set in a circle on the dirt floor. I scanned the room as technicians and communication personnel scampered hastily around the complex, busying themselves with the task of running a major political revolution.

"Ah, Dr. Jackson," a voice behind me said.

I craned my head around to see the source of the voice. An elderly man towered above his men at more than six feet tall, dressed in a plain olive green uniform. No medals, ribbons, or insignia of any kind adorned his clothing. His sallow face screamed of Mongolian ancestry and was darkened and leathery from years of working in the sun. His full head of silvery hair was well groomed with a part on the left side.

The newcomer's teeth shown brightly through paper thin lips as he grinned and extended his hand in welcome. I could only stare at him.

"Akim, please remove this man's bindings immediately," he said once he realized we were still tied up. Although tinged with a thick Russian accent, the man's English was impeccable. He'd obviously spent a great deal of time studying it. "Please forgive the enthusiasm of my soldiers, Doctor. I truly hope they were not too rough with you."

"Well, they blew us out of the sky," I said rubbing my newly freed wrists. "But other than that, they were pussy cats."

The old man smiled again.

"Come with me, Doctor," he said. Not waiting for a reply, he walked towards a set of doors in the back of the tent and stopped. "Your team will be well cared for, I can assure you."

I looked at my friends and stiffened.

"Go," said Randy. "I don't see you really having much of a choice. And maybe you can talk some sense into this guy. He seems reasonable enough."

"Yeah, for a James Bond villain" Vera chimed in.

Randy was right. There really wasn't any choice. For better or worse, we were in a pickle of a mess and at the mercy of a Dr. No wannabe.

"All right," I said, stood up and moved towards the old man. "Just take care of yourselves, okay? Oh, and Vera, tend Scott's wounds while I'm gone."

The newcomer gestured for me to walk through the doors, followed me through and closed them behind us. I found myself in a plush office with exquisite furnishings. A large mahogany desk sat in the center of the room on top of an expensive looking Persian rug. Two fine leather chairs sat in front of the desk. A Van Gogh, two Monets, and a Rueben adorned the office walls. I had no reason to doubt their authenticity. The only thing out of place in my exquisite surroundings were the florescent lights mounted overhead on the ceiling, giving the office a clinical, sterile feel.

My guest gestured to one of the chairs and I sat down warily, keeping my eye on him the entire time. The old proverb about wolves in sheep's clothing kept popping to mind and I was unnerved.

"My name, Dr. Jackson, is Sashe Abdulla Krenkin," he said with a wry smile. The Russian name seemed a contradiction to the Asian features of the man.

"I see that surprises you," he said. "While my mother was Malaysian, my father was a scientist from the Russia. I was born in Novgorod many years ago at the height of the Soviet regime. My parents were executed as political dissenters when I was only two years old."

I said nothing, biding my time and hoping Krenkin would give me the inside scoop as to what in the world was going on. Now was no time to be the smart mouth that I usually was. Realizing that I would make no comment, he continued with his diatribe.

"After my parent's death, I was raised by state institutions and given a classical communist education. Even became a renowned scientist, well respected by my peers," he said. "I'm so sorry. I've lost all sense of manners in this bloody rebellion. May I offer you something to drink?"

He turned to a side table near a clear plastic window and raised a decanter towards me.

"A very fine 1965 Merlot," he said proudly.

"No thank you," I said. "I'm a Silver Bullet man myself."

He smiled at that and poured a glass, bringing it to his nose, inhaling deeply. Taking a sip, Krenkin turned back to me and sat down in the second chair.

"As I was saying, I was raised to be a loyal party member. It wasn't until my twenty-third birthday that I found out the truth about my parents political beliefs," Krenkin said. "You can't imagine the anger I felt. My parents taken away from me simply because their views did not mesh with the government's idea of the utopian society they were trying to build. I vowed at that very moment to leave the Soviet Union and make my way back to my homeland and my people."

The back of my neck began to tingle as unseen fingers danced lightly down my spine. Something about this whole mess wasn't right. Something just wasn't adding up.

And he knew my name! He knew exactly who I was and I was willing to bet the farm he knew exactly why we were there. So what on earth is this charade about? I wondered.

"How do you know who I am?" I interrupted.

Krenkin mouth gaped at the sudden change in subject. I'd apparently taken him off guard.

Good. It's about time I start changing the rules in this little game.

"I'm sorry?" he asked.

"How do you know me? When you walked into the room, you called me by name."

"You're a well known scientist, Doctor. Your face has been on magazine covers and television interviews. I knew you at first glance."

"I think you knew me before you had my plane shot down."

"I can assure you that was not my doing."

"Look," I said. I was tired of playing nice. I was fed up with whatever was going on. All I wanted to do was take my team and leave this crazy country. Missionary girl could fend for herself. There'd be more jenglot to investigate. I had had it. "Let's get something clear. I may not be the brightest bulb in the pack, but I know when someone is conning me. Now, let's have it. Straight up. What's all this about?"

Krenkin stood from his chair, went back to the liquor table and filled another glass. He turned, leaning against the table, and lit a cigarette. His mouth a tiny red ribbon, pinched at the sides in thought. He blew a stream of smoke from his nostril and moved around the other side of the desk and sat down.

"All right, Dr. Jackson," he said grimly. "You want the truth. Up front. I'll oblige you. But I can assure you...you won't like what you hear."

For the second time in a day someone told me that I wasn't going to like something. Redundancy. Irritation was clawing at the back of my throat. I knew he was right. I wasn't going to like it. But I wanted to know anyway.

5

"I think I'll have that drink now," I said, figuring I would need it before our conversation was finished. "Mind if I smoke?"

Not waiting for a response, I fished in my pocket for a cigar and bit off the tip. Before I could react, he was at my side with a silver-plated butane lighter, firing up my stogy. There was just something about the guy I didn't like. He was too polite to be a revolutionary. Too well mannered. And the way his eyes looked at me forced somersaults in my stomach.

After the generous gesture, he produced a glass of Merlot. The aroma itself was intoxicating. I rarely ever drink alcohol, but I figured the situation called for it.

"Are you ready for the answers you seek?" he asked, waiting for me to get comfortable as I fidgeted in the chair.

"Sure. Why not? Let me have it," I regretted the choice of words the moment they slipped from my lips.

He smiled broadly, walked back to his desk chair and sat down, leaning forward with his arms extended towards me.

"The truth, my friend, is that you are in grave danger," he said. "There are certain people who are automatically inclined to mistrust westerners of any kind. But it's even worse for scientists and adventurers. It was not my men that shot your aircraft down, but the Malaysian military."

Granted, we hadn't arranged for proper clearance to fly through the region, but I found it hard to believe the official government would gun down an unarmed plane without warning. There were just too many ramifications in such an act. It could bring closer scrutiny by various national governments, if not serious sanctions.

"The Malaysian government wants me dead?" I asked. "I'm sorry, I just don't buy it."

"It's true, Doctor. Despite your attempts at entering the country undetected, your entire trip was already being investigated by the secret police before you were even out of Hong Kong," he waited a minute for the new information to settle. "Your connection with the Texas senator and a possible spy marked you as a danger to Samir's regime, which in turn, marks you for execution."

"Spy? What spy?"

"The senator's daughter, of course. She has been promoting propaganda against the Sultan's government. It is believed that she is a CIA operative attempting to topple the Malaysian power base from its core inhabitants."

"She's a Christian missionary," I said blowing a cloud of smoke towards Krenkin's incessantly smiling face. "Of course she's going to be propagating a message that goes against an Islamic government. That doesn't make her a spy."

"Obviously," my host said, ignoring the smoke. "But the Sultan isn't as level headed as we. He has an ever-crumbling empire to keep together. He's suspicious of everyone."

I leaned back in the chair, its plush leather upholstery contouring to the shape of my back. I closed my eyes, trying to sort through what I was being told. It made sense. With a rebellion threatening Sultan Samir's control, he would consider anyone—especially anyone with ties to the backbone of the nation's citizenship—as a threat. What I couldn't figure out was Krenkin's role in the whole scheme.

"And because the missionary's father, a United States senator, sent me here to get her out of the country, it's assumed that..."

"It's assumed that you are also working for the government and that you are merely pulling an asset out of a dangerous situation," he interrupted. "Your reputation as a cryptozoologist seeking some sort of local legend would make the perfect cover for such an operation. The fact that you tried to sneak into the country...well, you can see how it looks."

I swallowed the rest of the wine and sat straight up in the chair, eyeballing Krenkin to make sure he was paying attention.

"And I suppose your men just happened along our crash site and decided to rescue us from the Malaysian military that was hot on our tails...is that it?"

The Russian laughed as he stood and walked over to my chair, gripping my shoulder.

"Actually, our encounter was purely serendipitous," he said. "A routine patrol spotted your plane being shot down and went to investigate. My men had no idea who you were and like the government, are highly suspicious of westerners, as I've already explained."

I wanted to stand. I wanted to get out of there. The whole thing made no sense. I understood Samir's attitude towards Stromwell's daughter and anyone sent to retrieve her. I could handle that. It was Krenkin. I found it hard to believe his soldiers just happened upon our crash. It was even more improbable he just happened to know who I was when he saw me. It was a good bet that he'd been expecting me.

Something inside me railed against trusting the man.

"So," I said, looking up at the Russian hovering next to me. "What's your stake in all this then? What's in this thing for you?"

The old man bent over to look me square in the eye. The florescent lights above flickered and I suddenly I faced someone altogether different than the man I walked in with. Krenkin's smile was gone, replaced with thin, bloodless lips pressed tight against a haggard face. His weathered features merely skin and muscle clinging to brittle bones. The light's flickered again to reveal the strong, virile man I'd walked into the office with. It was unsettling to say the least.

"Actually, Doctor, what I want from you is rather simple," he said. "I want you to travel to the Pingitti village and capture one of the jenglot for me. It's as simple as that. It's a task you already planned on doing anyway."

"That's all? Find one of the jenglot and bring him back to you?" I asked, ignoring the nagging question that burned in my skull. *How did he even know about the jenglot?*

"Exactly," his smiled had returned. The large white teeth of a Cheshire cat grinned wildly at me.

"And if I refuse?"

"You won't."

"Let's say I do. What happens? You kill us? Hand us over to Samir's secret police?"

Krenkin considered the question for several seconds, raised himself to his full height and downed the remainder of his wine.

"Now why would you refuse six million dollars, U.S. currency?"

If I'd been speechless when Stromwell had offered a cool three hundred thousand, I'd lost my entire vocabulary at Krenkin's figure. Six million...for a little runt of a creature. I'd have given him Nessie for a quarter of the price.

Naturally, I was wary of the bargain. My dad and I rarely ever saw eye to eye on anything my entire life. But one of the few things we both agree on is that it's generally a mistake to believe in deals too good to be true. Another thing we both agree on is to always take chances when the outcome really matters. Of course, we always disagree on what "really matters", but that's a moot point.

I didn't trust the creep standing in front of me, but he had a valid point. I was going after the jenglot anyway. Why not try to make a fortune along the way?

"Just one jenglot?" I asked. "No hidden clauses? No agendas? Just one jenglot and my team and I go free...with six million dollars in our pockets and any other jenglot I happen to catch?"

"Well, actually, there are two conditions, Doctor Jackson," he said, holding out his hand. "Two rather insignificant conditions." He smiled, tilting his head slightly.

"That's what I thought. Let's have them."

"First, I require a very special specimen. Just any of the creatures won't do. I need the eldest of the group," he said, his face sober. "The second condition is that I expect you to hand the creature over to me, no questions asked." His last comment sounded ominous, but I was willing to let it slide. The sound of crisp dollar bills rifling through my fingertips had deafened me to anything else he was going to say.

I'm not saying that I'm greedy. But that much money goes a long way in funding research projects and truth be told, we were tapped out. Nelson Daniels had been the last investor in my proverbial pot.

But there was one problem with his conditions I couldn't wrap my brain around.

"How will I know the oldest jenglot? What if we bring the wrong one?"

He smiled again. "That won't be a problem, Doctor. You'll know right away when you see the creature I seek."

I pondered his answer for a second, before stretching out my hand and shaking his. "All right, Krenkin, you've got yourself a deal," I said grinning broadly with the cigar clamped down between by teeth. I'm sorry. The money was just too good to pass up.

"Excellent. I'll prepare for your team's transportation to Pingitti immediately," he said. "But be careful, Doctor. There are many more dangers in the Malaysian jungles than the jenglot."

As Krenkin ushered me out into the darkened operations room, I couldn't help feeling as though I'd just made a horrible mistake. I'd hoped it was one I would live to regret.

"So, he's just letting us drive out of here?" Randy said as he steered the Jeep over a rugged trail that Krenkin had assured me would lead to the main road. "Just like that?"

"Well, he's not doing it out the goodness of his heart," I said, clinging to the roll bar with one hand and holding Arnold's collar with the other. He was having a great time, head hanging over the edge of the backseat, tongue flapping in the wind. "He wants one of the jenglot."

After meeting back up with the team, Krenkin's second in command, Akim, returned our weapons, restocked our supplies, and provided us with an all terrain vehicle to make our way to the isolated village of Pingitti. He'd even given us surveillance equipment, both day for night and thermal imagers, and brand new top of the line computer equipment to enhance the chances of tracking our prey.

I'd been reluctant to tell the group of the deal I'd made. The whole thing smelled bad and I knew it wouldn't go ever well with them. I'd been right. As usual, Randy had been the most vocal in his protests. But they understood that there'd really been no other way. At best, we'd earn a heck of a lot of money if we were successful. At worst, we'd have not only the Malaysian government aiming to put a bullet in our heads, but Krenkin's rebels as well. But we were free for now.

"Krenkin," Vera said. She sat in the front passenger seat of the jeep. Strapped in tight with a wrap-around racing harness, she seemed relaxed on the bumpy terrain we were now driving over. "The name sounds so familiar to me. I just can't place it."

"Perhaps he was an old boyfriend," Randy jibed.

Despite the fact that Vera was an excellent physician, she'd struggled to survive in the streets of St. Petersburg before meeting me eight years before. Doctors in Russia don't enjoy the same prestige and income as their counterparts in the United States and many of them are forced to take various menial jobs just to pay the high rent. Vera had succumbed to prostitution and had profited on her lithe muscular build and drop-you-to-your-knees gorgeous face. She'd done many things that, even now, she loathed discussing.

"Not funny, Randy," I smacked my friend across the back of his head. "Knock it off."

"It's all right," Vera said, leaning back in her seat. "I've come to expect it from him."

"Ah, come on," Randy protested. "You know I didn't mean anything by it." He jerked the wheel sharp to avoid a large tree that had fallen onto the dirt path, nearly flinging me from the jeep. "So where do you think you know this guy from?"

"I'm just not sure. But it's a name that doesn't invoke good feelings, I can tell you that."

"Well, just think on it," I told her. "It'll come to you."

Marc's nose was pressed deep in another book, holding absently onto the roll bar. Landers sulked in the back seat, checking over the bandages Vera had secured to his injuries. At first, I thought his pride had suffered the greater wounds of his ordeal, but the more I watched him, the more I became convinced his silence was caused by something else entirely.

When pressed, he'd only scowl and say he didn't want to talk about it, so I finally gave up and left him alone.

As a matter of fact, there wasn't much talking by any of us for the two hours it took to find the main highway, if you could even call it that. It was just more dirt road, slightly more level, but snaking its way down a steep hillside into a canyon our map indicated to be the home of the Pingitti people.

. . .

THE SUN WAS SETTING over the horizon when we rounded a curve and saw the first two straw huts that comprised the outskirts of the village, nestled on a bank of a broad river. It had taken us practically a full day to get from the rebel camp to the village and we were exhausted. All I could think about was finding some place to lay my head, close my eyes, and fall into the oblivion of sleep.

As the jeep skidded up a slight embankment, six children, dressed in tattered soccer shorts and hand-me-down T-shirts bolted towards our vehicle, laughing and waving to us. The noise of the children brought others and soon, we were forced to stop the jeep as the entire tribe surrounded us with broad, warm smiles and gentle nods.

As a people, they were rather short, the average height being around five and a half feet tall, with dark skin. Their foreheads were broad and stretched over black oval eyes and wide, flat noses.

Three of the children jumped on the vehicle's hood, shouting greetings to us as they tendered offerings of fruit from over the windshield.

"No thank you," Randy said, clearly uncomfortable with the energetic swarm of friendly natives. "Please get off the hood of the car. Watch it."

Arnold leapt from the vehicle and chased the other children around the village to squeals of delight. Two adult males reached towards us, gesturing that they would assist our extrication from the jeep.

A soft, female voice arose over the clamor of the villagers in a strange tongue that even Marc found difficult to translate. Whatever language the people spoke, he later informed me, wasn't standard Malay, but was probably a mixed tribal dialect.

The crowd parted like the Red Sea to reveal a stunning thirty-something blonde striding up to us. She was petite and wore a dark green T-shirt that covered far more than I would have preferred and a pair of khaki cargo shorts, brown hiking boots, and a maroon baseball cap with a pony tail hanging from the back. She wore no makeup, but then, she didn't need to. Her full lips eased back to reveal a set of white teeth that any orthodontist would have given his right eye for.

"I'm Nikki Jenkins," she said as she extended her hand in welcome. At five, three she stood nearly four inches shorter than me. "And you're Dr. Jackson, I presume."

I took her hand, which was gentle, but definitely not soft. Her fingers and palms were calloused from toiling in her Malaysian mission. Her grip was strong and confident and I couldn't help but divert my eyes from hers as she sized me up with a glance.

"You'd presume correct. It's nice to meet you." I turned my grin up a notch as I subjected her to some scrutiny of my own. Great smile. Legs that go on forever. Nice, tanned skin. I was beginning to think I was actually going to enjoy myself here despite the trouble we'd already gotten ourselves into.

"I'm glad to meet you too. When you didn't show at the airstrip, I'd assumed you'd changed your mind and weren't coming."

"We'd never even think of it." My smile widened.

"Oh geeze," I heard Vera mumble under her breath behind me. I turned and glared at her.

"Shouldn't you all be unpacking the jeep?" I asked, eyeing the rest of my team.

"Oh yes," Nikki said. "Of course. Hyon, Misha. Help Dr. Jackson's friends unpack and show them to their huts, please."

Two young men in their early twenties rushed to the jeep and began pulling our equipment from the back.

"Watch it. Watch it," cried Randy as he scurried around to them to supervise the unloading. He looked over at me. "We'll be setting up."

I watched the team follow the rest of the villagers and our gear towards the center of the village. Arnold hopped after them, yapping at the children who kept tossing fruit at him.

Landers, hefting a large suit case full of camera equipment onto his shoulder, stopped to look at me, his mouth opened to say something. Then, thinking better of it, he turned around and followed the group up to the village.

Yep. Something is definitely wrong with that guy. I need to keep my eye on him.

I turned back to Nikki.

"Actually, it's Jack," I said.

"Excuse me?"

"My name. I go by Jack. Never been fond of my given name."

"Oh, I'm sorry. And you can call me Nikki."

"Jenkins?"

"Yes. The senator is actually my step-father. He's raised me and loved me as a real dad, but I've always chosen to keep my name.

"That's understandable," I said as we meandered towards the village. "Stromwell's just not a pretty enough name for someone as beautiful as you."

Nikki stopped short and turned to face me.

"Look, Dr. Jacks...Jack. We need to get something straight. I really have no interest in being swept off my feet right now. The only things I have any interest in caring about at the moment are the Pingitti people. I'm sure you're used to women fawning all over you with your boyish good looks, bright blue eyes, and rugged complexion, but you won't find me as willing a target. So you can just turn down the charm a notch or two, okay?"

I suddenly craved one of my cigars.

"Well, maybe you shouldn't flatter yourself, lady," I said, shuffling my boots in the dirt and cramming my hands into my pockets. "I'm a professional and I'm here on business. Any charm you think you detected is just all natural."

I flashed another broad grin at her, winked, and stormed towards the rest of my group—leaving her to soak in her own embarrassment. It didn't work.

"We need to discuss your 'business' before you turn in for the night," she called over my shoulder, skidding me to a halt. "They're due for another attack."

I turned around, looking at her silhouette now shadowed by the torch light that lined the village center. It was a shame. Such a gorgeous, intelligent woman and wasting it all out here in the middle of no where.

Come on, Jack. I thought. *She's right. Get your head screwed on straight. You're here for a reason.*

"You're right," I said. "Give us thirty minutes to eat and relax a bit and then come by our tent. We'll talk there. As a team."

I strode off into the village, examining the little community that had brought me half-way around the world. It was comprised of a few shanty huts scattered hodge-podge throughout the village, as well as three "long-houses" built on stilts on the river's edge that were used to house several families within the tribe. A handful of chickens clucked their way around a few rusted bicycles and wooden toys littering the mud-caked streets.

The team was already setting up the oversize tent we would use as a base of operations. The village shanties were fine for sleeping, but they were no where big enough to support the electronics and surveillance equipment we were going to use to track the jenglot. Krenkin had been kind enough to loan us one of the rebel barrack tents for that reason.

As I approached the team, Arnold scampered over to my feet, pawing at my leg. I hauled him up in my arms and looked at the group.

"Okay people," I said. "We've got to get ready. It looks like we're going to be in for a long night."

6

"All right," I said. Leaning against the computer table in the front of the tent, I gestured toward the missionary standing next to me. "You all have met Nikki Jenkins. She's going to be briefing us on what we're up against. I'd suggest we pay close attention to what she has to say."

Randy bit down into a strange concoction given to him by a little village boy. Nikki had explained that the food, which resembled macaroni salad without the actual macaroni, was a special treat for the people in Pingitti. She'd refused to reveal the ingredients, but Randy didn't seem to mind. He feverishly licked at the spoon as he looked up at the missionary.

Vera busied herself inventorying the medical supplies and survival packs. I knew I didn't have to worry about her. Of my entire crew, I trusted her the most. While Randy was my oldest friend, Vera and I had developed a deeper affection for one another—a bond of complete trust—over the years. She was a consummate professional and the one person in the world I knew I could always rely on.

Marc and Scott sat at another table, tinkering with the portable generator that Krenkin had loaned us. The surveillance and computer equipment rested patiently beside them. Arnold merely shuffled around the tent, sniffing his new digs.

"Thank you," Nikki began, standing up from the folding chair she'd been lounging in. "First of all, I'd like to extend my deepest gratitude to you all for coming here and helping us get to the bottom of whatever is truly going on."

"But we haven't done anything yet," Vera said, looking up from a suitcase full of anti-venom. "Your thanks is a bit premature."

"Well, the fact that you're even here is enough. Trust me. The truth is we're all terrified of what's happening around here. Five people are now dead, in this village alone. If the jenglot keep to their present pattern, more may die tonight. We've got to be ready for them."

"Five? Your father informed us that only three were deceased," Marc said, wheeling the roaring generator out the tent's door. Landers flipped a switch and the computer equipment hummed to life.

"And what do you mean by 'in this village alone'?" added Randy, helping himself to another portion of the not-so-macaroni salad.

"Well, he was basing the figure on an email I'd sent him last month. Although I have a satellite link for the Internet, it's not reliable. I get maybe five, six days out of the month to connect with home," she said, downing a glass of treated water. "The jenglot tend to attack each village in the area—there are a total of four in the valley—every two weeks."

She let the team absorb the information before proceeding.

"They always attack each village on a specific night of the week. Today is Tuesday, so they'll come here tonight. They'll attack Baik Orang on Saturday, Tuhan Kampong on Monday, and so on."

"But that's crazy," I added. "I can understand the bi-weekly cycles. They may be dependent on moon phases or something similar, but the specific day just doesn't make sense."

"It would if they were traveling around in a pack. It might take a full two weeks to circle the region. They'd just swoop in on villages in order and you'd have a steady pattern," said Vera.

"But what about unforeseen mishaps? Illness or injury of any one of the creatures? There are just too may variables to consider for such a precise migration pattern," I replied. Turning back to Nikki, "And you're saying they always attack Pingitti on Tuesday evening?"

"Exactly," she said. "I know it sounds strange, but it's true. Of course, there have been stories about them for centuries in these parts, but I'd only seen evidence of them in the last six months. The older villagers say they used to only take one or two victims a year. Now, they're raiding the villages like clock-work…every two weeks."

My brain raced, scouring the facts for patterns, answers, to the attacks. Why had their feeding schedule escalated? Why did they follow such a precise path? What was causing them to push into greater danger by more frequent attacks? The answers just wouldn't come.

I grabbed a dry erase marker and began scribbling the facts on the clear board we'd mounted to the wooden tent poles.

"Okay. First, there appears to be more than one jenglot involved," I said aloud as I scrawled the words "*More than one*" across the board. "Second, they attack every other Tuesday evening. Third, they follow the same pattern each migration cycle. Fourth, five people in Pingitti village have died as a result."

I scribbled the notes and turned back to Nikki. "You said they've been attacking twice a month for the last six months?"

"That's right."

"Then why aren't there twelve or more victims here?"

She walked over to the table with Marc and Scott and sat down in an empty chair.

"Because they don't always feed on humans. A number of times we've found chickens and oxen dead. The one thing they have in common though...they're all drained of their blood."

"Do we have an estimate for the total number, including all the villages?" Vera asked.

"Last I heard it was around twenty-three."

I marked the number down and circled it in red. I also wrote the phrase *"Blood drained"* on the upper right hand corner of the board.

"Do we have any idea how the blood is being drained? Any marks, abrasions, or cuts on the bodies?" I asked.

"None. I have no idea how they're getting to the blood. All I know is that each victim is bled dry."

"What assurance do we have that our quarry is indeed a jenglot?" asked Marc, an expert in Asian folklore, rifling through his journal. "No recorded legends depict them as being so organized...so precise. And only a handful portray them as a wandering tribe."

"That's a good question," Nikki said. "At first, I must confess, I chalked the whole thing up to superstition. This may be a Muslim country, Dr. Leeds, but these villages still practice their old animistic religions, despite pressure from their government. Magic and superstition are a mainstay in this region, so I just assumed the shamans and elders were attributing these mysterious deaths to some form of demonic creatures set in their tribal memories."

She reached in the side pockets of her shorts and retrieved a small digital camera. Flipping it on, she scanned through a number of pictures before stopping and handing the camera to me.

"I thought it was superstition until I took this picture," she said.

The photo was grainy...about the same quality as your average UFO or Bigfoot picture, but my eyes quickly picked up the image of two strange figures darting towards the underbrush along a rocky trail. The creatures' outlines were obscured by the cover of night, but whatever the camera had captured was not anything I'd ever seen before—not even during my jenglot hunt in Borneo. These were entirely different.

"These aren't jenglot," I said curtly, passing the camera over to Randy.

He looked at the photograph and passed it to each member of the group.

"They're too big," he said looking over at me. "Much too big."

The camera came back to me and I scrutinized the picture once more. The creatures were walking upright, with long, slim legs and sharp, pointed spikes protruding from their backs. It had been night time when the photo was taken, but it appeared that their hide was black or dark brown and made of some chitin-like material—like the carapace of an insect. At first sight, their framework and skeletal structure did indeed resemble what I'd chased through the rain forest in Borneo several years before. But these creatures were enormous in comparison.

"The jenglot of legend is typically only about six to nine inches tall," I explained to Nikki. "Actually, I'd say they were more like one and half to two feet tall. These things are a good three or four feet in height and much too muscular. Legend and my experience have them as little more than rag dolls. These guys here…" I tapped the screen, "they're all muscle. Strong. Powerful."

"That doesn't make any sense," she said, taking the camera from me and staring at the image on the back. "I was told that these were definitely the jenglot. It was even taken on a night when one of our villagers was found dead…near the victim's home."

"Who told you they were jenglot?" I asked.

She flipped the camera off and stuffed it back into her pocket. Sliding from her chair, she walked over to the entrance of our tent and peered out, looking around. When she turned back to us, her face was ashen and sweat glistened across her forehead.

"I had to be sure no one was listening in," she explained. "Shantili is not someone you talk about around here."

"Shantili?" I asked.

"He's a witchdoctor. An old shaman expelled from his own village for practicing dark magic. He's sort of nomadic now. Travels around the valley, living in caves and the hollowed out remains of dead trees. He's about as crazy as they come and doesn't like me one bit."

"Yet he informed you that your picture was a jenglot?"

"Well, not exactly. It was more like a warning," she said, filling her glass up with another draft of water and downing it in a gulp. "You see, Shantili blames me for his expulsion from the tribe he'd adopted several years ago. No one knows where he came from originally. He just appeared one day and entered a small village about twenty-miles from here and became their shaman.

"He believes my message of Christ and redemption has tarnished the people's respect for him and the old ways. He'd happen to come into Pingitti to trade for food and supplies on the night I took the photograph. He was right there with me when I snapped the shot. He warned me that they were jenglot and that they'd been sent by the spirits to remove me from the world."

"Well, he was mistaken," I said. "Whatever you caught in that picture, it was no jenglot. At least none like I've ever heard of or seen."

"Tell me something," the sudden sound of Scott's gravely voice made me jump. Except while setting up the equipment with Marc, he'd been a mere ghost since being released from Krenkin's camp. "How often does this witchdoctor come to Pingitti? Has he been seen around here on any other occasions when the creatures attack?"

"Good question," Randy said. "The soldier boy's got some

brains after all. Nikki, you said that he travels around a lot. Could he be following the same pattern as these...these...well, jenglot?"

"I've never thought of that before. I'm not sure if he's been around here every time they attack, but I know of at least two other occasions," she said. "I couldn't say about the other villages though. Nor do I know if he travels in a similar pattern as the creatures. But Gnali might. He's the tribal head. He makes it his business to keep tabs on Shantili."

"We'll ask him about it tomorrow," I said. "Right now, we have work to do. It's almost nine o'clock. We don't have much time. Nikki, about how many people are there total in Pingitti?"

"Sixty-seven, not counting us," she replied.

"Are there any large, communal shelters big enough to house all of them for one night?"

"Well, there is the feast hall. I use it for worship services and things, but it's large enough for the entire village, I think."

"Good. You need to start getting them in there then. There's safety in numbers," I said. "Besides, it makes it easier to keep an eye out when everyone's clumped together."

"Okay," she said, as she jogged from the tent.

"Randy, after you set up the transmitter tower, I want motion sensors set up in twenty yard increments around this entire village," I continued. "Marc, Scott, I need you guys to mount the infrared and thermal imagers in centralized locations. Make sure you get the entrance to the worship center where everyone will be staying. Oh, and mount the oscillating camera on top of the transmitter after Randy gets it up."

The three of them took off from the tent and busied themselves with their assigned tasks. Vera leaned back in her chair and looked at me with a smile.

"You like her, don't you?" she asked.

"Don't start." I withdrew an ammo box and handed it to her. "Check that, fill all the clips. We don't want to be short.

Unfortunately, we lost all our tranquilizer darts in the crash, so we're just going to have to make do."

Opening the container, she examined the rounds and slid them into the various weapon magazines we had available.

"She shot you down, didn't she?"

"No," I snapped. "She didn't 'shoot' me down. I didn't even try. We're here on a job. Besides, she's not my type and you know it."

"What type is she? Smart, independent, and has good taste in men?"

"Vera, if you like her so much, why don't you ask her out?" The comeback was immature, but I couldn't resist. She'd always been able to see right through me and sometimes, it just plain dug into my craw. I shrugged on my holster and cradled my gun with a growl. "And besides, she's a missionary...a Christian missionary. After seeing what my parents became after being born again, I want nothing to do with it. No thank you."

Now drop it, I thought to myself.

She stopped loading the magazines, stood up from the table, and walked up to me. Placing both hands on my face, she gave me a peck on the cheek and backed away with a smile.

"Honey, I've known you too long. I know you better than Randy or anyone else for that matter and I know when you're lying. Just don't let your feelings for her get in the way of why we're here. You lose your head over some woman on a job like this and it will be trouble."

"I know, I know," I said. She did know me too well. "I'll be okay. It's almost show time and you know how one track minded I get on the chase. I'll be fine."

"Yes, but the question is will you be chasing what really counts," she said as she strode out of the tent and into the night.

7

I mashed the off button of my satellite phone, tossing it on the computer table in front of me. I'd tried contacting Witz, my mercenary friend, in hopes of recruiting his help. I wasn't sure what was going on, but I knew Witz and his men would be incredible assets should the need arise.

Unfortunately, he was in no hurry to talk to me. Probably had something to do with the huge amount of cash he owed me from our game in Brazil. But after leaving him three messages explaining I wasn't concerned with his debt, he still hadn't called me back.

Come on, Witz. Don't be stupid.

I blew out a breath, glancing at the screen of the computer terminal. The clock at the bottom said it was 12:40 A.M. I'd taken the first watch and I was no where near tired enough to ask for relief.

It wasn't that I didn't trust anyone else to do it. They'd had a long day and deserved the rest. Besides, it gave me time to reflect on just when I'd taken a left turn into the Twilight Zone. I was used to the creatures I hunted presenting a certain amount of danger. That's just part of the job. It was another thing entirely to be shot out of the sky by a glorified bazooka and then be taken prisoner by a maniacal leader trying to overthrow a national government. Those kinds of things, thankfully, just don't happen very often and I had trouble keeping my head from spinning off my shoulders from it all.

Who had been responsible for nuking us out of the sky? Why on earth did Krenkin want me to catch the eldest jenglot? What was he up to? No matter how many times I spun the questions around in my head, I just couldn't wrap my mind around them enough for any clear answers. I was obviously missing some major pieces and hoped I'd have them soon enough.

I sat at the monitoring station; feet crossed and propped up on the table, munching mint leaves I'd snagged from a nearby tree. Randy snored behind me, rolling on his right side in blissful sleep. Arnold lay curled in a ball by my chair, one leg kicking the air as he dreamed.

Vera was curled on a cot in the corner of the tent. I couldn't tell if she was sleeping or not, but I doubted it. Of my entire team, she was the most compassionate and sensitive. I guess it goes hand in hand with being a doctor. But I knew she was seriously concerned for the Pingitti people. The death toll was just too high in the little village to allow her any peaceful slumber.

I'd sent Marc and Landers to sleep in the feast hall with the villagers. I'd insisted that some of our team join them, offering a modicum of protection in case the jenglot made it past our electronic perimeter.

I popped in another leaf and leaned forward for a better view of the video monitors. There were seven in all—one on the communications tower we'd erected, three scattered at key points along the village street, and two on opposite sides of the feast hall building watching the entrances and windows. So far the only thing that had passed by the cameras was a foraging bandicoot and a few strange looking birds.

"How are we doing?" Nikki whispered as she glided up next to me and took a seat at the screens. Her approach was catlike and would have startled me if I hadn't seen her leave the hall a few minutes before.

"You're supposed to be sleeping with the rest," I said, not taking my eyes off the displays. She had a way of throwing me off balance and I didn't like it. There was just something about her…"And you're definitely not supposed to be out wandering the village alone right now. It's nearly one in the morning. If they're coming, it'll be soon"

"I couldn't sleep. I wanted to check on you."

"I'm fine. Everything's fine. Now take one of the cots in here and go back to bed."

"You're awfully bossy," she said with a laugh, hitting me in the bicep with her fist. "I'm not one of your team. And I'm a grown woman. I don't have a bedtime."

"Okay, then please keep quiet, make yourself useful, and watch the monitors with me," I sighed, not looking at her. I wasn't sure whether I wanted to kiss her or gag her, tie her up and throw her in a deep well. It didn't make any sense. We'd only just met, but I already couldn't stand it when she wasn't around —which usually meant bad news for my love life. Which, of course, also meant problems for the mission. Vera was right. Scientific research, monster hunting, and infatuation can be a deadly combination.

We sat quietly for another twenty minutes without another word, our eyes fixed on the monitors waiting for living nightmares to stalk their prey once more. Nikki absently picked a mint leaf from the table and put it in her mouth.

"You know," she broke the silence. "You and your team remind me a lot of the story of Beowulf."

"Beowulf? We're hardly going after Grendel here," I said with a smile. "Whatever's out there is strictly zoological. An animal that has yet to be identified by modern science. I'm pretty sure they're not mythological monsters cursed by the gods to victimize those who do wrong."

"Still, you and your team are lying in wait in the stillness of the night for a creature that has been feasting on the flesh of a village. Sounds an awful lot like Beowulf to me."

"Look, I really think we should stop talking..."

Without finishing the sentence, I stood up and bolted from my chair, running out the door. I'd seen something on the video screen that had sent slivers of dread shooting down my spine. A black form with a row of spiky horns protruding from its back had slunk past camera three towards the Feast Hall.

I raced out into the street, drawing my Glock from its holster, oblivious to anything else but my quarry. After several yards, I stopped and craned my head around, trying to catch any glimpse of the thing that I'd seen on camera. Silence. No movement at all. I knew I'd seen something. My eyes scanned the darkness, digging through the steam of the jungle night.

Arnold trotted up next to me, his nose to the ground. Looking into the inky blackness of the jungle, he let out a subtle growl, his lips drawing back to reveal his yellowed teeth. Something was spooking him.

I reached into a pouch hung over my shoulders, pulled out a pair of night-vision goggles and placed them on my head. With a gentle hum, the eyewear sprang to life melting away the darkness in to a ghostly green world of light. I searched my surroundings which were now as crisp and vibrant as in the noon day sun.

"Nikki," I whispered into the walkie-talkie. "Come in."

"I'm here," she replied over the radio.

"Do you see anything on the monitors?"

"Nothing."

"Try the thermal."

Several seconds went by while I stood waiting for her response. The rainforest surrounding the village was deathly still. Only minutes before, it had been alive with a symphony of wildlife—now, the silence was deafening. Something was nearby.

The squelch of the radio caused me to jerk.

"I see nothing," Nikki replied.

"Wake Randy and Vera. They need to get out here. Now."

"Okay."

Walking on the balls of my feet, I padded towards the edge of the tree line, peering through with the day for night goggles. One step at a time, I moved through the underbrush with my pistol outstretched, aimed at anything ready to pounce.

Bram! Bram! Bram! The sound of automatic gunfire. I hadn't pulled the trigger. Turning towards the Feast Hall, I sprang forward and ran towards the sounds of screaming. I quickened my pace as I approached and ran headlong into Landers.

"It was in there," he said, bending over to catch his breath. "I think I hit it in the leg."

Marc ran from the building, panic in his eyes. He'd seen the creature too.

"Where's Vera?" he asked.

"I'm here." Vera, Randy, and Nikki sprinted up to meet us.

"Your assistance is required," Marc said, grabbing her wrist and pulling her up the steps into the hall. Nikki and Arnold followed close behind them.

"Okay," I said, my heart threatening to leap from my throat. "We need to split up. Scott thinks he may have hit the thing and that means there may be a blood trail. Search the perimeter in grid formation, then spread out towards the jungle. We can't let this thing escape. And be sure to keep your radios handy."

We fanned out. Landers skirted off to the north. Randy to the south and I took the west. The river ran the eastern border of the village and I didn't think the jenglot, if that was what we were chasing, would attempt to escape that way. Legends said the creatures hated water.

I flipped the IR goggles back on and scanned the ground for any signs of our intruder. I was uneasy about the whole thing. Nikki had said the jenglot traveled in packs, but we'd only seen one.

Where are the rest of them?

"Jack! Jack!" Randy screamed through his radio. "Get over here now!'

Gunfire erupted to the south, the familiar sound of Randy's rifle. I leapt several low shrubs and dashed towards the ruckus. Landers caught up with me just as we reached a clearing in the vegetation and the horrifying sight of my old friend grappling with four nightmarish creatures, hissing and snarling, on the ground.

The jenglot, black as pitch with a tough chitinous hide, snapped and slashed at Randy; never getting close enough to him for the kill. They were actually performing some sort of ritualistic dance around their fallen prey, playing with him before their full out onslaught.

Amazing.

"Jack! Help!" Randy yelled, fending off talon-like claws that shredded at his T-shirt.

The creatures were nearly four feet all. Their long, skeletal legs, bent backwards at the knee like a kangaroo, were connected to a stump of a torso. Course, straw-like stocks of hair adorned their heads and seemed to move on their own. The spikes I'd seen on the one in the video display were now clearly visible and resembled the thick versions of porcupine quills. But it was their faces, however, that wrought the most fear. Chalk-white, they appeared little more than fleshless skulls with two eyeless sockets. A lower set of long, needle-sharp teeth extended past their thin, upper lips in one heck of an overbite. They looked to me to be giant, grotesque, air breathing piranhas.

"Jack!" Randy's cries broke me from my paralysis. One of the jenglot's jaws snapped down towards his arm as he struggled to push the creatures away.

Drawing my weapon, I aimed towards the closest one. Landers hand came down quick against my aim, bringing my gun to my side.

"It's too risky," he said. "Shot's not clear."

"What am I supposed to do?" I asked as Randy's right hook belted one the jenglot across the forehead.

"Any time now guys!" Randy said.

I raised the Glock and fired four shots in the air. The explosions were deafening, but the jenglot hesitated only long enough to acknowledge our presence and then resumed their assault. Eight scaled talons flailed, trying to subdue their difficult prey.

Landers glared at me, a silent rebuke against such an idiotic stunt.

"Hey, you never know until you try!" I said, shrugging my shoulders.

Whatever these creatures were, they were not afraid of loud noises. Fortunately, they did not appear to be as strong as their muscular frame suggested. Although getting tired and a few cuts, Randy seemed capable of fending them off. *Maybe they'll tire out*, I thought.

Of course, I knew we couldn't risk that. What they lacked in power, the jenglot made up in numbers and tenacity. They were hungry and it wouldn't be long before they broke down my friend's defenses.

"Can you think of anything?" I asked Landers, who stood watching the scene in stoic contemplation.

"I'm trying, but every plan I come up with puts Randy in danger."

"More than he is now?"

"Good point. Still, you'd rather not have to kill them would you?"

"At this point, I don't really care. Stromwell just wanted us to get to the bottom of this and put a stop it. Krenkin just wants one of them."

"Guys!"

We turned to look at Randy, his hand around one jenglot's neck, his feet kicking another away. Two other creatures circled the frenzy, biding their time to pounce again. It was the creature limping through a thicket of trees, however, that shot an icy chill through my blood.

Oh wow, I thought. *This has got to be the Alpha.*

Most pack animals had a single male that acted as leader, protector, and judge for the rest. The Alpha. They were typically the largest. Most definitely the fiercest in the pack.

I had no doubt that the hulking black creature lumbering towards the others was the jenglot Alpha. By all appearance, the beast was identical to the others save its size, which was well over five feet tall, with a distended belly that protruded past its overdeveloped pectoral region, making the creature look strangely pregnant.

Its pale face bore down on Randy's struggling form, a hideous fanged grin stretching up its face.

That's why the others hadn't gone in for the kill, I thought. *It's not that they were weak. They were waiting for the Alpha to get here.*

The massive jenglot looked up at us as it crept, now on all four limbs, towards Randy. Its oversize belly dragging the ground as it crawled. The others backed away in deference to the dominant creature. The large jenglot crouched even closer to the ground, unhinging its jaw to reveal a massive gaping maw. A single barbed tendril flicked its way from inside the creature's opened mouth, slithering through the air towards Randy's exposed throat.

We were out of time.

Before I could move, Landers leapt forward, pouncing on the larger jenglot's back. With a squeal, the creature flung the Marine from his shoulders and lunged, snapping at his neck with its fangs. The four smaller creatures moved back towards Randy, keeping him pinned down.

"Oh, I knew I should have brought a bigger can of Raid," I muttered, as I sprang towards them, desperate. In unison, they wheeled around, hissing at me. In a full rush, I plowed into three of them, sending us all crashing to the ground in a pile of scale and flesh. In the tumult, I caught glimpses of Randy standing to his feet and grappling with the remaining attacker.

My three jenglot clambered to their feet, pushing forward, and lunged. Rolling backwards, I came up to face them as they renewed their attack.

Suddenly, a rustle of leaves and shouts from villagers carried through the thick jungle wall. They were searching for us. The sound of the fight drew them closer, but I wasn't sure the jenglot would be intimidated. They didn't seem afraid of anything.

A lucky talon slashed across my face, stinging my eyes and cheeks as one of the creatures leapt around me. The noise hadn't distracted them. They were not about to give up their prize—which I assumed was one or all of us.

A single shaft of light broke through the darkness and trees, filling the clearing with a halogen haze. The creatures surrounding me wailed, shrinking from the light, completely forgetting me. More beams flooded the area as Marc and a number of villagers plodded through the foliage carrying the high powered flashlights that Krenkin had given us.

One by one, the creatures hissed and howled, as they writhed against the phosphorous onslaught. A single bellow from the leader sent all five of the jenglot scurrying through the forest and into darkness.

When the crowd of villagers finally found us, we were alone, helping each other off the ground and dusting ourselves off. My face felt tender under the pressure from my fingers. Randy's injuries were far more severe. His chest, arms, and legs were shredded and bleeding. His eyes swollen shut; he was forced to lean on Landers as we made our way back to camp.

8

"We need to go after them!" I said, grinding a cigar with my teeth.

"And do what? Get yourself in worse shape than Randy?" Vera asked, rummaging through her medical bag and pulling out an opaque brown bottle labeled *Iodine*. "It's crazy. Those things are vicious. They killed an old lady before Scott managed to get a shot off."

"It," I said. "It, not 'they.' Only *one* of them actually did the killing."

"There were more than one waiting in the woods for you though, weren't there? It really doesn't matter how many were actually inside."

"My point is, only one of the creatures did the actual killing."

"The big one," Landers piped in. "It was the big one that snuck into the Feeding Hall tonight."

"Exactly," I said. "It was limping and you said you shot it in the leg. It had to be the same one."

The sun rose above the horizon, fingers of red-orange light clawed through the open canvas doors of the tent, ushering in the sounds of wails and cries of the villagers. Typical tribal mourning rituals. They were preparing the funeral procession for the jenglots' latest victim. Vera, Marc, and Landers diverted their eyes in respect as the line of mourners passed by carrying the remains. Nikki was walking in front, sullen and reading from the twenty-third Psalm.

"I think it's the only one that can actually extract the blood," I said once the procession had marched by.

"What on earth makes you think that?" Vera asked, turning back to apply iodine to Randy's injuries. "This is going to hurt a little, honey."

Wincing as she dabbed the swab across his chest, Randy lifted the ice pack from his swollen eyes, took a swig of water and cursed. "Geeze! Could you be any more brutal, Vera?"

"I'm not sure," I answered, ignoring the outburst. "Why did the creatures hold Randy down until the big one got there? Why did they back away as it approached and stuck that tongue thingy out at him? And the tongue itself is suggestive...it reminded me of the proboscis a mosquito uses to feed with. I think the Alpha is the only one capable of extracting their sustenance."

"Perhaps they were merely deferring to the Alpha's right for first blood," Marc offered, leaning back on his cot. "It might not mean anything at all."

"I agree," Scott said. "I don't think we can afford to assume anything at this moment. We just don't have enough intel on them yet."

Ignoring the peanut gallery, I dropped into my chair and cupped my head in my hands as the cries of mourning grew louder. The noise was nerve-wracking. I needed to think. I needed to reassess the situation. I bit my tongue, trying to contain the irritation building up inside me. We'd almost had them.

"I say we cut our losses and leave," Vera said.

"What? How can you say that?"

"Easy. We were paid to bring Stromwell's daughter back. Krenkin can go hang for all I care. I don't trust him anyway. The more I think about it, the more I know I've heard his name before and that he's bad news," Vera gently wrapped white gauze around Randy's waist, peeled off a piece of bandage tape and secured the bindings. "I say we just take the girl and get out of here."

A zillion hurtful words fluttered through my brain, desperately longing to lash out at Vera, but each one clung to the roof of my mouth. I was smarter than to let loose on her. She wasn't a woman you wanted angry with you and even I was rational enough not to pick a fight by resorting to spiteful words. Besides, she had a right to her opinions.

I spun around in my chair and rested my elbows on the monitor table. Exhaling a plume of smoke, I slammed my fist down on the table. She didn't understand. Not only were these things one of the greatest cryptozoological finds of my career, they were undoubtedly a key element in our own survival. Krenkin wasn't explicit in what would happen if I failed to deliver one of the jenglot, but I've learned to read between the lines over the years. Failure to capture his jenglot equals all the resources at the rebel's disposal gunning personally for me—and my friends.

"Guys?" I said to Marc and Landers. "Can we have a few minutes alone?"

Without a word, they walked from the tent and headed towards the river where the village was gathering for the funeral service. Randy lay in his cot, eyes closed, and pretending to sleep. He was never good at acting, but I didn't really care if he heard our conversation or not. Unlike the other two, he was a permanent member of the team.

I turned around to face her, willing my anger to dissolve. After all, she wasn't being stubborn on purpose. She truly had our best interests in mind.

"Look, the fact is that if we don't do something, more people are going to die," I said. It was a dirty move on my part. "We can stop this. We can."

Placing the iodine bottle back in her bag, she walked over to the cot where Arnold lay curled up in deep sleep and sat next to him. Awakening, he rolled over slightly, raised his legs in the air and grinned ecstatically as she scratched his underside.

"That's not fair," she finally said.

"I know. But you know I'm right."

"I also know you could give a rip about these people. You're always this way. It's always the hunt. Always the prey, the fortune, the fame. You're selfish, Jack. It's always about you."

She was right. It was a point of major contention with my folks and me. They'd always stressed the need to put others before myself; the idea of self-sacrifice for the well being of others. I'd never understood it. In a perfect world, it would be easy to do because I'd know that there was someone else looking out for me. But this wasn't a perfect world.

"Maybe." Knowing she was right doesn't always equal owning up to it. "But those jenglot are heading south to the next village. Are you willing to allow another person to die knowing we could have done something about it?"

Vera's eyes closed. Her jaws clenched tight, thinning her otherwise full lips. I knew I'd convinced her, but I felt the need to offer encouragement.

"Besides, we learned some things from last night's encounter."

"You mean your crazy theory about the Alpha?"

"More than that," I said.

"Like what?"

"Like their hunting pattern for one thing," I said with a smile. "They send one creature out while the others wait in the darkness. We also learned that these things are photosensitive… they hate light. That's a whopper."

"How does that help?" She tilted her head. I'd finally offered her something to sink her teeth into. She edged up on the cot and leaned forward.

"Well, it tells us that they are definitely nocturnal." I picked up a marker and added the word to the list I'd already started. "That means they probably need a dark place during the day to rest...a cave or a hollowed out tree...anything to protect them from the light."

I scrawled the words "*Photosensitive*" and "*Hiding Place*" on the board and wheeled around to Vera. Randy was sitting up in the cot gawking at the board.

"That's a good point," he said with a grin. "That gives us somewhere to start anyway."

"Absolutely not," Vera said looking over at her patient. "This nut job may go off chasing after those things, but you're staying right there. Your injuries may not look that serious, but I have no idea what kind of infection you've sustained. I'm not letting you out my sight until I'm confident you're okay."

"Ah, but mom," he teased, throwing himself back down to the cot in a feigned huff. "Jack always gets all the fun."

Yeah, I thought. *Real fun. Going after a pack of blood sucking mosquito lizards is hardly my idea of a good time.*

Then again, maybe it was.

Shouts from down by the river disrupted our conversation. The sounds were not the cries of mourners, but angry bursts of venom.

"What's going on?" Vera asked, running from the tent. "Don't move Cunningham!" she added to her patient.

Looking at Randy and shrugging, I chased after her towards the commotion.

"THEY DON'T NEED your protection, Shantili," Nikki said as we jogged down to the river bank where a crowd stood. "They have no need of your magic either."

"That is a matter for them to decide," the native witchdoctor said. His English was perfect and I had to wonder how he'd learned it. "You have no business here. The people have a right to choose who they will worship—your God or the ancestral spirits. But I warn you, the ancestors do not look kindly on those who turn their backs on them."

The little man leaned heavily against his staff. The rising sun glared from his smooth, shaved head. He wore a ragged orange tunic that hung low on his bony legs, with a red sash that crossed from his right shoulder to left hip. The few teeth he still had were dark and rotting with decay. A string of animal bones hung loosely from his vulture-like neck.

"It doesn't matter. These people are under my care now," Nikki shot back. "And under God's protection. You have no business here."

"This woman's death is upon your head, Christian." He pointed to the remains of the old lady lying on a wooden slab at the river bank. "The *darah botol susu* have been sent to drive you and your false religion from this country. They will not stop until you leave and the people return to their traditions."

I sauntered up next to Nikki, offering her support and glaring at the shaman that had turned the funeral service into chaos.

"You heard the lady, Mr., er, Little Creepy Shaman-guy. I believe she asked you to leave," I said.

"Its okay, Jack," Nikki said. "I can handle this."

"Oh, you're doing just peachy, I can tell."

"Look, this is our business, not yours. Your job is to track down the jenglot and do whatever it is you do. My job is to look after the people here, all right?"

"By all means," I growled, bowing and flaring out my arms in mock submission. She was really starting to rub me the wrong way and if not for the tantalizing lure of the hunt, I'd have been tempted to pack up our things and leave Dodge. "You deal with him."

I stepped back and walked over to Marc and Landers, who respectfully kept their distance from the other villagers. Without a word, they locked their attention on the old man. Landers hand unceremoniously gripped the handle of his P-90.

"Now, Shantili, we're in the middle of a funeral service," she continued, teeth grinding each syllable to powder. "If you're quiet, you can stay. If you can't remain silent, you need to leave."

The old man fixed his glare on me, muttering inaudibly and shaking the bone necklace around his neck. A sudden wave of nausea struck me, doubling me over to my knees at his silent words. Marc and Landers lifted me from the ground and helped me sit on a nearby tree stump as Shantili and the missionary continued their exchange.

"What in the world was that?" Marc whispered.

"I don't know," my voice shook, stumbling over the words. "A-All I know is he mumbled s-something under his breath and everything started spinning."

Marc's eyes snapped over to the old man and back to me. "What did he say?" he asked.

'I have no idea. I couldn't hear him."

"It's probably nothing," Marc said, taking a handkerchief out of his pocket and dabbing the stream of sweat glistening down my forehead. "It's nothing to worry about, I'm sure."

"Easy for you to say. Your insides weren't just turned to jelly."

We returned our attention to the argument.

"All right, Ms. Jenkins. I'm leaving. But mark my words. The jenglot will keep attacking until this place is cleansed of your false religion. I promise you that."

The witchdoctor turned and strode away without another word, leaving me feeling queasy in the building jungle heat. I already knew the guy was going to be trouble. We'd have to keep our eyes on the little guy through the rest of this whacked out mess.

9

The funeral ended without any further hitches and I brooded as we strolled back to the village. No one felt much like talking. We'd failed to save the life of an elderly woman in the village, Randy was brutally attacked, and we had nothing to show for it—not even good photographic evidence. The night had been a total disaster.

The team wandered off for some down time. I'd told them my plans of beating the creatures to the next village, a small village about thirty miles south called Baik Orang. I knew the next few days were going to be brutal and I'd suggested they all get some rest before we headed out at first light. I had a strange feeling that I wouldn't be able to follow my own advice. I was just too amped to sleep.

I wandered aimlessly into the tent, eyes cast down, trying to pinpoint the exact moment the world flipped inside out on me the night before.

"Would you care for tea?" said a pleasant male voice to my right.

I glanced up to be greeted by the warm face of the tribal chief,

Gnali. He wasn't smiling, but his bright eyes radiated a kind and jovial spirit, making it difficult to remain glum.

Gnali was holding a saucer and tea cup, its contents steaming. He had a dark, tan complexion with a neatly cropped mane of straight, graying hair. A thin mustache and beard adorned his face, hardly concealing the grin lines at the corner of his mouth.

"I said, would you like some tea?" he offered again when I didn't answer.

"Thank you." I took the cup from his hand and watched as he poured another for himself.

"I saw what happened between you and the shaman today."

"Oh, you mean when I told him to leave?"

He only smiled, turned, and sat down in a nearby chair, crossing his legs. "That's not what I meant," he said as he took a sip. "You know what I'm talking about."

I did. But I wasn't ready to admit it to anyone. Even Marc had no idea just how strange I'd felt when the old wizard had stared me down. It had been like someone taking a branding iron and churning my stomach with it—every nerve in my body had burned and it had taken all my strength to stop myself from throwing up.

I couldn't let Marc know. He'd let his imagination go wild, casting voodoo scenarios and half-cocked mystical hypotheses. I've been around. Seen a lot of things. But the one thing I believed in even less than some benevolent God looking to save my soul is magic. Everything has a reason. Everything an explanation cemented in reality and science.

"Ah, I see by your face that you don't wish to discuss it," Gnali said with a nod of his head. "All right, Dr. Jackson. I'm here to answer some questions. Sister Nikki told me you wished to discuss the jenglot with me."

I pulled a chair in front of his and plopped down, careful not to spill the tea. I looked at the wizened elder for some time before speaking. He was short, by American standards, standing just over five feet with strong, broad shoulders. His attire was different from the other villagers of Pingitti, wearing khaki shorts, flip flops, and a Hawaiian shirt that he left unbuttoned. His exposed torso was scarred with numerous markings, tattooed over the years to mark major feats in his life.

His face was dark and oval with a thick brow overhanging coal black eyes. Both of his arms were covered in a strange, black inked tattoo—similar to those on his chest—depicting a vine-like marking spiraling down from above his short sleeves to his wrists.

"Sure," I said finally. "I do have some questions for you. For starters, what do you believe we're dealing with? What do you think the jenglot are? Why are they so bold, so voracious all of a sudden? And how do I stop them?"

His smile broadened as he traced the tattoo on his left forearm. I leaned forward, taking a closer look. Along the spiral's line were several divots, set at regular intervals until it reached a spike at the base of his hand. A handful of red lines slashed across the spiral every inch or so down, marking through several of the divots.

"Do you see this line, Dr. Jackson?" He traced the tattoo a second time as he spoke. "This line represents my lineage. Each indention represents a fallen chieftain...my predecessors...dating back twenty generations. You see these red ones?"

I nodded silently.

"These represent each time the jenglot went on the warpath. They have always been around, Doctor. But feeding on very little. They rarely take more than they need to survive," he said, his face darkening. "But every three or four generations, the creatures go into a frenzy. They return to the region to mate, which stirs up their primal thirst for blood."

The chieftain took another sip of his tea, watching me from the corner of his eyes, before continuing.

"Each time they come, the strongest, bravest, and noblest of the tribe is chosen for the jenglot's final feeding. Usually, it is the chieftain, but not always," he grinned. "It marks a time of great celebration when the tribe's offering is found dead because the villagers know the rampage has come to an end."

Gnali's finger absently stroked the spike at his wrist, the smile fading. I said nothing. I'd heard similar stories in various regions of the world. Each tale was always a little different than the first, but the gist was always the same. A village is ravaged by fierce, mythical creatures for a time. The tribal leader offers himself as a sacrifice to appease their tormentors and the attacks cease upon his death. It was barbaric and superstitious and I loathed the very thought of it.

"Soon, it will be my time and I accept my fate gladly. I had hoped I would be chosen last night, but it wasn't meant to be."

"Stop right there." I couldn't take any more of this. "Look, you sound very intelligent...educated...."

"I studied at the university in Kuala Lumpur," he interrupted proudly. "Bachelor's in English Literature. I've taught my entire village to read and write."

"That's very admirable, but you're missing my point. Your education...your knowledge...should tell you that there is nothing supernatural about these creatures. They are flesh and blood. I hunt animals, not monsters. No need for you to die with honor. It's much better for you to live for your people."

"I am well aware of the jenglot's nature, Dr. Jackson. I am also aware of our tribal history and am ready to follow the will of God in this matter," he laughed out loud at some hidden joke in his sentence. I had no idea where he was going with his line of thought, but I had a feeling I wasn't going to like it. "He is sovereign in all things. If he wishes, I will gladly give my life for my people."

"I don't intend to let that happen," I said, a wave of anger washing over my face. "No one else has to die and they sure as heck don't have to sacrifice themselves to these things."

The old man smiled broadly at me, sat his cup down, and stood up from his chair. He stood next to me and placed one gentle hand on my shoulder.

"I know you will do your best," he said, chuckling. "But be warned. Things are not always as they seem and we rarely have as much control over the events of our lives as we'd like to think. There may well be sacrifices in *your* future, Dr. Jackson. Be prepared."

I cringed. Just when I was starting to like the guy, he transformed himself into an enigmatic fruitcake, of all things.

The old man turned to walk out of the tent.

"Wait," I said, willing myself not to ask him to explain his last few comments. I really didn't care to know. "I had one more question. The shaman, Shantili..."

"Yes? What about him?"

"Well, he seems to know a great deal about the jenglot," I said. "He's also known to wander around from village to village."

Gnali stood silently, hands in his pockets and stared at me. If he knew my next question, he didn't let on that he did.

"Do you think there's a connection? I mean a connection between the jenglot and the wizard?"

"I can tell you this," he answered, his smiling face growing grim. "Wherever the *Ahli Sihir*, the magician, is...you will find the jenglot. Wherever the jenglot are, there too is the *Ahli Sihir*. Are they connected? Yes. Is Shantili responsible? I simply do not know. But I believe you will find out soon enough, eh, Dr. Jackson?"

His smile had returned, beaming at me as he strode out of the tent, leaving me to think about all that I had learned. Or rather, what I hadn't.

"WHY ARE we back out here again?" asked Randy as we crawled on hands and knees through the jungle foliage. Vera would have killed him if she knew what he was doing. His injuries were no where near well enough for him to be out with me in the jungle, but I'd needed a second pair of eyes and his were the only one's I trusted. "I don't really like this at all."

The sun slunk down below the tree line on our second day at Pingitti Village and I'd decided to take a closer sweep of the area in which we were attacked by the jenglot. Randy had agreed to help, while the rest of the group prepared for our trip at daybreak.

"Don't worry about it," I said, digging at some leaves to reveal the soil. Arnold's snout huffed through the debris next to me. "They're not going to return. And I told you, those things may have left something behind...anything to add to what little we know about them."

I reached in my backpack, withdrew a UV flashlight, and powered it on. The ground radiated with a purple-blue haze in the dwindling sunlight. I knew I'd have a better chance if I'd used it at night, so I'd risked waiting to search the area until dark.

For twenty minutes, I poured over every inch of the patch of ground where we'd fought the jenglot the night before. Nothing. A few broken twigs, a button from Landers' shirt pocket, and a mess of ants were all that I managed to discover.

I was bringing the flashlight up to turn it off, when I caught something silver from the corner of my eye. I flashed the light in the same direction and found what I'd been looking for—a dried clump of blood shining silver in the UV beam.

"Randy, take a look at this."

My friend clambered up to his feet and walked over and looked where I was pointing.

"Is that blood?" he asked, taking off his cap and wiping his forehead with his shirt sleeve.

"I think so. Could it be yours?"

Randy looked at the stain on the ground and then back over

from where he'd just been searching. Crouching to one knee, he bent over for a better look.

"No, I don't think so," he said. "I'm pretty sure that patch of flattened grass is where the creeps had me pinned. I don't think I ever made it over this far."

My heart raced. This was it. If the blood didn't belong to Randy, then there was a good chance it came from the injured alpha. The first biological evidence of the creatures the natives called "jenglot"—blood sucking killers that had been terrorizing south Asia for thousands of years.

"Take a sample," I said, handing him a cotton swab and Petri dish from my pack. "We'll need to run a DNA test when we return to the states."

"I thought we planned on returning to the states *with* one of the creatures themselves?"

"Come on, Randy," I said with a wide grin. "You know how our luck runs. With a DNA sample, it's a win-win situation. If we capture one...great. If not, then at least we go home with a consolation prize."

"That is if we don't wind up going home in body bags," he said. "Like you said, we don't have the best of luck. If we don't catch one of these critters, you don't really think that rebel nutcase is going to let us waltz out of here do you?"

"Ah, he's a pussycat," I lied. "He'll understand. I don't think he's as bad a guy as we first thought."

I was so going to hell for the lies I was telling. But I couldn't let Randy or the others know just how much the old geezer had given me the heebie-jeebies. As far as they were concerned, Krenkin and I were tight. And that was the story I was going to take to my grave if I could help it.

"You go ahead and take the sample," I continued. "I'm going on ahead and see if I can follow their trail."

"Are you serious?"

I drew my gun from its holster and pulled the slide, loading the weapon.

"Sure. Besides, without you in the way, I don't have to worry about using this."

MY LUNGS PUMPED WILDLY AS I fought through the brush, plunging deeper into the rainforest. I'd been searching for nearly thirty minutes in the blackness of the jungle night, UV light in hand and infrared goggles strapped to my forehead. So far, tracking the small trail of blood left by the Alpha jenglot had not been as difficult as I'd first thought. There'd been a lot of it. The creature's wound must have been serious.

A well of hope surged through my veins at the thought. An injured alpha meant finding a place to hide until it was tended. The pack couldn't have gone too far in the leader's condition. But I had reached a point where the blood trail seemed to stop. I had no way of knowing which direction the jenglot had moved.

A rustle in the brushwood to my right, spun me around, my gun extended. Finger on the trigger. The movement bustled towards me. I pocketed the UV flashlight, placing my other hand around the gun for better aim. I held my breath. Frozen, my eyes peered through the vines and bramble that made up the jungle wall.

The sounds stopped. Whatever was lurking in the undergrowth in front of me had stopped moving. Tiny slivers of cold flashed up my neck, producing gooseflesh down my arms.

"Okay," I said under my breath. "It's probably nothing."

The foliage rustled again.

"Right," I whispered. "And the bushes are just dancing to the oldies."

I crept forward for a better look. The green haze of the IR goggles emblazoned my surroundings, giving me a clear view of the branches ahead. Inching my way through the brambles, I scanned right to left for the source of the sounds. My body jerked as a young pangolin, thrusting out its long sticky tongue, scurried from a nearby bush deeper into the forest.

I exhaled, relieved knowing the rustling had only been from the scale-covered anteater that thrived in the rainforests of Malaysia. I holstered my sidearm and moved forward, searching to make sure the pangolin had been the only thing moving around. My continued search turned up no other animals.

I turned to head back to the path when I caught the sight of something dark to the south. Taking a closer look, I discovered a small opening in the side of a ridge—an entrance to a cave.

I moved towards the small lip in the rock. My infrared enhanced eyes scanning for any signs of the creatures I had been tracking.

"There," I said out loud, walking to a dark patch on a pile of stones near the entrance. Stooping, I dabbed my index finger onto the spot and brought it up to my eyes. A sticky, dark red goo, congealed blood, clung to it.

The jenglot Alpha. I'd rediscovered the trail.

Steeling myself, taking a deep breath, I entered the ethereal blackness of the cavern before me. Hoping I'd find my prize inside. Praying that I wouldn't.

10

The cavern neck hung low, forcing me to belly crawl through the first twenty-five feet or so. Mud caked the stone floor, oozing around my arms and legs as I inched my way forward. The musty smell of mildew and guano mixed, stinging my nostrils and eyes.

Despite the tepid heat outside, the cave's chill sent uncontrollable shivers through my extremities as I moved. Water pooled around my neck and chin as I crawled through the muck.

The cavern entrance soon opened into a large domed chamber. Drops of water echoed through the maze of tunnels around me. I scanned the chamber, adjusting the day-for-night goggles to get a better view.

Nothing.

Except for the occasional flutter of bats clinging to the cavern ceiling, all lay undisturbed. I pulled up the goggles, engulfing me in tomb-like darkness. I reached into my pocket, pulled out the UV light and flicked it on. The bluish beam hovered over the stone floor and walls, projecting an eerie haze around me. Streaks of silver blazed around the chamber, the evidence of urine and other waste from the animals lurking in the recesses under the earth. There was no way to tell the difference between signs of the jenglot and the cave's denizens.

I jerked around at the echo of footsteps darting off down a low lying tunnel to my left—my light stabbing through the darkness in search of the source. Once again, I saw nothing. But nothing cannot make the sounds of flattened footfalls on the stone floors of caverns. Whatever it was, I knew it was large and possibly bi-pedal.

I inched towards the left passage veering, so caught up in the hunt that I smacked my head against a low hanging stalactite. A heated trickle wormed down my face and I detected the distinct taste of copper as it reached my lips.

I pushed on, straining to cut through the darkness, mindful that, besides the animals that usually haunted such places, I was not alone. Something else, something large, roamed the corridors of the cave with me.

After several yards, the tunnel narrowed, forcing me to turn and side-step my way through. It was a tight squeeze and I found myself thankful for meeting Jenny Craig after the holidays.

The slender throat of the passage twisted for another hundred yards until my eyes picked up something I had not expected.

Light.

I glanced at my watch, its florescent numbers glowing green in the darkness. It was nearly midnight. Still dark outside. The light I saw, just a few feet away around a curved wall, could not be coming from outside.

As I moved closer, I noticed the radiance rippling along the uneven surface of the stone ceiling. Fire. Somewhere deep in the earth, a single blaze melted away the gloom, calling me forward like a moth.

Coming to the end of the passage, I stepped out in a vast chamber. Its cathedral-like ceilings trailed higher than my sight would allow. Stalactites and stalagmites littered the walls and floor, appearing to dance eerily in the shadows cast by the large bonfire raging in the center of the room. Several pods of crystalline soda straws glistened in the light, projecting prismatic images around them.

I whirled around, taking in everything. A smattering of torches rested unlit in sconces along the walls. The chamber itself was a marvel any archaeologist would have salivated over. Paintings and pictograms were scrawled everywhere—on the floor, the walls, even the speleothemic formations scattered throughout the chamber. The drawings covered a wide spectrum, from simple daily depictions of agricultural practices to images of wars and battles.

I paced around the great hall, inspecting each of the pictograms in rapt awe. Grabbing my digital camera from my pack, I quickly snapped as many photographs my fingers could click. I stopped short, however, when the lens rested on one terrifying image—twenty jet black beings, carved from the very granite itself, long spindly spikes protruding from their backs and necks. The creatures in the picture formed a strange crescent shaped half-circle, standing idle as a larger, more menacing monster loomed in the center. The Alpha. The larger creature seemed adorned with a crown made of gold, its sharp, needle-like claws descended on what appeared to be a human villager. The depiction was uncanny, an almost photographic representation of the very creatures my team and I saw in Pingitti the night before.

"Amazing, aren't they?" A voice croaked behind me.

I spun around, hand gripping my sidearm and pointing it at the voice.

The first thing I saw were nine high-powered assault rifles pointed at my face, held steadily by stern looking men dressed in Malay ceremonial garb. The second thing I saw was the witchdoctor, Shantili, standing with arms behind his back in the center of the gun-toting locals.

A wave of nausea struck my gut as I looked at him, an aftershock of the attack from earlier in the day.

"You won't need your weapon," he said, palms extended upward. "The *darah botol susu* have already left this place. They were here, but left when the sun went down."

I stood stunned. The unnerving presence of the AK-47's paled in comparison to the shaman's sudden appearance. I willed myself to respond.

"The darah booboo whatnow?" I asked. Not exactly scientific. Not even remotely calm, but it was the best I could do under the circumstances. "I heard you use that word at the funeral earlier."

"The *darah botol susu,*" he replied, a chuckle slithering out of a sly grin. The old man waved a hand and his followers scattered around the cave, lowering their weapons. "It means *blood feeder* in Malay. I believe you call them jenglot, however. They are no longer here. Your gun really is quite unnecessary."

"I like my gun just fine where it is, thank you."

He walked nonchalantly over to the fire and sat down, crossing his legs.

"Suit yourself, but it makes my men a bit nervous," he said, looking over at me and stretching out his hand for me to join him. "Come. Sit. We have much to discuss, you and I."

I looked around the chamber, eyeing his henchmen before turning my attention back to the little old man sitting Indian style next to the blazing fire. Paper thin skin draped loosely over pronounced bones, jutting from his body. A slight hump pushed unceremoniously above his back. He looked at me and grinned. I half expected a forked tongue to slither out, but I was sure the old magic man knew more about the jenglot than anyone else. If I was going to catch one, he'd know exactly how to do it.

Of course, the distinct possibility that he was behind the blood suckers' attacks hadn't slipped my mind either. He might not like the idea of us catching one of his little pets.

Without a word, I strode across the chamber and squatted on the ground, holstering my Glock for the sake of easing the tension of the old man's soldiers. I shoved the UV light in my shirt pocket and pulled a canteen up to my lips. The cool water cascaded gently down my dry throat.

"All right, doc," I said, wiping my mouth on my sleeve. "What's up? What's this little pow-wow about?"

"You came to me, remember?"

I looked at him incredulously. I was determined not to play his game. The problem was I had no idea which game we were playing, or its rules for that matter.

"What are you talking about?" I sneered. "I didn't come here for you. I was looking for the jenglot. As a matter of fact, you give me the creeps. A dark cave is the last place I'd come if I was looking for you… Ripley's maybe, but not here."

"Needless to say, you did, in fact, come to me," he said, his smile fading into a scowl. "And I'm glad. It gives us time to talk… one on one."

He reached into his pocket and withdrew a dirty handkerchief, folded several times. He unwrapped it, plucked up an enormous, fur-covered spider and skewered it on a stick. The witchdoctor plunged the stick into the fire and let it sit for several seconds before drawing it out.

"That was quite a nasty bit of illness you suffered earlier today," he said, offering me a piece of the hairy little morsel with a gesture. I nodded, suppressing an urge to hurl. A malicious grin spread across his face as he bit into the char-grilled spider, tearing off two of its legs before continuing between mouthfuls. "There are many illnesses that come to those who explore these jungles without taking precautions."

"I'm up on my shots."

"I'm sure you are, American. But there are some things that medicine cannot cure."

If it was possible, I was beginning to the dislike the guy more and more, every second I was near him. He reeked of sweat and filth, and I cringed as several unidentified bugs crawled unnoticed across his bare neck.

"I'll manage," I said, wrinkling my nose in disgust. "Look, I need to get going. Don't think it hasn't been fun, but I'd rather have my teeth pulled than hang out any more with you."

I stood up from the cold floor and turned to head down the narrow tunnel that led back to the cave entrance. I wasn't sure what was going on, but something about the shaman was registering a perfect ten on my creeped out-o-meter. The old man might have information I could use against the jenglot, but I was beginning to wonder if it'd be worth it to find out.

"Wait," he said behind me. The crunch of his teeth against the hardened shell of the arachnid echoed in the cavern. "There are some things you should know, doctor. Things about the jenglot. And more importantly, things about Krenkin."

The name of the rebel leader stopped me cold.

"How do you know about Krenkin?"

"I know a great many things," he said, standing up and strolling over to me. "There is very little that happens around here that I don't know actually. For instance, I know that Sashe Krenkin has hired you to bring back one of the *darah botol susu*. I know he's offered you a considerable amount of money for it."

He paused, letting his words sink in.

"But I have to ask," he continued. "Have you not wondered what Krenkin plans to do with the creature once he has it? Have you not considered the reasons he'd pay so much, so easily, for a myth?"

Now that the old man mentioned it, I hadn't. I'd just assumed his interest was the same as mine—simple curiosity. But what would a freedom fighter, wanting to overthrow the current government, desire with a creature that fed on human blood to survive? From what I'd seen, the jenglot weren't even effective killers or hunters.

"I see by your expression that you haven't considered these things," Shantili said.

"No, but I suppose you're going to tell me."

The old man paced around me, hands behind his back and eyes staring up at the images plastered on the cave walls.

"Actually, I'm not," he said quietly. "But I will say this. The jenglot clans survive with a very delicate balance. Offset that balance by a hair and you threaten the entire species."

"What am I supposed to do? They're killing innocent people."

"Innocent?" His voice rose with his flaring temper. The bonfire seemed to burn even brighter with his words. "Hardly innocent Doctor. They have turned their backs on the gods that have served them for generations. Turned their backs on their ancestors to follow after a Man-god. Why would this Jewish carpenter care about the lives of some superstitious tribal miscreants?"

I'd touched a nerve. The old man obviously hated the Christian religion. At least we had something in common. But his response was surprising to say the least.

"That's kind of a harsh way of thinking about your own people."

"Hardly. The people of the village I served turned their backs on me. They kicked me out and stripped me of the privileges that go with being their spiritual leader...traditions that date back centuries."

"And so, you despise them now?"

"Absolutely. I'd rather spit on them as to look at them."

"Would you say you hated them so much you'd, let's just say, like to see them dead?"

Shantili turned to glare at me. His eyes burned white against the cavern darkness, reflection from the fire playing tricks with my own eyes. Then, his face softened a bit and a great smile edged its way up the sides of his face.

"Ah, I see," he said. "Why not just ask me what you are thinking?"

"Okay, I will. Are you responsible for the jenglot attacks on the villages around here?"

An earsplitting cackle broke out from deep within the old man's throat. His eyes, swollen with genuine mirth, locked on my own.

"You might as well ask if I can harness the power of the monsoon," he said between bursts of laughter. "Or whether I can take hold of the moon and use it to light my way through this cave. Your jenglot are not creatures that can be domesticated, contained, trained. They are a force of nature itself. They are the breath, the soul, the very source of darkness and despair."

"But are you responsible?" He hadn't answered my question and I wasn't going to let him off the hook with his arcane riddles. Why spiritual leaders and philosophical gurus felt compelled to speak in circles had always been beyond me.

The witchdoctor's smile broadened, distorting his features and creating a weird effect in the fire light. For a brief moment, I could swear his face had changed, jaws unhinged with sharp, needle teeth. Then, as quick as the image appeared, it was gone.

"The ancestors are the one's responsible for the jenglot," he said softly. "They alone have the power to control the Blood Feeders. And I am merely a humble servant of the spirits. I do as they instruct."

The nausea returned, doubling me over on the ground.

"Are you all right, Dr. Jackson?" he said. "You don't look well."

He reached down to help me up, but I slapped his hand away.

"I can manage, thank you," I growled. "Just got a bit dizzy, that's all."

"So it would seem."

I wasn't sure what was going on, but I didn't like it. Every time I got near or around the guy, my insides started doing somersaults and jumping jacks at the same time. My stomach pounded against my abdominal wall in spasms.

"Perhaps you should leave this place," the old man said.

"Leave this country. Go find yourself a well-trained American doctor and have yourself examined. It might be serious."

"I'll be fine. Don't worry," I said, leaning against the side of the cave. "Now, if you don't mind, I need to be getting back to the village."

"Ah, the village. Pingitti. I'm sure you're anxious to return to the beautiful Nikki Jenkins. It's really a shame about her when you think about it."

I had just slid myself into the narrow gap towards the exit when I stopped at his words.

"And what is that supposed to mean?" I asked, my head turning in his direction.

"Oh, nothing really. I suppose if you haven't questioned the motives of Krenkin, you definitely haven't delved into what forces have brought our young missionary friend to the jungles of Malaysia," he said with a smile. "So beautiful and intelligent. The daughter of privilege, prestige. And she finds herself in the lowliest of villages in Malaysia...a village that just so happens to land her in the middle of the jenglot hunting grounds. Does that not strike you as a bit odd, Dr. Jackson?"

I had to admit that it did. While her being here could have easily been coincidence, why hadn't her powerful father sent in a full blown strike team to get her out? Why send in a cryptozoologist? I was beginning to smell a rat and it wasn't necessarily coming from Shantili.

"Ah, I think maybe you are starting to understand," he smiled, bowing his head slightly. "I'm afraid that Ms. Jenkins is just as much a pawn in this mess as you. Caught up in a wave of deception by her own government, her own father. And she's not even aware of it."

I was getting tired of this.

"She's a missionary," I said. "She goes where they send her."

"But the question is...who sent her?"

This is getting ridiculous. The old man's playing mind games.

"And I suppose you're going to say someone besides Nikki's missions organization is pulling her strings?"

"It really isn't for me to say," Shantili said. "Perhaps it's something you should talk to her about."

"Whatever," I growled, looking back at the shaman's armed guards to make sure they would let me leave. They stood stoically in their places, unmoving and content to let me go. I looked back at Shantili, gave a curt nod of the head, and wormed my way back towards the entrance and open air.

The words of the shaman clawed their way through my mind, burning at my thoughts like an army of red ants. I'd spent entirely too much time talking with the crazy old coot and hadn't learned anything useful.

Yet, I couldn't help feeling that there was a great deal more to learn about my current predicament. I intended to find out everything I could—about both Nikki and Krenkin.

11

It was almost four in the morning by the time I made it back to the village. I'd expected to find the camp quiet and the team getting plenty of rest for the journey ahead. Instead, I found our temporary headquarters buzzing with activity.

Randy, still weakened by the injuries from last night, carefully checked the equipment, making sure each piece of gear was in optimal condition. Landers and Marc sat at a folding table, cleaning and loading the various weapons we would take on the trip to Baik Orang, the next village on the jenglot's progressive dinner party. Even Arnold was restless, spastically chasing a rubber ball around the room.

I looked around. No sign of Vera. I figured she'd taken her usual early morning run, so I walked out of the tent and into the brisk morning air. It had rained while I'd explored the jenglot caverns and the temperature had dropped dramatically.

The coolness felt sweet against my skin as I strode over to a nearby cluster of trees looking for my Russian friend. I needed to find her, discuss things with her. Fill her in on my encounter with the witchdoctor. Despite how long Randy and I had been friends, Vera was the one I depended on most. She was my closest, most intimate friend and through the years, had grown to become like a sister. She was wise beyond her mere twenty-seven years and always knew exactly what to do or say to help me see things in a clear light.

I wandered through a stand of durian trees, snatched one of its giant fruit from a branch, and cut into the thorny husk with my knife. After wincing from the disgusting odor wafting from it, I dropped a slice into my mouth, its sweet onion-like juice shooting down my throat, and I understood why the locals called it *King of Fruits*. I was about to take another bite when voices inside the grove caught my attention. Two women were talking—Vera and Nikki.

"It's all right," Nikki said in hushed tones. "It really is all right. He doesn't care what you've done in the past."

I crept towards the women, keeping myself hidden in the shadows of the trees. Vera sat on an old rotted log, both hands clasped over her face and heaving with sobs.

"How do you know that? Vera cried. "I've done horrible things."

Nikki sat next to her, putting an arm around her and drawing Vera's head to rest on her shoulder. For several long seconds, they just sat there quietly, rocking back and forth on the old log.

"Honey, you need to understand something," Nikki finally said. "Nothing you've done surprises him. Nothing you have thought or said or done can ever drive him away from you."

What are they talking about? I wondered, watching the scene from the security of the tree line. It occurred to me that eavesdropping was rude, but after the last few days, I wasn't very concerned with manners.

"That's hard to believe," Vera sobbed. "I was a whore, for God's sake! And that's one of the lesser sins in my life."

"It doesn't matter, sweetie. No one, not one single person in the history of man, has ever lived a life without sin. No one, that is, except Jesus."

Oh, no. This can't be happening. The last thing I need is this self-righteous little tart filling my team with this nonsense.

Despite my outrage, I found my legs unable to budge. I willed myself to move into the clearing and put a stop to the discussion right then and there. But I simply couldn't move.

"You see," Nikki continued. Vera's wet, blue eyes looked up at her. "God knows we can't live perfect lives. We can't measure up. He's perfect and we're not...plain and simple."

"But that's the problem," Vera said, wiping a tear away with her palm. "I can't measure up. How can He love me? How can He forgive me? I've never once thought about Him or what He wants. I've always lived for myself."

"That's exactly my point. That's the nature of mankind. Adam's sin was not eating the Forbidden Fruit, Vera. It was the fact that Adam put his desire over that of God's. That's what sin is. It's Man strolling right up to the throne of God and plopping down in it. It's Man thinking he can handle things on his own without consideration of what God desires for us."

"So, then how can He want anything to do with us?"

"He loves us, Vera. Just as any good parent loves a child. There's nothing that child can do that will drive the parent away. The good parent will always love their children. No matter what," Nikki said. The descending moonlight broke through a stream of clouds, reflecting off the missionary's eyes. She was crying too. "God is perfect, Vera. He expects perfection from us as well. But He knows we can't live up to his expectations. So what does He do?"

I need to stop this. I had heard all this a million times before. It was rubbish and Vera had had a tough enough life without having to hear what a "sinner" she's been.

"He sent Jesus, His son," Nikki said. "Jesus did live the perfect life. And he was killed because of it. He took the punishment meant for you and me, Vera. Our sins, our crimes against God, were punishable by death. But Jesus died in our place. In reality, we switched places. He became us and we, in turn, can take on His perfection. If we ask Him, God will no longer see us and our sin, but the wonderful beauty of His son's perfection in us."

The two sat quietly for several minutes, pondering what had been said. One look at Vera's face sent shivers of despair down my neck. She was buying into it all. She was actually considering the Christian rhetoric.

"All you have to do, Vera, is die to yourself."

I shuddered at her choice of words. Words eerily similar to those of Gnali. Self-sacrifice. Dying. Spiritual suicide. What in the world was she doing to Vera?

"You need to stop trying to live your own life," Nikki continued with a warm smile. "Give up control; give all that you are to Christ and ask Him to forgive you. That's all you have to do and I can help you. I can—"

"That's enough," I said, finding the strength to move from my hiding place and storm into the clearing. "Can't you see what you're doing to her?"

I moved over to Vera and pulled her gently to her feet, wrapping an arm around her and squeezing.

"It's okay, sweetie," I said, wiping a tear from her cheek. "You're fine just the way you are. You're a good, decent, and warm person. Better than any of us."

I glared at Nikki as I spoke.

"But, I..." Vera tried to protest.

"We'll talk more about this later, Vera," I said, squeezing her again. "Right now, you need to go back to the tent and get a little sleep. We'll be leaving in about two hours and you'll need to be rested up."

Vera looked at me, her big eyes glistening with tears. She then glanced at Nikki for a moment, wiped the streaks from her face, and dashed off into the Durian grove.

I turned to the missionary, eyes glaring.

"You need to stop." I growled.

"Stop what? I was just..."

"You know exactly what I mean," I said. "You have no idea what the girl's been through. No idea how much her past haunts her and you start unloading your sanctimonious drivel on her like she's some heathen from hell."

Nikki stood up from the log, arms crossed. Moving inches away from my face, she stabbed a finger into my chest.

"Listen," she said. "First of all, you don't tell me what I can or cannot do. Second, Vera came to me, not the other way around. I don't push my drivel, as you put it, on anyone. And third...third..."

"Yeah?"

She stiffened. Her eyes blazed as she glared at me speechless.

"What? I'm listening," I goaded, a grin spreading wide across my face. I'd been furious with her for trying to convert Vera, but now, I couldn't help think how cute she looked as she struggled to tell me off.

"And third," she continued, nodding her head in triumph as she came up with the perfect reply. "Third, you're a big jerk... that's what."

We both stood, unable to speak. Then, unable to control myself, I burst out in raucous laughter at her final point. She quickly joined me and after several minutes, we both heaved for breath and sat down on the nearby log.

"So I'm not good under pressure," she said between laughs.

"I can see that."

"But seriously, I never push my faith on people. I may be a missionary, but that doesn't mean that I seek out people to shatter their own belief systems. And Vera really did come to me. She wanted to know about Jesus."

I looked at her silently. She really was beautiful. Her long, blonde hair, no longer constrained by a baseball cap, hung loosely around her shoulders. A strand of it fell across her face, forcing her to pull it behind her right ear.

"I know," I said. "Vera's a complicated person. She's the strongest woman I know most of the time. But she has bouts with her confidence sometimes. She doubts herself."

"And that's a bad thing?"

"Absolutely. In our work, self-doubt can be fatal. We're scientists, Nikki. There's no room in it for faith."

"I see," she said, looking out at the durian trees. I didn't like the way she said it.

"What the heck's that supposed to mean?"

She looked back at me with a small smile.

"Well, it's a funny thing about scientists. They're always claiming that faith has no place in their disciplines, but it seems to me that it requires a great deal of it to do what they do," she said. "They have to have faith in their own methods, their suppositions, their theoretical conclusions."

I'd heard all this before—many times—and it never failed to grate against my spine like an elementary school band trying to play a Mozart concerto.

"Science is verifiable. It is tested and retested. If you can't duplicate results, then it's thrown out," I said. "That's not faith. That's science."

"Really? And what about evolution? The Big Bang Theory? Neither of those things is verifiable. You can't recreate creation. You can't duplicate the evolutionary process in a lab. On top of that, not one shred of physical evidence has been found to support it—not one transitional species discovered—yet all other science is based on the precepts. If evolution is wrong, then so many other disciplines will find their own suppositions distorted, if not out and out false."

She sounded so much like my parents. It was infuriating, but I remained silent.

"As a matter of fact," she continued. "Almost every aspect of our culture is centered around Darwin's hypotheses. Psychology, sociology, criminology. Even marketing and business is based on it. So tell me, what happens when we find out its all wrong? What happens to our culture, our societal infrastructure, then?"

I couldn't answer her. I knew she was right about evolution being the lynch pin of everything we were. But her argument was flawed.

"You're wrong though," I said. "Evolution is scientific. It is verifiable because it occurs in the natural world...not some spiritual one. We can see it, smell it. We just haven't uncovered enough evidence yet, but we will."

She let out another giggle. Not a laugh of incredulity, but one of genuine amusement.

"And there we have it," she said.

"Have what?"

"Faith, Jack. Faith. It's believing in what is unseen and hoping in what is intangible. It's the same for science as it is for Christianity."

I knew she had me, but I railed against the idea. Faith, by nature, was for the religious. And I wanted no part of it.

"Jack, you need to understand something," she said, her face hardened. "Before this whole thing is over, you may need faith. We're not just chasing monsters here. There are spiritual forces at work as well. I've felt it and so have you."

I looked at her wide eyed.

"What do you mean by that?" I asked.

"Yesterday. At the funeral. Don't think I didn't notice your collapse. Shantili was mouthing some sort of hex. I thought it was directed at me until I saw what happened to you. Jack, you were under attack. Spiritual assault. As soon as I noticed what was happening to you, I started praying silently. Then it seemed to ease up."

I didn't know what to say. The whole thing seemed so "out there." I didn't believe in the spirit world. It was all a bunch of hocus pocus—mind over matter. Superstition. But my analytical mind tried to wrap itself around the idea anyway. It really made the most sense, whether I wanted to admit it or not.

"I don't know about all that," I said. "But don't worry. No matter what happens, I'll be ready." I patted my shoulder holster for emphasis.

"I hope so," she said, offering a warm smile. "But Jack, you may need more than a gun to see this through. You may need to find your faith...or you might not survive the next time."

She stood up without another word and strode off back to the village, leaving me alone with my thoughts. Grim, unnerving thoughts.

12

"You're not going with us and that's final," I said to Nikki as I stuffed my pack with an assortment of gear I'd need on the trail. I hesitated, spinning my last four cigar cylinders in my fingertips, then slid them in the side pocket.

I'd returned to camp irritable, thirty minutes after my talk with Nikki and had gathered the team together to prepare for our departure to Baik Orang. I was floored when Nikki demanded to go with us. We were sent here to protect the spoiled little princess, after all, and I was in no mood to carry her around in the jungle with me.

Of course, some of it had to do with Vera. I was still steaming over Nikki's attempt at converting my friend. Vera and I still hadn't had a chance to discuss what had happened. Some things were just better left unsaid. But I hadn't even been able to tell her about my run in with the witchdoctor and that bothered me. I needed her guidance, but her latest episode of self-doubt had ruined my chances of any level headed advice.

"This is going to be tricky as it is. The last thing I need is an amateur tagging along and mucking things up," I continued.

"Amateur?" she spat. "You're one to talk."

Vera and the gang slid their packs over their shoulders and crept out of the tent to load up the canoes we'd be taking down river to the next village. They knew they'd be better off no where near Ground Zero when I went off on the little shrew.

"What did you just say?" I asked, watching Landers slip out the door.

"You heard me. So far you haven't bolstered my confidence in your methods, *Dr. Jackson*."

"Look, toots. I am very good at what I do. I'm very professional and I don't need some...some...some religious wacko telling me how to do my job!"

I grabbed my gun off the table, secured it in my holster, and slid my arms through my pack's straps. I chomped down on a Cuban, chiding myself for breaking my own smoking rule, but knowing it was the best way to vent the steam building between my ears. I strolled towards the tent's door, satisfied that the conversation was at end, only to be grabbed from behind and whirled around to a smack across the face.

"Look, buddy," she growled, pulling her baseball cap down over her brow and glaring up me. "You don't like me and that's fine. You don't like my faith...that's fine too. But like it or not, you need me on this."

"And why do you think that?"

"Because I know how to get to Baik Orang and you don't," she said with a smug grin.

"Oh." *Geeze*. I hadn't thought of that. I'd been so caught up in tracking the jenglot that it hadn't even occurred to me to actually map out the location of the community next on the creatures' take out menu.

"I don't suppose you're going to offer the location, are you?" I pinched the base of my nose, looking down at my mud-caked boots and pants.

"It's not about the location, Jack." Her voice softened. "It's the people. The locals have always been friendly and trusting, but with all that's been happening, they've become a little skittish. Closed off. They're not going to understand what you're up to and once they figure it out, they're going to freak. They'll think you'll stir up more trouble by hunting the jenglot."

"And how are you going to help with that?" Arnold scratched at my leg. Poor guy was feeling attention starved. "Not now, buddy. I'm in the middle of something." I reached in my pack and threw him a dog biscuit, which he snatched up and trotted outside.

With a smile, she watched the dog scamper away and turned back to me. "Because they know me. Most of them trust me... trust my message. Only the elders hold to the ancient ways now and you need me to convince them not to string you up as an offering."

The last bit elicited an even wider grin to curl up her face as she tilted her head. She knew she had me. I hated the thought of dragging her further into this mess, but she was right. We did need her.

"All right," I sighed. "Grab your things. We leave in ten."

EXCEPT FOR SPOTTING two massive crocs basking lazily on the river bank, the canoe ride wasn't nearly as harrowing as our jeep drive through the jungle. Nikki, Landers, and I drifted in one boat, while Vera, Marc, and Randy paddled in the other. Thankfully, I didn't need to worry about Arnold. He'd opted to stay with the Pingitti children and I couldn't really blame him—unlimited supplies of bones to chew on over facing blood thirsty jungle monsters wasn't much of a decision.

"How much farther?" I asked Nikki, putting all my strength to the oar to keep the boat from smashing into some outcropping rocks. Vera and Marc pulled their boat silently up next to ours, watching the rainforest speed past. Randy, sandwiched between them, checked his bandages and winced.

"I'd say about four more miles," Nikki said shifting herself on the creaking seat of the canoe. "Then we'll need to pull up on shore soon and hike the rest of the way."

"Hike?" Randy moaned. "Ah come on. I'm so sick of jungles and snakes and jaguars. Not to mention bugs!" He smacked something on his arm. "And I'm especially sick of the whole jenglot thing, I might add."

"Get over it," I said. "You knew about this before we left Pingitti. I told you to stay, remember?"

"And how would you be able to execute your brilliant plan? I'm your tech guy and last I checked, your idea is one hundred percent tech reliant."

"We would have managed," Vera said, spraying more insect repellent over her bare arms and then on Randy's. She passed the bottle over to Marc. "I haven't figured out why he's kept you around as long as he has."

"Shut up, Vera." He hunkered back in his seat, pulling his cap down over his eyes. "Just wake me when we get there."

"Are they always that way?" Nikki asked, looking at the other boat.

"Only when they're sober," I said. "Or conscious."

A gentle thud of an air-gun popped behind me. I craned my neck to see Landers bringing down his scoped CO2 rifle.

"Scott, how we doing on the GPS markers?"

"Not bad. Just shot off number seven. We still have twenty-three more."

With Nikki being the only one we had close to being a guide through the jungle, I'd decided to take extra precautions. The GPS markers would serve as our electronic bread crumbs, showing us the way back home should we loose contact with her or the rest of the team.

We coasted the remaining four miles without incident and pulled up on the river bank near a strange, run-down shack at the edge of the forest. The dilapidated building stood isolated from the rest of the world with only three walls and a ceiling sagging treacherously inward. Four sets of cryptic white markings were painted on the exterior for any travelers to see.

"They're warnings," Nikki explained, grabbing her pack from the back of the canoe. "They were here way before I came. Gnali told me the words indicate that death comes swiftly to those who enter the jungle."

"Well that's friendly," I said. "Okay people, we're on foot at this point. Grab the equipment and let's get moving. The sun will be setting in four hours and I'd like to get to the village before then."

If the jenglot kept to their schedule, they wouldn't attack Baik Orang for another two days. Our first encounter with the jenglot had proven that poor planning had led to disastrous execution. I refused to be caught with my proverbial pants down again. We'd timed our trip to give us plenty of time to set up a fool proof operation. But then, if experience has taught me anything, nothing is ever "fool" proof when it comes to me.

"So, if Baik Orang is so close to Pingitti, why do the attacks always come three days later?" asked Landers as we stepped into the thick vegetation.

"I'm not sure," Nikki replied. "Even on foot, the entire trip should take less than two."

"Maybe they only attack out of need." I hacked away at a large vine, cutting a trail. "They don't seem to be greedy. Only one or two victims at a time. I don't think they're killing for the thrill. Just the sustenance."

A barrage of howling and squeals erupted around us. Randy clawed his rifle from his back and pointed it towards the sound.

"Hold your fire," I said, pointing up to a nearby tree. A family of seven orangutan flitted playfully above us, curious of the intruders in their domain. Three others nested in the branches directly over our heads.

"Let's just hope they don't get playful," Randy said with a

grin, slinging his rifle over his shoulder. "I know what they like to use to play catch and I'm in no mood to clean poo off my nice clean duds."

Without responding to Randy's quip, we pushed on until the thick jungle opened slightly into a rarely used trail. I sheathed my machete and trudged forward, scanning fruitlessly for any signs that the jenglot had traveled the same path.

We covered nearly thirteen miles in four hours before coming to an opening in the dense vegetation. The grass covered clearing was roughly oval shaped and two hundred yards in circumference. The trees had been intentionally cut down years before. A vine shrouded stone altar rested silently in the center of the field.

"Look over there," Marc pointed towards the southeast edge of the clearing. Another isolated shanty tenuously leaned on age-damaged beams, threatening to topple with the slightest gust of wind. More markings, this time in red, were scrawled across the aging timber.

"Let's see," Marc said as he moved in for a closer look. "I can decipher the words *awas darah botol susu semangat*."

"I've heard part of that before. *Darah botol susu*," I said, not mentioning my encounter with Shantili in the cave. "Blood feeder. The jenglot,"

"Yes, actually, a rough translation of the entire phrase reads something like 'Beware the blood feeding spirits.'" Marc continued. "I'd say it's a good bet that's what the writer is referring to here. It's a rather broken form of Malay, so it's a bit difficult to determine the syntax necessary for proper translation."

"Well, try anyway," I said. "What else does it say?"

"Let's see. The next legible words read *jahat mati ...kampong Bait Orang*."

Marc turned to us, his face pale.

"What? What does it say?" Vera asked.

"Bad death to the village of Baik Orang," Nikki answered, walking towards the building. She swiped her index finger against the paint. "It's wet. This is fresh."

"Yes, but only the name of the village," Marc had recovered to continue his assessment of the letters. "The rest are quite old. Probably as old as the building itself."

Our linguist rubbed his hand over a loose board nailed diagonally across the façade of the shack. Taking his knife, he wedged the board loose, jarring it free. The plank fell to the grass with a thud, exposing one last word.

"*Orang nya-k raksaksa?*" he mumbled. "That doesn't make any sense."

"Why? What's it mean?" I asked again, wishing I'd bothered to spend a little more time on the airplane listening to my 'Learn Malay in Minutes' tapes. Instead, I'd opted to play '*Legend of Zelda*' on my Gameboy.

"I'm not quite sure, actually," he said. "The first word orang means 'man'. That's easy. So's the third word, raksaksa. It means 'monster.'"

"Man, monster," I repeated. "So what's the second word?"

"That's the problem. I'm not sure. Some of the letters have worn off with time. It either refers to some kind of insect or a heap of garbage."

"Well, for sake of argument, let's say it's not a trash heap. What kind of insect?"

"I don't know. The root word is connected to other insects. That's the only reason I can even guess it has to do with a bug. But without the missing letters, it's a shot in the dark."

I looked at Nikki. "Any ideas?"

She shook her head and leaned closer into the markings. "I couldn't tell you. But I'd bet that the recent message was meant for us."

"Yeah, that's just what I was afraid of," I said, scrutinizing the horizon for any signs of trouble and unsheathed the machete. "All right. We're losing light. Which way from here, Nikki?"

She looked around for several minutes and strode towards the setting sun. "This way," she said. "Baik Orang is only about five more miles west of here."

13

The team stopped long enough to wet their parched throats and snack on some bananas from a nearby tree before moving on. We'd spent entirely too much time examining the arcane shack and the sun was already dropping over the tree line.

The last leg of the journey was unbearable. The jungle terrain closed in on us once more, threatening to entangle the entire group in wild vines and trees. Sharp palmetto fronds thrashed at our arms and insects swarmed in the oppressive heat.

It was dark by the time we made it to a high ridge overlooking Baik Orang. I stopped to survey the terrain and the village down below. It was lit with a few fires and torches burning brightly on pikes scattered hodge-podge throughout the town.

"Okay," I said. "We're finally here. Nikki and I will head down to the village and talk to the chief; let him know what we're up to before you all waltz in and scare them half to death."

The jungle screeched behind us, waking up from its day time slumber. Insects buzzed, tickling our ears as they whisked by. A family of spider monkeys howled into the night.

"Um, you want us to stay here?" Randy asked, throwing on his night vision goggles and scanning the forest. His constant complaining was more a comfort than one might think. It told me he'd been healing nicely from the jenglot wounds.

"That's the plan," I said. "These people are friendly, but jumpy, Randy. We need to prepare them."

"It's okay, Jack," Vera said. "We'll take care of the big baby while you're gone."

I smiled at her with a nod. My old Russian firecracker was back. She'd sulked for the better part of the trip, distracted by her own issues. It was good to see her joking around again.

"All right. Give us thirty minutes and come on down. If there's a problem, we'll contact you on the radio." I said to the group before looking at Nikki. "Okay, this slope is steep, so mind your step. I don't want to have to carry you the rest of the way to the village."

The missionary glared, her fists clenched in white knuckled fury.

"Carry me?" she hissed. "You don't want to carry me?"

A frog-sized lump clogged up my throat, threatening to tear its way out through my nasal cavities.

Oh, boy. Foot. Mouth. Idiot.

"Er, you know what I mean," I stammered. "The slope's slippery, dangerous. I was only thinking of your personal safety."

"Let's get something straight right now, bub. I was hiking, camping, hunting, and fishing since I was five years old. I've climbed three class three mountain ranges. Skydived. I'm scuba certified and I won first place in the gymnastic nationals while in college." She was seething. "I think I can manage a little hill on my own, thank you very much."

I glanced over at the rest of the team. Marc covering his mouth to hide his complete amusement at the exchange. Vera and Randy weren't even trying. Only Landers remained stoic, unmoved by her outburst...bless him.

I cleared my throat, jutting out my chin in defiance. "Well, there should be no problems then," I said, hoping I sounded bolder than I felt. I stepped forward and started jogging down the hill, not bothering to wait for Nikki to catch up.

The quarter moon above us darkened, as ominous clouds drifted in from the sea to the east. Nikki and I skidded down the pebble-riddled slope of the ridge, careful not to tumble down the hill like the proverbial Jack and Jill. We were doing well until my foot snagged a root sending me sprawling on the ground and sliding several yards towards the village.

"Great," I grumbled, picking myself up and dusting the dirt from my clothes.

"Are you okay?" Nikki giggled, not able to hold back her amusement. "I'm not going to have to carry you am I?"

"Funny. Real funny." I rubbed a tender spot on my jaw, drawing back bloody fingers. "I'm bleeding."

"You're such a wimp. It's just a mild abrasion."

"Abrasions don't bleed. This is bleeding!" I pointed to the injury.

A rumble of thunder boomed several miles away.

"Well, we'll take care of it once we're set up in the village. Right now, we have more pressing matters to worry about," she said, nodding up into the sky where a streak of lightning blazed through the clouds.

The wind picked up, hurling leaves and woodland debris at our faces. A storm was coming and it was coming fast. I pulled my radio from my pocket and clicked it on.

"Randy, you copy?"

A brief pause of static and then his familiar voice blared through the speakers.

"Roger, I copy."

"Um, we need to switch to Plan B. We're about to get hit with some serious weather. We don't have time for manners. Pick up the gear and get moving ASAP."

"Ten-four," he said. "We're right behind you."

I looked at Nikki, concern painting her face.

"You know it's monsoon season," she said.

"It's always monsoon season around here. Only three months of the year is dry."

"Well, I have a bad feeling about this storm."

I looked up at the clouds, a clap of thunder clambered through the sky, drawing nearer. I knew what she meant. So far, the weather during our trip had been relatively mild. It looked as though things were about to get a touch rougher.

"Well, we need to run," I said, taking her arm and pulling her downhill. "Let's go."

14

The sky opened up, unleashing a wet deluge on us as we stumbled into the village of Baik Orang. My clothes and pack felt fifty pounds heavier as I plodded through the ankle deep muck towards the town center. A large crowd gathered in a two-tiered open pagoda, gawking at the travel weary westerners.

We padded up the two steps that led to the covered shelter, while running my hands through my hair, shaking out the excess water. Nikki, who was only a step behind, pushed forward, brushing past me to greet the villagers.

"Hello," she said to a wide-eyed villager who stood at the forefront of the group. "Is Denang here? We need to speak to him." She then repeated the phrase in what I assumed was Malay.

The man stared unmoving at us, silent. His dark face remained emotionless, his thick lips parted slightly to reveal jagged teeth. I watched as his hand descended slowly to the hilt of large machete attached to his belt.

"Whoa!" I said, holding up my hands, waving them in protest. "No need for that. We're here to help."

A crash of thunder exploded over head, jarring my teeth and turning my insides into knots. The wind, now blowing at nearly twenty miles an hour, tossed the grass covering of the village rooftops. It was about to get real nasty and the last thing we needed was an unwelcome welcome.

"Is...your...leader...here?" I asked, annunciating each syllable for clarity.

"Denang is no longer the chief of this village," said a voice from behind the crowd.

Sheesh. Does everyone in this country know how to speak English well? I thought, searching through the crowd for the source.

The villagers parted to reveal the large frame of a Malaysian man in his mid-thirties. Muscles rippled down his bare arms and chest. He sported a full mane of jet-black hair, bunched up in a pony tail that ran past his shoulders. A thick, unwieldy scar ran down the left side of his face, wrapping around the front of the neck to the right side. The man's massive hands white-knuckled the grip of an AK-47; its barrel pointing harmlessly towards the ground.

"I am called Jenglotti Membunuh," he said, a dark grin forming on his face. "I am chief now and you are trespassing in my village."

I glanced over at Nikki, her eyes wide in confusion. Since meeting her, I'd never seen her so...well, speechless. If it wasn't for the formidable, angry villager with the gun, I would have enjoyed it.

"Um, what did he say his name was?" I whispered to her. But she didn't hear me. Her eyes were staring past the crowd, glued to a pike in the center of the shelter. A pike with a hideous black and white, oval object impaled on it. A putrid stench wafted from the thing—the all too familiar stench of decayed flesh.

The object on the pike was a decapitated jenglot head.

"Let me guess," I said out loud. "His name means jenglot killer."

"Close. Jenglot slayer is the more literal translation."

Membunuh's chest bowed up, pride oozing from the grin on his face as he glanced at his gruesome trophy.

"This is your call," I said to Nikki. "We're in your ballpark here."

"Where's Denang?" she seethed. "I demand to see him. Now."

"What are you doing?" I hissed behind clenched teeth. When I'd said it was her call, I definitely didn't expect her to insult him. "The man has a gun. Maybe 'demanding' isn't exactly the best way to handle this."

She ignored me.

Typical. This broad's going to get me whacked. Just as sure as I have the dumbest name on the planet, we're going to die.

"I've always been welcome in this village," Nikki said, folding her arms across her chest. "Your people have accepted me. It is impolite to deny me safe haven in Baik Orang during a monsoon."

I looked around. Sheets of rain streaked diagonally onto the village, tiny balls of hale raged against the village shanties. The wind gusts were even higher than just a few minutes earlier. Not quite gale force, but getting close.

"Monsoon?" I asked. "Aren't you jumping the gun here?" Then, back to the armed men, "Not you guys. Your guns are fine just where they are."

"Trust me, Jack. We're about to be hit with one. And it is against the law of the local villages to cast someone out during these storms," she said. "Trust me. I know what I'm doing."

I scanned the darkness behind me. No signs of the team. I was getting worried. They should have been there five minutes earlier. But there was no sign of them and the weather was clearly not improving.

"You cannot see Denang," Membunuh said. "But you are more than welcome to stay. As a matter of fact, I insist."

I did not like the sound of that.

"Um, thank you," I said. "Well, if you'll just show us to our quarters, I'll grab my things..."

The new chieftain brought his gun up to his face, aiming it at us. Ten others brandished their own weapons, ranging from AK-47s to primitive pitch forks—all pointed directly at us.

"I don't think you understood," Membunuh said with a laugh. "You are not our guests. You are our prisoners. And soon, you will be offered to the jenglot as an atonement offering."

"A what?" I asked, not sure I'd heard the crazy man with the gun correctly.

"You will be an offering to the jenglot in payment for the death of their brother there." He pointed to the head on the pike. "With my bare hands, I slew one of the demons when they attacked our village last night. Denang protested, saying that I had brought death upon the village. But I quickly silenced him as well."

Membunuh paused to let the information sink in. Nikki's eyes glistened with unbidden tears. Wiping them away from her face, she glared furiously at our captor. Her lips moved in silent prayer, but she held her tongue.

"With Denang now dead, and my strength established by slaying the jenglot, I have been made chief. No longer do we worship your God," he continued, pointing a long, thick finger at Nikki. "We return to our old ways, our ancestral spirits who have guided us for thousands of years. It is they who told me of your coming. It is they who demand your sacrifice to the jenglot."

"Now wait just a minute," I said, holding out my arms in protest, backing up into the sturdy frame of a toothless, gun-toting villager. "There's no need to be rash about this. We've come here to help you."

No where to go, my head craned around, peering through the torrential darkness in search of my friends.

Where are they?

The chieftain muttered something I couldn't understand

resulting in five of the townspeople stepping towards us to snatch my Glock, machete, and backpack. Without a word, they shoved Nikki and me through the downpour to the edge of the village where two thick, bamboo poles stood wedged deep into the ground.

The villagers followed; a morbid procession through the whirling gusts and hale-heavy rain. A piece of ice struck me against the side of the head, bringing flashes of darkness dancing before my eyes.

"Nikki," I said as they set me down and wrapped straps of raw-hide around my wrists, fastening me to the pole. "Do something."

"What do you expect me to do? Bring fire down from heaven?" They were binding her feet to the base of the pole.

"That would be a good start."

I pulled against the straps, cutting deep in my wrists. They were solid. The wet weather might help to weaken them if we had enough time, but I doubt we had that luxury. If the rain didn't drown us or beat us to death with golf-ball size hale, we were now officially the jenglot's version of a *Happy Meal*.

"But I was thinking more along the lines of talking to the villagers," I continued. "That is, after all, why you convinced me to bring you along...so they wouldn't string us up as a sacrifice."

She grunted, struggling against her own bindings, her head swinging wildly as two of the villagers tried futilely to strap it to the beam. Sheets of rain continued railing against us as we finally found ourselves completely secured to the posts.

"Well, things are a bit different now, aren't they?" she grumbled, spitting a stream of rain water from her mouth. "With King Kong there in charge of the village, I don't have much clout now."

"Well, is that fire thing still an option?"

"Silence!" Membunuh shouted over an ear-shattering thunder

clap. "The spirits are now happy. Soon, the jenglot will be on the hunt and find you both acceptable offerings of peace."

The big man stalked up to Nikki, grabbing her chin roughly and inching his face close to hers.

"Where is your God now, witch? Tonight, you will see the power of my magicks and the terror of the jenglot," he whispered in her ear.

"Um, I don't exactly believe in her God and I've already seen the 'terror of the jenglot,'" I said. "Does that mean I can go?"

Without a second glance, Membunuh struck me across the cheek with the back of his hand. Black spots flashed in front of my eye as the buzz of thousands of bees swarmed inside my head from the blow. The village leader walked away, never looking in my direction.

"Mind your jokes," he said, moving towards the largest shelter in the village. "Your blasphemy will soon be dealt with."

The rest of the townspeople followed the hulking form of the jenglot slayer as he stooped his head and entered the long-house. After the last of the villagers had entered, the door slammed shut and the sounds of bars sliding across the door posts rang out across the village.

"Jerk." It was the only word my addled brain could come up with.

I GLANCED AROUND. Three men were left to stand guard. Two had positioned themselves in tree stands to the east and south of us. One guard, several bone and feather charms draped around his neck, stood warily in the shadows between two huts inside a bamboo cage.

Hmmm, I thought. *A dry land jenglot-shark cage. Interesting.*

"So, *Indiana Jones,*" Nikki yelled over the roar of wind and rain. "How are you going to get us out of this one?"

I didn't answer. I was too lost in thought. This was not

making sense. I couldn't for the life of me figure out what was taking the team so long to get to the village. With our weapons, skills, and experience, we would have had no problem taking these guys out. Randy would have probably freaked, but Landers would have handled the situation easily. But despite all that, there was no sign of them. Nothing. And with my pack gone, I didn't even have a radio to contact them.

But there was something else bothering me. I just couldn't put my finger on...

"Last night!" I said out loud.

"What?" Nikki asked.

"Membunuh said the jenglot attacked the village last night. He killed one of them...last night!"

"So what?"

"But you said they weren't scheduled for another attack for two more days," I said. "They follow a set pattern, a predetermined schedule. Yet they broke the pattern last night."

"Oh yeah," she said, a light coming on in her brain. "Why do you think they did that?"

"That's the hundred-thousand-dollar question, isn't it?" I said, clenching my eyes shut against a sudden gust of wind. "What would make them do that? What happened to change their schedule?"

We sat in silence for several minutes. I could almost see the steam rising from Nikki's head as she pondered possible scenarios to explain the irregularity.

"Hunger?" she asked. "That seems the most likely reason."

"It would if they hadn't already fed two nights ago. But they managed to obtain their usual amount of blood from the old woman then. The same amount they always get. So it can't be that."

"Cinta Tuhan," she said quietly.

"What?"

"Cinta Tuhan. That was her name. It means *God's Love,*" she said. "I'm getting tired of you referring to her as 'old woman'."

"Are you kidding me? We're stuck here, tied to poles, and waiting for the blood-feeding brigade to march in and turn us into giant Slurpies and you're worried about the woman's name?"

"Yes. She was a good friend."

A blinding flash of lightning zipped across the sky just as thunder boomed again directly over us. I decided to pass on responding to her last statement. She was right. I should show more respect for the dead. After all, I was well on my way to joining them if we couldn't figure a way out of this mess.

My hands were tied behind my back, so I couldn't see my watch. With the rain, it was next to impossible to figure out the time. I had no idea how long we had before the jenglot returned. I wasn't even sure they would. It wouldn't fit their pattern, but then, they'd already thrown a monkey wrench in that last night. But Membunuh seemed to think they'd be back. I had no choice but to believe him.

"Okay, we've got to figure out how to get out of this," I said over to Nikki. "Any thoughts?"

"Yeah," she replied. "Where's Vera and the rest of the group? Can't they bust us out of here?"

"I was wondering the same thing. I have no idea where—ow!"

A rather large pebble smashed against the side of my head. The nearest guard stiffened, re-focusing on us. The stone had come from somewhere to my right. I twisted my head, struggling against the straps, and looked into the murky outline of the jungle wall. A glimmer of light broke from the darkness for a split second, then another.

It was a message, a code using flashes of light. Randy and I had used a similar one in Nepal four years before when a group of yeti had wandered unusually close to a small mountain community.

"I mean, why didn't the team follow us down?" Nikki

yammered. She was oblivious to the stone, my throbbing head, and the illuminated code only twenty yards away. "You told them to come on. I mean, doesn't anyone in your group lis—"

"Hush," I whispered as I nodded to the right, drawing Nikki's vision towards the team, now hidden in the tree line.

"Oh."

My current dilemma shrunk against the surge of hope that coursed through me at the appearance of my friends. They must have somehow caught wind of what was happening in the village and decided to lay low for an opportunity to rescue us. Things were going to be all right. I let out one massive breath and relaxed against the post.

"Well, now what?" Nikki's voice shattered my calm. If she wasn't so good looking, and I'd been raised to actually hit women, I'm pretty sure I would have punched her in the nose. She was really beginning to annoy me.

"Now, we wait until Landers and Randy breaks us out of this mess. Just be patient. They know what they're doing."

"Do they?"

I glared at her. She was soaked to the bone, her clothing clung loosely, heavy from rain, to her small frame. Her hair strung around her face as beads of water streaked her cheeks and chin. She really was beautiful. It was such a shame her mouth always got in the way.

"Yes, they do. Believe it or not, this isn't the worst predicament I've gotten myself into," I said. "Randy's always found a way, despite his griping, to get me out."

There was a soft thud above in one of the tree stands. I looked up to see one of the guards slouch and fall forward, a tranquilizer dart lodged in his neck. If not for the rope tied around his waist, he would have fallen out of the tree.

Landers' work.

Another thump from the south drew my sight to the second

guard slumping over, his right leg catching the safety rail. He hung unconscious upside down by his pants leg.

"Two down," I whispered. "One to go."

The third guard, sensing trouble, opened his makeshift cage and stepped out, scanning the rain and wind swept night for the source of the sounds. His eyes kept focused on the ground, never looking up towards the dozing forms of his companions.

Bringing his rifle to his shoulder, the man walked, eyes darting around wildly. Alert for any signs of danger. Visibly shaken, the guard trudged on wobbling legs towards us.

I grinned. Any second, the group would make its move and we'd be out of there.

My smile faded at the howl belting from the jungle. Close. The guard screamed at the sound, dropped his rifle and ran towards a nearby shanty, slamming the door behind him. Another howl answered, closer—only yards away from the village.

"Oh crap," I said, wrestling against the ropes binding me to the post. "Cut me loose, cut me loose!"

Three more wails erupted in as many directions, closing in on us.

"Guys," I shouted into the tree line. "I'm serious here."

Landers and Randy bolted from the jungle towards us, spinning around every several yards to watch for the approaching creatures lurking nearby.

"What took you so long?" I asked Randy as he pulled a knife from his boot and cut away at the leather bindings. Landers started freeing Nikki, his eyes taking in the terrain around us, searching for any signs of the jenglot.

"Sorry, we got a little tied up with something," Randy said. "I'll explain later."

Several more shrieks leaked through the rolling thunder. They were there. Somewhere in the village, the jenglot now lay in wait, ready to pounce on any one dumb enough to be caught out in the rain.

Moments later, I was free and rubbing my wrists, trying to coax my circulation back.

"We've got to get out of here," I said, holding out my hand. Catching my meaning, Randy handed me a .357 revolver. *Only six shots. Great*. "Where's Vera and Marc?"

"Well, that's part of why we were so late getting—"

Gunshots exploded from the longhouse, forcing the four of us down behind a massive feeding trough. I peeked warily over the rim. Eight high powered rifles were pointed at us from Membunuh's shelter.

"They must have been watching," Nikki said.

"You think?" I asked, cringing as a bullet whizzed by my head. "Sheesh! When this is all over, remind me to tell the Malaysian Tourist Commission about this place."

The good news was the howling had ceased. The bad news was that the gun fire didn't. And they had us pinned down. No place to run. We couldn't move. I glanced around, looking for a way out. Nothing. But fortunately, no sign of the jenglot either. Still, the creatures' silence unnerved me even more than the villagers' barrage of bullets.

"Keep your eyes open," I said to no one in particular. "These things are smart. They may be flanking us."

"I'm already way ahead of you," Landers said, flipping on night vision goggles and scanning our surroundings.

I pulled off three rounds from the revolver and ducked back down behind the trough.

"And why can't you carry a gun with more than six rounds?" I asked Randy, who smiled sheepishly at me. "I've got to get my gun back." I fired two more shots behind us without looking over the trough.

Randy dug into his pack, pulled out a box of ammo, and dropped them in my hand.

"There," he said. "Stop whining and start shooting."

But the shooting had stopped. Only the sounds of the monsoon tearing away at the village could be heard.

"Landers," I said. "What's going on?"

No response.

"Landers?" I turned to my right where he stood crouched, looking in silence around the corner of the trough. He removed the day for night goggles, his face a mask of fear.

I poked my head up above the wooden feeder and froze. At first, the thick black veil of night prevented me from seeing anything. Then, a burst of lightning blazed above, brightening the streets of Baik Orang in one, brief, terrifying flash. In the center of the village stood nine jenglot, hunching down, malevolent predators coiled to strike. With the lightning discharged, darkness regained its ominous control on the world, shrouding the creatures once again.

Oh, crap.

My head spun around just as another flash streaked across the sky and caught glimpses of nearly ten others huddled in the shadows all around us, their sunken eyes merely hollow pockets of darkness. They shrunk back at the sudden brilliance of the ionized night before darkness again oozed around us.

Nikki stiffened beside me. She'd seen them too. Only Randy appeared oblivious to the intrusion as he inserted shells into his rifle while whistling an unforgivable rendition of the Eagle's song 'Take It Easy'. He raised his head to look at us, staring back at him in disbelief.

"What?" he asked, turning around to see what was going on. His mouth dropped into a silent scream as he caught his first glimpse of the jenglot in Baik Orang. "Oh. Bite me."

15

The twenty jenglot surrounding us tensed, coiling to spring. Shards of yellow needle-teeth glistened as lightning streaked across the cloud-heavy sky. A low snarl hissed from the non-existent lips of the nearest creature as they glared at us.

Randy cocked his rifle and pulled it to his chest, aiming with his back against the trough.

"No guns," I said.

"What?" Randy and Landers spoke as one.

"No. Guns." I wanted to be perfectly clear.

My brain raced, trying to sort out the mess we were in. None of this made sense. The creatures weren't acting according to the patterns we'd established. They were animals. Intelligent, but not sentient—meaning they hunted for food, not revenge. And, they had completely changed their feeding schedule. Why?

Maybe they're not animals.

The voice inside my own head startled me. It was the most ridiculous thought I'd had in a long time.

Of course, they are.

Why do you think that?

Sheesh. My own internal monologue was rebelling against me.

Because they're certainly not human. Since I don't see leaves growing off their arms, I'm pretty sure they're not plants either, And I don't believe in goblins, spooks, or demons, so that pretty much just leaves animal, now doesn't it? I thought, a smile creeping up my face. *Ha. Guess I showed me.*

But are you sure…

"Jackson!" Randy said, snapping me from my panic-deluded thoughts. His eyes stretched in absurd proportions, watching the jenglot inch towards us in tandem. "If we can't use guns, then what are we supposed to do?"

"I don't know. We've got catch at least one of them alive. Something about killing any of these things just doesn't feel right."

"Are you kidding me?"

"I wish I was. But the truth is, until we figure out what these things are and what's going on, it's best to just cut and run for now."

"That's easier said than done," Landers said, pulling himself up to one knee and looking behind him. "These things are all around us."

I looked over at Nikki, head bowed, eyes shut tight and mumbling what I assumed was a silent prayer for our protection.

"Where's the Alpha?" I asked, searching the group of jenglot. "The Alpha's not here."

"That's probably why they're not attacking," Randy said. "They're waiting for it to get here."

A scream erupted above us, drawing my eyes to the southern tree line where one of the guards Landers sedated had awakened. The horrified sentry stared helplessly up at the gruesome face of a jenglot clinging to the trunk just above his dangling form. Unable to defend himself, the creature lashed out, snagging him from his perch and leaping to the ground below, pulling the thrashing guard behind him.

Two other jenglot jumped in the fray. Pain-filled cries exploded from the guard's mouth as razor sharp claws tore through clothing and flesh, savagely shredding him. The other creatures stood in their place, watching patiently at the carnage. The screams faded as the man was torn to pieces before our eyes.

I took Nikki in my arms, shielding her from the sight. Her cold, wet body shivered uncontrollably against my chest.

"So much for them not attacking," I said. "Okay, change of plans."

Landers and Randy turned to me.

"Shoot anything that moves."

"Now you're talking," said Randy with a stupid grin.

"But only if you have to," I said. "We're making a run for it. If they get close, shoot them. Otherwise, leave them be."

The four of us pushed up from the ground onto our haunches, as I glanced around the corner of the trough and looked at the idle jenglot. The creatures had moved only a few feet from where we first saw them, their arms hanging low to the ground as they sniffed the air for signs of their prey.

"I don't think they can see," I mumbled. "I think they use other senses to hunt."

"That would explain why they haven't moved in on us," Landers said. "Maybe the wind currents are too strong. They can't catch our scent."

"If you're right that gives us quite an advantage then, doesn't it? All we have to do is stay down wind from them and make as little noise as possible."

The others crouched silently, gripping their weapons tight.

"Okay, on the count of the next lightning flash we move," I said.

My reasoning was rather ingenious, I thought. The creatures had already demonstrated sensitivity to light. I'd already seen the creatures disoriented during the last few streaks of lightning. It might just give us the cover we needed for dashing into the jungle on the eastern edge of the village.

We didn't have to wait long. A mere four seconds passed before another flash of light streaked across the blackened sky. Jumping to our feet, we ran in unison to the nearest stand of trees. My logic, however, had been flawed. I hadn't counted on the sheer number of creatures lurking around the town.

Stooping in the shadows of the tree line, three more jenglot snarled. I floundered forward, trying desperately to stop before I crashed into the salivating creatures. But it was too late. I plowed straight into them; our limbs tangling in a knot of bone, claws, and teeth.

"Shoot! Shoot! Shoot!" I shouted.

Two loud pops and two of the creatures lay dead on each side of me. The third skirted off to the safety of the others. Unearthly howls pierced the air as the family of jenglot turned in our direction.

"Oh snap," I said as Randy pulled me to my feet. "Run!"

My heart pushed up my throat as nearly twenty-five pair of black scaled, gnarled feet pounced towards us. Randy, still grasping my hand, pulled me forward into the forest as the jenglot came after us.

Jerking free of Randy's grip, my legs pumped furiously as I navigated the unfamiliar terrain in gale force winds and rain. Water streaked past my eyes, blinding me. I had no idea where I was heading and I didn't care as long as it was away from the gore-swilling creatures that hunted me. I turned and fired the revolver twice, not aiming at anything, but hoping to get a lucky shot.

My lungs, rebelling against me, heaved for breath as ear splitting shrieks propelled me through the dense foliage. I wasn't sure how long I'd been running when I finally came to a halt. The howling had died and the only sounds around me were the pounding of my own heart inside my head and thunder and rain above.

Bending over, I caught my breath, heaving and hacking. After a few minutes, I looked up, hands still on knees and breathed in one great lungful of air.

"That was close," I said.

No one responded.

I looked around wide-eyed. I was alone.

16

The rain teetered to a drizzle, but the wind still howled through the vine covered branches of the jungle. I wiped away excess water from my face and turned a three-sixty to catch my bearings.

There was no sign of Landers, Randy, or Nikki. I was alone with only a swarm of mosquitosauruses and a handful of vampire bats fluttering through the gale to keep me company. And perhaps something else.

Hearing the crunch of wet soil behind me, I spun around bringing my gun up. I'd forgotten how many bullets I'd fired when fleeing the jenglot. I could only hope I still had a few more secured in the cylinder.

Another crunch. Footsteps.

The panic of the jenglot attack was fading fast. My heart rate ebbed to tolerable levels and my mind cleared. I'd been tempted to shout out to the foot falls, hoping they belonged to my friends. But wisdom was once more prevailing in my jenglot addled brain.

That'd be real bright, you bonehead. Just lead the piranha-heads right to me.

I held my breath, straining my ears to break through the wheezing gusts of monsoon-birthed wind.

Another step, drawing closer—slowly—to my left.

I extended my right arm to full length, balancing the butt of the gun's grip with my left palm, trying futilely to steady the shaking barrel. I squeezed my left eye shut tight and focused on the sites of the revolver for better aim. Whatever was coming towards me would find itself looking down the barrel of one of the most lethal handguns ever to be made.

I smiled nervously at the Dirty Harry joke flashing unbidden through my mind.

A rustle of leaves from a tree above me brought my aim up high, probing into the jungle canopy. Thunder rumbled lightly several miles away. The storm was abating and only wind obscured my senses now.

More footsteps from behind jerked me around. My gun darted wildly in every direction. Rain-mingled sweat streamed into my eyes, burning them, causing me to squint.

A long hiss leaked through the foliage in the tree tops above. I struggled against a desire to succumb to my parents' and Nikki's own superstitions by praying that the noise was only a python or a nice semi-hungry panther.

But I knew it would do no good. I already knew without looking what lurked just several feet above my head and at least in two different directions on the jungle floor.

The jenglot had tracked me.

"Great," I muttered as I lifted my head back up to the tree.

A chalk-white face looked down at me, a hideously fanged grin twisted around a lipless mouth. Its wiry hair whipped against its face in the wind. The jenglot clutched the bark of the tree with its sharp-edged talons, hanging upside down. Its chitinous hide covering spring-loaded sinews. Its eyeless orbs gazed hauntingly through me.

Two others skittered out of hiding, on all fours, into the

narrow clearing where I now stood. Saliva oozed from their mouths as they flanked me on both sides.

I froze.

Where is the wind? I wondered. *Can they sense me? Smell me? Hear me breathe?*

The tree-bound creature slithered down the trunk a few feet before jumping to the ground to land on its wiry legs. For the first time, I noticed that this particular jenglot was different from the others. It was not the Alpha, but it had distinctive markings over its body. Thin, almost imperceptible scars lashed on nearly every surface of its frame. One thick scratch traced diagonally down the creature's face.

This one's seen some action. It reminds me of some sort of warrior class creature, I thought. *But that's crazy. That would imply a culture.*

The Tree Jenglot reared upright, unleashing a savage roar towards me. Its arms stretched upward, revealing thin skin-like membranes stretching from its wrists down the sides of its body to the ankles.

I stood spellbound. My mind raced with a cocktail mix of awe and terror. The jenglot had different classes. Different kinds with specific functions. Much like an ant colony.

Amazing, I thought. Then, a sudden burst of clarity struck my thick noggin. *What am I thinking? I'm about to be drained dry like a Capri-Sun pack and I'm actually admiring the creepy thing. I really must be nuts.*

The creature's arms dropped to its side as it lumbered towards me. Fortunately, the other two jenglot were content to watch the impending massacre from the sidelines. I was definitely not in the mood for a tag-team bout.

Suddenly, the Tree Jenglot lunged forward, throwing me off balance. My finger squeezed the trigger of the revolver, releasing a single shot into the air. The bullet whizzed past the creature's head by a mile. I fell backwards, bringing the gun back up to aim. I pulled the trigger again.

Click. Click.

Empty.

I rolled, coming back up on my feet. The creature lashed its claws at me, swinging with its full fury and striking me across the chest. My flesh screamed as talons raked deep into my flesh, doubling me over. The useless .357 flew from my hand.

The jenglot lunged again, barely missing me as I rolled to escape its advance. I came up behind the thing, grabbed it around the head and pounded against the back of its ribs with my right fist.

The two on-lookers howled and hissed in demonic fury, scrambling forward, then backward in fits of indecision. The rules of the hunt were clearly defined and unbreakable. They could not interfere.

The Tree Jenglot wriggled, its legs kicking wildly in the air as I lifted its four and a half foot frame from the ground. Its arms flailed, reaching behind to lay hold of any part of my body it could grasp.

But I held on, pummeling against the creature's side. It screamed in frustration and pain, found some footing against a nearby branch and pushed backwards, pinning me against the trunk of a large tree. The wind knocked out of me, I released my grip and fell to the wet soil.

It's stronger than it looks, I thought, heaving for breath.

The jenglot spun around, lurched forward and grabbed my neck. Finding a large rock, I snatched it from the ground just before the creature hauled me to my feet to meet its gnarled face. It sneered, revealing long rows of spiny teeth.

The solid feel of the stone in my hand quickened my courage.

"Ah, what the heck," I said to the creature just as I slammed the rock against its mouth, shattering several of the fangs with the blow.

It howled, releasing me, bringing its claws up to its splintered jaw. The two on-looking jenglot screeched sympathetically, but still did not interfere.

With the creature distracted, I bolted through a clearing in the trees and ran as fast as I could away from the hideous creatures that hunted me. Branches and thorny brambles slowed my progress through the jungle as they lashed at my face. It was as if the entire forest sided with the jenglot, trying to prevent my escape.

Sounds of pursuit rushed to my ears. I stole a glance behind; the Tree Jenglot had recovered and was already making up the distance. Closing the gap, it lashed out with its claws at my back just as my foot caught a low hanging vine, sending me sprawling to the ground.

Okay. So I'm not graceful.

I quickly rolled over to face the creature, hands raised defensively, but it was no where to be found. I hopped to my feet and scanned the surrounding trees. Nothing. Not a sign of the jenglot.

Even the howling had stopped.

"That was freaky," I said aloud, stepping slowly ahead, glancing in every direction for any signs of an ambush. "Yeah, this is really weird."

I inched forward, cautiously searching for traces of the jenglot. I looked into velvety darkness of the sky. The sun wouldn't rise for another five or six hours. What had driven the creatures away?

The *rat-a-tat-tat* of a submachine gun blasted through the jungle, one or two miles south of my current location.

"Landers," I murmured, pushing through the underbrush in the direction of the gunshots. More shots went off, followed by shouts from the distinctive voices of my friends. "Just keep firing away and I'll find you."

Turning around for one last glance and still seeing no bloodsucking creatures from hell, I darted off towards the rest of the team.

THE GUNFIRE CONTINUED UP AHEAD. I could now hear the distinctive single shots of Randy's .30-06 echoing in the distance, along with the singsong rhythm of Lander's own P-90 submachine gun. Shrieks and howls of the jenglot followed each lull in gunfire and I knew my team was in trouble.

I'm almost there. Question is what am I going to do once I get there?

I was out of ammo. I'd even dropped the revolver in my tussle with the Tree Jenglot. With no weapons of any kind, how was I supposed to deal with an army of super strong, bloodsucking monsters bent on tearing us apart?

A rustle from above halted me mid-step. A hiss. I looked up to see my old pal Chuckles, the jagged toothed jenglot, perched on a nearby branch, sniffing the air. A cock-eyed grin splayed up one side its face. It had been following me the whole time. Playing with me.

These things are smarter than I thought.

Not giving me time to react, the jenglot pushed off its perch, spread its arms wide, expanding the skin-like membranes. A gust of wind, catching the creature's underside, propelled him out towards me.

I stood, gooseflesh lifting up from my arms, as I watched the jenglot barrel towards me on currents of air. It could fly. Or at least glide.

The jenglot swooped down just barely missing my head, rode back up to a higher altitude and dove towards me again. I ducked and rolled out of the way seconds before the jenglot's talons slashed where my face had been.

The creature folded its arms, the slimy membranes contracting, bringing it gently to the ground with a soft thud. Its shattered jaw oozed darkened, congealed blood as it snarled and gnashed the remainder of its teeth towards me.

"All right," I said, defensively raising my fists up to my face. "Enough's enough. You want me? Come see if I taste like chicken."

What the heck are you doing? The voice inside my head screamed.

The jenglot took one tentative step forward, its talons raised for attack.

Now's not the time for a discussion on this, I told the voice. *I'm sick of this whole mess. It ends here.*

Another step.

It's your funeral.

You know, when this is all over, we're going to have a serious talk about your attitude.

A third step, the creature was only two feet away from me now.

Um, maybe you should be concentrating on the ugly mean monster that's about to tear you to pieces rather than worry about what I think.

I had a good point.

The jenglot pounced, landing directly on a right hook I'd thrown only seconds before it lunged. Its clawed hand slashed at my back, tearing through clothing and flesh, as we both tumbled to the ground.

My fist smashed into its already broken jaw, eliciting shrieks of agony as the creature leapt away, freeing me. I jumped to my feet, glanced around for anything that could be used as a weapon.

I grinned almost maniacally as I dashed for a patch of bamboo grass and yanked a sturdy shoot from the ground. The piece was long, about four feet with a jagged end and I brandished it in two clenched hands like a baseball bat.

"All right, Sparky," I said. "Game's even now. Let's play."

Without waiting for a reaction, I stormed the jenglot, screaming like a madman—bamboo rod swung high above my head. The creature hesitated, not expecting the move, giving me enough time to bring the highly flexible stalk of grass crashing down against its head.

It screamed, reeling back from the blow. Not letting the monster recover, I pressed forward, wailing against it with all my strength. My arms swung furiously, pounding against the lithe form of the jenglot, now cowering down to the ground.

I swung down against the creature's head one more time, but it dodged, twisted, and leapt up around me. I spun around to face it, but not fast enough. One powerful blow by its clenched fist sent me reeling. Dark spots flashed before my eyes from the impact. Unable to maintain my balance, I collapsed helplessly to the ground, willing my eyes to focus on the jenglot now standing over me.

But my eyes betrayed me, growing darker with each second. I was about to pass out. I knew it. And once that happened, I'd be completely helpless.

The creature let out a long guttural hiss, hovering over my inert frame. Its bloodied mouth once again formed the outline of a grin as it raised one fierce claw high over its head and lashed down towards my head. Without thinking, I thrust the bamboo staff forward.

My attacker stopped mid-swing, looking down at its chest in surprised pain. The shoot had pierced through the tough carapace of its abdomen, pushed upward beneath its thorax-like torso and penetrated its heart. A stream of dark crimson, mixed with bubbles of air, inked from the corners of its mouth.

The jenglot stood three heartbeats longer before dropping to the ground in a lifeless heap. A rustle of underbrush, and the two on-looking jenglot materialized cautiously from the shadows, in silence.

They stared eyelessly at their fallen comrade, then back up to me. Their faces expressionless, showing no reaction to the sight of their Tree-bound brother's demise. And then, beyond my expectations, they turned silently around and walked back into the darkness of the jungle.

I smiled, watching them leave. I picked myself off the ground and squatted down for a better look at the quarry. Pulling the bamboo shoot from its chest, I lightly tapped against the side of the creature's head, checking for reaction.

Nothing. He was dead. My grin drained away from my face.

"I so didn't want to kill you," I said aloud, standing up and dusting myself off.

"I don't think that makes it feel any better," came Randy's voice from behind me.

"Took you all long enough to find me," I said, not turning around and wiping the bloody piece of bamboo off on my pant's leg. "And I want my gun back."

I turned my head to see Randy, Landers, and Nikki limping up a small embankment towards me. A nasty gash bled out over the Marine's forehead. Randy appeared to only have a few cuts and bruises.

And Nikki. Well, she was something to see. Covered in mud, nearly head to foot, her hair matted and tangled, she looked almost comical. One glare from her upon seeing a grin forming on my face told me not to make any jokes.

So I didn't.

"Would someone please tell me where Vera and Marc got off to?" I asked.

"We're right here," Vera said pulling up the rear as Randy, Landers, and Nikki cleared the hill. "Sorry we weren't around for the fun, but we got a little distracted."

Marc trudged the final few feet up the hill, hands on his waist and heaving for breath.

"O-on the way down to the village, w-we caught sight of a cluster of buildings," he huffed. "A-about three hundred meters east of the village. Just a few dilapidated shacks, really, but we discovered something quite intriguing while we were there. A stone trail."

I stared at him without saying a word, trying to decide whether I should be angry or too tired to really care.

"So?" I asked. "It was a good visit, was it?"

"Actually, yes," Vera replied, surveying the team's injuries and setting to work at mending them. "Very interesting. We followed the path through a dense region of jungle. Probably walked two miles southeast of here. We found a large abandoned settlement nestled in a cluster of durian trees. I think you'll want to check it out."

"Well, okay then. But first, I want my Glock back."

The five of them stared at me, unsure of what to say.

"I'm serious," I said. "I want my gun."

Randy walked up to the body of the jenglot, hands in his pockets, and gave it a tap with his boot.

"Yep, it's dead all right," he said, turning to look me in the eye. "And you can't get your Glock back. The local yokels in the village confiscated it, remember?"

"Oh, I remember all right. That's why we're going there to get it back." I looked down at the bloody remains of the creature I'd killed, eyeing its neckline. "I need to borrow someone's knife. A big one."

17

Dark clouds rolled swiftly through the sky, smothering the rising sun's light as we returned to the edge of Baik Orang. I found myself incapable of stopping my teeth from grinding inside my skull. Randy stood beside me, fidgeting and double checking the rounds in a small .380 Walther that Vera had loaned him.

There were no signs of the rest of the team, hidden as I'd instructed on the ridge nearly four hundred yards above the town.

Good. At least we have an ace in the hole, I thought. *These jokers are about to wake up to a really bad day.*

The left side of my lip curled up, the start of a grin. I rarely allowed anger to dictate my actions and made it a point to avoid revenge at all costs. It just had a way of making things messy. But then, this wasn't about revenge. It was about right and wrong. It was about my gun.

The villagers slowly emerged from the safety of their huts, gazing around at the signs of destruction strewn haphazardly around the small village. It was in shambles; torn asunder from the high winds, hail-filled rains, and blood-thirsty creatures prowling the night.

A group of large men set to work, clearing the debris from the storm, as well as dragging the corpses of the fallen guards to a make-shift platform to be used for funeral preparations. A number of women—mothers, wives, and daughters—wailed up at the sky, cradling the shredded remains of the dead men in their arms in mourning.

I stepped from the shadowed protection of the tree line into full view of the villagers. An instant hush fell as eyes darted up to ogle the intruder entering into their camp. Work halted. Slowly, every head of the mourning villagers lifted up, mouths gaping, to watch me walk through the med-caked street. Straightening my shoulders and taking a quick breath, I lurched towards the pagoda in the center of town where the decapitated head of the jenglot still rested on the pike.

A rumble of thunder to the east reminded me that the monsoon driven rains had not dried up. We were sure to have another storm passing through soon and I knew that I needed to take care of business before that happened. Landers would need clear skies for my plan to work.

A young boy, wearing only a pair of ragged shorts, loose around an emaciated waist, bolted into the village longhouse. A few moments later, he emerged with Membunuh and three muscular men bearing assault rifles. The chieftain's head swept the area, looking for something before stopping at me. His hand gripped the handle of my Glock sticking out from the front of his pants.

Stoically, I approached the pagoda, now only a few feet away. The shuffle of footsteps behind told me Randy was close on my heels. As I strode forward, I reached behind, grabbed the bamboo spear I'd strapped to my back and stepped up into the open air shelter.

Membunuh and his men stepped down in the muddy soil surrounding the longhouse, eyeing us as we entered their sacred construct. Strutting up to the pike, I tore the skewered jenglot head from its mount and tossed it into a nearby puddle.

Gasps echoed through the village at the desecration of their holy relic and the symbol for the new leader of the people. I turned to face the villagers, bamboo spear gripped firm in the air. With a free hand, I reached inside my backpack and withdrew the bloody head of the jenglot I'd killed. I stretched it up into the air for everyone to see before slamming it down upon the point of the bamboo and securing it into the floor mount.

Silence. The wind even ceased for the moment. No one moved. I turned around to face the four well-armed men gawking at me.

I grinned back at them defiantly.

"I want my gun back," I said to Membunuh, motioning to the Glock with my head. "And I want an apology."

I glanced back at Randy who absently twirled his pistol around his finger, gunslinger style. His eyes fixed on the three men that made up the chief's entourage. I turned back to my enemy, smile even broader.

"Oh yeah, and I want you to step down from your office" I said, glancing over at my trophy on the bamboo spear. "I'm Jenglotti Membunuh now."

I was goading him. It was probably not the brightest of moves but then, the guy had really ticked me off. He'd murdered the village's own chief, had set himself up as its dictator, and had thrown me to the piranha heads as a midnight snack. It was time someone taught him a little good 'ole fashioned Southern reciprocity.

Membunuh shuffled forward, eyes glaring at me. His dark face reddened as his mouth twisted into a hideous grimace.

"You are in no position to spew such insults at me," he growled.

The chief looked over to his men and nodded. Without hesitation, each man raised their rifles and took aim. I stood motionless, raised three fingers into the air and counted down to zero.

On cue, a perfectly round, dime sized hole, bore into the forehead of the farthest rifleman on the right. Two breaths later, a clap of manmade thunder rumbled nearly four hundred yards behind on the ridge overlooking the village. The percussion blast of a high powered rifle. Blood trickled from the bullet wound into the dead man's wide eyes before he crumbled to the soft earth with a thud.

The chieftain and his two remaining men stood frozen, staring down helplessly at their fallen comrade. Before full understanding dawned on them, a second man's head snapped back, blood streaking backward as he fell to the ground. A second gunshot echoed a breath later.

Sheesh. Note to self: don't stand in a firing range with Landers looking down a barrel at you, I thought staring at the two dead men at the feet of Membunuh.

Two nearly perfect shots with a .30-06 from four hundred yards were amazing. The best hunters I knew wouldn't have been able to get close to the accuracy at nearly half the distance.

Membunuh drew my Glock from his waste and pointed it towards me in a brilliant display of speed. His remaining partner slowly brought the AK back up to his face.

"I'd reconsider, *Kemo Sabe,*" I said, forcing a cool grin across my face. I'd kind of hoped the gruesome deaths of his friends would have stopped the big lug in his tracks. I was beginning to think I'd miscalculated. "My Marine friend up there is one heck of a shot."

The remaining member of Membunuh's entourage couldn't control the shaking of his hands. The AK faltered up and down.

"I'm pretty sure he's a touch steadier than your friend there." I motioned towards the fear-addled rifleman. "And that Glock's got great aim, but the columns in this pagoda give me plenty of cover. I'm pretty sure I could outlast you."

I glanced around. The villagers had scurried off to safety. Randy stood, guarding my back against anyone trying to flank us. The clouds rolled past high above, darkening the early morning light, bringing a ghostly orange haze through the settlement.

Membunuh glowered silently for several seconds. His aim, as well as his wrath, fixed on me. His rifle-wielding partner turned to the chief, eyes pleading, but saying nothing.

Then, the big man lowered his head, dropped the gun and walked away, turning briefly to scowl at me.

"You have not won, American," he said. "The jenglot have your scent now, as do the spirit elders. No amount of sharp-shooting can save you from them. Your life is now over. You just don't know it yet."

Grabbing his partner by the hair, he turned again and strode past the shanties and longhouse and stormed into the jungle to the south.

I turned around to face Randy and let out a deep breath.

"YOU CAN'T FIND THEM ANYWHERE?" I asked Marc who was chugging a pitcher of water. The wind howled outside the shaky timbers of the Baik Orang longhouse. Thunder boomed over head, followed by several stifled cries from the village women. "They've got to be there."

"And I'm telling you they're not. Vera and I searched up and down the jungle ridge and were unable to discover a single body anywhere. Not even the one you beheaded."

"This makes no sense," I said to no one in particular.

At last count, between Landers, Randy, and myself, we'd managed to take out at least four jenglot the night before. I'd wanted to find at least one of the bodies to examine and to give to Krenkin if we couldn't actually catch a living specimen.

But Marc insisted that their search had turned up nothing. As much as I hated redundancy, I had to say it again. "This just makes absolutely no sense. Dead jenglot just don't get up and walk away," I insisted. "And I'm not ready to believe that a group of animals are in the habit of carrying their dead off for burial."

"I don't know what you'd like me to say," Marc said. "All I know is that the remains of the jenglot were nowhere to be found. Whether they absconded away of their own volition or were carried off, I have no idea. But they're not there anymore."

Nikki sat on a wooden cot, her back against the wall. Several children sat in rapt attention at her feet as she told them Bible stories. Apparently, she had better things to do than worry about the jenglot.

"The way I see it, there are three possibilities," Vera piped in from the opposite side of the room. "One, scavengers carried the remains away. Two, they weren't dead. Just injured. Or three, these 'animals' as you call them are much more socially advanced than we've given them credit for. Personally, I'm hoping for option one."

I stood up from the bedroll a villager had given me, walked over to the window, and gawked out at the rain-soaked afternoon. After Membunuh had fled the village, we were greeted with a much friendlier welcome from the people of Baik Orang. They'd explained that after the murder of their former chieftain, they'd had no choice but to follow the leadership of his killer. No one in the village was strong enough to challenge the large man.

We'd helped clear their village of the dead and debris from the previous night and were about to make our way down to the abandoned village Marc and Vera had discovered when we were hit with another storm. The villagers had insisted we stick it out in the safety of their longhouse until the tempest blew over.

The door of the house flew open, jerking me out of my reverie, and Landers stepped into the room. Stamping his feet to remove excess mud from his boots and shaking the rain from his thinly cropped hair, the Marine secured the door again. He then turned to me.

"I tracked them as far as the western bank of the river," he said, taking the towel Vera offered and wiping his face. "Then the tracks disappear."

"Any signs they might be carrying there dead?" asked Randy. "We seem to have misplaced a few of their bodies."

"It's hard to say." He didn't appear surprised at all. "These things are crafty. They know how to cover their tracks. It's as if they're aware I was tracking them."

"But they're animals," I said. "Just animals. They're not sentient. They're definitely not supernatural."

"Maybe they're getting help," Randy said.

"What kind of help?"

"I don't know. Maybe someone who'd like to see them kill a few more villagers around here? Someone like that kooky witchdoctor."

"Not likely," Landers said. "There were no human tracks at all. Only one set of tiger tracks, some elk, and the jenglot. If someone's helping them, they weren't standing on two feet."

"Does no one find it interesting that the jenglot attacked the village two days earlier than schedule?" Nikki rose from her cot and pushed into the conversation. "And then come back the very next night? Since they started their attacks, I've never heard of this happening before. They've always stuck to their routine. Never once have they attacked a village twice in a row."

I'd already questioned that very thing myself. The more we dug into this whole mess, the more confusing it seemed to get.

"She's right," I said. "Even stranger is the fact that the creatures didn't seem to feed at all in the past two nights. They were pure destructive attacks, not hunting parties. Anyone have any suggestions? Possible solutions for the aberration?"

"Not a clue," Randy said leaning back in a wooden chair, pinching the bridge of his nose.

"What about the Alpha?" Vera asked. "It didn't seem to be here last night. Last we saw it, Scott shot it when it attacked the

Pingitti woman. You found some blood, so we know it was injured. Could that have thrown them off schedule somehow?"

"I don't know how it could," I answered. "Unless it's dead. Maybe it bled to death and now the jenglot have no direction, no leadership."

"And that's why they organized a rescue party and carried their fallen back to God only knows where?" Vera eased up next to me at the window, clutched the sill with her hands, and looked out into the rain. Water splashed through the window, drenching her face. "It's just so hot in here."

I recognized the signs. Vera was getting itchy. She was excited and on the hunt for answers and I knew she was finally digging her teeth into the crazy mystery we'd stumbled into.

"No, something's going on that we haven't accounted for yet," she continued. "There's something we're missing. Something we haven't considered. But I think the village we found may help shed some light on what's going on around here."

"How come? What's so important about this village?"

'It is rather problematic to explain," Marc interjected. "It's something you'll really have to observe for yourself."

"Try me."

"Okay, well, for starters, it looks like the place has been abandoned for more than thirty years or so, given the amount of vegetation that's sprouted up all around," said Vera. "But the people apparently didn't go of their own free will. There's some major fire damage to the buildings and shell casings all over the ground. Looked like AK-47 ammo to me."

"And what does this have to do with our situation?" I asked.

"*Punya semangat kampong,*" Marc uttered in Malay. "*The Village of the Spirits*. It was inscribed in several of the ruins in red paint."

"But what does that have to do with jenglot?"

"Think about it you knucklehead," Vera hissed. "Wherever we go...whoever we talk to about the jenglot, one thing keeps popping up over and over again."

"The spirit ancestors," Nikki piped in. "They're central figures in the mythology of these parts. Ancestral spirits that disappeared from their village one day and believed to have ascended to some higher plain. They've become gods."

"Exactly," Marc said excited. "And according to the legends, these ancestors seem to have an intricate connection with the jenglot. It is an oversimplification, but true enough, to say our quarry is their enforcers or something similar."

"But you said this village has only been abandoned for around thirty years," I said. "They're not exactly 'ancestors' now are they?"

"It doesn't matter," Marc answered. "The myth has obviously been in their collective consciousness for centuries. The sudden disappearance of these particular villagers may have drawn some sort of parallel. The locals might think another ascension had taken place."

Thunder rumbled high above as I considered what I was being told. I still couldn't wrap my brain around the whole thing. Too many holes.

"But even if the locals see these disappearing villagers as some sort of new spirit elders, why would it have anything do with the recent jenglot attacks? What's the connection?"

"That's why we need to check the place out," Vera said. "We were in a hurry last night. We wanted to get back to you as soon as possible. We didn't have time for a thorough investigation."

The longhouse swayed in the wind, the bamboo timbers creaking with the strain as the rain pounded against the rusted tin roof above us. We all stared silently at each other, unsure of what to do or say.

Suddenly, I became aware of a bent over, old woman hovering patiently around us holding a bowl of rice.

"Can I help you?" I asked, a little steamed at the interruption.

The old crone smiled a toothless grin and extended the bowl towards me.

"Eat," she said. "Eat. Hungry."

I glanced at Vera, a warm smile spreading across her face. Nikki moved over to the woman, spoke to her in Malay for several minutes, and took the bowl. She passed it to me and nodded.

"You need to eat it," Nikki said. "She's showing her appreciation to you for liberating her people from Membunuh. It would be an insult for you to refuse."

I studied the brown rice, bringing it to my nose and sniffing. I couldn't remember the last time I'd eaten and my stomach snarled in protest. I dipped two fingers into the dish and shoveled a handful into my mouth.

It tasted like four day old dishwater—don't asked me how I'd know that—and I strained not to spit the stuff from my mouth. Whatever ingredients she'd added to the rice was definitely not on the menu at *Chinese Bob's Authentic American Chinese Grill and Bar*. I willed myself to smile at the woman, rubbing my belly.

"Mmmmmm," I lied. "Very good."

I handed the bowl over to Randy. "Eat. Pass it around to everyone."

The crone smiled back, spouting a string of Malay words excitedly. Nikki responded in turn, gesturing to me intermittently. Marc asked the woman several questions himself, which encouraged an even more frenzied reaction from her. Soon, the exchange ended, the woman turned around and walked to the far end of the Longhouse and sat down. Her warm grin beamed across the room at me.

"She wanted you to know about the abandoned village," Nikki said. "She said the place is cursed. The people there were apparently taken by demons in the night. The villagers themselves escaped the demonic assault, but not before learning the secrets of Life itself. They ascended, according to local legend."

"She hasn't really told us anything we don't already know," I said. "Now has she?"

"Actually, she did," Marc said, pushing his glasses up onto the bridge of his nose. His face was stricken in a rigid frown. "She said that the jenglot are not the Spirit Elders' enforcers as I'd supposed."

I stared at the bookworm, waiting for him to continue. His face grew even paler.

"Well? You going to fill us in or what?"

"She said the jenglot *are* the Spirit Elders," Nikki said, face just as grim. "She said that the spirits are shapeshifters—spiritual beings capable of taking physical form at night."

"That might explain some things," Randy said, still stuffing his face with the rancid rice. The guy would eat anything.

"No. As a matter of fact, it doesn't explain anything," I snarled. "It's the stupidest thing I've ever heard. There's no such thing as spirits or shapeshifters or bogeymen. It's insane."

"I'm not finished," Nikki interrupted. "She also explained why the jenglot had altered their feeding pattern. She said that the Elders are now on a warpath. They are no longer concerned with just feeding. They have been insulted and seek retribution."

"Insulted?" I asked. "By who?"

"You, Jack," Marc answered. "And Landers. He shot the Alpha. It was an affront to their honor and now they seek to annihilate the entire team. Er, that is, according to the old lady."

"So what you're saying is that we've just gone from bad to 'put a bullet in my head' worse, is that it?" I asked, rubbing my eyes. I was getting real irritated with all the hocus pocus talk.

"Essentially," Marc said. "At first, they were content to just feed to survive. Now, they're killing out of malice and the villagers believe things are just going to escalate."

"That's just great," Randy said between a mouthful of rice. "Fantastic."

I wasn't sure he was talking about the jenglot or the empty bowl he put down on the dirt floor of the Longhouse.

I was tired of talking about this. I turned and walked over to my bed mat and dropped onto it, pulling a light jacket from my pack and wrapping it around my shoulders.

"Well, we're not going to figure anything out tonight," I said, turning over on my side to face the wall. "Let's get some sleep. Tomorrow, we'll check out that abandoned village and then make our way to Tuhan Kampong before those things attack again."

"But, what about..." Randy tried to protest.

"Get some sleep," I commanded, looking at the shadows between the bamboo walls. "I have a feeling we'll need it."

I closed my eyes, willing myself to sleep, hoping to escape the maze of riddles pummeling my mind. The disembodied head of my winged attacker flashed through my mind's eye, followed by the words of Membunuh as he limped out of the village: "Your life is now over. You just don't know it yet."

18

I couldn't sleep. Visions of the shredded remains of the Baik Orang villagers, mauled by the jenglot, haunted my dreams. Vicious teeth and claws slashed across my scattered thoughts. The shrill cackles of Shantili thumped in time with the crescendo of my pounding pulse.

But the mind wrenching revelation of the village crone nagged at me the most. I refused to believe the jenglot were anything more than a biological species of animal yet to be discovered. Shapeshifters. Wrathful spirits. It was all so ridiculous.

But I just couldn't let what she'd told us go. I had to admit that there was something definitely weird going on with this hunt. The jenglot behaved...well, almost human. They collected their injured or dying. They recognized and recalled potential dangers. And if the old lady was right, they'd marked me for a serious case of revenge. These were not the actions of mere animals.

These thoughts kept tossing and turning through my mind as my weary body huddled restlessly on the straw mat of my bed. Staring up the thatched roof above my bed, my thoughts shifted to Witz and whether or not I should call him again. But I thought better of it. Although things had definitely been crazy the past few days, I wasn't really sure a mercenary army was even needed. With Landers backing us up, we'd handled ourselves pretty well.

Through the rest of the night, I drifted in and out of dream-filled sleep, thoughts spiraling out of control in my mind. I was thankful when the sun finally rose above the mountainous terrain and the rain let up just enough to begin the two and a half mile trek to Marc and Vera's newly discovered village. The going was tough, thanks to the drizzle and slippery mud, as well as Liana Creepers choking their way through the dense vegetation. After a little more than an hour, we finally came to the Durian grove that surrounded our destination.

Nine decaying shanties sat in a horseshoe pattern around the village. Like Baik Orang, a small two-tiered pagoda rested in the center of town. Liana vines crept up the wooden beams supporting the structure, branching out near the top with several flowering blossoms peeking up at the sky.

"Landers," I said. "Take Randy and Vera and search the perimeter of the village. Look for anything that might shed some light on what happened here."

Without a word, they turned to walk back towards the jungle edge. I grabbed the Marine's arm and pulled him close.

"And keep your eyes open," I whispered. "Something's not right here. I feel like we're being watched."

"I've felt it too," he said. "Don't worry. I'll take care of it."

I watched them walk into the forest and turned to Marc.

"All right, show me what you've got."

We followed the linguist around the shell of an old hut, towards the remains of the village longhouse. Walking around the building, he stopped at the doorway and drew back a clump of vines and shrubs standing sentry through the years. Malay words were etched into the door of the ruins, scrawled in quick shaking strokes by some sort of chisel and red paint.

"These look different from the markings we saw yesterday,"

Nikki said, running the tips of her fingers across the letters. "What do they say?"

"You're right. They are different. Different method of writing. Different hand. Different message altogether," Marc answered. "These," he pointed to the top most words, "I've already told you about. 'The Village of the Spirits.' The next few lines are difficult to make out, but something about the 'Red Demon' taking the peaceful villagers who lived here back to Hell."

"That sounds promising," I quipped. "Not only do we have to deal with bloodsucking monsters, but now we've got a demon to deal with as well. It's about par for the course at this point."

"I don't think it was a literal demon, Jack," Marc said seriously, pushing his glasses up to the ridge of his nose. "Not unless demons have taken to brandishing AK-47s and perforating jungle villages."

Marc had never developed an ear for sarcasm. I let his explanation go without a word and just nodded at him to continue his translation.

"Anyway, the villagers were apparently taken prisoner by this red demon and they later escaped," he said. He drew closer to the last few words as he brushed a stray palm frond away from the door. "It says they had changed during their ordeal. They had attained what the Buddhists call Nirvana and had been allowed to ascend into the spirit world."

A steady stream of rain began to fall from the overcast sky, soaking through our clothes. By now, I was pretty much getting accustomed to the one million percent humidity. At least the wind was minimal and there was no rumble of thunder anywhere nearby.

"Anything about the jenglot?" I asked, brushing water from my face.

"Nothing at all. There is a reference to some sort of guardians and the 'draining of the river of life,' which could refer to the blood stream since it's universally recognized as the source of life. But I see no specific mention of jenglot."

"Well, good job. I'm not sure what this, if anything, has to do with our expedition, but it was a good eye."

"Are you kidding me? It more than confirms the old lady's story," Nikki said. "Maybe we should go back and see if she can tell us anything else."

"It doesn't confirm anything. For all we know, she read the same inscription herself and was just passing on the folklore. Look," I decided to change the subject for now. "We've got to get to Tuhan Kampong, the next village on the jenglot's feeding pattern, before sundown. With the jenglot mucking with their dinner schedule, I don't want to risk not being there tonight."

"Then let me go back," she said. "You guys can go on ahead. Tuhan Kampong isn't that far away. I can meet up with you by morning."

"What about introductions? The whole reason you came along was to pave the way with the villagers?"

"You'll be okay. There's actually another missionary in Tuhan. A guy named Terry Greenholm. Just tell him you're with me and he'll fix you right up."

"I don't like you going back to that village alone."

Her face lit up, a wide grin spread across her face.

"Why Dr. Jackson, are you worried about me?"

"Of course I am," I said with an equally large smile. "Your rich daddy is funding this little expedition. I'd hate to go back without getting paid."

"Say whatever you want," she beamed. "You care about me whether you admit it or not. As for going back alone, could you spare someone? I have a feeling this is really important." She pointed to the writing on the door.

I knew she was right, but I didn't like it.

"All right," I said finally. "But Vera will go back with you. I don't want you going it alone and forcing me to turn around and save your irritating little butt again."

"Sure."

"I'm serious. This has nothing to do with liking you. It's purely practical."

"Okay."

I stared at her smug grin for several seconds before wheeling around with a grunt for a better look at the strange markings on the hut. Marc stifled a smile, trying desperately to appear unamused at our exchange.

"Jack," squelched a static-filled voice of Randy over the hand held radio. "Do you copy?"

"Roger," I said into the mike, thankful for the reprieve.

"Er, no. My name's Randy, not Roger, in case you'd forgotten," he quipped. His sense of humor was really starting to rub me the wrong way. He'd just stolen one of my best lines.

"You know what I mean. What do you have for me?"

"Oh, just an uninvited guest." I could hear the grin in his voice. Geeze, everyone was having a great time on this little outing.

I looked over at Marc, who stiffened at the news.

"Roger, er, okay," I said. "We'll be here."

I heard rustling in the foliage to my right and turned, gun ready, to face the noise. I didn't need to wait long. Soon, the scrubby head of Randy poked through the underbrush, still grinning ear to ear, followed by Vera. Four seconds later, the mortified figure of Shantili waddled into the open with Landers' beefy hand gripping the witchdoctor's shoulder. A small gash marred the squat ridge of his nose, a small stream of fresh blood trickling down his cheek.

"Well, well," I said, holstering the gun. "You do show up in the darnedest places, don't you, Doc?"

The little man scowled, looking down at the ground in

defiance. A trickle of blood streaked across his brow, rolling down his right cheek.

"What happened?" I asked Landers.

"We were searching a cluster of strange mounds just east of here near the river bank," he said looking down on his captive. "When this little piece of…"

"Watch it," I nodded my head towards Nikki.

"Sorry. When this little creep here jumped out of a nearby tree and tried to skewer me with this." The Marine held out a nine inch double edged dagger, intricately engraved with images uncannily similar to the jenglot. I took the blade by the hilt and twirled it in my fingers, scrutinizing the exquisite craftsmanship before handing it over to Marc.

I turned around to face Shantili, giving him a huge grin.

"Well, Shorty, what do you have to say for yourself?" I asked.

His dark eyes, filled with malice and hate, lifted to meet mine. A sudden rush of nausea swept through my body, striking the smile from my face, and playing havoc with my equilibrium. Gentle hands gripped my elbows to steady me. I looked over to find Nikki at my side, concern etched over her face.

"Whoa," I said, shaking the wooziness from my head. "Guess I'm a bit dehydrated."

Now it was the shaman's turn to smile as he looked back down at the ground in silence.

"What happened?" Vera asked, bringing me a canteen of water and placing two fingers across my wrists to check my pulse.

"I'm not really sure." I eyed Shantili who refused to meet my gaze. "Dizziness. Nausea. Black spots flashing in front of my eyes like I'm about to pass out. It's hard to explain, but every time I get around this guy, something weird happens."

"Well your heart rate appears normal. When we get to Tuhan Kampong, I'll need to check your blood pressure. Other than that, I don't know what else to do."

"Medicine won't help," Nikki whispered, sidling up next to us. "It's not a medical condition."

Vera and I stared at the missionary in silence.

"It's spiritual."

"Oh come on," I laughed. "You can't possibly expect me to believe this guy is putting some hocus pocus on me. There's no such thing. I've been around the world a few times. Met hundreds of people and seen a lot of weird things—including so-called voodoo hexes. It's not real."

"I never said it was magic. I said it was spiritual. There's a difference."

"Look, we're getting no where fast," I said, walking away from Nikki and Vera towards Shantili. I motioned my team to spread out to give a little more privacy. "Now, listen Shorty, you and I need to have a little chat. Just the two of us."

The old man looked back up at me and smiled...warmly. The sudden change in demeanor unnerved me even more than his malicious gaze earlier.

"What would you like to talk about American?"

"For starters, what do you know about this place? What happened here?"

The shaman, his hands now tied securely behind his back, walked to a nearby stump and squatted down.

"You'd like to know about this place?"

"That's what I said."

"I can tell you. Or I can show you. It's up to you."

"Show me? What do you mean?"

The malice oozed back into his gaze once more as he snickered.

"I can show you the answer to all your questions. I can show you what happened here. Most important, I can show you the jenglot."

My heart pounded inside my chest, threatening to tear it

inside out. I felt sweat rise against the bristly hairs on my upper lip.

Could it be true? Would he be willing to give me...no, not give...show me the answers I was seeking?

Somehow, I doubted it. But there was no way I could resist his offer and he knew it.

"All right," I said. "I'm up for show and tell. Let's go."

I stepped forward to lift the old man up by the arm, but he resisted.

"Not yet," he grinned. "There are some conditions."

I knew it. He is up to something.

"And what are your conditions?"

The shaman looked down at his bare feet, wiggling his big toes amid little bursts of giggling.

He's insane, I thought. Why on earth am I even listening to this geezer?

He looked back up to me, licking his lips.

"I'm thirsty."

Oh for crying out loud. Without a word, I reached for my belt, pulled the canteen Vera had given me and held it to his lips. The clear liquid poured down his chin as he lapped at it with a pale tongue.

"Okay. The conditions," I said, screwing the top tightly on the canteen and re-attaching it to my belt.

His eyes lifted to meet mine as decayed, yellow teeth glistened in an even broader smile.

"First. Only you and the Christian witch are allowed to see what I have to show."

"No deal," I said, turning away and walking back to the team.

"I give you my word," he coughed. "You'll both be safe. No harm will come to you. But I can't have your entire team seeing what I have to show you."

He curled his index finger at me, drawing me closer, and whispered, "After all, one of them will betray you."

That stopped me in my tracks. I spun around and glared at the little man.

"Betray me?" I knew exactly what he was trying to do and I didn't like it. "Shut your mouth. I'm not going to let you set us against each other."

"Think what you will," he said, his eyes boring into my own. "The spirits have assured me. One of your team is a liar and a traitor. The only ones true for sure are you and the Christian. It is for that reason that I will only show the two of you."

It was crazy. No one on the team would betray me. The old man was playing mind games, sowing doubt and paranoia. I was an idiot to even entertain him, but he sat on his stump dangling the tantalizing ambrosia of Truth in my direction. There was no way I could possibly say no to his demands. But I wouldn't allow his lies to influence me either. Of that, I was sure.

"All right. Next condition."

"I will not ask you to leave your weapons behind. The jungle, after all, is a very dangerous place," he said, licking his lips once more. A faint wave of nausea struck me again, but I brushed it aside, waiting for him to continue. "However, I will only allow one weapon, and that to be carried by the woman."

"You've got to be out of your mind."

"Possibly. But I'm also serious. I will not compromise on this."

I pulled the Glock from its holster and looked at it, absently rubbing the barrel with my index finger.

"If it makes you feel any better, if the need arises, she can hand you the weapon. But she will be its caretaker on our journey."

"Journey? But I thought you were going to show me what happened to this village?"

"Precisely," he laughed. "But this is where it started. You want to see where it concluded, do you not?"

"I'm not sure. I don't even know if any of this ties into the jenglot. For all I know, you could be leading me on a wild goose chase."

"That's a chance you'll have to take, just as it is a chance... ever so slight...that the mystery of this village has a great deal to do with the creatures you seek."

I looked over at the rest of the group, idly biding their time, allowing me privacy with the shaman. Two of them, I loved as family. The rest were definitely growing on me. The thought of one of them betraying me slunk back into my mind, causing a shudder to ripple down my back.

Glancing at the old man, I said, "Why didn't you share any of this with me back in the cave? Why didn't you 'show' me then?"

"Because, Dr. Jackson," his giggling seemed incessant. "I never expected you to get this far."

"Any other conditions?" I asked, shoving his last comment aside.

"Only one," he said, his grin faded, darkening his face. "When you see what I have to show you, you and your team will leave this country for good. You will not follow through on your mission for Krenkin. You will leave and not return."

"I can't promise you that."

"Oh, but you will," his malicious smile returned. "You will have no choice in the matter."

19

"You've got to be kidding me!" Randy yelled, scowling at Shantili. "You can't possibly trust that weirdo."

"It's not like I have a choice," I said.

"Sure you do. You can just leave him hog-tied here and hope an orangutan comes along and makes him its girlfriend."

"Randy, shut up," Vera interrupted. "Jack, we're just worried. That's all. It's just a little strange that he'll only let you and Nikki go with him. It seems like he's trying to split us up."

If she only knew. I hadn't told the group about Shantili's prediction of betrayal. It wouldn't have done any good and this way, at least, the only one who had to worry about it was me. I knew that the shaman's words could not possibly be true, but the venomous seeds had been planted, just as he intended.

"It works out great actually," I said, looking at them with the biggest smile I could muster. "This way, we can cover more territory. You guys can move on to Tuhan Kampong, meet up with that other missionary guy Nikki told us about, and get ready for the next jenglot attack."

I paused to let the words sink in.

"While you're doing that, Nikki and I will be investigating this craziness from Shantilli's angle. And if he tries anything hinky," I turned to look at Shantili, "I'll feed him to the jenglot myself."

"I still don't like it," Randy said.

"I don't either, but my mind's made up. We're doing it this way."

"All right, but keep your radio handy."

"I was already planning on it," I said out loud for all to hear. "Actually, I want regular check-ins. Every hour on the hour."

"Sounds good to me."

I motioned for Randy to come closer and we walked out of earshot from the rest of the group.

"Look, something's not right here," I said. "I know it, but I need your support on this with the others."

"This really *is* stupid, Jack," Randy whispered.

We both glanced back at the witchdoctor. His dark eyes closed, head swaying in tight, concentric circles and mumbling something under his breath.

"I just don't like it. But I'll follow your lead. Just let it go on record now—this plan sucks," my friend said.

I smiled, placing a hand on his shoulder and squeezing.

"I'll be careful. But listen. When you get to Tuhan Kampong, you need to be proactive," I said. "I want one of these things caught ASAP. So far, they've run circles around us and I'm sick of it. We're about to go on the offensive."

"What do you have in mind?"

"You know how I work, Randy. I never have a plan until I see what I have to work with. You'll just have to figure it out when you get there."

"Well, you're a big help," he said, scratching the stubble on his chin. "Guess I'll think of something."

SHANTILI LED us deep into the jungle for several hours before coming to the base of a massive, steep hill carpeted with thick vegetation. A red-orange glow cascaded around the peak, as the sun sank down from sight.

"How long until night fall?" Nikki asked, huffing for breath behind me.

I glanced down at my watch, stumbling over a branch jutting up from the ground. I teetered forward, swinging my arms to catch my balance, took two steps and steadied myself.

"About an hour and a half," I said, hoping she hadn't seen. One glance at her amused face told me that she had. "Don't say a thing."

She burst out laughing.

"I'm sorry," she said. "It's just that you've got to be the clumsiest man I've ever met. How in the world have you survived for as long as you have?"

I glowered silently at her, increasing my stride and leaving her to trail behind as I moved up closer to Shantili, who had halted at the hillock's base.

"We must climb," the little man said, looking up at the peak and wiping sweat from his brow. "It is near the top that you will find your answers. And we must do so before the sun sets."

"How come?" asked Nikki, pulling up the rear. "The way you make it sound, the jenglot won't attack you."

"And they won't," he said. "It is the two of you that I'm concerned about."

Blocking the sun from my eyes, I looked up the nearly forty-five degree arc that led to the top. Thick stands of lichen-rich jungle trees lined its ascent, twisting and turning along an ancient trail. Strange, angular stones jutted here and there up the steep embankment, at regular intervals, creating a type of narrow staircase.

"This is an odd looking hill," I said, surveying the angular striations along the ridge. "It almost looks like a..."

"A what, Dr. Jackson?"

I tore my eyes away from the peak to bring them around to Shantili. A cruel grin etched deep in his face.

"Like some kind of pyramid," I croaked.

"And that's precisely what it is," said the witchdoctor, carefully placing a sandaled foot on the first step. His head craned around to look at us. "Thousands of years ago—well before Siddhartha Guatama, Christ, or Mohammed walked the earth—my people erected this temple to worship the true gods of this world."

He turned back to the foliage-covered structure and clambered up five more steps. I looked at Nikki, gestured her forward, and followed close behind.

"My ancestors revered this place for nearly thirty-two generations, tending to the pleasures of the gods and performing strong *ilmu sihir* in its bowels."

I glanced up at Nikki, who'd turned to me.

"Magic," she answered my unspoken question. "*Ilmu sihir* means magic."

"Ah," I nodded, moving on and letting the old man continue his rant.

Shantili crouched, ducking past a low hanging vine and continued, "We led a peaceful existence. There were no wars between tribes. No warrior class. Only a civilization of priests dedicated to preserving their way of life.

Even after Islam and Christianity pushed its way into our world, we managed to maintain our purity with anonymity."

"So what happened?" Nikki asked, heaving for breath.

The shaman paused, catching his own breath. I glanced down and discovered we'd scrambled up nearly a quarter of the pyramid already.

"As the country became more populated and western influences seeped into even the most remote places of the jungle, my people were forced into a nomadic way of life to avoid detection," he said. "The nation's leaders outlawed ancient religions for the more civilized way of Allah."

Shantili looked back at us, his eyes blazing in the orange haze of the sunset.

"We must hurry," he said. "We've only a little further to go and it will be dark before we know it."

For the first time, I noticed a surreal hush that had settled over the forest. The air hung motionless around us. There were no signs of movement anywhere—not even birds flew over the place. Talons of dread raked down my back eliciting goose bumps over my arms and neck.

"But what does this place have to do with the abandoned village near Baik Orang?" Nikki pressed as we continued our ascent. "What happened there?"

"Oh, this temple has everything to do with the people of that village," he said, pulling himself up onto a short three-foot ledge. He turned, stretched out a spindly hand and dragged Nikki up. He allowed me to fend for myself. "The inhabitants of that village were the nomadic descendents of those who built this place. I, myself, was born and raised there."

"So were you there when…when…" she couldn't get her question out.

"When it was assaulted and pillaged? Yes. I was there." The old man's words oozed with venom.

"But…"

"Nikki, enough questions for now," I interrupted. Her curiosity was insatiable and my gut was screaming for caution. For some reason, I didn't like the direction the conversation was heading, but I couldn't put my finger on why. Maybe it had something to do with what the old woman in Baik Orang had told us about the Spirit Elders and their connection to the jenglot. "I'm sure he'll answer all our questions in time."

"Ah," the old man said, beaming from ear to ear as he peered in the waning light at strange markings carved on the stone walkway. "Here we are."

I glanced up again. We were a little less than half-way up the structure. I clambered up to where Shantili crouched, sweeping debris from a stone.

"Are you sure?" I asked. "I thought we needed to get to the top."

The old man cackled.

"Oh heavens no," he said. "At least I was hoping we wouldn't have to. I knew the entrance was somewhere nearby, but I wasn't sure. If I hadn't found this, then yes, we would have needed to climb the entire temple. But not now. Oh no, not now."

The sun was completely on the other side of the pyramid, blocking out all light from us. I reached into my pouch and pulled out my flashlight and the radio.

"Jack to Randy," I said, pushing the transmitter button and speaking into the mic. "Can you copy?"

Static.

"Jack to Randy, are you there?"

A squelching roar of radio waves blasted through the speakers. For an instant, I thought I heard the familiar tone of my old friend's voice, but it was gone just as quickly.

"Randy, you're not getting through," I yelled. "Please repeat."

More static erupted from the tiny speaker.

"Guess we're out of range," I glanced over at Nikki.

"I'm sure they'll be okay," she said with a warm smile. "Besides, my missionary friend, Terry, knows the area well. He'll take care of them."

The cold, hollow echo of stone grinding against stone spun me around. The white beam of the flashlight revealed the old shaman struggling to push a slab of rock from a hidden entrance behind a veil of shrubs near the pyramid wall.

"Here, let me help you," I said, moving beside him to lend a little muscle.

The stone slab fell forward revealing the entrance to a dank tunnel leading into the temple. The putrid stench of decaying flesh tinged with mildew and stagnant air struck me in the face, nearly doubling me over.

"What's down there?" I asked, forcing bile back down my throat.

"Answers, Dr. Jackson," Shantili said. "Answers."

20

The blinding beam of my halogen flashlight cut through the darkness of the shaft leading toward the recesses of the ancient temple. I was leading the way down a winding staircase, with Shantili behind and Nikki in the rear.

Except for the shuffling noises of our own feet and the occasional flutter of insect wings, the structure appeared devoid of life.

"How far down are we heading?" I asked over my shoulder, carefully maneuvering a shallow drop off. The walls of the tunnel, supported by thick wooden beams, narrowed, forcing me to move at a sideways angle down the steps.

"Only a few meters more," the shaman hissed. "Be quiet. There are things in this place that you would not wish to disturb."

"What kind of things?" I felt my Adam's apple pushing towards my mouth, trying to get the heck out of the creepy pyramid. A little more coaxing and I might just follow it out.

The old man ignored my question, so I walked on, searching the shaft ahead for any signs of trouble. Various paintings marked the walls, depicting strange rituals and ancient customs. Bizarre images of tiger-like horned animals battling against giant armored gods adorned the murals, stirring up my curiosity.

"These animals," I said, stopping briefly to point at the markings. "What are they? I've never seen anything like them."

"And you never will," Shantili said. "Most of the creatures have long since died off from the land, but many make up the rich legends and myths of the Malaysian people. Once they prospered in the jungle. They are now little more than a vague memory. Please, let's continue. We really haven't much time."

"Aren't we safe in now?" Nikki asked. "I thought we'd be protected from the jenglot in here."

"It's not a matter of safety at this point," he replied, adeptly sidestepping Nikki's jenglot comment. "But I have much to show you. Much to reveal. And it is almost time. The *Dara Ratu* will be here soon."

"Dara Ratu?" I asked, turning to look at the old man who suddenly seemed withered with age, almost wraithlike with fatigue. "What the heck's that?"

His grim smile faded but he said nothing.

This deal was getting hinkier by the minute. The old man was up to something. Whatever this "Dara Ratu" thing was, I'm sure it wasn't good. I was determined not to let this weirdo get the upper hand.

"Look, let's get something straight right now," I stopped walking, turned, and shoved a finger into Shantili's brittle chest. "If you double cross me, I'm going to put a bullet in that bald little head of yours. And I won't lose any sleep over it either."

A weak chuckle croaked from his throat. "Don't worry, Dr. Jackson. All will be revealed soon enough." He pushed my finger away. "As for betraying you...I swear upon the ancestors I will do exactly as I've promised. I will show you the answers you seek."

I felt Nikki's hand slide across my shoulder, drawing me to look at her worried worn face.

"Jack, come on," she said, trying to smile. "We need to get

moving. I don't like this anymore than you do, but we really have no choice now."

"Listen to your woman," the old man said. "She speaks wisely for a change."

I glared at Shantili a while longer before turning back to the staircase. We marched down another fifty feet or so before coming to a landing with a dark tunnel veering off to the right.

"We are now almost a hundred feet below the surface of the jungle floor," Shantili explained. "At the end of this corridor, you will discover some of the answers you seek. However..."

He trailed off, twisting his head to one side as if listening for something. He jerked forward towards the arched doorway of the corridor and poked his head into the darkness, sniffing the air.

"What is it?" I asked, shining the light through the tunnel. The shaman ignored me, shifting to his left for a better listen. I looked over to Nikki who silently gripped the handle of my gun that was now strapped to her belt.

Good girl. Keep that thing handy.

"What is it? What's wrong?" I repeated.

"Nothing. Nothing is wrong at all," he finally said, pulling himself away from the tunnel door. "As I was saying, the answers you seek are down this way. But I must warn you, the path is treacherous."

The beam of my light splayed across his features, his jet black eyes sunken deep within his skull, and jagged yellow teeth shined through his cadaverous lips.

"Treacherous? I suppose you're going to tell me that one false step will send a huge boulder barreling down on me or thousands of poison tipped darts whipping past my head."

The old man took another look down the darkened corridor before turning back to me. His legs quivered under his weight. Something was spooking him.

"Oh, nothing quite so insidious," he said. "But the temple is protected. Jenglot do, at times, stalk these halls, protecting the secrets that lay within," Shantilli continued.

"So the jenglot are here," I said, glancing back at the gun tucked away in Nikki's belt.

"Yes, they are. Oh, not all of them, mind you," he cackled at his attempt at humor. "But there are some. Some left behind. Left to defend the secrets."

Nikki inched closer to the tunnel and flashed her light down the corridor, before turning to me.

"Well, we might as well get started," she said. "The sooner we get through this, the sooner we get out of here."

"This place gives you the creeps too, huh?" I asked with a troubled grin.

"Oh, that's a bit of an understatement."

I moved towards her, adding my own light to hers. A thick haze of blackness engulfed the beams, as if the very air smothered any illumination that entered into its realm.

"All right, old man," I said without looking back at Shantili. "Let's get moving."

Silence was the only response.

"Shantili?" I turned around to find the witchdoctor gone. "Shantili! You little twerp! Get back here."

I glared at Nikki.

"I thought you were supposed to be watching him," she said, flashing her light up the narrow staircase we'd just descended.

"Me? You're the one with the gun."

"What do we do now?" she asked, changing the subject.

I walked to the edge of the stairwell and drew the beam of the flashlight up, scanning for any signs of the slippery little weasel.

Nothing.

Turning back around, I moved to the edge of the tunnel and stepped forward.

"We move on," I said, the weight of the words dropped like

lead in the dank corridor. "Like you said, we don't have much choice if we want some answers."

"That's assuming Shantili was telling us the truth about this place," she said. I heard the echo of her footfall directly behind me.

Courage too. I'm really starting to like this girl, I thought. *Maybe she really is different from all the other Christian pin-heads I've met in my life.*

"I don't see any reason for him to bring us all this way for a lie," I said, stumbling over a slab of rock jutting from the stone floor. "It doesn't make sense."

"Unless this is where the jenglot nest," she whispered. "And he's brought us here for dinner."

"Maybe. But one way or another, I guess we'll get the answers the old man kept promising us."

"Yeah. One way or another."

"UM, you mentioned something earlier about rolling boulders and poison tipped arrows," Nikki broke the silence I'd enjoyed for nearly twenty minutes as we hiked down into the netherworld of the temple. "You don't suppose there really are any booby traps we need to be watching out for, do you?"

I halted our march, opened up my canteen and took a swig. The moment we first began our trek down the tunnel, we noticed a steep decline descending deeper into the ruins. There was no way of knowing how far down we had to go, but I was beginning to hope it wouldn't be far. The heat was unbearable. It wasn't something I expected this deep underground. I handed the container to Nikki and wiped my brow.

"I don't think so," I said, taking the canteen back from her and hanging the strap around my neck. "I've met a lot of archaeologists, treasure hunters, and out right grave robbers and each time I talked with them, they assured me of one thing—there were no such thing as ancient booby traps."

"That's good to know," she said with a slight smile, betraying the fact that I hadn't eased her mind on the subject.

"Look, it's like this," I turned around to face her. "Even if some place did sport some kind of crazy anti-personnel devices, they would have been the pride of the builders and celebrated with great big neon signs flashing: 'Look at the cool booby traps we came up with. Aren't we smart?' Ancient rulers loved tooting their own horns that way and since we didn't see any signs of the sort, we don't have anything to worry about, do we?"

I wheeled around and walked down the tunnel a bit further, but stopped when I realized Nikki was no longer following me.

"What now?" I asked, without looking at her.

"It's nothing."

"No, really. What's wrong now?"

"Okay, it's just that the whole 'neon sign' thing..."

"Yeah?"

"That has got to be the dumbest thing I've ever heard in my entire life. You thought that something so inane would make me feel better?"

Well, yeah, I thought, grinding my teeth to stifle the biting comment begging to spew from my mouth.

"Okay, how about this then," I said, quiet pride for my self-control welling inside my chest. "If there are any booby traps in this place, they must be hundreds, if not thousands of years old. Right?"

"I suppose."

"And what do you think centuries would do to mechanical devices?" I asked. "Centuries of wear, tear, and debris would play havoc with anything relying on gears, chains, or triggers. What would happen if you buried your car in the sand and dug it up again a week later? Would you be able to start the engine?"

"No, I guess I wouldn't."

"Exactly. Same concept," I finally turned to look at her. She was smiling again.

"Now that, Dr. Jackson, made me feel much better," she said, leaning forward and giving me a peck on the cheek. "Thanks."

Grinning from ear to ear, her lithe form brushed past me, flicked on her flashlight, and moved into the darkness of the tunnel. I could only stand, speechless, watching her backside grow smaller into the dimness before realizing how foolish it was for her to be wandering through the temple ruins unescorted.

I quickly closed the distance between us, mentally reflecting on just where everything in my life started falling apart.

I can't believe this is happening. In less than a week, I gave up on a nice, easy expedition searching for a cute little elusive creature with no violent tendencies. I substituted it for hunting an ugly little elusive creature who'd love to drain every last drop of blood from my bones.

Moving along side her, I peered into the murk before us and wondered how much farther the tunnel would descend. Scraping and the sound of scattering pebbles against stone echoed several yards behind us. It wasn't the first time I'd heard the noises since Shantili had disappeared, but it had been the most obvious. A sound distinctly like footsteps. I looked over at Nikki, who appeared oblivious to the shuffling.

Glancing behind, my eyes tried pushing through the dense shadows, but could see nothing. Not even the slightest hint of movement.

I probably lost my job, I thought, pushing the thousand possible explanations for the sounds from my mind. *It was such a great job. Oh, and my airplane was blown up. That's something you don't hear every day.*

The tunnel that had descended for nearly a mile from the stairwell landing began to taper off, making the going a bit easier.

Let's see, what else? That little voice in my head just kept chattering away. *Oh yeah, I met a would-be communist dictator bent on overthrowing the Malaysian government, been hexed by a crazy old witchdoctor with an axe to grind, and have been viciously assaulted by the vampire version of Rocky the Flying Squirrel.*

I couldn't help but shake my head at the insanity of it all.

And now, here I am, walking blindly into an ancient ruined temple with a hot, but completely ungrateful missionary who's irritatingly full of herself. Did I leave anything out?

More footfalls shuffled through the blackness from behind. A distinct sound of a low guttural growling.

Oh yeah, and I'm currently being stalked by an unknown number of monsters intent on ripping my throat out. This just keeps getting better and better.

"Okay, you've got to have heard that," I said, grabbing her arm and turning her to face me.

"I did," she replied, her eyes grim. "I was hoping if we ignored it, it would just go away."

The sounds ceased with our whispers, but soon a completely new set of noises echoed from somewhere in front of us. Nikki jerked at the sound and drew closer into my arms.

Well, well. Maybe she's not as frigid as I thought. There's a chink in her armor. She does have emotions after all…albeit fearful ones.

"It's okay," I said, pulling her away from me and looking her in the eyes. "But we need to move on. I'm not sure how much farther we have to go, but we're sitting ducks just standing here in the open like this."

With a brave nod, she turned and walked forward, her hand absently gripping the butt of the gun in her waistband. Upon venturing into the tunnel, I'd decided to let her hold onto the Glock. It seemed to make her feel more comfortable.

My decision, however, was now beginning to trouble me. As we inched our way down the never-ending corridor to the bowels of the temple, I was increasingly wondering if perhaps I could use a little cobalt steel comfort myself.

21

We trod another twenty minutes before the tunnel completely leveled off. The tepid heat finally submitted to the cool temperatures of the subterranean depths, bringing great relief to our nearly dehydrated bodies. My eyes strained in the darkness. For an instant, the beam of my flashlight dimmed, before brightening again.

"How far down do you think we've gone?" Nikki broke the silence.

"I'm not sure," I said, slapping the flashlight against the palm of my hand.

Ah, crap. Please God, don't let the batteries die now. Not now.

The beam grew even brighter with the impact.

A shudder coursed through my limbs at the sudden thought. I'd just prayed for the first time since...well, for a really long time. And what was worse, I'd actually believed He answered.

This girl is definitely messing with my head.

"I'd say we've walked a good mile from the stairwell, wouldn't you?" she asked, ignoring my bout with the flashlight.

"Er, probably more like two," I said, climbing up on an overturned stone pillar in the middle of the walkway and reaching down to haul her up. "I'd say we're getting pretty close. I can't imagine it'd be much further."

"I kind of hope not. Jack, I'm getting really creeped out."

"Feel like we're being watched?"

"Yeah. Kind of. But it's more than just being watched. It's like we're being..."

"Stalked," I said, helping her down the other side of the pillar and turning to peer into the darkness behind us. "Yeah, I feel it too."

I hopped down beside her and pushed on.

"At least the shuffling footsteps have stopped," she said, forcing a grin.

"That, actually, makes me even more nervous," I said. "Makes it harder to know where they are."

Her head turned back the way we came, obviously searching for any signs of our pursuers.

"And who do you think 'they' are?" she whispered, as if her very words could make our stalkers materialize from the shadows.

"My first guess would be the jenglot. But I'm not sure. Shantili's lurking around too. But whatever is, it'll probably just try to eat my face off."

She stifled a laugh at the joke.

"Somehow, I have a feeling you get that alot," she said.

"Yeah, Vera says I just have a way with monsters—"

I skidded to a halt, forcing Nikki to stumble against my back.

"What is it? Why'd you stop?" she asked as she peeked around my shoulder and beamed her flashlight forward. "Oh."

"Yeah. *Oh* is right."

We'd come to a dead end. The walls of the tunnel had collapsed ages ago and had erected a stone barrier between us and our supposed destination. I crouched down, grabbed a chunk of stone and tried to lift it from the rubble. It wouldn't budge.

"What are we going to do?" Nikki's voice sounded hollow, exhausted.

Ignoring her question, I scanned the walls and the pile of stones blocking our way.

"Look at this," I said, pointing to a portion of the tunnel wall still standing. Its edges were blackened, charred by intense heat.

"What could have caused that?" she asked.

"Oh, it's pretty characteristic of black powder burns. These walls were intentionally blown down."

"With black powder?"

"Yeah. But the scorch marks aren't that old. Probably no more than fifty years or so ago, I'd say."

The sound of a pebble skidding across the stone floor jerked our attention away from the debris, spinning us around. Then a barefooted step. No more than a few hundred feet away.

Nikki turned back to the barricade, tucked her flashlight into her pocket, and tested the weight of any stone she could grab hold of.

"That's not going to work," I said. "It's too heavy. Even if you manage to roll of a few rocks away, it'll just crash down on itself under the stress of its own weight."

"Well, we've got to try. Don't we?" She sidestepped to the left edge of the debris, pulled down on another stone and brought it crashing to the floor. "Ah ha!"

"That's only one of them,' I said, flashing my light back and forth, scanning for any movement behind us. "You're wasting your time..."

The crash of another rock exploded through the confines of the tunnel.

"Jack!" Nikki shouted. "It's some kind of a vent!"

A what?

I turned just in time to see the upper portion of Nikki's body disappear into a tiny opening in the rock barrier. Her feet kicked against the stone floor as she shimmied her way deeper into the crevice.

"What the heck are you doing woman?" I yelled. "Get back here."

Ignoring my command, she scrambled forward into the unknown. When she had fully disappeared, I crouched down and examined the narrow cleft of rock she'd crawled through.

The crevice was obviously handmade. Whoever had blown the walls apart, had erected a shallow stone tunnel to bridge the gap to the other side. The rocks from the blasted wall had camouflaged the fissure enough so that only someone who knew where to look would have been able to find it. Or someone with some blind stinking luck.

"Are you okay?" I said into the opening, shining the beam of my light through the small cleft.

I can't believe she's doing this, I thought, stifling the urge to give her a good verbal lashing for her stupidity. I decided to give it to her later. *This girl is nuts and she's dragging me right along with her*.

"Yeah," she grunted, clambering on her elbows to pull her forward. "It's a little tight, but I see an opening on the other end. It's definitely a way through. And it appears pretty sturdy. It's safe."

Numerous growls hissed through the chamber behind me as the padded steps of multiple feet echoed through the tunnel.

Great. Here comes the munchkin blood brigade, I thought, climbing to one knee and tentatively poking my head into the tiny opening. My dormant claustrophobia clawed its way up my spine, crushing against my thoughts like a massive, invisible vice.

A howl erupted nearby, followed by the full onslaught of pounding feet against the stones. I cast my light back for one final look and reeled at the sight of three dark shadows charging full speed at me. Flashes of blood-stained fangs reflected in the beam of my light.

Without a second breath, I plunged head first into the stone crevice and clawed my way forward. The sounds of snarling hisses followed me through the shaft and I scurried even faster.

The crevice was tighter than it seemed from the outside. My shoulders barely squeezed through the sides, forcing me to struggle my way through. My stomach and back scraped against the stone floor and ceiling, shredding my shirt and quite a bit of skin in the process.

This must be what it feels like to be in a sardine can, I thought as I scrambled on. *Wait a minute. Something's not right. Nikki!*

She was no where to be seen. The heavy breathing and growls of the jenglot tore through the tunnel behind. They'd entered the tight crawl space and were now only yards away.

"Nikki!" I yelled ahead. The beam of my flashlight flickered and dimmed, before brightening again. "Where the blazes are you?"

No response. The sounds of the jenglot were growing louder. They were closing the distance quickly, having much less body mass to contend with in the narrow confines of the tunnel.

"Nikki!"

A taloned claw latched onto my left ankle, pulling me back with more strength than I would have thought possible for the agile little creatures. Instinctively, I tried turning around to get a better look at my attacker, but forgot the height of the ceiling and struck my head against it.

My head throbbing, I kicked furiously at the unseen creature forcing him to release my leg and pulled myself forward.

It was then that the batteries of my flashlight gave up the ghost and went completely black, eliciting howls of glee from my pursuers. I'd forgotten their abhorrence to light and had failed to use it to my advantage. I knew it wouldn't happen again…one way or another.

"Nikki!" Panic ripped through from my words. At this point, I wasn't exactly concerned with appearing manly.

"Jack?" the soft and irritatingly distant voice of my

companion drifted through the tunnel from the other side. "It's absolutely amazing. You're not going to believe what I'm seeing."

"And you're not going to get to show me if you don't...ow!" The creature clawed against my leg again, tearing through the cloth of my pants and sinking its talons through the tough leather hide of my boots.

"I need your help here!" I shook my leg, striking the jenglot across the jaw, but his grip held firm. More hissing snaked its way through the tunnel. At least two more had entered the crevice with me. "Any time now!"

"What's the problem?" Nikki materialized at the opening, her light barreling through the tunnel directly into my eyes.

"Ah geeze! I'm blind! Turn it off."

Screeches from behind erupted just as the creature's grip let go of my leg. Nikki flicked the switch of her light off, the darkness swallowing us once again. More growls again.

Darn it! I forgot about the light again.

"Turn it on! Nikki, now."

"Make up your mind, will you?" She said as she flicked the switch again bombarding me with the sweet blissful rays of blinding light.

They say if you ever find yourself in a dark tunnel near the end of your life, don't go into the light. Obviously, anyone who says that has never been hunted by a brood of blood ravenous creatures from the jungles of Malaysia.

I quickened my pace for the remaining fifty-yard stretch of tunnel and found myself barreling out of the crevice as fast as my elbows and knees could move.

Nikki reached down, pulling me to my feet. I spun around, found a good size stone from the debris, and pulled. It dislodged with minimal effort and crashed against the opening of the crevice, temporarily sealing the jenglot creatures in.

"Quick, help me get more weight against the opening," I

demanded, searching the rocky barricade for large, but manageable stones.

Three minutes later, Nikki and I had managed to build a pretty sturdy blockade. I stood up, cracked my back, and dusted myself off.

I looked around, speechless, at the vast chamber I found myself in. With a ceiling nearly twenty-five feet high, the oval shaped chamber gleamed in the dull firelight of six wall torches hanging by sconces. Shadows from the torchlight swam across smooth, stone walls adorned with fantastic, mythic paintings... more of the same, strange creatures we'd witnessed upon entering the temple. Thick, sturdy columns, lined in gold symbols and letters, supported the domed ceiling. Near the back of the chamber, a set of large wooden doors hung agape, allowing a glimpse of eerie green and red lights flickering from the room beyond. A low hum of electricity buzzed behind the doorway.

Wow. What the heck is this place? I wondered, turning around full circle, absorbing as much of the vault as I could. *It's absolutely amaz...*

Then I remembered the verbal lashing I'd promised to give Nikki and shifted my train of thought. I let loose.

"What the heck did you think you were doing back there?" My right thumb pointing behind me towards the tunnel we'd just crawled through. "I turn my back for one second and the next thing I know, you're worming your way down that stupid crevice."

She walked ahead about ten feet before turning around to look at me without a word.

"I'm serious. That was the most reckless, idiotic thing I've ever seen in my life and then, when I needed you most, you weren't anywhere to be found. I kept hollering and screaming for you and nothing. Not a thing. I can't believe you."

"Jack..." Her eyes widened.

"Don't interrupt. I'm not finished. You and I are going to have to establish some major rules if we want to go on with this whole thing. I..."

"Jack, you really need to..." She shook her index finger at me, but I continued before she could turn the tables.

"I told you I'm not finished. I'm really mad. And yes, I was worried about you back there. And that's why we're going to set up those rules right now. Rule Number One..."

"Jack, I really think you should..." Her finger kept at it.

"Number *one,*" I was determined to ignore her. Actually, I was enjoying the verbal thrashing. Poor little rich girl had probably never been told off in her entire life. Well, now was the time and I was just the man to do it. "In no way, shape, or form are you to do anything dangerous without first consulting me. Rule Number Two..."

The look on her face twisted into a scowl of sheer horror as she reached to her belt and drew out the Glock, pointing it directly at me.

"Now see...that right there. That's exactly what I'm talking about in rule number one...don't do anything dangerous. Pointing a gun at me kind of falls into that category," I said, gesturing for her to lower the gun.

The gun barrel remained level at my head. She squinted, lining up her shot

"Now come on. Let's be reasonable about this. Now, this isn't funn..."

"Jack, would you shut up and look behind you!" she screamed.

I turned, just as a slithering, scaled talon wrapped itself around my neck, pulling me backwards. The jenglot hissed in my ear, its putrid breath nauseating me, throwing me off balance.

She wasn't shaking her finger at me! She was pointing behind me.

My eyes flashed to the side, catching the glimpse of a second, much smaller creature crouched low behind me.

Where'd they come from?

"Don't move," Nikki whispered. She steadied the gun's barrel, still aimed directly at me.

"What the...Don't shoot!" I screamed. "For crying out loud, don't shoot!"

"Don't worry. You'll be fine."

Oh crap. I squeezed my eyes tight, as the creature wriggled around onto my back, its claws digging deep into my flesh. I felt the second jenglot brush against me as it pounced onto my right arm and sunk its teeth into my shoulder.

"Ow! Shoot! Shoot!" I felt a surge of blood rushing through my shoulder and into the small creature's mouth. The first and larger one, held me tight, its strength completely immobilizing me.

Bram!

I froze as the Glock blasted through the chamber. Both creatures leapt away from me, as I patted down my torso, checking to see if I'd been shot. I found the strength to slowly open one eye and peered down.

No bullet holes. That's a good thing.

Then, I saw the impish creature that had been feeding on my shoulder. It lay crumpled in a heap, blood oozing from its mouth and just behind its right ear. It wasn't breathing.

Wow. She's actually a pretty good shot.

A howl from behind reminded me we weren't out of the woods yet. The first jenglot leapt onto my back, keeping me between itself and Nikki's gun. The beast roared with rage as its claws once again dug furiously into my back.

"I can't get a shot!" Nikki shifted her stance to the right and then left. "I can't hit it."

My arms reached around, desperately grabbing at the jenglot attached to my back, but it wriggled away from my grasp. I spun wildly, trying to sling it away, but only succeeded in making myself nauseous.

Okay, Jack. Think. Use that thick head of yours for more than just a punching bag for a change.

Since no inspiration came, however, I decided to take a more primitive approach. I leapt backwards, hoping to slam the creature into the stone wall, but it swung around at the perfect moment, avoiding the impact.

The jenglot clung fiercely to my injured shoulder, using my body as a shield. Its fanged maw snapped at my face just as I twisted a second time, trying to give Nikki a shot. At this point, I didn't care if she hit me or not. I just wanted the creepy critter off my back. But every move I managed, the jenglot countered, keeping itself out of a clear shot.

I glanced around the chamber. The torches blazed, emitting a warm, dull glow across the room. Apparently, the light wasn't strong enough to hurt the creatures.

That's when the idea hit me.

Swiveling wildly, as fast as I could go, I leapt into the air and slammed backwards into one of the torches. The creature screamed, but hung fast to my shoulder. The smell of burning flesh wafted towards my nostrils, threatening to gag me.

The jenglot, reeling in pain, slithered around to my other side, once more removing itself from Nikki's aim. Its claws dug deep into my flesh, but I could tell its strength and fierceness were teetering out.

"Nikki? You know what to do."

"Are you serious?"

The creature, as if sensing my plan, howled viciously into my ear before renewing its assault. I could only scream as its fangs plunged into my bicep.

Not waiting another second, Nikki leapt towards another torch, snatched it from the wall and charged at us. The torch's heat singed the flesh of my arm as she plunged the pitch fueled flames directly at the creature's head.

It leapt into the air, pouncing at Nikki in a savage attack.

Faster than I could have imagined, she brought the barrel of the Glock up and fired, the projectile plowing directly through the center of the jenglot's forehead. It fell to the floor with a thud.

I stood motionless for several seconds, looking down at the thing at her feet. I shook my head, trying to clear the haze from my eyes as the room began swimming in all directions around me.

"Are you okay?" Nikki asked, looking over the edge.

No, I am not all right, I thought, unable to coax the words from my mouth. I was pretty sure I'd have to change my pants and frankly, that was a bit embarrassing. *Not to mention major blood loss and a sure fire infection to boot.*

Then my strength completely left me and I collapsed to the floor. I managed to roll over on my back, look up at the concerned face of Nikki.

"Rule Number Two..." I managed before the darkness overtook me.

22

"Jack? Wake up," I heard the ethereal voice echoing through my haze addled head. "Come on, wake up. Please."

My eyelids felt as if they were glued to my face. The roar of blood pounded through my skull like tribal drums just before battle. The cool rush of water poured over my lips, seeping into my mouth. I drunk deep, letting the liquid run down my throat.

Absently, I reached up to my throbbing shoulder, feeling the soft texture of linen wrapping. Nikki had apparently dressed my injuries while I was out.

"Are you okay?" Her voice sounded a thousand miles away. I tried opening my eyes, but they wouldn't budge.

A low groan escaped my lips, as I reached into my shirt pocket and pulled out a cigar. Before I could get it into my mouth, it was snatched from my fingers.

"No way," she said. "Those things are going to kill you."

"That's kind of the point," the sound of my own voice thundered in my head. "Now give it back." I squinted at the beautiful missionary hovering over me.

"It's the last thing you need."

Struggling to push myself up to my elbows, I wrenched open the other eye.

"Oh yeah. Now I remember," I said, grabbing the cigar from her hand and gripping it between my teeth. "Rule Number Two. Never take away one of my smokes. I've only got three left."

I dug into a side pouch pocket, pulled out my Zippo, and enjoyed the savory flavor of the cigar burning down my throat. The chamber still swam in front of me, but for the moment, I was feeling like my own self again.

"How long was I out?"

She leaned over my head, wiped my brow with a damp cloth, and pulled a pack of antiseptic wipes from her pack.

"About an hour," she said, dabbing a cool wipe over the abrasion on my forehead. "I was beginning to really worry."

Oh yeah. I hit my head on the tunnel wall.

"But I have to say it was very peaceful too," she continued with a smile.

I looked around the room, ignoring her barb. It was the same as I remembered. Oval shaped, torches blazing on the smooth paint covered walls. Two jenglot lay motionless on the stone floor only feet away.

"I'm glad to see they didn't get up and disappear like at Baik Orang," I said, nodding over to the dead creatures. "Nice shooting by the way."

"Thanks," she beamed. "But it comes with the territory of growing up with four brothers in Texas. I learned to shoot before I even owned a dress."

"Well, for that," I said with a grin. Then a wince. It even hurt to smile. "I am definitely thankful.

I looked back at the jenglot on the floor.

"No signs of the others?" I asked.

"No, thank the Lord. But I figured out where these two came from."

Nikki rose and walked over to the Southeast end of the

chamber and pointed up. A small hole gaped from what looked like a rather modern ventilation shaft—the same kind of ventilation you'd find in air conditioned buildings.

"That's odd," I said, rubbing my aching head. "Since when do ancient jungle tribes use central air?"

"Since when do they use vintage IBM computers and laboratory equipment?" she asked, walking back over to me and holding out a hand. "Can you walk?"

I clasped her hand and let her pull me to my feet. "Computers?"

After a regaining my balance again, I let go of her shoulder and turned to the heavy doors I'd seen when entering the chamber. The same green and red lights flashed from around the corner, followed by the electric buzz I'd heard before the jenglot attacked.

"That's what I wanted to show you," she said, moving towards the door. "Jack, this is getting crazy."

Reaching up to a sconce and taking a torch, I followed her through the entrance and felt the breath wheeze from my lungs at what I saw. The stone floors of the tunnel gave way to institutional, black and white linoleum. The walls of the new room gleamed sterile gray. Thirteen long operating tables, complete with arm and leg straps, sat unused in a semi-circle near the center of the room.

Monstrous computer terminals, green and red LEDs blazing synchronously, lined the wall to my left—the letters IBM etched into their metal frames. The humming sound I'd heard came from the giant wheels of computer tape whirring around their ports. A few panels on the enormous machines lay open, revealing large vacuum tubes buzzing with electricity.

The machines looked as if they'd come straight out of an atomic age B-movie. I half expected to find a hunched-back ogre named Igor hefting pieces of a dead corpse over his back. Or at least, the classic lightning gizmo zapping arcs of electricity through the air.

Pushing the images aside, I stepped towards the computer and found tiny lettering identifying the make and year: IBM 700 SERIES, MANUFACTURED 1956.

What in the world is going on here?

Nikki strode casually over to the door and pulled up on a large lever sending currents of electricity to five florescent overhanging lights dangling from the ceiling. The room blazed to life.

To my right, several tables, complete with beakers, Bunsen burners and Petri dishes lay covered in dust and cobwebs. A large, green chalkboard with strange, archaic mathematical equations scrawled across the marble, hung snug against the wall.

Nikki glanced over at me and smiled.

"I'm glad to see I'm not the only one amazed at all this."

"Are you kidding me?" I asked, moving over to the operating tables and absently running the arms straps through my fingers. "This is..." I couldn't get the words out.

Nikki strolled over to the lab tables and rummaged through the dry, yellowed papers still scattered across their surface.

"I can't make head or tails of this," she said. "But it looks Russian."

"Russian?"

"That's what it looks like to me. Take a look for yourself," she said, walking over to me and handing me some of the papers.

I scanned them quickly. She was right. They were Russian and the pieces of the puzzle we'd been struggling with were beginning to come together for me. And I wasn't liking the picture it was making at all.

My Russian, as I've mentioned before, is very limited. It had been years since I'd studied the language and it would have been ridiculous to even try to decipher them. I folded them neatly and placed them in my pocket with a mental note to show Vera.

"I'm really getting a bad feeling about this," I said out loud.

"What is this place Jack? What did they do here?"

"I don't know. But I think it's time we get..."

A sudden wave of nausea struck me in the gut, doubling me over until my knees buckled and I fell to the floor. My half smoked cigar dropped from my mouth to the linoleum.

"Jack! What is it?" Nikki asked, crouching down to offer assistance.

"Shantili," I muttered, clutching my gut with both hands as my insides turned somersaults. *How does he keep making me sick like this?*

"You are perceptive as always, Doctor Jackson," hissed the grating voice of the witchdoctor from the lab's doorway. "And quite difficult to kill as well, it would seem."

"Oh, I'm as easy to kill as the next guy, actually," I said, grinding my teeth to ward off the fit of vertigo swarming through my head. "I just get lucky from time to time."

Nikki remained crouched, looking at me, eyes wide.

"Help me up, would you Doll?" I said to her. Without the anticipated rebuke for what I'd called her, she reached down and hauled me to my feet. Not only was she a straight shot with a pistol, she was a lot stronger than she looked as well. "Thanks."

We both turned to the shaman and three of his followers grasping AK-47s. I recognized one of them from the cavern I'd found back near Pingitti. The other two, I'd never seen before, but they definitely didn't look friendly.

"So, what now? I can't believe you brought us all this way just to kill us," I said, bending over to pick up the stogy. I walked towards Shantili, drew from my cigar, and puffed a ring of smoke into the old man's face.

"Actually, I haven't quite decided what we are to do with you," he coughed, fanning the smoke with a hand. "The Christian witch, on the other hand, will not leave here alive. I had hoped my jenglot brethren would have taken care of you, but since you've gotten this far, I think we might find a good use for you."

"Brethren?" Nikki asked, apparently unconcerned about Shantili's intentions towards her.

"Yes, brethren," he said, circling around us with his arms clasped tightly behind his back. "They are, after all, survivors from my ancestral village."

I glanced back at the operating tables and then at the dust covered lab equipment.

"The jenglot were once...human? Your kin?" asked Nikki, a look of horror filling her eyes.

"Yes, they are my kin, as you put it," he said, turning to her and lifting up her chin with his index finger. "But now, they are so much more than human."

"The ascension," I said, trying to take his attention away from Nikki. "An old lady from Baik Orang told us the abducted villagers had ascended. They became some sort of shapeshifting gods."

The little shaman smiled at me. "There is some truth to that, yes," he said.

"So they were brought here? To this place?"

The old man laughed, moving over to stare me in the face. His three henchmen remained still, stern, hard faces glaring at us as their guns rested easily on their shoulders.

"Actually, we are the one's who brought them here," he said. "It's been fifty-three years ago now, but I remember it as clearly as the day they first came to us.

He walked around us and traced the edge of the operating tables with his finger, eyes closed, rifling through the memory.

"It was actually my seventy-sixth birthday."

"Seventy-six?" I asked. "That would make you..."

"One hundred and twenty-nine years old, yes," he said, smiling. "But that is inconsequential. My story now is about them. They claimed to have come to us in peace, desiring to learn more about our culture, our history. Naively, we believed them. We brought them to our most sacred of places and they built this." He waved his arms around the room.

"Who was it? Who came?" Nikki asked, drawing closer to me and grasping my arm at the elbow.

"Sounds like aliens to me," I said with a sarcastic smile.

"Soviet scientists," Shantili sneered.

Nikki and I glanced at each other.

"Jack, the writing in the abandoned village," she said. "It said the Red Demon snatched the people away. It could have meant the Soviets."

My mind raced, recalling the Russian documents we'd just discovered. Things were just getting too weird.

"But that doesn't make sense. The Soviets never occupied Malaysia. They were never here in force."

Suddenly, the old man screamed in howls of rage, his little feet pounding the floor in short hops like a child wanting a toy in a Wal-Mart. I had no idea what I'd said to set him off, but he'd definitely gone up three notches on the loony scale.

"That's some temper tantrum, you got there," I said, taking a step away from the crazed shaman.

"Do you really think territorial issues would stop them?" he growled, ignoring my comment. "Would it stop your own government? No. They came here, befriended my people and tricked us into showing them this place. A temple dedicated to our ancestral spirits. A monument to the spirit creatures they'd become."

Spirit creatures? Familiars.

"The animals on the walls," I said, connecting the dots. "You mean that the paintings on the walls depict representations of your ancestral spirits?"

The old man didn't answer. He merely stared up at the ceiling and hummed a strange tune.

Of course, I knew many similar legends. Many who practice

magic believe the spirit world reveals themselves in the form of various animals. They're called "familiars." In Western culture, the obvious example is the black cat most often associated with witches.

"But what do these legends have to do with Russians? This lab? Your people?" I asked. "I'm not seeing a connection here."

Shantili allowed a thin smile to spread across his face. His yellow, jagged teeth flashed in the florescent lights.

"You haven't figured it out? I'd have thought the answer would be obvious by now," he said, strolling casually to stand only inches from my face. His foul breath wafted up past my nostrils. "Actually, we harbor no ill will towards the scientists who brought us here. We've even turned our birth place into a shrine, maintaining the power and keeping the laboratory operational."

"Birth place?" I asked, feeling Nikki's grip tighten around my arm.

"Yes, for it is here, that we were truly born. Or rather, we attained our ascension. The Soviets helped us, of course. They helped us become like our ancestors, transcending mere mortal flesh. We'd become completely new beings. Powerful. Fierce. They'd helped us to become gods."

"But you're no jenglot," I protested. "You act as if you were one of their test subjects...one of them. But you're as human as we are."

I looked at his men standing guard at the door and turned back to Shantili. "Only a lot creepier."

"Joke all you like, Doctor Jackson. But you will see soon enough just how *creepy* I can be."

The old man glanced back at his guards and nodded in our direction. Without a word, they hung their rifles around their shoulders, moved towards us and grabbed Nikki, pulling her away from me. She struggled to break free from their grip, but their strong hands held firm.

I leapt forward, throwing a right hook against the man nearest me. His face snapped to the side and came around to face me again. He wore no expression. The hit hadn't even fazed him.

It was then that the nausea struck again and I dropped harmlessly to my knees. Doubled over, I glared at the witchdoctor who once again mumbled silent words.

"What are you doing to me?" I screamed, grabbing my stomach in agony. "How are you doing this?"

His words grew audible, increasing with each phrase until the old man shouted the strange incantation into the ceiling above. The pain was unbearable. My stomach clenched tight in sharp throbbing stabs, causing me to collapse completely on the ground.

"Jack!' Nikki screamed from somewhere far away again. "Listen to me. This is spiritual. The only way to beat it is prayer. You've got to pray, Jack. Pray to beat this!"

A million thoughts, ideas, memories, and emotions roared through my pain-wracked mind as I curled up on the cold, checkered floor. Flashes of childhood, my parents lovingly holding me in their arms as I lay feverish in bed. My father crying at the gravesite of my older brother, who'd died when he was sixteen. Our pastor's sweat covered face as he yelled from the pulpit, warning sinners of the doom they all faced if not for the mercy and grace of God's love.

I screamed. The pain was growing more severe, the world spinning out of control. The old man's words grew even louder, but now they seemed audible only in my own head. It was as if Shantili projected his incantations directly into my brain.

"God help me!" I shouted aloud.

Words my dad told me years before swept through my mind. *"Son, know this. Belief in God isn't enough. Even demons believe in God. No, it's only through the sacrifice…the blood of Jesus Christ that we can be saved. It's only through faith in Jesus, and no one else."*

"Jesus, please. Please. Help me."

With the remaining strength I had left, I glanced over at Nikki, no longer wriggling desperately to break free from her guards' hands. Her head bowed, eyes closed, her mouth moving silently.

Then, the pain, nausea, dizziness were no more. They were gone. Completely. My strength rushed through my limbs like a raging torrent cascading over the edge of a dam and I jumped to my feet.

This time, I didn't care that I'd been humbled. I didn't care that I had fallen to the crutch of Christianity and prayed for help. I wasn't even sure it was my own prayer or Nikki's, but for whatever reason, I knew that God had helped me. I wasn't quite ready to completely believe, but He'd at least given me something to think about and more importantly, a second chance.

Without hesitating, I lunged towards Shantili, grabbing him by the neck and slamming my right fist against his jaw. He stumbled backwards and I was about to pounce again when large, meaty hands grabbed me by the waist and threw me into the archaic computer terminal.

Wiping away the stream of blood from my lip, I pushed myself up to my feet, shaking my head to clear my vision. And saw Membunuh towering over me.

"I told you, American," he growled at me as he bent down and hauled me up by my neck. "You didn't win. The jenglot will indeed feast on you and your friends."

"Membunuh. Stop," Shantili commanded as he picked himself up from the floor and walked towards us. I glanced over at Nikki who still struggled to slip free from her captors.

The room was getting crowded. Not only had Membunuh managed to slip in unnoticed, but now three other Malaysians crept through the large doors. My eyes widened at the sight of an attractive female who stood in the center of the newcomers.

The old man, followed by Membunuh, bowed at her sight. I

could tell by the expression on the faces of Nikki's guards they would have done the same had their hands been free.

The woman's two escorts veered off to the left, as she glided over the checkerboard floor towards me. I couldn't tear my eyes away from her. She was easily the most beautiful woman I'd ever seen in my life, though no words could truly do her justice. Raven black hair, framing a tanned oval shaped face with thin, but lustrous lips. Her almond shaped, emerald eyes gleamed in the light. Perfectly straight, white teeth peeked through a warm smile as she approached. Her sheer, linen robes billowed loosely around her frame, opened partially to reveal portions of the soft, round curves of her breasts.

"This...is...one?" she asked in broken English, turning to Shantili.

The old man rose and walked over to the woman and nodded.

"Yes, he is the one, Mother Dara Ratu."

"Him is to be mine?" she asked, circling around me, eyeing me up and down as she ran her index finger over my chest. I have to admit, being hers wasn't an altogether unpleasant idea at the moment.

"If you so choose."

"What?" I said, embarrassed that my voice squeaked two octaves higher than normal. "Don't I get a say in this? I mean, she's hot and all, but I..."

"Silence!" Membunuh's thick paw flashed across my face, shutting me up with a sting. He then turned to Dara Ratu. "This is madness. He is a Westerner. The privilege should go to one of the Malay people."

"Mind your tongue, simpleton," spat Shantili at the large man. "Or you will find it removed from your mouth."

Dara Ratu ignored the exchange as she continued her scrutiny of my physique. Her right brow rose as she turned and looked at me with a seductive smile. Her silky arms wrapped themselves over my shoulders as she lightly swayed her hips around my legs.

Her firm, toned frame lightly rubbed against me as she arched her nose up and sniffed at my neck several times.

"Him will do," she said, turning around and heading out a set of swinging doors in the back of the laboratory. "Prepare him. Prepare the others."

Others? What did she mean by that?

"Shantili, what the heck is going on?" I asked, eyeing Nikki who hung limply, held up by the strong arms of Shantili's men. She'd exhausted herself to the point of submission.

"It is simple. Today will be a glorious day for my people," he said to me before turning to the men who held Nikki. "Take her away. Place her in a cell with the others and see that she is fed and watered. And don't harm her. We still might need her."

They carried her off through a second set of doors on the far side of the lab. Membunuh's powerful hands clasped my shoulders, warning me not to try to anything funny—which was okay, since I'd lost my sense of humor hours ago.

The witchdoctor then turned back to me.

"That's the second time someone's mentioned 'others'," I said. "What others?"

"Why your companions, of course. They never made it to Tuhan Kampong. My people captured them shortly after we left my village," Shantili smiled. "Oh, don't worry. They're safe. For the moment."

There's an expression that describes intense anger. The blood boiled. I'd always found the phrase clichéd, over used. At that moment, the words made perfect sense to me. I felt the rush of blood coursing through my veins, my arteries. My heart pounded heavily against my chest, threatening to tear itself away from my flesh. Heat rose from my core to my face. The very thought of my friends being held by these…if I'd had any chance of success, I'd have torn the smug face from the witchdoctor's skull at that moment.

Instead, I chose to change the subject entirely.

"You never explained to me what's going on around here. Who is that woman? What did she mean when she asked about me?"

The shaman stared up at me with the same passionless smile.

"We really haven't the time now," he said. "We have many preparations to make." Then, looking at Membunuh and a new goon that had entered the lab, "Take him to the others. I'll come get him when it is time."

Two sets of massive hands jerked me by the collar towards the small lab doors in the back. Stomping down on my new guard's right foot, I tore free from their grip and wheeled around to Shantili.

"I'm serious. Tell me what the heck is going on!" I demanded, as Membunuh's backhand sent me sprawling to the floor.

"Membunuh, stop. All right, Doctor Jackson. The answer to your question is rather simple. As I was saying earlier, today is a glorious day for my people," the old man said, as if the imprisonment of my team wasn't important. "Today, the Sister Queen has chosen her mate. You."

With two great beaming smiles, my man-handlers hauled me to my feet. The muscles around my voice box clenched up like a major case of lock jaw and I found myself completely speechless at the news. The blood that had been coursing through my body, suddenly drained away. My face flushed.

Oh, crap.

23

"She did what?" Nikki squelched, shoving me back against the padded wall of our cell with her hands.

After Shantili's startling revelation, Membunuh and the guard had escorted me to the same cell holding Nikki and the others. I had been led down a winding series of hallways, resembling more a hospital wing than an ancient temple. The Russians had completely gutted the old structure and refitted it with the modern sensibilities of 1950's living when they started playing Dr. Frankenstein.

After a warm, but tenuous reunion with my friends, I filled them in on the crazy queen's choice of potential mates.

"You've got to be kidding me!" Randy laughed. "A beautiful queen of some jungle tribe has actually picked you to be her boy toy?"

My eyes narrowed at my old friend.

"Hey, you don't have to sound so surprised," I growled. "I'm as good a catch as the next guy."

"Yeah, if a girl doesn't mind what she catches."

"Knock it off, you two, this is serious," Nikki said, moving over to me and staring me down. "This bimbo thinks she can just march into a jenglot infested layer and snatch you away, just like that? I don't think so!"

Snatch me away? Away from who?

"Um, Nikki? What the heck are you talking about?" I asked, having an uncontrollable urge for another cigar. Our captors had taken them away, as they'd taken anything else of value to our team...from our backpacks and supplies, to our guns. "Last I checked, there wasn't anyone in my life to snatch me away from."

Fire burned in her eyes for a half-second, before they were extinguished with a rather unattractive snort. She turned away from me and walked over to an unoccupied corner of the room and scooted down to sit on the floor.

Sheesh, I came to Malaysia with zero girlfriends and all of a sudden, I have two. I puzzled over the mental math. *This is getting ridiculous.*

Taking a breath, I glanced at my surroundings for no other reason than to think about something else. The holding cell we were trapped in was apparently built by the Soviets for very distressed, or angry, subjects. The nearly twenty-five-foot square room was covered from ceiling to floor with padded leather. Four twin-sized cots rested parallel to one another near the southern wall, their mattress shredded to pieces by rats years before.

Vera and Marc sat silently on one of the cots. Randy crouched two feet away, peeking through the thin crack between the door and the floor.

"So? What happened?" I asked the question that had burned in my gut since Shantili told me they'd been captured.

They all glanced at one another, drawing mental straws to see who'd be the one to tell their story. Apparently, Vera lost.

"We were ambushed," she said, glaring at Randy. "I wanted to get back to the river and use our canoes to coast our way down to Tuhan Kampong, but Mr. Wizard there thought it would be quicker to make a bee-line through the jungle paths."

"It would have taken us forever to hike back to the boats,"

Randy protested. "We'd be back-tracking and we didn't have that kind of time."

Vera rolled her eyes and continued. "We'd walked maybe five or six miles when Scott realized we were being followed. He snuck off into the underbrush to investigate and that's when we were attacked."

"Jack, it was amazing," Randy nearly shouted. "I mean, we've seen the jenglot in action, but never like this. They were hunting us with incredibly sophisticated tactics. It was..."

"I'm not interested in their tactics," I said. "I just want to know what happened."

"A group of them flanked us from the east, another from the west. They hemmed us in," Vera explained. "But Jack, that's not the strangest part."

I stared at her, wishing she'd get on with it.

"There was a human leading the group," she finally said.

"That's what I was trying to tell you, dude," Randy said. "There was a man, typical tribal attire, directing the critters like they were his own personal blood hounds."

Oddly, with everything we'd learned in the last few days, the revelation wasn't as shocking as I'd thought it would be.

"How was he leading them?"

"Verbal commands. Malay words," this coming from Marc. "And the man's clothing was not 'typical', as Randy suggested. They were ceremonial. Their hunt was ritualistic."

"What do you mean ritualistic? Are you saying the jenglot hunt was an act of worship?"

"I haven't enough data to be sure," Marc shook his head. "But every movement was planned. Rehearsed and deliberate, in much the same way as a worship service would be."

Now that bit of information was blowing my mind. A human —a priest maybe— leading the jenglot hunt as an act of some ceremonial observance. It was just too wild to even fathom.

"And when the jenglot caught you, then what? They didn't attack? Didn't try to feed?"

"No," Vera said. "They just herded us together, keeping us from running away. The human bound our hands together with vines and we were marched to this…this place."

This just keeps getting weirder and weirder. Why didn't the piranha-heads bleed them dry? Why did they even bother to bring them to the temple?

I glanced around the room again, suddenly aware that someone was missing.

"Uh, where is Landers anyway?" I asked.

Once again, my three teammates exchanged glances at one another before turning to face me. For several long seconds, the question hung unanswered in the cramped and increasingly uncomfortable room.

"We're not sure," Vera finally said. "When he went to look for whatever was following us, the jenglot attacked. Everything just kind of fell apart. We were doing everything we could to fend off their attacks. We never saw him again."

I let the information to sink in before allowing a glimmer of hope to seep its way into my brain.

If anyone can take care of himself in a fight, it's Scott. And if he made it out alive, that means we still have a chance.

"We'll just hope for the best on that," I said. "Right now, we have more pressing matters. We need to figure a way out of this dump and fast."

I flashed a rakish grin at Nikki. "I don't plan on being on time to the wedding chapel, if you know what I mean."

"I'm afraid it's no use, bud," Randy said, rising from his lookout position at the base of the door and dusting his trousers off. My bravado-forced grin faded. "We've been in here a lot longer than you have and as far as I can tell, whoever built this place knew what they were doing. There's no way out."

"They were Russians," I said, looking over at Vera for a reaction.

"What did you say?" She asked, tilting her head as if unsure of what she'd just heard.

"I said, the Russians built this place. Or at least, this portion of the temple."

I proceeded to fill the team in on what Nikki and I had learned since coming to the ruins, with the intrepid missionary recounting my less than flattering exploits. When it was all over, I dug into my pockets and pulled out the documents I'd manage to smuggle in from the lab. I handed them to Vera.

She read the gibberish typed over the crinkled papers with wide eyes, flipping to the next page every so often. When she finished, she sat open mouthed without saying a word. She then read through the documents for a second time with the same results.

"Oh for crying out loud, Vera," I said, walking over and sitting down next to her, forcing Marc to move to the next cot. "Just spill it. What's it say?"

"Yeah, it can't be that bad," Randy piped in.

"Can't it?" she said, still dazed, gawking at the documents. She dropped her head into her hands, taking several deep breaths before looking at the group again. "It's actually worse than we could have thought."

"We already know a lot," Nikki said, pulling herself up to her feet and drawing into the conference circle we'd unconsciously created. "We know Shantili's people invited the Soviet scientists to this place. We know that horrible experiments were done to some of the villagers, turning them into the creatures we've been calling the jenglot."

"Yeah, and we also know that Shantili and his kin have placed a certain reverence on the jenglot," I added. "They seem to be both adored and used as menial servants to do their bidding. So, I ask you, Vera, what could really be worse than all that?"

Without looking at me, she let out a deep breath she'd held since Nikki had begun her discourse and slapped the stack of papers with her other hand.

"For starters, does the name Dr. Ilya Ivanov ring a bell to anyone?" she asked.

Nothing but blank stares met her question, so she continued.

"In 1926, this doctor, not really much more than your run of the mill mad scientist, was commissioned by Stalin for a very specific and potentially devastating task," she said, scanning the room to see if anyone showed recognition. Negative. "We're have you all been? This only came out a couple of years ago. Made big news.

Anyway, it seemed that recently declassified documents revealed Stalin had been unsatisfied with his Red Army. He wanted something bigger. Tougher and more fierce. He wanted soldiers who felt no fear, who didn't complain when they were hungry or tired. He wanted an invincible army."

"Enter Doctor Creepy McCreeperton," I said, nudging her on.

"Exactly, Doctor Ivanov was an expert in the field of artificial insemination. As a matter of fact, he'd pretty much fathered the field. No pun intended," she said, a joyless smile creeping across her face. "He'd theorized that the similarities between men and apes were so close, he could cross-breed them—create a race of Man-Apes."

She paused, letting us take in the full significance of what she was saying. She stood up, walked over to the door and leaned against it, looking at us.

"Stalin loved the idea. Imagine. An entire army comprised of loyal mutated soldiers, part man, part ape. The power, strength, and endurance of a primate mixed with the cunning, intelligence, and adaptability of a human."

"It truly would have been an unstoppable army," Marc chimed in, sweat glistening from his brow. "It's just too incredible to imagine."

"Did this doctor succeed?" I asked, realizing how stupid the question was as it slipped between my lips. *Of course it hadn't succeeded. I'm not Charlton Heston and the creatures we keep running into are definitely not Roddy McDowall in a chimp costume.*

"No. Ivanov never could get the cross breeding to work," she said. "Of course, we've only recently come to understand how the laws of genetics protect each species from intermingling. It's a virtual impossibility. Or at least it's supposed to be."

"So what does this Ape-Man army have to do with this place and the jenglot?" Nikki asked.

"It seems that the Soviets never gave up on the idea," she said, scanning the pages once more. "Although they rethought their strategies of cross-species breeding. They turned their attentions to pure genetics, deliberate mutations. They were working on an actual Super-Soldier serum right inside this temple. And if the jenglot are any indication, it seems that they succeeded."

"But why here? What was it about this place that they would risk an international incident by seeking their gene cocktail here?" I asked. "And why did they just abandon the project? If it was successful, then why just shut it down and leave the creatures to fend for themselves?"

Vera shook her head at my question.

"That, I can't answer for sure," she said. "The documents are far beyond even my knowledge of science. I'm a doctor, not a geneticist, but from what I gather, they used some sort of early form of gene splicing."

"Gene splicing? How is that possible?" I asked. "Splicing is a relatively new concept. As far as I know, it's not even a process that's possible with modern science."

She stopped, carefully scrutinizing the notes.

"This is amazing," she said, looking up at us. "Look, I don't have an answer. Scientists didn't even discover that DNA existed in the form of a double helix until 1953. Three years later, two doctors discovered that humans had forty-six chromosomes. The sky was pretty much the limit in genetic research after that. But, there's no question that whoever came up with this technique was far beyond his contemporaries. He was an absolute genius."

"It wasn't Ivanov?" I asked.

"No, not by this time," she said, folding the papers up and handing them back to me. "From what I can remember, he was already dead before these particular experiments."

We all stood in silence. The entire thing was just too impossible to imagine.

"Pardon me," Marc broke through the hush that had thickened in our cell. He was looking through the crack under the door and then stood to face us. "Has anyone else observed that since being escorted to our cell, there's not been one sign of a jenglot out there?"

We stared at him, but no one spoke.

"I mean, an entire army of them practically marched us into this cell. Jack and Nikki were swarmed by them in the ruined section of the temple," he said, pacing to the other side of the room. "And now, none are to be seen anywhere. In addition, where did all the people out there come from?"

I crouched down for my own look. Sure enough, the hallway was filled with people, dressed in ceremonial tribal attire. I assumed they'd been invited to the big wedding. I found myself wishing I hadn't.

"You're right," I said to Marc, pulling myself to my feet. "The only things out there right now are people...just normal, every day humans. No monsters. No jenglot."

"Maybe they're sleeping," Randy said, glancing down at his watch. "It's about noon now. We know they're nocturnal."

"Perhaps, but there is something perplexing about the whole thing," Marc said.

"I guess that's just one more puzzle we're going to have to figure—" I couldn't finish the sentence.

The rattle of keys and the creak of the door's lock unlatching stifled our discussion. The padded door opened and the grinning face of the shaman peeked around the corner. Three of his goons stood stoically in view, brandishing their Russian-made rifles.

"Doctor Jackson, it is nearly time," he said with a raspy chuckle. "But first, I still have some things to show you. Great things. You will want to see them before..." he trailed off in thought. "Come, come. We haven't much time."

The rhythm of my heart quickened as I turned to look at my friends. They stared helplessly at the door. I could almost hear the grinding gears of their collective brains turning.

"Don't worry," I said. "We'll figure something out. We always do."

I forced another smile at them, wanting to reassure each one that I'd be fine. The problem was, I wasn't particularly reassured myself.

"But guys," I whispered over to them with a wink. "Maybe you should start thinking a little quicker, eh? Seriously. Snap snap."

THEY'D SHUFFLED me out back to the lab and I watched as Shantili conferred quietly with four more women dressed in fine ceremonial garb. I hadn't moved in the five minutes since they'd hauled me back there, the events of the day racing through my thoughts. We were prisoners in the Jenglot temple. My friends were captives, awaiting possible death, and I had been chosen to become their queen's personal consort.

How do I get myself in these messes?

The women turned from the witchdoctor and marched purposefully out of the room. Shantili looked over at me and smiled.

"Now, we still have some time," he smiled. "As I said, there are still some things to show you. Come with me."

The shaman turned and walked towards the doors we'd just marched through, but I willed myself to remain glued to my place. I wasn't going anywhere. The whole business was way out of control and I was determined to regain some composure before it was over.

"Doctor, you really have no choice in the matter," the old man said without looking at me. "I urge you to make this as easy as possible on yourself. For the sake of your friends if for nothing else."

Membunuh, who seemed to me to have become an ever present shadow, squeezed my shoulder with his powerful hands.

Resigned for the moment, I let out a breath and walked towards the shaman.

"Okay, let's go."

The old man preceded me through the now familiar corridors, making our way in the opposite direction from our cell. After taking a series of left corners and a curve to the right, we came to the expanse of the all too familiar stone walls and floors that comprised the majority of the temple proper. Torches once again replaced the soft humming comfort of florescent bulbs and it took some time before my eyes adjusted to the bleak confines of the temple again.

The old man, slouching under the weight of his age, shuffled through a set of stone doors and entered a dark room. I stopped, looking around, unsure whether I should proceed. The rough nudge to my back by Membunuh told me I really had no choice.

I stepped through the threshold and into a vast circular chamber, completely bare except for a cooler-sized limestone chest laid perfectly in the center of the room. Several paintings lined the walls, depicting priestly figures bowing to a strange, diminutive creature in black.

Shantili nodded towards the single torch lighting the chamber from a sconce near the doors. Understanding his intent, I reached up and snagged the light and drew nearer to the shaman.

"This, Doctor Jackson, is where it all began," he said, circling the box. He reverently placed his palm on it, gently brushing its surface. "This is the resting place of our Mother Queen and the progenitor of our species."

I eyed the old man up and down.

Species? This is getting crazy. He's as human as I am.

"Go ahead," he said, sensing my hesitation. "Open it."

I moved over to the box and swiped the dust from the lid with my hands. The chest was plain. No markings or symbols could be seen on any of its surface. My fingers found a crease in the lid where I could get a good grip and I lifted. The witchdoctor grabbed the other side and helped me lower the lid to the ground.

When I looked inside the chest, I stood mesmerized, unable to move, unwilling to say a single word lest the body of the strange being inside should shrivel up into dust. There, laying long ways in the box, was the mummified remains of a tiny humanoid creature no more than two feet in length. Its straw-like hair, more like the antennae of some strange insect, still clung to an oversized head, chalk white with numerous black orbs around the region where its eyes should have been. It was covered, head to feet, by a chitinous exoskeleton. The body was segmented into three separate sections, sporting two normally proportioned arms, and four shriveled ones underneath. The creature had no teeth, that I could see from its thin lips, but garnished nasty looking pincers arching upward from its jaw.

I stared, awestruck, at the creature.

"This is a jenglot," I mumbled, remembering the one I'd tracked several years before in Borneo. "But not anything like the ones we've seen for the past week. Nothing like the ones that attacked us."

It looks like some humanoid shaped bug, I thought, restraining the desire to reach out and touch it.

The old man chuckled softly as he struggled to bend down and lift the sarcophagus lid from the floor. I helped him secure the lid and waited for him to speak.

"As I said, this is our Mother…our Eve if you will. She was the first. All others are merely imitations of her perfect form."

"And it was she that the Russians desired to see? She was the reason you brought them here?" I asked.

"Exactly," he said, once again stroking the contours of the chest. "They'd heard rumors of the jenglot. After following one false trail after another, they were given the location of this temple by a fisherman not too far away from Pingitti Village. They came to us and asked to see the Mother Queen."

The old man stiffened, a cruel scowl contorting his face.

"The elders of our village refused," he said. "The Queen was too sacred to us…a goddess mother to the ancestors. To bring outsiders into this place would have been the greatest sacrilege."

"What happened? What changed their minds?"

His scowl was replaced by a gentle smile as he heaved a sorrowful sigh.

"There was one on the elder council who saw the Soviet interest as an opportunity," Shantili explained. "He was a man with a voracious thirst for knowledge. In his many years, he'd never even left the jungles of his homeland and he had a great desire to learn what the rest of the world had to offer. He saw the Russian scientists as the answer to obtain that knowledge. After hours of debate, he managed to convince the rest of the council to allow a select handful of their researchers into the temple, into this very vault. From that point on, our lives have never been the same."

I stood quietly, moving over to the walls to examine the paintings more closely. It wasn't difficult to figure that the Faustian character in the shaman's tale was himself. Without looking at the old man, I asked, "So did you gain the knowledge you sought?"

He merely grunted and moved over to stand beside me.

"Most definitely. Through them, I learned several new languages, including your own. I studied mathematics, physics, and world history. I was schooled in philosophy, rhetoric, and civics. It was the most wonderful time of my life...that is, until I discovered what the Russians were doing to my people. I protested. I tried to protect them. But in the end, I was powerless to do anything about it."

"Shantili, tell me. What exactly did they do here? What did they do to your people?"

"They used the Queen, her hair and blood, to change us," he said stoically.

Gene splicing.

"They used her DNA?" I asked. "But how is that possible? She's mummified. There wouldn't be anything useful to extract DNA from."

The old man gave a knowing smile, crossing his arms behind his back.

"She's not mummified, Doctor," he said. "As a matter of fact, she's not even dead. She merely sleeps through the ages, waiting for a time to be revived. Her blood still pumps through the veins underneath her armored skin."

I stared at the sarcophagus just inches away.

The creature is alive? Impossible.

"I have shared answers with you," he continued. "Not all of them, but more than I was allowed. Now it's your turn...you answer a question for me."

"Shoot," I said absently, still spellbound by the sleeping creature hidden in the chest.

"When I was casting my spell against you, the hex that made you ill, what incantation did you use to defeat it?"

I looked down at the old man, who now looked thoroughly weak and mild compared to the savagely maddened sorcerer that had attacked me in the Russian lab.

"Honestly, I'm not sure. I prayed. Nikki prayed. To Christ.

And then it was all over. No more nausea or dizziness. It just vanished."

Shantili stared down at his bare feet, scratching his chin in thought.

"This must be how the Christian witch has managed to avoid my hexes all this time," he said, turning towards the door of the vault. "This power she wields...I must learn more about it."

The pounding of several drums echoed through the stone corridors causing the old man to stop in his tracks. His head craned slightly as he listened to the hidden message behind the beat.

"I have more questions," I said, sensing the drumming marked the end of the time I had left.

"You have all the answers you need," he said, glancing back at me before stepping through the door and beckoning for me to follow. "All you must do now is put the pieces together."

Sure, this whole thing is one big jigsaw puzzle and someone keeps swiping all the edge pieces away every time I get close to seeing the picture.

"That's no answer. I want more," I said.

Membunuh, who'd remained outside, stepped into the vault. Gripping my arm with vice-like hands, he pulled me out the door without a word.

"There's no more time," Shantili said, scurrying off towards the laboratory wing. "The ceremony is about to begin."

24

I was ushered into a large, glass-enclosed amphitheater, very similar to the observational operating rooms found in many hospitals. The drab, gray floor was tiled with two water drains positioned strategically near the center of the room.

The room was bare except for a single operating table pushed to the far wall and a small table used for storing surgical tools. A small, gas powered generator sat idly in the far corner. Four metal gas cans lay stacked next to it.

The overhead lights remained dark, the room lit only by three torches, once again held by sconces. The torchlight revealed the presence of three newcomers I'd never seen before and the Sister Queen standing to the far right. I assumed the strangers were part of the village council Shantili had told me about.

Dara Ratu smiled at me as I stepped through the doors, and glided gracefully towards us. Taking me in her arms, she embraced me, her nose sniffing at the base of my neck. My nerves buzzed with raw energy from her touch.

*Wow. I can't remember seeing anyone so...so...*the words jumbled in my head. None could describe her with any real sense of aesthetic justice. The only word consistently whizzing through my lust-numbed brain was...*hot*.

The queen practically dripped with sensuality. She was dressed in a sheer, red gown revealing every inch, every curve, every muscle in her taut frame. Her long, supple neck was as dark as mahogany, her rare emerald eyes radiating unbridled lust. And her scent. Though I couldn't figure out how, there was just something about her scent that hurled missiles of heat through every nerve of my body. My face flushed as she held me in her arms. Molten lava rushed down my spine, nearly knocking the air from my lungs.

Then, looking into my eyes, she kissed me and turned to Shantili.

The two spoke in Malay, the queen quickly becoming agitated at something the shaman had told her. Her arms flailed wildly as she yelled in contempt. Then, as quickly as it began, she looked to me, smiled, and held out a hand.

"It is to begin now," Shantili said, backing away from us. The three strangers in the room moved to the door and walked out without a word. I turned to the old man, who was also backing towards the exit.

"Wait a minute," I said. "Don't I get a say in any of this?"

Dara Ratu waited patiently, her smooth fingers curled gently around my elbow.

"No, you do not," the witchdoctor said with an understanding smile. "But rejoice. You are honored among men."

"Then at least tell me why? What's this about?" I pleaded. "You owe me that much."

Shantili looked at his queen, bowing his head in a silent, but reverent question. She nodded back and he turned to me.

"All right. I will tell you," he said, tucking his hands behind his back and circling me as he spoke. "My people have become tainted...marred...by the curse and the blessing the Soviet scientists bestowed on us."

I glanced around the torch lit room, looking frantically for anything that could be used to get me the heck out of there. Shantili's discourse was buying me a little time, but I was afraid it just wasn't going to be enough.

"...so when they left," he was saying when my mind wandered back to the conversation, "we found ourselves completely barren, unable to produce offspring of any kind. Only the Sister Queen was granted the privilege of bearing our children. Of course, it also requires a father, not of our tribe. So, you see, we need you to help continue my people."

Oh great. I have enough trouble balancing my own checkbook and these loons want to turn me into Ward Freaking Cleaver.

"But I'd make a horrible dad," I protested. "I cuss. I stay out 'til all hours of the night playing poker with my pals. And I always leave the toilet seat up. I'm pretty much the worst role model a kid could have."

"Dr. Jackson, enough." He said. "You really don't have a choice. You might as well accept it."

"But what about a preacher? Who's going to marry us?"

"You already are," he said, chuckling. "You were betrothed the moment she chose you. She is, after all, the Queen."

Married? Oh geeze, Nikki's never going to let me live this down.

"But my religion demands a ceremony. A ritual with a priest," I lied. Hey, when you're about to be forced into marrying some weird jungle queen, you'd say anything to weasel out too. "This is so wrong."

"I'm sorry, Doctor," he said as he stepped through the threshold. "Our laws are specific and you really have no choice."

The doors swung shut behind him, followed quickly by the sound of locks grinding into place, securing it. I turned to face my new bride.

"Uh, hi." I said, with an unsteady wave and a smile. "Look, I think there's been some sort of mista..."

My blushing bride lunged at me, grappling me to the floor.

Low growls rumbled from her throat as she straddled my lap, bent over and showered my neck with hot, wet kisses.

"So, what's your sign?" I asked, wriggling away from her mouth, saying the first thing popping into my head.

I really can't do this. This is nuts, I thought, trying to unhook her hands from my backside. *I'm not sure what's going on, but this crazy broad's tied to it all and I've had enough bad relationships to know—this one will never work.*

Her hands glided up and down my chest, ripping the buttons from my shirt. Her long, silky hair hovered tenuously above my skin, exciting every nerve ending. She looked down at me with a savage smile.

"Hey! That's one of my favorite shirts!" I said, eyeing the buttons on the floor. The shirt had already been ruined while crawling in the crevice that led to the lab, but it was the principle of the thing that had torqued me.

Dara Ratu said nothing, continuing her exploration of my chest and neck.

"Look, I'm not really that kind of guy," I grinned from ear to ear. "I haven't even met your parents yet."

She glared at me, clamped one hand over my mouth and continued her tactile examination of my chest, shoulders, and neck.

Oh what the heck? I thought, her intoxicating scent pounding against all reason. I wrapped my arms around her waist and quickly returned her affection in spades. *What could it hurt?*

We kissed deeply, lying uncomfortably on the cold tile floor. I didn't mind the discomfort. There was something about this woman...something primal, something savagely carnal. A few soft, gentle touches from her hands and mouth, and I'd melted into gravy. I was out of control.

My arousal grew, burning deep inside me. I wanted her. Badly. And from what I could tell, the feeling was definitely mutual.

I grabbed her wrists, shifted my weight and rolled on top of her, staring deep into the pool of green that welled inside her eyes. Her lips, blood red, pulled back into a hungry smile. I lowered my face and kissed them hard, her fingers clawing deep into my back.

My mind was ablaze. My ability for coherent thought evaporated as I gave into the fleshly desires and tested her silky skin with my hands. I shifted to her side, caressing her arms, her neck. My eyes taking in every curve, every bead of sweat, every... a scar on her leg.

That's weird. She's got a scabbed-over wound on her right thigh. Looks recent. Exactly in the place where Landers said he'd shot the Alpha.

Suddenly, Dara Ratu pulled my face to hers, sweeping me towards oblivion with another heated kiss. For a quick second, I glanced up and saw a line of faces watching from the observation lounge above the operating room.

Those weirdoes are watching us, I thought, completely forgetting the scar.

Sensing my hesitation, she threw me off of her and climbed on top, her hands pushing up my chest to caress my exposed neck.

"Er, Queen," I said, struggling to remember English. "Dara Ratu. I can't. They're watching us."

She looked up, but not seeming to mind, continued her pawing.

"This is wrong. I care for...I kind of belong to someone else."

What am I saying? Who do I belong to? Nikki? I don't think so.

But through my entire ordeal with the queen, one face kept popping up in my mind—Nikki. Thoughts of betrayal. Hurting her. Something just wasn't right. Nikki and I had done nothing but bicker since we met. Sure, I'd entertained sowing some wild oats with her when I first came to Pingitti, but that was before I got to know her. After five minutes with the uptight broad, I'd wanted nothing to do with her. But that, I was beginning to realize, wasn't quite true.

But it wasn't just Nikki that concerned me. The more I became enflamed, the more a single Scripture verse I'd been forced to memorize as a kid kept popping into my head.

'He made Him who knew no sin to be sin on our behalf, so that we might become the righteousness of God in Him.' Darn it, Dad! It's really hard to...well, you know...with Bible verses bouncing around my brain. Especially that one.

"Look, we need to stop this," I said, looking to the peeping Toms above and then back to the lustful form of the queen straddled on top of me. "This isn't right."

I tried to rise, but she pushed me back to the ground with a snarl, pinning my arms to the tile. Then a blood freezing howl came, erupting deep within her lungs. With a scream, she tore at her gown, throwing it to the side and I stared helplessly as she changed before my eyes.

Her once, gentle smile was now replaced by a scowl. Her perfectly white teeth stretching beyond their limits, grew to razor sharp fangs.

Oh no, I thought staring up at her. *Talk about bi-polar*!

I struggled to throw her off of me, but she held on tight, as the metamorphosis continued tearing her beautiful body to shreds. Her shoulders arched, elongating, large bony spikes ripping through the flesh of her back. The skin around her collarbone and breasts split apart, as hardened plates of black scales swelled from somewhere inside her chest.

It was the change to her face, however, that left me spellbound. Captivated. I forgot my struggle, the danger, and watched helplessly. Her dark skin dissolved, leaving the bare remains of a chalk-white skull with large, black cavities where her eyes had only recently been. Her long, lustrous hair tumbled in clumps from her scalp, replaced by straw-like fronds.

In a mere twenty seconds, the transformation was complete. The once stunning beauty that had been the queen was no more.

In her place, crouched the slithering, scale hided form of what I'd come to call the jenglot.

It snarled, as a long thin proboscis snaked through her lipless face and wriggled its way towards my neck. That's when the recognition hit me like a cartoon anvil on the head.

The scar. The proboscis.

Dear God, no. This is the Alpha. It's not an Alpha Male. It's a queen.

Images of the hibernating jenglot Mother flashed through my mind. Her chitin-like skin. The pincers. The antennae. The real jenglot didn't just resemble some weird form of humanoid insect. They were insects. Some type of mutated mosquito or other blood feeding bug.

The feeding apparatus from the creature's mouth was only three inches away from my shoulder. I wish I could say I thought of something clever at that point, but truth be told, I panicked. It's not really the heroic thing to say, but its at least the truth. I just flat out went ballistic.

Tearing one hand away from the queen's grip, I slung my fist against her face, sending her flying off my prone form. Without thinking, I was on my feet, lunging for her. Both fists pounded against her skull, willing it to shatter from my blows.

What was I thinking? Yeah, she was hot, but you knew something like this was bound to happen.

My brain played reruns of Discovery Channel documentaries as I raged against the monster I'd almost let seduce me to death, trying to figure out what on earth had turned me into a raging hormonal teenage boy again.

Pheromones.

The word popped into my head, as I drove a right hook across her jaw.

One show I'd seen had revealed how insects emit pheromones to entice their mates. A chemical exuding from special glands, designed to drive potential mates wild.

But pheromones had to be how the queen had done it.

Of course, it could be that I'm just a guy, too.

Another show flashed through my memory. It had dealt with the mating customs of the praying mantis, where the females always kill their male counterparts after the fun was over. That had been their plan all along. I was supposed to have my little fun time and then become the main course for the wedding banquet.

The realization fueled my rage as my hands flailed against the writhing form of the Alpha underneath me. Screams and shouts from above told me the on-lookers were on the move, coming to their queen's rescue. I only had seconds.

I searched the room in my fury, looking for anything that could be used to end this madness once and for all. My eyes stopped, locking on the generator and gas cans in the corner of the room. Smiling, I looked down at the pulverized queen, stood up, and raced to the cans. Unscrewing one of the fuel caps, I jerked it over my head and heaved it at the rising form of the queen. It struck her full in the chest, gushing stale gas all over her bleeding body.

She screamed a piercing shriek that would have probably shattered the glass in the observation booths had they been closer. The beast wiped the excess fuel from her body and glared at me, taking a single step forward.

"I just want you to know," I said with a rakish grin as I set the can down by my feet, "when we first met, I thought you were drop dead gorgeous. But then we got hitched and all you did after that was nag, nag, nag. I just don't think it's working out."

The jenglot snarled, stepping to the side and taking another step closer.

"I mean, look at you now," I taunted. "Baby, you just let yourself go."

I reached up to the sconce above my head and palmed the pitch fueled torch.

"So consider this our divorce."

I hurled the torch at the creature, now dashing towards me at full speed. The flames erupted in a great wall of flame. The blast of heat knocked me backward, into the wall behind.

The pathetic cries of the creature echoed through the room. The doors burst open, Shantili, Membunuh, and four hulking men rushed in with thick blankets, trying to smother the flames from their tortured queen.

A single guard, gripping his AK-47, watched helplessly at the room's exit, blocking my escape.

After several minutes, the flames were extinguished, leaving only the charred remains of the jenglot laying motionless on the tile. Steam and smoke billowed up to the ventilation shaft in the ceiling.

I leaned back against the wall, nursing my battered knuckles. I'd managed to escape the bride of Frankenstein, but I didn't think I was going to be as lucky with the six men who turned to stare at me at that moment. Their eyes burned with hate.

"What have you done?" Shantili spat, crouching down to caress the crispy remains. "What have you done?"

Normally, in a situation like this, I would have played the role of complete submission. It was a no-win situation for me. I definitely wouldn't have tried to agitate my captors. But this wasn't a normal situation and I was ticked. They'd tricked me. Lied to me. Planned on letting their crazy jenglot queen feed on me and frankly, that's the kind of thing that really gets me steamed.

"Look," I said, pointing my index finger at the old codger. "I have had it. Don't blame me for this. I wasn't about to sit by while she drank me like a super-sized slushy and you knew it when you threw me in here with her."

I tensed, not knowing what was about to happen...how they would react. All I knew was that I had to be prepared to act, to run if I could. Or fight. That was about all my options. But I'd watched as they entered the room. I'd kept my eye on the door when it closed. It hadn't latched. It was open and my one-way ticket to freedom...if I could get past their guard.

"You knew that crazy woman was a jenglot and you didn't warn me!" I growled.

Who'd have thought she could change into one of those things? Suddenly, I remembered what the old woman in Baik Orang had said about the jenglot being shapeshifters. *Ah, geeze.*

The shaman only glared at me. Membunuh and the three other guards sidestepped, trying to flank me on all sides.

This is definitely about to get real ugly.

"Geeze, this whole thing is crazy!" I said, trying to keep them off balance with my chatter while I gauged their next move.

"More *crazy* than you know," the old man growled, stepping towards me.

I eyed him warily as I backed slowly towards the door.

"Okay guys, this isn't funny. You're starting to freak the nice cryptozoologist out here."

Shantili snarled as he reached up and tore his robe, wrenching it free from his skeletal body. The four others followed suit. Then the growling started. Low, guttural, sounds I'd heard a number of times since coming to the Malaysian rainforest. Jenglot growls.

Without warning, the witchdoctor's face elongated, changing. Sharp fangs sprouted up from his bottom lip. Scaly hide replacing his pale, thin skin. I looked over at Membunuh and the others, the same transformations sweeping through their own bodies.

Oh snap. I'm so screwed.

I looked at the door. The guard was on his knees, convulsing, as spikes exploded up his spine. Without waiting for the metamorphosis to complete, I leap-frogged over his back, darting towards the door, and threw it open with a swipe of the hand. Once through, I slammed it shut, pulled the belt from my pants, and tied the door shut with the good old Jackson knot.

That might hold them off for, oh, say two seconds, I thought as my feet pounded against the tile floor. My mind raced to remember the layout of the place.

I had to get to the others before it was too late. Howls and screams echoed from behind as my pursuers scurried to catch up to me.

This is so *not my day*.

I took a left, darting past a couple of clueless, but normal-looking, villagers. Without warning, the entire complex went black, the florescent lighting shut down, making my frantic search for my friend's cell more difficult.

It was a brilliant move on the part of the jenglot. Without the lights, I would have greater difficulty making my way through the maze of corridors, while providing them with the comforts of pain-free hunting.

Letting out a sigh, I sprinted down the shadowy hallways, zipping around three right turns before reeling to a halt. I smiled grimly to myself. I'd found the hallway.

Now, just to find the right room.

Without skipping a beat, I ran down the hall, pounding on each door I came to, screaming for my friends to answer. I came to the last door at the end of the hallway, when the foundations of the temple shook, knocking me to the ground. The delayed sound of an explosive blast from somewhere above followed seconds later.

That's when things really went nuts.

25

I had hit the deck the moment the blasts rocked through the temple, covering my head with my hands. When the bombardment stopped, I raised up and looked around the trembling hallway. A handful of locals in the hallway screamed as the sound of gunfire erupted somewhere above. Short blasts thundered in every direction, knocking chunks of stone free from their foundation.

"Jack!" Nikki shouted, pouncing through the cell door that had been ripped open from the first explosion. "You're okay."

She ran to my side and helped me to my feet. Vera, Randy, and Marc jogged up to me, probing the hallway with puzzled expressions painted on their faces.

"What in the world did you do?" Randy and Vera asked at the same time. Marc stood silently, running his fingers through his disheveled hair, a look of bewilderment plastering his face.

"I didn't do it!" I said, turning around to get a better look of the hallway, keeping my eye out for the jenglot that had been so hot on my tail. "Why does everyone automatically assume I'm responsible whenever things start blowing up?"

"Well, bud, you do have a history of this sort of thing," Randy grinned.

I looked over at Nikki, before turning, red faced, back to Randy. "Now's not the time to bring up the past. We need to get out of here. I kind of ticked the whole jenglot nation off and they're pretty much ready to kill us all."

Two mournful howls belted through the darkened halls several feet away, freezing my blood solid.

"That's our cue," I said, grabbing Nikki's wrist and pulling her blindly down the corridor towards the old Russian lab, ducking every so often when sounds of gunfire drew nearer.

"Jack, what exactly did you do to get them so riled up?" Randy asked, huffing for breath behind me.

I glanced over at him, then at the rest of the team.

"I sort of killed their queen," I said, smiling sheepishly and picking up the pace.

"Sort of?" Nikki asked from behind. "How can you 'sort of' kill someone?"

"It was a shotgun wedding," I growled back at her. "Look, we can discuss this later. Right now, I kind of need all the breath I can pack into my lungs, so for now...just zip it."

We bounded down the hall, dodging an assortment of scrambling villagers and not a few bewildered jenglot, darting for cover from the gunfire that was steadily coming closer. I rounded a corner, just as a massive jenglot tore into me from out of no where, a jagged scar stretching down the left side of its skull-like face.

Having seen the transformations, I knew what to look for in my attacker and I recognized the oversized mosquito-man as my old pal Membunuh.

I opened my mouth for a smart comment, but clamped it shut again as the beast snarled, snapping its fanged maw at my face. If I hadn't managed to snag him by the throat as it lunged towards me, my pretty scientific face would have been shredded into ground chuck. Still, Membunuh held tight, sinking his claws into the flesh of my already injured shoulder.

I could do nothing but let a scream explode from my lungs over the agonizing jolt through my arm.

Of course, that's when a second creature hurtled towards the others, howling in fury as it lunged into the air on a direct course at Nikki.

Pata-pata-pata! A stream of gunfire rang out to my left, shredding the torso and head of the creature in mid-air. Its momentum carried it forward, landing on Nikki and splattering her with dark, gelatinous blood. The missionary screamed, pushing frantically at the blood spattered corpse on top her and crying desperately for help. Vera leapt to her aid, heaving the carcass to the side and helping Nikki to her feet.

Membunuh craned his head in the direction of its new adversary and roared. Landers stood motionless at the far end of the hall, his P-90 pressed tight against his shoulder.

With the creature distracted, I clenched my right fist and slung it against the jenglot's jaw, sending it spiraling off me onto the floor. I quickly rolled twice, away from the Marine and shouted, "Fire!"

As the jenglot rose to its feet, a second series of shots barked from the muzzle of the submachine gun. The barrage hammered against Membunuh's body, sending him reeling. With a whimper, he crashed to the floor, the same thick gooey blood oozing from his mutilated carapace.

"Sorry I'm late," the Marine said with a smile. "But I had to stop for some help on the way."

The team ran towards Landers, allowing a brief moment of relief and excitement over seeing our new friend alive and well. Ignoring the reunion, I stooped down over the fallen jenglot and scooped my index finger into the thick, congealing blood.

"Interesting," I said to myself.

"Jack, we need to go," Landers shouted. "Krenkin and his

army are laying explosives around the temple's foundations. They're going to bring this place down."

"Krenkin?" I stood, wheeling around and looking at the soldier.

"Yeah. We needed help and I figured he was about the only one with enough fire power to get us through," he said as I walked over to regroup with the team. "I followed the creatures and the team here and then booked it to some high ground. I managed to raise his camp on the radio and he sent in one heck of a strike team."

Krenkin. Invisible, ice cold fingers danced over the flesh of my scalp at the name.

In the mess of the past few days, I'd almost completely forgotten about our mysterious benefactor. Our newest patron and his strange request. A single jenglot specimen.

Up until that point, I'd never bothered asking the obvious question…why? Shantili had. He'd even posed the question to me, but I'd simply let it go. I pretty much believed I was better off not knowing. Now, I wasn't so sure.

Krenkin didn't want just any old jenglot. He was after a very specific one…the eldest. And he knew I'd eventually end up leading him right to it.

I couldn't stop the bone rattling dread inking down my back. The puzzle pieces Shantili had spoken of earlier that day were finally starting to drop into place.

Soviets. Krenkin. His words from our initial meeting echoed eerily in the empty cells of my idiotic mind: *"After my parent's death, I was raised by state institutions and given a classical communist education. Even became a renowned scientist, well respected by my peers."*

I'd been used and I didn't like it one bit.

"And is he here too? Did he come with the strike team?"

"Yeah," Landers said with a puzzled look. "He's leading the group himself."

I looked at Vera, the look in her eyes blazed with understanding as well.

"What?" Nikki asked, glancing back and forth at the both of us. "What's going on?"

"Come on. We need to move," I said, disregarding Nikki's question and bolting away from the lab in the direction of the Mother Queen's tomb. The others followed close behind, voicing their concern about the new change in destination.

"Jack?" Randy said between breaths. "If this place is going to blow, shouldn't we be heading towards the exit and not away from it?"

I quickened my pace, refusing to answer. Time was running out and I couldn't stop to explain my reasoning to the group. One more corner and we were at the stone doors of the circular burial vault.

I stepped through the opened doors and stopped, staring at the sight of a thin, miserly jenglot snarling at the tall form of Krenkin and his lieutenant, Akim. Krenkin's shoulder bled freely, as he trained his sidearm at the creature that I now recognized as Shantili.

"Well, look who we have here," I said, cutting through the tension with sarcastic flare. "We've got the sleeping princess," pointing to the sarcophagus in the center of the room. "And there's Grumpy, Sneezy, and Dopey. It looks like the gang's all here."

I grinned at the scowling face of Akim, just as the rest of the team stepped through the door, struggling for air. Only Landers remained unwinded.

"Dr. Jackson," Krenkin said, drawing his lips into a grand smile. "It's so good to see you alive and well. I trust we arrived in time."

I moved forward, towards the box containing the hibernating form of the Queen. Shantili snarled, but backed up two steps, allowing me to draw near. His eyeless face fixed pointedly at the sarcophagus.

I decided to take a risk. Easing towards the transformed

shaman, I laid one hand gently on his shoulder and turned towards Krenkin. My heart pounded from somewhere inside my throat, waiting for the jenglot to tear my arm off, but it never happened. Shantili seemed to have no desire to kill me at that point.

"Mr. Krenkin," I said, glancing back at Nikki, relieved to find her doing exactly what I'd hoped. Her eyes were closed. Her mouth muttering silently. She was praying. *Good girl.* "I'm afraid we have a bit of a problem."

The man's smile faded. His almond shaped eyes, narrowing in a harsh scowl.

"And what would that be, Doctor?"

"It's like this. You hired us to do a job. Catch you a jenglot specimen," I said, moving away from Shantili and around the sarcophagus, rubbing its contours with the palm of my hand. "Problem is, you lied to us. To me."

"Uh, Jack?" Randy asked from the door. "What are you doing?"

"Randy, we can't give him what he wants," I said, never taking my eyes off the rebel leader. "And I can't let him take it either."

"What are you talking about it, Dr. Jackson?" Krenkin snarled. "We had a deal."

"That's true. But the deal was built on a lie," I said, glaring at him. "You told me that you had neither the men nor the resources to attempt your own hunting party for one of these things. But that's lie number one. You, in fact, had sent hunters out before us. You sent them out hunting for the Queen herself, in fact."

I paused, allowing the thoughts to cascade over my brain, spinning swiftly on overdrive.

"And your hunters were successful. They caught you a queen," I winced at the thought. "Only it wasn't the Queen…it wasn't the Mother. The queen they'd caught was one of the hybrids, not the original. But the damage had been done."

Krenkin's eyes burned as he stood quietly, absorbing each word of my diatribe. Vera, Nikki, and Randy inched closer, waiting to hear what was coming next.

"You see," I looked over at my team. "The jenglot feed on blood, but they're not all capable of producing the something—maybe an enzyme—that keeps the blood in liquid form. I figured that out when looking at the congealed blood of Membunuh. They can't process it as food. For that, they need the Alpha...or rather a queen. She is the huntress. She is the feeder. She takes the blood into herself, processes it, and then distributes it among her people."

"So what happened?" Nikki asked, drawing closer to me and grasping my hand. "How did the loss of their queen affect the jenglot?"

A low growl hissed from Shantili's paper thin lips, a distinct expression of sadness.

"They needed to find a new queen and fast. The problem was that they had no candidates mature enough. My guess is that their queens are typically old. Very old and their digestive systems are better able to process their food supplies. The new queen wasn't able to handle as much at one time. And because of that, it required more hunting parties...more blood...more deaths."

I turned to Krenkin, forcing the rage building inside me to quiet for a little while longer. The rebel leader, for his part, remained unusually calm as he moved his gun in my direction.

"Please, go on," he said, his smile returning. "You're doing quite well."

"You're responsible," the words oozed through my lips. "For all of this. For the deaths. For the suffering. And most importantly, for the jenglot themselves."

The shaman hissed from behind me at the words.

"Vera?" I looked at her.

"I knew I'd heard your name before," she said, scowling. "In hushed whispers during my time at medical school. Of course, the government at the time kept such talk to a minimum, but rumors spread about a scientist, displaced from his own country, who had become the intellectual successor of Russia's own Dr. Ilya Ivanov.

Before anyone ever heard of Ivanov's experiments for Stalin, he had been well known for his genius in the early stages of genetic engineering. And just a few years before he died, he'd discovered a brilliant new protégé. His name was Sashe Krenkin."

Krenkin's smile broadened, as he lowered his gun and slipped it into his holster. He glanced at Akim and then turned his attention back to me.

"You and your team are definitely as good as your reputations suggest," he said. "Yes, I was the fool Ivanov's pupil for a few years before he died. But my own research went far beyond anything he'd ever imagined. Where he worked with the basest form of life and cross-breeding, I began delving deeper into the very framework of creation itself. The human gene."

He strode casually towards the sarcophagus, allowing his hand to hover inches above its surface, as if the very mysteries of the universe were locked away inside.

"And this is the Queen you've been seeking all this time," I said, glancing back at Shantili, who'd suddenly tensed behind me. "You used her, an actual jenglot...her DNA...to fuel your genetic experiments. You twisted Shantili and his people into monsters, hoping to use them for the sake of Mother Russia. And for whatever reason, you were forced to leave here in a hurry... experiments unfinished...and head back to the Soviet Union."

"But you made your way back as soon as you could," Nikki said, catching on. "You built up an army in the name of overthrowing the government, but it was really for the sole purpose of coming back here and finishing what you started."

"And to do that, I need the progenitor...the true Queen," he said. "And we'll be taking her now, I think."

"Not on your life, buster," I growled. "You're not going anywhere with that box."

"Dr. Jackson," Krenkin said. "Please don't make this any more difficult than it need be. You really have no choice."

"Everyone keeps telling me that today. But I'm not letting you out of here with the Queen. I'm not sure exactly who the bad guys and good guys are in this fiasco, but I'm pretty sure you'd give Hannibal Lecter a run for his money."

"Have it your way," he said, giving a curt nod behind us.

A sliding click echoed through the chamber, the sound of a submachine breaching a round into its chamber.

"Jack, he's serious," Landers said gravely from the doorway. "You really don't have a choice."

26

One of your own will betray you, Shantili's words from the abandoned village echoed through my mind. *Landers? No.*

We all turned around slowly to see the Marine, poised to fire at us. Marc stood next to him, his eyes wide, completely baffled at the unexpected turn of events. He glanced at Landers, then at us, and without another word, bolted down the two steps near the door into the chamber to stand next to us.

"Landers," I said, bile rising to the throat as I looked at the man who'd quickly become a good friend. "Scott. Don't do this."

"I have to."

"Why? What does this guy have over you?"

"It's not that, Jack," he said, letting out a breath. "I'm under direct orders."

Krenkin moved around the group and walked up to the Marine, putting his arm around his shoulders with a great smile on his face. Landers scowled, jerking himself free of the other's touch, but kept silent.

"That's right, Jack," the scientist said. "It would appear that your government has an interest in my research. They sent Agent Landers here to assist me in my search for the Mother."

"But Stromwell said he'd sent you to help protect his daughter," I said to Landers, averting my eyes away from Krenkin's smug stare. "Was he in on it too?"

Landers shook his head. "Not that I know of. He really did send me here to bring his daughter back. But shortly after our meeting in Brazil, I was approached by...a superior...who gave me the orders. I was supposed to help Krenkin find the jenglot Queen and then take them to a special research center we'd built for him."

He stepped down, away from the stone doors, pointing his weapon at me and nodding to Akim. Krenkin's second-in-command heaved the sarcophagus from its stone pillar, balanced it on his broad shoulders, and walked towards the door.

With a howl, Shantili leapt into the air, his fangs and claws bearing down on Akim. Before he was three feet from his target, Landers pulled the trigger, armor piercing rounds hurling through the air, plowed into the shaman's chest. With a shriek, the jenglot fell to the floor, sliding several feet before striking a nearby wall.

"I'm sorry, Jack," Landers said, shrugging his shoulders. "I tried to get you out of here before any of this happened, but you were just too stubborn for your own good."

Krenkin smiled as he sauntered over to me and laughed.

"You really should see the look on your face right now," he said. "You were good, my friend. Very good. But I have no further use of your services. Good bye."

He wheeled around and strode out the door.

"Seal them in," he said, walking into the hallway with Akim and three heavily-armed guards.

Landers eyes widened as he turned to look at his boss.

"You can't be serious. You're going to blow this place up. It'll kill them."

"You're a soldier," Krenkin stopped walking, but didn't turn around. "Collateral damage is part of your job."

"But it's not my job to murder. I'm not doing it."

The rebel leader leaned over and whispered something into his lieutenant's ear, before turning back to face Landers.

"Now isn't the time for you to have a bout with morality, Agent Landers. You've been given your instructions and you will follow them to the letter. Come with me. Now."

The Marine didn't move.

"I have my orders, but they don't involve killing innocent people," he said. "The only way I'll go along with this is if you let them go."

"Impossible. They're now a liability. You know, as well as I, that Dr. Jackson will not rest until he's secured the Queen."

"Then we'll make sure they don't have a clue where to find you. I'm serious, Sashe. They go free or I walk...and you know ENIGMA will back me up on this. One word from me and they'll pull the plug on your entire operation."

The Russian glared at Landers, curling his hands into fists. Judging by his reaction, I knew that Scott had him over the barrel. It didn't make up for the betrayal, but he at least wasn't going to stand by while the creep blew us to smithereens.

"Very well," Krenkin finally said, glancing at his watch. "We'll deactivate the detonators. But they'll remain sealed in this tomb to give us time to depart to the base. Agreed?"

Landers looked over at us, his steely eyes betrayed no emotion.

"Yeah, that will work," he said, walking up to me with a face like granite. "For what it's worth, Jack, I'm sorry. But my mission is clear. Priority one is to secure the Mother Queen and that's exactly what I intend to do."

"I'm sure you'll sleep well tonight, knowing you jumped when you were told," I growled. "But you should know...I'm going to find you."

"Of that, Jack, I have no doubt."

"Agent Landers," Krenkin said, looking at his watch a second time. "We need to leave."

"Yeah, Corporal. Your boss is getting antsy," I said. "Don't want to keep your boss waiting."

Landers looked over his shoulder at the Russian before turning to me again.

"Look," he said. "There are some things you should know before I leave."

"Oh this is so going to be interesting," Randy said, leaning against the wall, arms crossed.

He ignored the comment, his eyes fixed on me.

"First, I'm not a Lance Corporal. I actually don't have a rank at all." He looked at each of us, measuring our reactions. "Heck, I'm not even in the Marines. At least, not any more."

"And let me guess, your name isn't Landers either," I said, coaxing the bile back down into my throat.

"No, actually it is. You see, I did join the military five years ago, but after a barrage of tests and psychological assessments, I was transferred to another area of service."

"Black Ops," Randy ventured a guess.

"It's not quite that simple, but to make a long story short, yes. The program I belonged to was special. Very special. Maybe only sixty people in the world knew of its existence, including the twenty-three operatives that were employed with it."

"Agent!" Krenkin demanded.

"Shut up for one lousy minute!" Landers barked, glaring at Krenkin and his goons. "I owe them this much."

I ignored their exchanged, a nagging feeling in my gut forcing me to ask the question that raked against my mind.

"And what did this *special* group do? What was your primary focus?" I asked, fighting against the dread bubbling up from my gut. I had a feeling that I knew the answer before he said it.

"We were assigned to watch you, Jack. Or rather people like you," he said, forcing a weak smile. "We were supposed to keep track of groups of cryptozoologists, UFO enthusiasts, paranormal investigators and—"

"Holy crap!" Randy said. "They're the Men in Black!"

Landers eyed Randy and shook his head. "Not exactly, but I suppose you could draw some parallels there. We were assigned the task of watching these different researchers and—."

"And keep an eye out for anything that might be useful to good old Uncle Sam," I interrupted him again, rising to my feet and stalking to the edge of the camp. "That's just swell."

"It isn't as bad as it sounds. We've done a lot of good. There have been some incredible projects, beneficial advances that have come out of our mission. I thought the jenglot expedition would reap similar benefits."

"Oh, it's reaped plenty," I said, struggling not to reach out and throttle the pompous jerk where he stood. "Death. Mayhem. Yeah, there's plenty to look forward to with more of these things in the world."

Landers could only stare at me, struggling to find the right words to make me understand. We both knew it was pointless. Nothing he could say would justify what had been done.

Finally, he leaned towards my ear and whispered a single word, "Siberia." He then turned back to Krenkin and his entourage and jogged up the steps to the door.

"Oh, and Jack, hope you don't mind, but I thought I'd keep this as a little souvenir of our time together," Landers turned around to look at me again, holding up one of the GPS tracking units I'd given him. "Never know when it might come in handy some day."

"Son of a—" Randy said, just as Landers, Krenkin, and Akim moved out of view. Two of Krenkin's goons materialized from the shadows going to work on securing the large stone doors of the vault. With a crunch, the doors closed tight.

"A warning, Dr. Jackson," Krenkin's hollow voice shouted from behind the doors. "Though I've promised your friend Landers that I'd refrain from blowing up the temple, I can't have you free too soon. Your exit is now being wired with C4 explosives. Any attempt to open these doors will detonate them, killing you all. Horribly. In five hours, I will send someone to release you, so you really have nothing to worry about. Sit back, relax, and enjoy some much needed peace and quiet. Good bye again, Doctor."

I stared at the door speechless, my hands lifting slowly in the air, before falling to my sides in frustration.

"Why don't bad guys ever just shoot the good guys and get it over with?" Randy snarled under his breath.

"We don't have time for jokes, Randy," I turned to the rest of the group. "We need to figure out how we're getting out of here. And fast. I've been through too much today to die now."

"But Krenkin said he'd send someone to let us go in a few hours," Nikki said, lowering herself to the floor to sit. "Why not just wait it out?"

"Because he's got no intention of keeping his promise. To us or Landers. I'd say we have a few minutes before he brings this entire place down on our heads."

27

I walked over to the door, placing my hand gently on the cold stone. I couldn't hear a thing on the other side. No voices. No movement. Nothing.

Great. This is just absolutely fantastic. My brain raced, struggling to stabilize the whirlwind of thoughts zipping through my head. *Just when was it that I lost complete control of this crazy mess?*

"Um, so how much time do you think we have exactly?" Randy asked, ambling up next to me. "I mean, no pressure or anything. Just kind of curious."

I shook my head. "I'm not sure. Ten, maybe fifteen minutes. They won't blow the temple until Krenkin is well outside the blast zone," I said, running my fingers along the crack of the stone door. "I don't think they came in the same way Nikki and I did. And from the sound of the explosions when they attacked, I think they may have blown a way into the side of the temple."

I looked at the others, each face a mask of fear and doubt.

"All right people," I said in the most confident and commanding voice I could fake. "I know things look bad. Really bad. But we've been in tighter places than this."

My brain flipped through the mental files storing all my past dilemmas, searching, pining, for any situation I'd encountered that proved my last comment. For some reason, all I could think of was our trip to the Congo in search of a pack of ravenous panther-men. Turned out, it had merely been a litter of half-starved feral cats. I just didn't see how I could draw any parallels, so I kept it to myself.

"But we do need to think. Any suggestions?"

The silence in the tomb thumped with the rhythm of my own heart.

"Randy?" I asked without looking at him. Despite his cavalier attitude at times, Randy had a great mind for trouble shooting his way out of jams. He'd pulled my butt out of the fire more times than I could count.

"I've got nothing, Jack," he said, his eyes closing as he raised his face to the ceiling. "If they really did wire these doors, I can't think of any way we can get out of here...not without someone..."

He didn't finish the sentence. He didn't need to. One shove of the hinge would break the connection to the C4 and set them off. The only hope we had was if someone volunteered to open them with us far enough away to avoid any major injuries. That would mean someone sacrificing their lives and I wasn't about to let that happen.

I spun around, pacing the edges of the circular wall, searching for any signs of a hidden door or vent. Anything that would lead to a way out. I knew it was useless, but I had to try.

"Jack!" Vera cried, darting over to the prone form of Shantili. "Get over here. He's still alive."

I moved towards them, gawking in disbelief. The old shaman lay on the cold floor, his head and shoulder leaning up against the wall. Congealing purple blood globbed from the bullet hole perforating his bare chest. But it was his face that took the wind out of me...stuck somewhere between man and jenglot, the metamorphosis not quite complete. His body writhed on the floor, Shantili's torso, covered in chitinous armor. His legs remained thin and skeletal with claws extending from raptor like feet.

The old man looked at me and coughed, the same purplish ooze trickling out the side of his mouth. His clawed hand clutched at the wound to his chest.

"There was a time," he croaked, "that we would not have been so easily killed." His coughing intensified, blood gushing from his nose and mouth. "Before Krenkin's return and his capture of the first Sister Queen, we were nearly perfect. We needed only to feed once a year and that one feast would heal our ailments, mend broken bones...even reverse the aging process."

The shaman scrambled to stand. Vera, extending a gentle, but firm hand, kept Shantili from rising.

"You need to rest," she said. "Lay back down. We might be able to save you."

The witchdoctor gave one of his world famous cackles, waving her hand aside. "It's too late for that, woman. I'm already dead. I'm just too stubborn to accept it."

Shoving Vera aside, he wobbled to his feet and stood, and stared at the team. He then turned back to me.

"And our strength. Our strength Dr. Jackson, was beyond your wildest dreams," he said. His face seemed to shift uncontrollably. One second, he appeared more human. The other, more jenglot. "But when the Russian murdered our last queen, all that changed. Then he sent you."

"And I killed your new queen and let that creep walk out of here with the Mother," I said, a lump swelled up in my throat. As terrifying as the jenglot were, I was beginning to think I might have had them pegged wrong to some degree. They'd done horrible things, yes, but only out of instinct, in the name of survival. The real horror had been what Krenkin and the Soviets had done to them. "And I plan to get her back."

Randy walked up next to me, leaned over and whispered in my ear. "Um, Jack? What the heck are you talking about?"

I looked at my old friend, giving him an encouraging grin.

"Just what I said. We're going to get out here. And after that, we're going to track down the Mother and we're bringing her back."

"Are you crazy?" Marc blurted out, uncharacteristically colloquial.

Randy glanced at the addled folklorist and smiled, then turned back to me. "The little guy doesn't say much, but when he speaks, he's pretty darn smart. So I'll repeat his question: are you crazy? Why the heck should we stick our necks out on the line for these freaks who've done nothing but try to suck us dry from the moment we got here?"

"Why you selfish pig," Nikki piped in.

"Hey! Who you calling selfish?" Randy yelled back, a look of pure incredulity on his face. Her comment had actually stung. Who'd have thought?

"The jenglot are people to, at least they were. They've been forced into this situation…they've been manipulated. It kills me to think of the good people…" Nikki continued, pausing for a second to wipe a stray tear from her eyes, "friends of mine, people I've loved and bled for…killed for the sake of feeding their thirst, sustaining them. But now that I know what they are…well, I can't help but sympathize a little. We need to help if we can. Besides, it will save lives in the long run."

"But it won't necessarily save ours!" Randy said, throwing his hands into the air.

The room suddenly erupted in heated words, each person in the group demanding their concerns be addressed. The commotion raged into chaos, insults and names hurled at anyone near by as the tension and stress of our dilemma ebbed from their mouths.

"Shut up!" I yelled. The room, except for the residual echoes of the last few syllables screeched into silence. "Please. When we get out of here, we'll discuss this. For now, we have a more pressing matter to figure out."

"Uh, yeah," Randy said, tapping his watch. "The clock's ticking."

I knew he really didn't care whether we went after the Mother Queen or not. Randy's the kind of guy who loves just stirring up trouble. I turned and smiled at him, before looking back at the shaman.

"Shantili, is there any other way out of here?" I asked.

"Strength, yes. Great strength," the old man mumbled in a half-snarl, the vestiges of his jenglot form struggling for control. "We were gods among the people. Yes. Gods."

"Looks like the witchdoctor is out for nine holes at the Goofy Golf," Randy said, twisting his finger around his ear.

"Give him a break," Nikki snapped, stepping over to him and wrapping an arm around his shoulder. "He's lost a lot of..." she hesitated, looking at the violet-colored gelatin dripping from his wounds. "blood."

Randy, taking the reproof in stride, walked over to the door and placed an ear to the stone.

"How much time now, do you figure?" he asked over his shoulder.

I glanced at my watch, pinching my lips together in thought. "I'd say we still have a good ten minutes. But we're going to need every one of them we can get."

"So what are we going to do?" Marc asked. "I'm not hearing a plethora of ideas being presented for our dilemma."

"Plethora?" Randy mocked. "Okay, am I the only one who can't understand half of what this guy ever says? I mean, who talks like that?"

I glared at my friend in rebuke before turning my attention back to the room. We just didn't have many options. I looked at each of my friends, hoping some ray of inspiration would—I saw it. Around Marc's waist.

"Marc, your fanny pack! They didn't take it?"

The little scholar looked down at his belt, the bright red pack draped casually on his hip.

"No," he smiled, getting where I was going and unzipping it. "They must not have known what it was."

He reached into the pouch and pulled out its contents, discarding everything to the floor. A line of rope. A flashlight, matches, and a pack of rations. That was it. The pool of hope that had risen in my chest evaporated.

Throw in some duct tape, some chewing gum and MacGuyver and we might have a chance, I thought, scratching my head, trying to prime any other idea from my atrophied brain.

"Strength and power," Shantili continued chanting, nearly inaudible now. "Gods we were."

With a sudden scream, the old man wheeled around and glared at me, new found clarity burning in his eyes.

"Dr. Jackson," he whispered, his fanged teeth shining in the torch light. "You must save her. My people depend on it. The villages of the jungle depend on it. If she's not returned, the jenglot cannot crown a new Sister. Without her, my people will starve and rivers of blood will course through Malaysia as they frenzy to sate their hunger."

My eyes rolled at the comment. As I've mentioned before, stating the obvious ranked right up there with redundancy.

"Kind of know that," I quipped. "But we've got to get out of here first."

"But that's not the worst of it," he said. "If Krenkin should synthesize his experiment...if he should duplicate it outside the confines of the Malaysian jungles, the carnage would be catastrophic."

Now that, I thought, *piques my curiosity.*

"Jack!" Randy demanded, tapping his foot. "Tick-tock."

I waved him off and eyed the old shaman. "What do you mean by that?"

"He means the seclusion," Nikki piped in. "We're in a valley here. It helped to isolate them. Take them out of the jungle, into civilization and just imagine what could happen."

"Or worse yet," Vera said, stepping up to us. "Some U.S. government agency using them for any number of Black Ops campaigns."

I turned towards her, eyes narrowing as I strained to subdue the rage burning in my gut.

"Landers knew. The jerk knew about this and never said a word." I clenched my teeth, fighting the urge to slug the stone wall in front of me.

"Hey, guys?" Randy said again. "Come on, already. I don't want to stick around to become a primo discovery for some lucky archeologist one day."

I ignored the comment, cursing under my breath and turning back to Shantili. "Okay, old man, I get it. There's a lot at stake. Now, how do we get out of here?"

The shaman's eyes closed as he arched his head towards the dome ceiling above. His jenglot lips quivering, shaking, as inaudible words poured through his throat. I'd seen him do it many times before, and instinctively I braced myself for a bout of nausea that never came. After several seconds of whispered chanting, Shantili's eyes snapped open.

"There is one way," he said, coldly as he stumbled towards me and placed one shaking claw on my shoulder. Gooseflesh rippled down my arm at his touch. "Only one way. Save her. Honor me and save her."

"Yeah, I will, but that doesn't explain how we're going to..."

The old man started hobbling towards the door as quickly as an aged man in his condition could manage.

"Oh, cripes!" I shouted, realizing the shaman's plan. "Someone stop him! He's heading for the door!"

Marc spun, trying to grab him, but Shantili regained some of the old strength he'd been spouting about and hurled him across the chamber and against the far wall, never breaking his stride.

"Everybody against the wall!" I shouted, dragging Nikki and covering her back with my body. The others followed close behind just as the shaman shoved against the doors with all his might.

I squeezed my eyes tight, bracing for the blast that could very well shred us to pieces with debris. The creak of the doors echoed through the chamber, like great heralds of doom. I tensed, squeezing Nikki's small frame with all my strength. One heartbeat. Two. After the third, one of my eyes popped open and I winced.

Where's the kaboom?

But the explosion never came. The doors had just swung harmlessly apart.

I turned around to see the old man grinning from ear to ear, still holding his bleeding chest with his hand. Two jenglot lurked silently just outside the door, one holding the remains of the C4 detonator, the other moving to their leader to keep him from tumbling over from his weakened state.

With a muffled laugh, the old man looked up at me as I strode forward, red faced. "I got you good, didn't I, Dr. Jackson?" He laughed again. Then in the span of a single wink, his face shifted to one of dour sternness. "Now, please Doctor…Jack. Go. Find her. Save her."

Shantili crumpled to the floor, his jenglot crony, gently easing him to the ground. The old man's face twisted, contorting into an amalgam of human and jenglot features. His claws lengthened and retracted within his hands as he wriggled on the floor and coughed up more blood.

"I will, old man, I promise."

It was then that the light flitted completely from Shantili's eyes. His heaving lungs settled. His face relaxed, transforming once more to his human form. His entire body shuddered as it twisted and morphed back to the man I knew him to be. The man that I had somewhat learned to respect, if not kind of like.

"I promise."

WE BOLTED for the temple exit, led by three jenglot guides, directing us through a maze of ancient, neglected tunnels. I'd imagined that no human had tread on the stones we'd move across for years...even longer than the path Nikki and I had entered through.

Dehydrated, burning for breath, I wheezed as my legs pummeled against the uneven stone floors. Three times, I nearly knocked my own head off, when low hanging ceilings materialized in the dim light of the torches we held.

In minutes we were out and free of the ruined temple, hurtling through the underbrush and vines of the jungle to escape the blast radius of Krenkin's explosives. We'd managed a quarter of a mile when a series of explosion rocked the foundation of the jungle, sending a wave of heat and debris towards us, knocking us to our knees.

When the shockwaves had settled, I stood and surveyed the team. Thankfully, no one had been injured and I found myself praying once again (it was becoming a real habit) that the jenglot had made it out in time. Our guides had already turned back and headed towards the ruins.

"Well, what now?" Randy asked, dusting himself off.

"What?" His voice had been drowned by the intense buzz echoing through my ear canal.

"I said," he yelled, cupping both hands to his mouth. "What do we do now?"

"I'm not sure," I hollered back, wiggling my index finger in my ear. "But we need to figure out what we're going to do now."

"Oh for crying out loud," Nikki mouthed the words at me.

"What?" I shrugged, reaching up to my shirt pocket, I rifled through it in search of a cigar. *Great. I forgot. The little runts took my Cubans.* "By any chance, does anyone have a smoke?"

Four sets of eyes glared at me in silence.

"I'll take that as a no," I grinned, holding in my frustration and forcing myself to appear confident, in control. "All right. Here's the plan. I say we head back to Pingitti, get my dog, find Krenkin's hideout and save the day."

"In that order?" Nikki asked, rolling her eyes. "That's not much a plan."

My hearing was coming back and I easily detected the sarcasm dripping from her lips.

"Care to share a better one?"

"I might." She gripped her hips with her hands, defiantly.

"Well, let's have it *sweetheart.*"

She paused, struggling to come up with something better than my own inane plan. I wouldn't admit it to her, but she was right. My plan really sucked. It wasn't really a plan at all in the technical sense...more like a moron's to-do list. But it was the best I could devise with the ringing bells still clanging inside my head.

"Okay, I can't think of one," she said, folding her arms across her chest. "But it doesn't mean that yours is the best one we can think of."

I couldn't help smile at the fierce tenacity burning in her glare. I moved close to her, defiantly, pushing a stray strand of golden hair from her face. Her warm, blue eyes drifted towards mine and I found myself wanting to dive in and never come up for air.

She softened for a millisecond before shrugging me off with a snort and walking towards the tree line.

"I'm telling you, honey, she meant nothing to me!" I laughed out loud at the joke, but the laser beam glare she threw at me, shut me up quick.

"You two through?" Randy asked, glancing back and forth

between us. "'Cause some of us are seriously working on a real plan here."

My face grew stern, grim, as I nodded at my friend to continue. "Okay, shoot. What have you got in mind?"

"All right. If you're bent on saving the hides of the scaly-skinned mutant mosquitoes," he said. "We can high tail it back to Pingitti. Pick up Arnold if you still insist on the mangy mutt's company, and radio the Law. Let them deal with Krenkin."

I had to admit, his plan was infinitely more appealing. But I wasn't sure we could trust the government to do anything about it. If Krenkin was acting on a deal he'd made with the United States, the Malaysian government might not risk a confrontation. Worse yet, they might go in gung ho, guns-a-blazing, and kill the hibernating jenglot Queen. I just couldn't risk it.

"Not bad," I said. "But it's too dangerous. There are just too many unknowns."

Marc paced back and forth in the clearing of trees.

"I can't believe you all are serious considering this," he said, running fingers through his hair as he walked. "This whole affair stretches the limits of sound reason. I never signed up for any of this, Jack. You and I have been rather close associates for a while now and you know I'm not one to cringe in the face of adversity or danger. But this is just...well, stupid, for lack of a better word."

I stared back at him, rummaging my brain for words of encouragement that I knew would invariably sound ridiculous.

"You're talking about going up against not only a crazed Russian scientist with a god complex, but the entire United States government here," he continued ranting. "So far, it's been bad enough. Blown out of the sky. Shot at. Attacked by mutant bloodsuckers. I'm just not like you. I'm a scholar. A scientist."

His last comment burned like acid.

"What's that supposed to mean?" I asked, stalking up to his face. "I'm as much a scientist as you."

"I didn't mean to imply…Look, Jack, you know what I mean. You're an adventure craving junkie. Yes, you're a scholar, but you strive on action. You thrive on all this insanity and I'm just not cut out for it. I can't go on with you."

For a brief moment, my heart pounded heavy against my rib cage, as thoughts of a second betrayal edged its way in the corners of my mind.

No. That's no fair. Marc's been there with us the whole way, I thought, a sly grin forming on my face as he struggled to defog his glasses with his shirt. *He's helped us more than we can possibly repay…more than earned his money. And he's right, the little guy just isn't built for this kind of thing.*

"It's all right, Marc," I finally said, gripping his shoulder with a nod. "I understand. And there's no hard feelings. But there is something I want you to do for me once you get back to the States. I'll fill you in on the details when we get back to Pingitti."

He just blinked as I turned to the rest of the group.

"Whatever we decide to do, it's all up to us," I said. "We can't let Krenkin continue his experiments. We definitely can't let anyone, even the U.S., get their hands on a fully functioning army of jenglot." I paused, letting my words sink in. "When we get back to Pingitti, Marc's heading home. Anyone else who doesn't feel comfortable with what we're doing is free to go too. No foul."

They all stared in silence. Waiting for me to give them something, anything to hold on to…to bring any amount of hope that we could succeed. I had nothing.

I looked them over. Bruised. Battered. And scared. Not exactly the rescue dream team, but it was all we had.

"Just one problem," Randy said, scratching the stubble on his chin. "We don't even know where Krenkin is. Scott said they'd built him a lab and I doubt he'd run back to his fake guerilla camp."

"That's true," Vera said, walking up to me, an encouraging

smile forming on her face as she wiped a smear of blood from my forehead. "He could be anywhere."

"I know where he's going."

"What? How?" Nikki asked.

I tried swallowing the gigantic lump in my throat. I couldn't quite figure out why Landers had told me. Couldn't figure out what he was up to. But he'd given all the information they needed to track down Krenkin and grab the jenglot Queen right out from under his nose.

"Landers pretty much told us exactly where to find him," I said. "What's more, he's carrying our GPS tracking device with him. Once we get within range, we'll be able to track him down easy enough."

"Jack? I know that look," Randy said, rolling his eyes at me. "Where exactly are they going?"

"They're heading to Siberia."

A frigid chill washed through my bones as I spoke the words, icing my veins. It was the worst possible place they could have gone. Jungles were fine. Tropical beaches were better. But the frozen tundra of Siberia was not on my short list of vacation spots. I hated the cold.

But I made a promise, I thought to myself bitterly. *And I never welch.*

28

The frigid wind bit clean through the thermal clothing and parka draped over my shivering body. The high-tech goggles slowly frosted in my hands as I scanned the valley below. I thumbed the electric switch, zooming in on the complex below.

The GPS tracker had worked beautifully, leading us directly to the dilapidated military installation hidden as if a giant neon sign stating "MAD SCIENTIST SECRET LAB" was erected above the complex. I was still puzzled over Landers' assistance, but I wasn't going to look a gift horse in the mouth.

I turned my attention back to the grounds on which Krenkin's laboratory rested. It was huge, stretching nearly ten miles in every direction, and contained by thick lines of evergreens on every border. Twenty-five foot fences loomed around the perimeter, humming with bone-frying electricity and topped off with looping cords of wire, barbed with razor-sharp blades. At least eight squads of guards, some walking dogs, patrolled the area at random intervals.

"Looks nasty down there," Randy whispered in my ear after crawling through the few tufts of dried grass we were trying to use for cover.

"It isn't going to be easy," I squinted through the eye piece. "That's for sure."

One of the dogs halted in his tracks and looked towards us, sniffing the air. It crept forward several paces, tail wagging slowly from side to side, until being yanked by the sentry and set back on course.

I let out a breath and flipped another switch on the goggles, transforming the dusk covered landscape into a deep shade of blue. Dozens of ghostly spheres of white haze buzzed in various locations down in the camp. In this mode, the goggles could pick up the signatures of electromagnetic devices such as spotlights, cameras, and electronic trip wires scattered about. From the looks of things, the compound was a veritable fortress.

"Sheesh," I said, watching my breath hover above my head as I rolled onto my back. "What was I thinking?"

"Not sure you were, bud," Randy chuckled cautiously, looking around for any signs of approaching guards. "This has got to be one of the dumbest things you've ever talked me into."

I stared up at the thick gray canopy of the Siberian sky. A swift cross wind was blowing in from the east, snaking its way up my pants leg. I shuddered, wishing myself back into the bug infested sauna of a Malaysian rainforest, bloodsucking monsters and all.

Everything had made so much sense when I'd decided to follow Krenkin and Landers back to Siberia to steal back the jenglot Queen. The insane Russian was about to resurrect a horrible experiment bordering on the realms of abomination. His plan, whatever it truly was, could potentially cause untold damage in human lives. I just couldn't let it happen.

At the same time, I had no idea what we were going to do.

I'd wracked my brain over similar doubts for the three weeks since leaving Pingitti and chartering a small airplane to fly us to the outer rim of the Siberian western plains. There were just too many unknowns...too many variables to consider. Landers' duplicity didn't help matters any. And the only assistance we might get was a long shot—a little gambling debt I'd asked Marc to collect on.

"Jack?" Randy shook my shoulder, breaking my train of thought. "Are you all right?"

I looked over and gave him a warm smile. "Yeah, I'm fine. Just thinking."

"So, *now* you start thinking," he joked. "Look, it's getting dark. We need to head back to camp and start sketching out some kind of plan." He pushed up from the ground to his hands and knees. "Besides, your girlfriend's going to start worrying. She'll probably think you've got yourself hitched again."

He gave a sly wink and chuckled quietly.

"Girlfriend? You've got to be kidding me! That crazy broad's been nothing but trouble since the moment we laid eyes on her," I said, hoping it sounded more convincing out loud than it did in my head.

"I kind of think thou dost protest a little too much, bud," he said, turning around and crawling back to the forest wall towards our campsite, nestled in a stand of trees. I let him go without another word.

Nikki. God, why did I let her come along? I closed my eyes, the image of her bright, warm smile filling my mind.

I was getting accustomed to the prayers now. I really didn't believe He was listening, but I found an odd comfort in just knowing I could talk to someone about my doubts. He was open ears, so I decided it was high time I'd take advantage of it.

Nikki would find it funny if I ever got the courage to tell her. If I ever had the opportunity. But with the odds stacked against us, I wasn't so sure I would. The thought of losing her in this mess sent a stab of regret burning in my chest.

Why wouldn't she listen to me? Why'd she have to be so dadburn stubborn?

I'd tried talking her into flying back to the States with Marc, but she'd have none of it. She wouldn't even consider staying in

Pingitti, picking up her mission where we'd so unceremoniously interrupted her work. She'd insisted on seeing this through to the end. I just prayed that the end wouldn't mean her own.

Dear Lord, I'm falling for her. As irritating and bone headed as she is, I don't know what I'd do if I...if I lost her.

My eyes opened with a snap and I scrambled on hands and knees toward the camp. It was time to put such thoughts aside. Randy was right. It was time to make a plan. My usual method of stumbling along waiting for things to work themselves out just wasn't going to cut it. If we were going to succeed...if I was going to keep everyone, Nikki, alive...we needed a real, honest to goodness strategy.

I just hoped I was smart enough to come up with one.

"I'M TELLING YOU, our point of entry should be here," my finger tapped at the digital photo on the laptop's screen as I glared at Randy. "There doesn't seem to be as many cameras or electronic eyes around. The biggest problem we'd have is the guards and those mutts of theirs."

"And I'm telling you, it would be a mistake," Randy said, shaking his head. "Those guards down there aren't your average rent-a-cops. Their weapons, the way they move...they're U.S. special ops if I've ever seen one. Probably some Russian special forces as well."

I stared blankly at him. "And your point is?"

Randy growled, throwing his hands into the air and storming to the other side of our makeshift shelter.

"I swear, you're about the dumbest...look, these guys aren't going to be pushovers. I'm sure Landers' organization has hired the best," he said, turning back to me, his arms flailing wild in frustration. "That means they're trained to recognize weak points in security and compensate accordingly."

He paused, letting me absorb the information.

"That means that you can bet they've got something covering that area...something you haven't seen."

"Like what? Werewolves?" I asked. The drunken local we'd hired as a guide had spouted off gibberish about the land being inhabited by werewolves just before he'd decided to high tail it only five miles short of Krenkin's camp. He'd taken the horses his chieftain had loaned us, as well as the wallet right out of my back pocket.

I'd seen real werewolves before and although this was their kind of place, I had a very bad feeling they weren't exactly what the locals had seen lurking around.

I pointed once again to the photo before tapping the space bar, bringing the electromagnetic field image on screen. "Look. There's nothing there."

He spun around, breathing deep as he tried to get a grip on his irritation.

"Jack, I think you should listen," Vera said, putting her arm around my shoulder and squeezing. "You're not thinking straight. Too wound up. Randy knows about security technology. He's a professional and I think you should trust what he has to say."

"But he's just being stubborn about this!" I spat, slamming a fist against the stone I was sitting on.

The team jerked at my sudden outburst, each one dropping their head in silence. The bitter wind howled through low hanging branches above us, creaking and groaning in harmony with my mood. The canvas walls of our shelter flapped harmlessly in the air.

"Jack, grow up," Nikki whispered, almost inaudible in the frigid night.

"Excuse me?"

"I said, grow up!" Her glare locking on me defiantly. "What he's saying makes sense."

I stared at her, struggling for a comeback that would put the missionary in her place. The problem was, she was right. So was

Vera. I was too high strung. There was too much at stake and the pressure was weighing me down. Randy knew his stuff and if he said my way was too dangerous, I had to believe him. He'd never let me down yet.

"All right," I said. "Randy, the mission is yours. Let's hear your plan."

He stared at me for a moment before clearing his throat. "Okay then," he said, straightening his coat before continuing. "I do have an idea. But I really don't think you're going to like it."

I rolled my eyes, de javu playing havoc with my equilibrium.

Great. Every time someone starts a plan like that, I end up getting shot at.

29

Randy was right. I didn't like the plan. As a matter of fact, it stunk. And I told them so repeatedly, but was overruled. Everyone felt his plan had the best potential for success and far outweighed the dangers. But that was exactly what I didn't like about it. Especially when the dangers involved Nikki.

Nikki. Since when did I start caring so much for her? This isn't good. At least not now…in the middle of all this.

"This plan is stupid!" My voice thundered, making me wince involuntarily. "I'm not go along with it."

"Hey, bud," Randy said, gesturing for me to keep it down. "Take it easy. It's a good plan. It'll work. If you're yelling doesn't give us away first."

"I don't care, Randy, this is nuts!"

"The whole thing is *nuts*, Jack," Vera said. "This whole hair brained scheme of yours. We should have never come here in the first place. But we all listened to you and now we're up to our ears in this craziness."

A low snarl rumbled inside my throat.

"Lighten up, Jack," Nikki whispered as we hunkered down in a patch of grass, a mere fifty yards away from the compound's main entrance. "Remember, you said you'd go along with whatever Randy came up with."

"Yeah, but I never thought he'd think of something as idiotic as this."

My friend turned back to his surveillance without another word, crouching in the grass, his gaze intent on the movement of the guards and a large transport truck rolling up towards the gate. If the words I was spouting bothered him, he made no sign. His face was grim. His thin lips curled down in quiet contemplation. If not for the rise and fall of his chest beneath his Kevlar vest, he would have made a fantastic statue.

"Would you please keep it down," Vera whispered.

"What difference does it make? If we go along with this, we're as good as dead anyway."

"Jack, this doesn't sound like you," Vera whispered. "It sounds more like...Randy."

"Hey! Now that's not cool," Randy protested, his cheeks reddening. "I'm the guy who's being the responsible one here now."

"You know what I mean," Vera rolled her eyes. "Come on, Jack. This is ridiculous. You're jeopardizing everything and you're acting like a spoiled child."

"And I'm telling you, this isn't going to work and I'm not going to sit around and watch you all get caught because of him. I can't do it."

No one said a word.

"Look, I've had enough of this," I said, scrambling to my feet, being sure to stay crouched below the tall grass. "I can think of some other way. A better way. Anyone who cares to join in, follow me."

"I'm serious Jack, cool it," Randy said. "Or you're going to have every half-cocked soldier in the place breathing down our—."

"Necks?" said a deep, gravely voice behind us.

"See?" Randy said, scowling. "I told you."

In unison, we turned our heads to find ourselves staring at the barrels of six rather large looking rifles clutched tight in the hands of six equally large looking men dressed in black fatigues.

"Oh, hi there," I said lamely, lowering myself onto the ground again and placing my hands behind my head.

I really really hate this plan.

"No one move," said a large, muscle-headed monstrosity of a man with two marble sized eyes hiding under a thick Neanderthal brow.

"Easy, sergeant," came a familiar voice, eliciting a fury in me that threatened to turn super nova. Scott Landers marched up from behind, a cold glare in his eyes as he looked at me. He raised a radio to his mouth. "Delta Hub, Delta three. We have intruders in sector twenty-one. Count five."

Landers touched a finger to a hidden receiver in his ear and nodded. "Roger. Repeat, count five."

The muscle-headed sergeant glared down at us as the Marine...um, agent...listened to the inaudible voice squawking in his ear. I watched his knuckles grow white as he tightened his hold on the rifle's grip.

"Understood," he said, looking up at me. "We're assessing potential danger. Stand by for further intel."

I leaned in towards Nikki, placing an arm around her shoulder. She glanced at me, smiling, trying desperately to be strong. Her bright blue eyes gleaming with hope. She'd never doubted the plan for a minute. I wondered if she was having second thoughts about it now.

"Jack, you have got to be the lousiest sneak I've ever seen," Landers said, shaking his head in disappointment. "We've been tracking you since you entered the perimeter."

"Sorry to disappoint," I said, clenching my teeth. "But we're not a professional spook like you. We don't typically backstab our friends to get the job done."

"Think whatever you want. I have a job to do and I'm going to see it through, no matter who I have to walk over to do it. Especially you."

What's he playing at? He helped us find them, yet he's acting like he could give a rip about us? I wish someone would fill me in on the score card around here.

Suddenly, the rage over his betrayal bubbled up my chest like an erupting volcano. I walked over to my former friend and slammed a right hook across his face. A snap echoed around us as Landers dropped to the ground, bleeding.

The butt of a rifle slammed the back of my head as I swung at Scott, driving me to the ground. My ears rang from the blow, growing louder with each thump of my heart. Spikes of white danced in front of my eyes, as I was hauled to my feet by one of the guards. Muscle Head said something to me, but I couldn't get past the buzzing sound whirling behind the planet sized lump growing on the back of my head

The sergeant glared at me for a second more before placing two big, beefy hands around the grip of his weapon and leveling it at us. The other sentries encircled us, their rifles trained at our heads.

Landers clambered to his feet, tenderly pinching his now crooked nose. Blood trickled down his hand, wrapping around his wrist and arm to drip from his elbow. "Stand down," he gasped nasally to Muscle Head. Then, he looked up at me, eyes nearly crossed from pain. "I guess I deserved that."

Every muscle in my body tensed. I couldn't believe this was happening. I couldn't believe I was letting it. But I forced myself to stay still and let the whole thing play out.

"You know these guys?" Muscle Head asked Landers, still pointing his M4 assault rifle at me.

"Yes, I do. Now, stand down. I won't ask again." Landers pulled his sidearm from his holster and leveled it at the sergeant.

The barrel shook slightly, but the threat to his guard was still very clear. "That's an order."

Muscle Head hesitated, glaring at us for several seconds before lowering his gun. "You know our protocol, sir. Secure any intruders we find. Search the area for others. And then eliminate the threat."

Landers' eyes never wavered from the massive soldier, thumbing his weapon's hammer back. Blood still drained from his nose, but he didn't seem to notice. "I'm in charge of security, not Krenkin. Now, Sergeant, we need to take them into the complex where I will interrogate them. And Krenkin is not to be told, is that understood?"

"But sir—"

"This is *not* open for discussion. One more act of insubordination and you'll find yourself before a firing squad. Now, do we understand each other?"

"Yes, sir," the sergeant said, scowling at his superior. It was clear that the big galoot didn't like his boss very much. At least we had that in common.

Muscle Head turned to his men, "Search them. Make sure they're secure."

I really hate this. God, please don't let this be a mistake.

Landers glanced over at me with an arrogant smile, before stepping up to the first guard.

"You'll find a sidearm stashed in a shoulder holster underneath his parka," he said, before turning back to us. "You'll find similar weapons on each of them."

"Landers, you jerk!" I yelled, feeling Nikki's reassuring hand grab my wrist as I lurched forward.

The guards searched all of us thoroughly, finding each weapon we'd smuggled in our clothing.

"Hey, that's no weapon," Randy said, grasping at a small silver thermos they took from his pack. "That's my fortitude."

The guard glared at him, unscrewed the cap, and took a whiff.

Crinkling his nose at the acrid odor of Russian vodka, he capped the thermos and started to hand it back until Landers opened his mouth.

"Um, let me see that," he said, taking the thermos from the guard. He sniffed the contents, shined a flashlight into it, and handed it back. "Don't give that back. I believe there are some explosives hidden at the bottom."

"Scott, what the heck are you doing?" Randy cried, trying to snatch the thermos again.

The guard twisted around, backhanding my friend to the ground. He handed the thermos to his sergeant before stooping down to pull Randy back to his feet.

"I'll have the demolitions team examine this later," Muscle Head said, turning to his men. "Secure their hands and let's move out. That is," he glanced at Scott, "if it's okay with you, sir."

Landers merely nodded and moved towards Krenkin's laboratory complex without a word.

We quickly followed, trudging through the heavy underbrush towards the compound's gate in silence, heavy hands and butts of rifles pressed into our backs, pushing us closer to our destination.

"Don't worry, Jack," Randy said, pulling up beside me. "We'll be okay." He gave me that crooked smile that always seemed to precede disaster.

"If that's true, then why are my insides twisting around like I just ate four bowls of your infamous Fireballs of Hell Chili?"

"Mmmm...Fireballs of Hell Chili," he licked his chapped lips. "I could go for some of that right now."

"Be quiet," one of the guards slapped the back of Randy's head.

"Ow, watch it, buddy!" he growled. "Apparently, I'm an invited guest of your boss. Best treat me with some respect."

The guard's smile snaked up one side of his face as he chuckled. "Yeah, right."

We pushed on towards the gate, which loomed larger with every passing step. Its strong iron grating etched black against the darkening sky. A guardhouse lay just behind the gate, its light revealing two guards bent over security monitors. Two blinding spotlights flashed down on us as we approached.

"I really hate this," I whispered over to Randy, making sure our watchdog was out of earshot.

"I know, but you're doing the right thing."

The squeal of gears echoed in the darkness as the gate slid open before us.

"This had better work," I hissed as we stepped through the open door of the compound.

"It already has," Randy said quietly. "The plan worked perfectly."

30

We were ushered down a series of corridors through an ultramodern, underground facility dug deep below the Siberian frostline. The white tile floors and walls gleamed from the rows of bright overhead lights humming above us. Everything appeared shiny, sterile—I couldn't remember any hospital I'd ever seen cleaner.

"Gene-techs to Station 12," droned a shrill, feminine voice through loudspeakers mounted into the ceiling panels. "Containment field operational. Commence experiment designation J-82."

I glanced over at Nikki, who shrugged wearily, as we strolled through the labyrinth of disinfectant-heavy hallways. To my left, we passed a large picture window looking down on a lab filled with techs dressed in flabby, white suits, hoods drawn over their heads, and thick, purple rubber gloves. The techs scurried around the room like ants building a hive, hunching over microscopes, twisting knobs on some super high-tech gadgets, and meticulously taking the measurements of a strange orange liquid contained in five beakers.

"Huh, what do you know?" Randy said, peering down into the lab. "I didn't know mad scientists had their own university."

"Good ol' Mad Science U," I grinned at my friend, before being shoved yet again by the goon behind us.

Landers, who walked casually in the front, alongside Muscle Head, turned his head and glowered at us, the expression on his face unmistakable: *Knock it off, you two. You're prisoners, not tourists.*

"Dude, Captain America up there wants us to behave," Randy whispered with a grin.

"And he's right," I said, the rebuke sobering me. The rush of what we were doing, the fear and anticipation, had me drunk with adrenaline. I hated agreeing with Landers, though. It just somehow felt...blasphemous to do so in light of his betrayal. "We need to get serious before we blow this."

We bit our tongues and continued our tour of Krenkin's facility. After several minutes, we were led into a large, simple library; each wall covered by floor to ceiling bookshelves filled to the brim with ancient leather bound tomes. The walls, what little of them edged out from the shelves, were comprised of ordinary cinder block. The floor was concrete, painted in a pale shade of blue. The room was sparsely furnished with two metal folding chairs complete with canvas footstools laying parallel near the center. A TV tray sat next to one chair with an empty mug and a filled ashtray resting on its surface. Hanging unceremoniously from a frayed wire, a single, shade-less bulb radiated the room with a harsh, burning light. A long, metal table with more folding chairs sat unceremoniously underneath the bulb.

The library seemed starkly institutional and I shuddered at its lack of warmth. I looked around, half expecting to find my ninth-grade English teacher, hair bunched up in a rigid bun, pointer in hand, demanding that I pay attention to the lesson on Dickens. But she wasn't there. Only books, and shelves, and the smell of death in the air.

"That will be all sergeant," Landers said, waving his underling away. "I need some time with the intruders for interrogation.'

Sergeant Muscle Head walked towards the door, grumbling his disapproval. He motioned for the five other goons, who followed him out the door without a word.

Landers turned back to us, a grim smile turning up one side of his face.

"It really is good to see you again," he said. "Please, have a seat."

He pulled out a chair at the head of the table, sat down, and motioned the others to their seats. None of us budged.

"What's going on Landers?" I snarled. "I want some answers."

"And you'll get them, I promise." He motioned once again at the seats. "Now, please, what we have to discuss may take a while. You might as well make yourselves as comfortable as you can."

"We'll stand if it's all the same to you," Randy said, wrestling with the cuffs binding his hands from behind his back. "Besides, I don't feel much like getting comfortable with a creep like you. Gives me the willies."

"Cunningham, shut up," Landers said, pointing his gun at Randy, causing us all to stiffen. "First of all, you're hardly in a position to be hurling insults. Second, you need to know that appearances can be deceiving. I may have betrayed you guys personally, but it was for a good reason."

"Did he just call me Cunningham?" Randy asked, shrugging his shoulders.

"If that's the case, then why not take our cuffs off?" Nikki asked. "Not to be rude, but having to wear them doesn't really bolster our confidence in you, right now."

Landers shook his head, holstering his gun. "I'm sorry, Nikki, but they have to remain on for now. I've got to keep up appearances. Don't worry though; I'll take them off as soon as I can."

"Well, since you're being so agreeable," Randy said, holding up his cuffed hands behind his back, "my nose itches like crazy. Care to give it a scratch?"

Landers merely rolled his eyes and looked back at me.

"Jack, I'd like you to hear me out all the way. Just give me a few minutes to explain what's happening."

I glowered at him, struggling with the two opposing battles being waged in my head. On the one hand, there was nothing I wanted more than to learn what was going on. On the other, I only wanted to see Scott's smug smile ripped from his face as I pummeled him. Fortunately, Randy beat me to the punch.

"Um, excuse me," Randy said, moving up beside me. "Let me get this straight. Now you're playing nice, wanting to open up for a big pow-wow. But aren't you the same guy who stabbed us in the back and almost let us get blown to bits in a big, dilapidated jenglot temple?"

"What are you talking about? Krenkin didn't blow the temple."

"Tell that to Jack's ear drums and about twenty-five jenglot villagers that didn't make it out in time."

Landers' eyes narrowed as he craned his neck to look back at the complex. "Why that little, creepy, double crossing..."

"Snake?" I piped in. "Is that what you were going to say? Pot. Kettle."

"Look, Jack, it's not like that at all. I even sent one of my own guys, another agent to release you from the vaul—oh, no."

"What?" Nikki asked. "What's wrong?"

He glanced at his watch, standing up from the table and moving to the door. He swiped a keycard across the electronic lock and punched a numeric code in a pad. The sound of a deadbolt clacked.

"That'll buy us a bit more time," he said, looking back at us, worry scrawled in his eyes. "I sent that agent to get you safely out of the temple. He'd informed me that he did and never mentioned that Krenkin has demolished the temple."

"Which means?" Randy asked, his voice rasping with nerves.

"It means that I may be compromised. Look, Jack, you may not believe this, but I really was trying to help."

"And just how do you figure that?"

"It was when we entered the vault that I knew what I had to do. One look at Krenkin told me that I had to make things right at all costs," he said, pacing back and forth as he spoke. He seemed to be trying to convince himself more than us. "Listen, we don't have much time now. Sergeant Gonzales has probably already informed Krenkin that you're here."

I stared at the spook, not speaking, trying to decide whether to hear him out or attempt to take his head off and deal with the goon squad as best I could. But I decided to hear him out. I nodded at him to continue.

"Good. Okay. You need to understand that from the get go, I really thought we were doing something good. I thought teaming up with Krenkin would accomplish something beyond mankind's wildest dreams," he said. "You see, Shantili was right about the jenglot. The creatures we were fighting were only shadows of what they'd been before Krenkin kidnapped their mature queen. Since the Russian experiments in the fifties, not one single subject seemed to age more than a handful of years. Disease was practically unknown inside the confines of their tribe. They exhibited strength and agility far greater than any humanoid ever to exist."

He turned to Randy, Vera, and Nikki, staring at them unapologetically.

"Just imagine the implications," he said. "I had no idea how the loss of the Mother or the sub-queen would effect them. There was no way to know the imbalance would cause so many deaths. I truly believed we were doing the right thing. That is, until I realized the madness that consumed Krenkin. I knew right there in that burial chamber, when I looked into his eyes…I knew what kind of man he truly was. I also knew the government had made a grave miscalculation in trusting him. That's why I had to leave you guys and go with him."

I shook my head, a weak chuckle hissing between my lips. "Now see, that's where things get fuzzy for me. You leaving. With the bad guy."

"I *had* to. I needed stay with the Queen and keep an eye on Krenkin's experiments. I also had to make sure to leave a trail of crumbs for you to follow," he said. "Of course, things haven't worked out exactly according to plan. The moment we arrived, Krenkin sequestered himself in his own private lab. I don't have a clue what he's been doing or how far along in the process he's come.

"It didn't help matters when my superiors placed me in charge of security either. But now, I'm beginning to understand why. I've reported my doubts about the project to some of them. And after finding out the other agent lied to me…well, let's just say I now know exactly where my superiors stand on all this."

He stared at us, holding his ground and waiting for our response. No one moved. No one said a word. I have to admit, I struggled to find something clever to say myself, but after hearing Landers' full story, I just couldn't bring myself to say anything.

I found myself asking if I'd have done something similar in his shoes. The possible benefits of jenglot physiology to medical science were staggering. Disease could be completely wiped out. Aging would be a thing of the past. My mind reeled with all the implications.

Still, I wasn't ready to forgive and forget just yet. Unfortunately, Nikki had no such qualms.

"It's okay, Scott," she said. "We understand. I think."

"Nikki!" I growled. "Speak for yourself. The creep left us to die in that temple. He's lied to us from day one."

"But he helped us get this far," she protested. "He told you about Siberia. Used the GPS tracker. His story makes sense."

A flurry of footsteps outside the library's door jerked Landers' attention away from us. The knob jiggled as a flurry of beeps from the other side of the door told us that someone was punching in their own code. The lock still held.

"I used a security priority one code to lock the door. It'll take them a few minutes to get in," he said, his face grim. "Look, I know you don't trust me. Frankly, I don't care what you think of me. But we really are out of time. We need to find the Queen and get out here now."

"I think I'd rather take my chances with them," I said, nodding towards the locked door.

Nikki pressed up against me with her shoulder. "Knock it off, Jack. We'll deal with him later. For now, we need to be figuring a way out of this mess."

"Actually, there's only one way out, my dear," crooned the heavy handed voice of Krenkin to my left. We turned to see him, standing in the doorway of a hidden tunnel, cut from a line of bookshelves in the wall.

"Well, I'll be," Randy whistled. "Secret passages and everything. This guy really takes his mad scientistry serious."

"Randy, not now," I said, watching as Krenkin stepped into the room, letting the door swing closed behind him. He spoke quietly into a radio and the noise at the library door ceased. He then walked casually over to one of the reading chairs, and dropped into the seat, crossing his legs on the stool with a flare that would have put P.T. Barnum to shame.

"Dr. Jackson," he said, a sickly toad kissing smile twisting up his face. "It is definitely good to see you again." He glanced at Landers and then back to me. "But then, I knew I would, didn't I?"

I stood, looking down at the old codger, as he raised both hands and placed them behind his head.

"Though, I must admit, I was sorely disappointed in your role in all this, Agent Landers," he continued, directing the comment at Scott.

"I'm not sure what you're talking about," Landers said, strolling behind me and dropping something heavy in the pocket of my parka. "We discovered them outside the perimeter and I was merely interrogating them to find out what they knew."

The Russian's face twisted in a hideous scowl as he slammed his fists down on the arm rests of his chair and exploded from his seat.

"Don't think me an idiot, boy!" he roared. "Your communications with ENIGMA were intercepted. I've known of your duplicity from the moment we left Jackson and others to die in the temple."

I took a step towards Krenkin, wishing my hands were free so I could throttle him where he stood.

"Look, Doctor...Krenkinstein," I said, forcing my most 'Dirty Harry' voice to gravel from my throat. "I hate to interrupt this little boss-employee chat session of yours, but I came here for the Queen. If you give her to me, I'll let you live. If you don't...well, I don't even want to think negative."

"Dr. Jackson, you really do have a certain crassness about you, don't you?" Krenkin asked, turning his pale eyes towards me. "I've come to respect you a great deal, but you really are in no position to demand anything from me. I have very special plans for you and your friends." He grinned maliciously. "However, there are some things I'd like to show you beforehand."

"Sheesh. Why does everyone I meet think they can just keep making these special plans for me?" I asked, rolling my eyes. "And why can't these plans ever involve a tropical paradise with the Swedish bikini team?"

Smiling at my lame attempt at humor, he pressed a button on a small remote control in his palm and the door we'd entered made a loud pop before beeping open. Akim, Sergeant "Muscle

Head" Gonzales and seven other guards stomped into the room and leveled their rifles at us.

Geeze, enough with the guns already.

"Secure Agent Landers' weapon and take the two females and the skinny male to laboratory seven and tell Lazlo to begin the preparations," our captor said to his lieutenant. "Dr. Jackson and our ENIGMA liaison will remain with me."

Landers froze, hands raised above his head as two guards patted him down, removing his P90 from around his neck and a 9 mm sidearm strapped to his belt. Then, I watched helplessly while Akim and his thugs seized Randy and the girls, shoving them out of the room and closing the door again.

This was definitely not part of the plan, I screamed silently. *We were supposed to stay together.*

"Alone at last," the scientist said. "Now, I think it is time that I show you just how far my research has come since our return from Malaysia. Would you like that, Dr. Jackson?"

Without waiting for a response, he turned towards the bookcase, stepping on a tiny button set into the hardwood floor. The disguised door whirred to life, swinging open.

"Hold it," I said. "I'm not going anywhere until someone tells me what the heck is going on. What's ENIGMA?" I scowled at Landers again. "And more importantly, what's happening with my friends?"

Krenkin chuckled, strolling around me, laying a shriveled, age-spotted hand on my shoulder. His spindly fingers could definitely use a manicure. "Once again, you're demands are rather foolish, but I will placate you for now. First, ENIGMA is the agency your friend Landers works for."

"He's no friend of mine."

He ignored my comment and droned on. Real life bad guys aren't really like the ones you see in movies—they generally don't jabber on in long monologues that reveal their plans for taking over the world. Fortunately, Krenkin wasn't your average real-life villain. He liked talking and I liked the fact that he liked it. At the moment, I wanted him to use up as much air as possible because I needed to buy us a little more time. And a good ol' fashioned, villainous diatribe was just what this doctor ordered.

I wasn't sure how much time we needed, but I knew I had to buy every second I could until the diversion we'd set up inside Randy's thermos could do its thing. Then it was a simple matter of hoping the cavalry would be on time for the fireworks, finding the jenglot Queen and my friends, and sneaking out of here with as little bloodshed as possible.

What could possibly go wrong?

"...so when President Nixon recognized the potential dangers, ENIGMA, or rather the Entity Identification and Global Management Agency, was formed," Krenkin continued despite my limited attention span. "In essence, it is a U.S. think tank designed to take cryptozoological research and assess the possible military applications each new creature you discover might provide." He smiled, dropping his hands into the pockets of his lab coat as he leaned against one of the bookcases. I kind of wished he'd lean against the secret doorway and fall through onto his pompous rear. "They've already developed a number of promising innovations just from your work on the Mongolian Death Worm alone."

That caught my full attention.

I glared at Landers, balling my fists still handcuffed behind my back. The death worm had been a pet project of mine a while ago. I'd sweated blood and tears for three years to prove the thing existed and when I finally got the proof I needed, POOF, it just disappeared.

"You're the reason I couldn't publish those findings," I growled, no longer faking. "I was laughed out of that symposium and it was all because you wanted my research for yourself?"

"Now's really not the time for this," Landers croaked. "Perhaps you should answer Jack's other question. I'm kind of curious about it myself. What are you planning to do with his friends?"

Krenkin's eyes tightened, edged with nauseating joy as his lips curled up one side of his face in a grotesque sneer.

"Oh, that," he said, turning towards the hidden passage leading to a stairwell. "Well, as I said before, I'd rather show you." He gestured me towards the door. "After you, Dr. Jackson."

I knew I had no choice but to follow.

31

I stepped through the bookcase door and made my way down three flights of stairs before coming to another door leading into another series of white, sterile halls. The scientist led us through the hall to the first door on the right.

"Please," he said, swiping a keycard through the magnetic lock, punching in a code, and opening the door.

Landers lead the way this time and we entered a cramped, dark room with a large rectangular table and seven leather office chairs. A single ceiling fan whirred softly above us, circulating the stagnant underground air. A fifty-two-inch flat panel monitor hung ominously in one corner of the room.

"Have a seat, gentlemen," Krenkin said, pulling a chair for me to sit down in. With my arms cuffed to my back, it was uncomfortable, but I made the most of it and leaned back in the chair, trying to look indifferent. Landers took the chair opposite me and turned to the scientist.

"Okay, now I'd like some answers," he said. "You've kept me in the dark for too long."

"Is it any wonder?" Krenkin chuckled. "You've already

betrayed one group. I had a feeling you'd do the same with me as well."

"Knock it off, you two," I said. "Where are my friends?"

"I will show you your friends, Dr. Jackson, but first I have something far more entertaining."

With a glimmer in his eye, Krenkin palmed his remote and mashed a button. The monitor hummed to life, drawing my eyes toward the screen as it slowly brightened into a crystal clear picture of a dank, shadowy room.

I scanned the picture, but found it rather anticlimactic. The room was large, nearly the size of a high school football stadium from what I could see on the monitor, with smooth tile floors. Its walls, unlike the rest of the complex, were painted in dark shades of green and brown. Several massive trees had been planted in each corner, as well as the center of the room, their branches adorned with dense vegetation. Although I couldn't see the ceiling from the camera's angle, my mind completed the mental image by capping it off with an abundance of skylights for the trees.

"It's a greenhouse," I said. "So what?"

The scientist's eyes continued twinkling. "Have a closer look."

I stood from my chair and strode towards the monitor, focusing in on a strange shadowy mass in the lower right corner of the screen. I jerked when the mass moved, slithering away from the camera's view.

My head twisted briefly to look at our host and then fixed back on the screen. Another shadow flickered down the side of the central tree, pushed off the trunk and grabbed the limb of another.

"Jenglot," I mumbled, moving closer for a better look. "You've already synthesized your original experiment." I turned around to face Krenkin.

"Actually, I've improved it ten fold, Doctor. I've had over fifty years to prepare, to perfect my research. All I needed was the Queen," he smiled as he stood from his chair and walked over to me. "This brood of jenglot is far more powerful than their counterparts. Stronger. More fierce, And much larger."

I glanced back up at the screen to catch a whir of motion as one creature leapt on the back of the other, ravaging the smaller beast with hind claws.

"Why are they so hard to see?" I squinted at the image. It reminded me of one of those paintings you had to look at cross-eyed in order to see the sailboat. "The Malaysian creatures were kind of hard to miss."

"Ah, I will answer that in a moment. But first, you undoubtedly noticed that the jenglot were extremely sensitive to light upon some of your encounters with them," he said proudly. "That's because in their metamorphosed state, they do not have eyes the way you and I think of them. The chitin used to produce their exoskeletons has hundreds of photosensitive sensors that allow them to see their surroundings like nothing else on earth. Every inch of their skin is used to observe their surroundings. In essence, they have three hundred and sixty-degree perfect vision."

"So when we flashed our lights at them—" Landers began.

"It was more than the creatures could take," Krenkin said. "That's why they prefer dark places and night time hunts. Some of the Malaysian brood, like our friend Shantili, evolved to some degree over the years. They became more accustomed to light."

"So, besides the size and strength of this new breed, what's different?" Landers asked as I stood spellbound in front of the monitor.

"Well, a significant improvement is that they no longer metamorphose. Once they transform, they remain in the jenglot state. Always in the bloodlust, they have forgotten their human sensibilities and have truly become the perfect hunters. The second advancement may be a bit premature to discuss. Up until recently, I had not found an adequate female to process the blood for the others. This brood," Krenkin reached up and tapped the monitor, "is still young. Inexperienced..."

"Screw all that," I yelled, freaking out as a blur of motion darted across the TV screen.. "I want to know why they're so hard to see!"

Krenkin drew back at the outburst, a cruel smile creeping up his face.

"Very well, Dr. Jackson," he said. "Early tests seem to confirm that these new jenglot are able to use the photosensitive sensors in their armor to act as a sort of cloaking feature. They are able to take what little light is available and bend it around them, making them virtually impossible to see."

"Dear Lord," Landers gawked at the television. "If your early notes I read are true, the jenglot's armor protects them from losing body heat, so they'd cast virtually no heat signatures for thermal cameras. And with their innate camouflage—."

"They're almost completely undetectable by any known security system, yes," Krenkin almost giggled.

I listened to the conversation, detached. Something he'd just said was nagging at me. Buzzing through my mind like a swarm of angry bees. Something was wrong. Something...

'Up until recently, I had not found an adequate female to become the queen,' he'd said. Recently?

"Nikki and Vera," I said, scowling at the scientist. "Where are they?"

Krenkin merely smiled, placed both hands behind his back and walked over to the chair at the end of the table. He sat down and gestured to the chair I'd taken upon entering the room.

"I'm serious, you creep. Tell me where they are. Now!"

"I'll show you, but first, please take a seat." He pointed to my chair again, completely calm.

I sat down and tried to burn holes into the man with my eyes, but I never had quite got the knack of heat vision. *Superman has all the fun.* Without another word, Krenkin nodded to the television and pushed another button. The screen dissolved for a second and reappeared to a new room.

This time, the monitor showed a lab. Nothing odd. It was similar in every way to any lab I'd ever seen before. Beakers, microscopes, busy lab techs scurrying here and there in the tedium of their scientific endeavors. I thought it was just a regular, run of the mill laboratory until I noticed a set of five operating tables in a semi-circle fashion to the left of the screen.

Just like the one in the temple, I thought. *These guys should really watch more Home and Garden television. Maybe add a little feng shui to the place.*

You ever notice how your eyes and brain plays tricks on you when you see something you hope just isn't real? At that very moment, both my brain and eyes decided to simultaneously go out to lunch. I didn't want to admit what I was seeing, but it was there in all its high def glory. My friends. Strapped to three of the tables.

My jaw dropped, stricken paralyzed, as I watched Randy, Vera, and Nikki squirming against the leather straps fastening their arms and legs. A lab tech moved over to Randy, stabbing the largest needle I'd ever seen deep into his neck. In three seconds flat, my old friend lay motionless on the table, eyes closing slowly on the screen.

He's planning on using either Nikki or Vera as the new queen. This can't be happening.

But I knew it was and white hot fury rose towards my throat like magma

"Krenkin, you're a dead man!" I exploded from my seat, propelling myself over the table towards my tormentor. I felt the trickle of liquid heat running down my hands, as I struggled to break through the cuffs behind my back. "I swear, I'll tear your head right off that puny little neck of yours."

It was at that precise moment the complex shuddered from a massive explosion above. Claxons sounded, braying their warning through the loud speakers over head. Witz and the cavalry had finally arrived and it was high time to kick a little Russian butt.

"Now it's my turn to play mad scientist," I grinned, moving around the table.

32

Landers, who didn't appear in the least surprised by the chaos rumbling above, darted towards me, reached into my parka, drew out a small caliber pistol. Without hesitation, he trained the weapon at Krenkin. The scientist sat smoldering in his chair, unmoving. The ceiling fan above wobbled uncontrollably as more explosions ripped through the foundations of the complex. I just prayed that Randy's thermos was no where near the lab that he and the girls were being held.

"Scott?" I said, not taking my eyes off the scientist. "You know I don't like this, but I hope I can trust you."

Keeping his aim leveled on Krenkin, Landers moved behind me without a word and unlocked the cuffs. I rubbed my wrists, as I walked around the table and leaned down in the cruel face of the man I'd grown to loathe. "Where are they? Where's that lab?" I pointed up at the screen.

The old scientist sneered, closing his eyes in defiance. Another blast from the surface rocked the room, knocking me off balance. I tipped forward, catching the edge of the table to steady myself.

"Those explosions up there have your name written all over

them," I whispered in his ear. "The only way you're getting out of here alive is if you cooperate. Now where are they?"

Krenkin opened his eyes and slowly turned his head toward me, his smile slithering across his face.

"Still making demands," he said, baring his teeth. "You are overconfident, Dr. Jackson. This little military coup you've set up won't save you. Or your friends."

He turned the channel of the TV with his remote back to the greenhouse where the jenglot had hunted each other in the darkness. I watched, waiting for the shadows to flit across the screen, but they never came. Pressing another series of buttons, the camera panned, revealing large garage-style doors hanging open.

"The moment your friends began their attack, the doors were automatically opened, letting my new brood out into the battlefield," Krenkin laughed. "And they're thirsty. Without a queen to process their blood intake, they are perpetually famished, starving to death. I'm afraid your rescuers above are decidedly outmatched."

I looked up at Landers, still aiming at Krenkin's head.

"We've got to move. Witz and his men aren't going to last long up there with those jenglot on the loose and neither are Randy and the girls," I said, pulling Krenkin's arms behind his chair and fastening them with the handcuffs. As much as I'd like to plant a slug in the guy's head, I was no killer. "Any ideas where they are?"

He shook his head. "Not really. This place is huge. He's kept most of the scientific wing on lockdown even from security."

"Then, I guess we'll just have to do it the hard way."

"What about the Mother? Should we split up to cover more territory?" Landers asked.

"Haven't you ever watched Scooby Doo? Splitting always seems to lead the monsters right to where Shaggy and Scoob are. In our case, I'd be Shaggy, so I don't think so!" I said, searching the scientist, grabbing his remote and a nice little Walther PPK hidden under his lab coat. I looked down at Krenkin. "A James Bond gun? Really?"

Smacking the scientist on the back of the head with my palm, I tucked the weapon into my waistband and ran for the door. I heard Landers coming up behind me but stopped just as the foundation of the complex shook again.

Geeze, Witz. Lighten up, will you? There are good guys in here, you know.

I looked right and then left, shrugging my shoulders. "You were part of this whole thing," I said to Landers. "Any idea which way to go from here?"

He shook his head, checking the magazine in his gun. "I've never been in this sublevel before."

"What kind of security guard were you anyway? You kind of suck at it."

"It was never my forte actually," he smiled.

"Okay, I guess we do this the super-irritatingly hard way," I said. "I figure that since they didn't take Randy and the girls down the bookshelf stairs that we came through, they're probably somewhere on the library's level."

"Sounds reasonable," he said.

We turned to the left and jogged towards the stairway that led back into the library The air horns, howling through the complex, were even louder on the upper levels. Each blare of the claxon pounded deeper into my skull and I checked my ears to make sure they weren't bleeding.

"Would someone turn those things..." I shouted, clamping my hands over my ears, "off!" The cacophony from the alarms ceased abruptly just as I yelled the last word. I winced, hoping no one heard. Landers threw me a glance, pointing his pistol at the library's main door.

For several seconds, neither of us moved, waiting for the

inevitable henchman to burst through the door with guns blazing. For a change, I got lucky.

"So, why do you think they stopped?" I whispered, edging towards the door and leaning against the wall to one side.

"Maybe you're telekinetic," he mocked, moving to the other side.

I reached for the knob, twisted, and cracked the door a hair. Landers sight followed the line of his barrel through the opening, scouring the hallways beyond. All the lights were off. Only the crimson waves of emergency lights flashing silently along the walls provided any semblance of illumination.

"Clear," he whispered, pushing the door open further.

"Why is that not comforting to me?"

"Because it probably means that several large blood sucking mutant bugs are lurking inside every nook and cranny from here to the lab we're looking for," Landers said.

I pulled up beside him and watched as he cocked his head to the side.

"Do you hear that?" he asked.

"Hear what?"

"That's my point, exactly. The explosions have stopped," he said, crouching down, his eyes closing as he listened. "But I do I hear gunfire above us. Faint, but its still there. Your friend and his men are still fighting the good fight...at least for now."

I stared at him for a few seconds, my mind whirling through questions and doubts, trying to piece everything together.

"How did you know?" I asked.

"Know what?"

"When Witz and his men attacked...you didn't even flinch."

"Oh, that," Landers grinned. "Easy. I know you. How you think. How you operate. You've mentioned this mercenary friend a few times so I figured you were probably going to recruit him. Of course, I didn't expect you to just walk in and get yourself captured."

"Er, that's because it was Randy's idea."

The agent laughed quietly, peaking through the door to peer around the corner. "Sounds like something he'd come up with."

"Trust me, I wasn't too happy about it," I said. "But, we need to hurry. I'm not sure how much longer Witz and his men can hold out once the jenglot show up." I pointed to the right. "I think we came in from that direction, so my best guess would be that we go left."

Landers swung the library door open, stepping out into the pristine hallway and swinging his gun around in a three hundred and sixty-degree arc.

"Still clear," he whispered.

We crept down the corridor, opening any unlocked door we came to, and listening for signs of approaching sentries. I was beginning to get spooked. I figured that if the Christian rapture had come, the bad guys wouldn't be the one's getting zapped up to meet Jesus, so that couldn't account for the absolute stillness that echoed through the compound.

Eventually, we came to a bright green door on the left. I cracked it open, and couldn't stifle a grin threatening to break across my face. The twelve by twelve foot room was completely devoid of life. A handful of coats, uniforms, and towels lay draped over long wooden benches mounted securely on the tile floor in front of a row of foot lockers lining the left side of the room. A narrow door at the back led to what I imagined was a series of showers.

The locker room, however, was not what had captivated my interest. It was the right hand wall that excited a seditious smile to spread across my worried features. Four large gun racks hung at head level on the wall. Two army green crates rested closed on the floor. Although most of the racks lay empty, one still contained an M4 assault rifle and a 12 gauge shotgun.

I moved into the room, snatching the weapons from their slots and slung their straps around my shoulders.

"Check the lockers," I ordered Landers. "See if you can find anything useful."

While Scott busied himself with his search, I crouched down, opened one of the crates and would have probably cried at the sight, if Landers wasn't in the same room. I reached in, snagged five fragmentary grenades and stuffed all but one in the pockets of my parka. The other crate was empty.

"That's what I'm talking about!" I grinned, tossing the remaining grenade in my palm like a baseball.

Landers glanced over his shoulder, eyes so big the space shuttle would probably get sucked in. "Be careful with that, you idiot!"

"Hey, I know how to handle these babies." I missed the grenade, cringing as it clattered to the floor. One eye slowly opened, glancing down at the pineapple shaped bomb laying dormant at my feet. "See, that's exactly the kind of thing someone who doesn't know how to handle them would do." I reached down, picked it up, and stuck it in the side pocket of my cargo pants.

Landers finished his search and turned around

"Here. This might come in handy," he said, throwing a Mag-Lite towards me. It fumbled on the tips of my fingers, before I managed to snatch it in my hand. Okay, so the grenade thing made me a little nervous.

"Thanks," I said, heat rising to my face. I then turned around, revealing my new found arsenal clinging to my back. "Um, you want one of these?"

"I'm good, thanks," he said, shaking his head and holding up a P-90 he'd found in one of the lockers. "Found my gun."

He moved silently out the door into the hallway again. "Now, we need to get moving. Time's running out."

WE'D WEAVED through the corridors slowly, dodging into the shadows to avoid a patrol of guards running to the battle above, when we finally came to the laboratory we'd been searching for.

The electronic doors whizzed open as we approached, revealing the same pristine lab we'd seen on Krenkin's television monitor. As with the rest of the facility, the lights were darkened, casting the room in orange and red shadows from the rotating emergency lights.

Twisting the front of the Mag-Lite, a brilliant beam shot out into the dim room, revealing abandoned workstations with beakers boiling over lit Bunsen burners. We moved over to the far right corner of the room and found the operating tables.

Nikki and Randy lay dormant, resting peacefully under their restraints. Vera, however, was no where to be seen.

I nodded at Landers, who understood my meaning, moved over to Randy and released the bindings around his wrists and ankles. When he switched to Nikki, I turned around and searched the lab for any signs of the Mother Queen...and of Vera.

"Vera?" I whispered into the darkness. "Are you there?"

The whirr of the facility's heating vents kicking in was the only response. I moved, crouching low below the lab tables in case we were interrupted by any stray guards who might wander in.

I caught a glimmer of light, a reflection from the Mag, out of my peripheral vision. I twisted in that direction and saw her. The jenglot Queen, sleeping soundly in a thick glass container, various colored tubes pumping thick gooey liquid in and out of her prone form. I dashed to the high-tech sarcophagus and examined it, trying to figure out what the contraption was designed to do.

Can't go pulling out wires all willy nilly, I thought, scratching my head. *I have no idea if this thing could kill her.*

"Jack!" Landers shouted from the opposite end of the room, jerking my attention away from the Queen.

I turned around, nearly bumping head first into the gorgeously serene face of Vera, standing only inches behind me.

"Vera!" I said, beaming from ear to ear. "Thank you God. I was so worried about you."

Vera glanced down at my shoes, humming a strange tune I'd heard her singing before. A song her mother had sung when Vera was a young girl growing up in communist Russia...a song of joy taught to a child before the tragedy of her parents' death scarred her for life.

"Vera? Are you all right?"

She looked up at me again, a strange gleam in her eyes.

"I—I'm not sure," she whispered, bringing her hands to her face, running her fingers through her short, chestnut hair.

"It's okay," I said, forcing a smile and putting an arm around her shoulder, pulling her against me. The thump, thump, thump of her heart pounded against my chest. "We're here now. Witz is up top. We're getting out of here."

I looked over at Scott, helping Nikki sit up on the table. She looked dazed, drugged. Randy was already standing, moving towards us in slow, deliberate steps. Although his balance swayed, he appeared to be fine.

"Look, Randy and Nikki are fine," I said. "We're all fine."

"I—I feel strange," Vera said, closing her eyes and spouting a string of sentences in Russian I couldn't follow. "Help me, Jack."

Then, she collapsed to the ground, curling up in a ball and sobbing uncontrollably. "Help me. Somebody help me."

I dropped to my knees, rubbing her back with my hand, shushing her with gentle words. "It's all right, Vera. We'll help you." I looked up at Randy, who now stood next to us. "What happened? What did they do to her?"

"I, uh, I don't know," he said, turning briefly as Landers and Nikki approached. "They stuck me with some needle and I've been out ever since."

"Nikki?" I asked, lifting Vera up and cradling her against me.

"I don't know either," she said. "But besides a major hangover, I feel fine."

Vera's body tensed beneath my grasp—every muscle, limb, and tendon constricting in rigid torture. A low steady snarl rumbled from somewhere deep inside her throat.

"Vera?" I asked, pulling her away from me to look at her face. "Oh, God, please no."

Her gentle, blue eyes turned up inside her eyelids, rolling back in her head. Her mouth convulsed into a hideous deformed scowl, her straight, white teeth elongating before my eyes.

God no! Please. I'll do whatever you ask, just not Vera!

She pushed against me, throwing me away from her with strength easily more powerful than Lou Ferrigno when he played the Hulk. Landers leveled his gun at her head, his finger tensing on the trigger.

"Don't!" I screamed, tears running down my cheek. Vera and I had been friends for a very long time. She'd had such a hard life, had been so caring, loving despite years of abuse and neglect she'd suffered. Over time, she'd grown to become like a sister to me. She would have easily died for me, without a second thought. And I, just as freely, would have done the same for her.

Her screams melded into deep, guttural howls, bounding off the corrugated walls that confined the lab. Large, bony spikes ripped through her spine, shredding the flesh from her back.

"Behold," came an acidic voice from the doorway of the lab. Krenkin. "The new jenglot queen. Beautifully terrible. Ravishingly savage. Beauty and Beast in one." The old man strode casually towards us, flanked on both sides by Akim and Sergeant Muscle Head. He stopped a foot away from Vera's contorting body, looked down and smiled.

"If the subject struggles against it, the transformation of this brood is decidedly longer, and excruciatingly more painful than the original," he said, dropping the handcuffs I'd used on him onto the tile floor next to Vera's writhing head. "But even still, the results are stunning."

I glared at the three men standing over the tortured form of Vera and gripped the handle of the pistol I'd taken from Krenkin.

"Landers," I said.

Without comment, the ENIGMA agent raised the barrel of his submachine gun at Krenkin. Akim and Muscle Head followed suit, bringing their M4s up, targeting both Randy and Nikki.

"I'd be careful if I were you," Krenkin laughed. "You may well put me down, but your friends would follow seconds after."

Landers aim remained steady, unwavering. His eyes focused on a small liver spot near the center of the scientist's head.

"He's not going to lower his weapon," I said, nodding over at Landers. I still wasn't completely convinced I could trust the agent, but he was the only hope I had left. It was a gamble I had to make.

"And neither will they," Krenkin gestured at both his men.

For several seconds, we stood, staring at one another in complete silence. Only Vera's writhing body made any noise at all. Snarls, growls, and high pitched shrieks burst from her lungs, shattering the last vestige of hope that I would ever see my friend again.

Then, all was truly silent.

Vera was no longer wriggling on the tile floor. In her place, breathing shallowly, in a fetal curl, lay the crisp black armor of a jenglot. Her head snapped up, glaring at me with an eyeless chalk-white skull. A low growl whispered from her mouth as she stood up, steadying herself with her new, sleek, skeletal legs.

She was the largest jenglot I'd seen so far, standing nearly a full six foot tall—practically six inches taller than Vera's human form. Her lower fangs poked up and forward in a sinister overbite designed specifically for shredding the flesh of her prey. Paper-thin, transparent insectoid wings fluttered uselessly behind her. She was obviously too massive for the thin membranes to lift. I figured they were more for show, vestigial structures from her insect-like DNA. What little skin remained over her emaciated flesh, sagged, particularly around the belly region that I deduced was used to store blood for processing.

She whirled around, scouring each of our faces with primal fury. Her long, spiny proboscis snaking out of her mouth as if sniffing for the nearest source of sustenance. I glanced over at Krenkin.

With any luck, he'll be the first to go.

But my short streak of good luck had just ran out.

The Vera-jenglot's eyes rested on me, as she lurched forward, bending her knees in slow, steady arcs.

"Vera? It's me, Jack," I said, holding out my hands, palms up. "Please, don't do this. We can save you. We can figure out how to reverse this."

Lord God, please. She's my friend, my sister. If you love me…if you love her, then you'll stop this. You won't let this happen.

But I knew what his response would be before the words were ever formed in my head. He wouldn't help us. He didn't care and I hurled all my hatred, all my anger towards the heavens at Him.

Then I leapt at Krenkin with my own snarls of hunger.

33

I landed on Krenkin, wrenching him down to the ground, my fists pounding against him in a feral, unthinking salvo. Before anyone could react, Landers and Randy lashed out at the two goons gawking at the sudden fury of my attack. The lab erupted into chaos of fists and feet flailing mercilessly at each other.

Pushing the others from my mind, I wailed against the scientist's body, unleashing every ounce of frustration and anger I'd kept bottled up inside through most of our expedition to Malaysia. My rage was fueled all the more by Krenkin's incessant laughter, gleefully mocking me with every blow.

We rolled on the floor, my right arm pounding against his ribs in a series of blows that would have shattered a younger man's bones. But his laughter only increased. Then, with the same effort he'd have used to swat a yapping mutt, he threw me off of him and rolled to his feet.

Vera crouched low, snarling as she watched the fray unfold before her. Her head tilted to one side as if trying to discern her next move.

"You idiot," Krenkin laughed, tearing his lab coat away and

unbuttoning his shirt. "You insignificant, little imbecile. Even now, you still haven't figured it out."

I pushed myself to my feet, wobbling slightly to regain my balance and cool the jets burning white hot inside my gut. Landers and Randy were still struggling with Akim and Muscle Head, holding their own despite the massive strength of their opponents. Nikki had moved back behind one of the lab tables, watching.

"I've figured out enough," I growled. "I pretty much figure you're a whacked-out loon who could care less about the lives you destroy."

Another bellow of mirth erupted from the scientist's lungs. "You really are a simpleton," he said, wiping a stream of saliva and blood from his chin. "This goes so far beyond sanity or insanity. It transcends what is good or evil. Those are obscurities used by the weak of mind and heart."

We moved around in a tight circle. My muscles tensed for another strike. I caught Vera moving in tandem with us out of my peripheral vision, wondering if any vestige of the woman I knew still resided in her bestial form.

"This whole thing...the experiments in Malaysia, my agreement with ENIGMA...they were all for one purpose, one goal," Krenkin said. "I could care less how the governments of the world choose to use my research. Politics. National security. Those things are as beneath me as your contempt for what I've done."

His bony chest heaved as he spoke, his hands balled, whitening his knuckles. He looked at Vera and then back at me.

"It's been about me the entire time," he said. "I know I don't look it, but I am ninety-five years old, Dr. Jackson. Age is the devourer of us all. Time ravages even the best of men. But not me. Not now."

I glanced over at Landers, bringing down his thick soled boot against the head of Akim, knocking him out. Muscle Head already lay prone on the floor, unconscious with Randy crouched above him.

Great. They manage to bring down King and Kong and I can't even take a sickly old man. Wait a minute…what did he just say?

"What do you mean…not you?"

The scientist erupted in a fit of uncontrollable laughter, pulling out a syringe and injecting himself with a strange, orange liquid. Vera hissed behind me.

"You've seen the queen," Krenkin bellowed, collapsing to his knees. "Now, meet the king!"

HE ROSE UP, spreading his arms into the air and arching his back. His thin skin ripped down his chest, like of a fault line snaking a fissure during an earthquake, revealing shiny, black armor underneath. Fangs grew from both upper and lower jaws, as razor sharp claws extended from his upraised hands. Spikes burst from his back while stringy tendrils of hair sprouted from his graying head and down his back.

Son of a…I can't believe this is happening…this is just un-crazy-believable.

Krenkin's mass expanded, growing taller and larger during every second of his transformation. Already he loomed above us at nearly nine feet tall and it didn't look as though he was remotely close to finished.

"Landers?" I nodded at the metamorphosing scientist with a weak smile.

He nodded back, each of us raising our weapons in unison and firing. Thirty rounds of armor piercing rounds flashed from Lander's barrel, hurling a scant ten yards towards its target. The half-changed creature arched back, stumbling over and crashing to the floor.

The boom of my shotgun echoed through the lab as I pumped

at least five more rounds of 12-gauge buckshot into the fallen scientist.

Smoke and gunpowder burned my nostrils as our weapons cooled in our hands. I looked down at the twisted form of Krenkin, laying still on the cold, tile floor of the lab. His chest wasn't moving. He made no sound.

"Um, a little overkill, isn't it?" Landers asked, popping in a fresh clip. He checked his pockets and grimaced. "Go easy on the ammo. We're nearly out."

Ignoring the comment, I twisted my head, taking stock of everyone, making sure they were safe and secure.

Randy. Nikki. Good. Vera?

"Where's Vera?" I whirled around, looking for her lurking in the shadows. So far, she'd watched idly as her friends and enemies fought for their survival. I had no way of knowing what she'd been thinking. Or if she even had the capacity for human thought any more.

"I didn't see her leave," Nikki whispered, peering around her shoulder.

"Neither did—" Landers cut his sentence short as several growls reverberated from different areas of the lab in unison. "This might be bad."

A single howl bellowed through the smoke-filled air, prompting the pounding of at least three separate pair of large, clawed feet to flit through the shadows. My eyes caught a glimpse of one creature just as it hurled itself up the wall, clinging to the ceiling. It disappeared as soon as it moved past the field of the emergency lights.

"Randy," I said, holding out the M4. He snatched it from my hand and spun around, wary of the hidden creatures encircling us.

"Nikki, get under the table," I said.

"Why? I can fight just as well as you."

You know? She's probably right.

But I wasn't about to take the chance. "Nikki, we're fresh out of guns, now get under that—" Before I could finish the sentence, she swooped down next to Muscle Head, scooping up his fallen M4 rifle. "Geeze, woman, sometimes you can really be a pain in the—"

A snarl from the ceiling above my head cut me off, sending gooseflesh up and down my back. I looked up just as a seven-foot-tall jenglot, its chitinous armor absorbing the dim light in the room, dropped down on top of me. Its claws and talons slashed, tearing through my parka. Three unused grenades rolled out from the torn coat, harmlessly to the floor.

The beast picked me up over its head and hurled me towards a series of lockers on the far wall. I careened against them, knocking the wind from my lungs.

"Holy cow!" Randy shouted. "These things are gigantic! Someone's been eating their Wheaties."

The jenglot turned in the direction of my best friend's annoying voice and pounced.

One by one, the team leveled their weapons at the attacking jenglot and fired. The jenglot shrieked as the maelstrom of bullets shattered its hide, digging deep into its flesh. It dropped to the floor, convulsing wildly and then was still.

"Randy, cut the banter for now, okay?" I said, picking myself up off the ground and cutting my hand on broken glass in the process.

Another howl erupted to my right. I couldn't be sure, but I sensed it came from their new queen—Vera. In answer, two more jenglot burst through the haze of gun smoke, hurling themselves at my friends in a hunger induced frenzy. Nikki swung her barrel around, targeting a large creature that bounded over one of the lab tables. A cluster of beakers and test tubes crashed to the floor, shattering into thousands of flesh tearing shards.

A single shot to the creature's forehead plowed through its skull, tearing through brain matter like a blender to hamburger.

"Vera stop!" I yelled, wheeling around. *Every time she yells another jenglot attacks. What's she doing?* "Please."

But it was too late. Two more creatures fell from the shadowy ceiling and landed in a crouch between the team and me. We couldn't shoot without the risk of hitting each other.

Okay. So they're smart too, I thought, letting out a breath.

The jenglot, on all fours, circled around like wolves biding their time before taking advantage of their prey's weak point. Saliva glistened from their teeth as their bony spikes heaved up and down on their backs.

"Vera, stop this," I pleaded into the shadows around me. "I don't want to..." I swallowed the rest of the sentence. I couldn't even think about what was running through my mind. If things kept going this way, we'd have only one option. "I can't."

But I knew what she was doing, or rather what she was trying to make me do. She was forcing my hand, sending her brood in short, easy-to-deal with bursts. Forcing us to defend ourselves. Forcing me to take action and end the nightmare that had become her life.

I won't.

A shrill howl exploded in front of me...but not from the two creatures we were now staring down. And not from Vera either. The fallen, mutilated form of Krenkin rose to his taloned feet. His huge form reared back unleashing an ear-shattering roar. The scientist's jenglot body was warped, shredded from the lead we'd filled him with. Black, goo-like blood oozed slowly from gaping wounds. One of his fangs had broken, leaving a jagged stub where a razor tooth had once rested. His right arm hung limp against his side.

Still, despite his marauded flesh, his body exuded raw, unquenchable hatred. He was a walking, living, breathing nightmare on two, boney legs.

Krenkin craned his head at an impossible angle and shrieked. I clenched my ears as the cacophony pummeled against me like fists. Then he bounded to the ceiling and disappeared.

The other two jenglot stared up, watching their king skitter across the ceiling and turned back, focusing their attention on me. They crouched again, growling softly, like two cats playing with the same mouse. I tensed as they prepared their attack.

I had one shot. It was an idea that could very well save my life and avoid any unpleasant shooting of my friends in the process. My hand fell to my hip, finding the Mag-Lite I'd tucked into my belt and pulled it out. Without waiting for them to strike, I powered on the light and shined it at them in a brutal wave of luminescence. Taking my cue, Landers did the same, surrounding the two gruesome creatures with a field of pure, white light.

The jenglot writhed and screamed on the floor, covering their heads with their scaled arms. Keeping my light trained on them, I darted around and joined the rest of the group.

The second I was there, Landers lowered his light and unloaded a full clip from his P-90 into both of them without even flinching. His eyes never blinked. His face, a mask of stoic gravity, unfeeling, unmoved. Perfectly rational. I'd never seen the man so brutal, so impervious to killing. Looking down at the wriggling bodies of the dying jenglot, I couldn't help but wonder who they were...who their families might be and whether they'd be missed. One look at Landers' serene face told me, he just didn't care.

A shudder rippled through me at the thought. *Just who is this guy?* He was the true wolf, not the jenglot. Landers knew how to wait it out, watch his prey, and take advantage of any weakness he found. I knew at that moment, he was someone that should never be crossed.

The two creatures lay still. The lab was now a graveyard, reeking of death and congealed blood. Four jenglot, once real life human beings, lay dead around us. I looked over at Nikki, tears streaming unchecked down her soft, tanned cheeks. Her mouth muttering a silent prayer.

God, why are you letting this happen? Why would you allow so much death and destruction happen to people you claim to love?

"It's not God", I heard the voice of Dad. A forgotten memory from years long gone. Zachariah, my older brother, had just died. A victim of leukemia. It had never made sense to me. He'd been my hero, so strong and brave. I hadn't thought anything could stop him...until that moment.

"God hurts when we hurt, son," Dad had said, tears staining his cheeks as the words dripped from his lips. *"He never wanted us to live this way. Never wanted us to suffer. To hurt."*

"But he lets it happen!" I'd screamed. *"If he was so powerful, why can't He just stop it?"*

A flurry of motion to my left jerked me from the memory. The Krenkin jenglot hurled his massive form towards me, his claws lashing across my face, sending me reeling backward. His hind claws dug deep across my chest, as he leapt on top of me, thrashing wildly.

"Shoot the creep!" I screamed at anyone with a gun. But they stood motionless, watching the carnage in terrified awe. "Kill him!"

The beast's salivating jaws snapped at my face, its fangs cutting a deep gash down my left cheek. Its jaw extended further, unhinging like the jaw of a viper, to release a long, spiky tongue.

A proboscis? But I thought only the queens could have those.

I pushed against the hulking figure pinning me down, forcing every muscle in my body to react to the impending, and gruesomely ugly death that slithered my way. But it was useless. The jenglot outweighed me by a ton and my frantic movements only served to enflame his bloodlust.

The tongue suddenly lashed out, striking just under my collarbone and worming its way deep into my neck. Agonizing pain shot through me as if thousands of super charged electric eels coursed against every nerve, every synapse in my body.

"Shoot him now!" I screamed again, as my vision clouded over the edges of my vision. A new terror filled my veins as Akim and the muscle bound sergeant clambered to their feet behind my friends.

Dear Lord. It can't end this way. Not like this.

My mouth opened again as I screamed a silent warning. My vocal cords paralyzed by toxins emitted by Krenkin's proboscis. *Why won't they shoot? Why won't they look behind them? God, please, do something.*

Of course they couldn't shoot. They wouldn't. They were afraid they might hit me. But I was dying anyway. My fingers and toes grew cold, as if cut from my limbs and stuck in an icebox next to the popsicles and two-week old lasagna. The blood was draining quickly from my body and Krenkin was growing stronger by the second. His battered hide seemed to mend itself in front of my dimming eyes.

And Akim and his goon inched closer, stalking, in their minds, the weakest of the pack—Nikki. I stretched out my hand, willing my fingers to stretch, to pull her away from danger. But it was no use. The haze of blood loss and the jenglot's poisons were taking their toll...my vision was going. My limbs no longer responded to my mental commands.

And just as Krenkin's lieutenant reached out one rippling arm to seize Nikki from behind, a shadowy form streaked across my field of weakening vision, its claws slashing at Akim's torso, gutting him from the crotch up. The big man fell forward, landing on Nikki, pinning her to the ground.

The sergeant turned and ran out the door.

And Vera swiveled, her skull-like face burning against the dim light, her attention locked on me. On Krenkin. And then she howled. It was a shriek straight from the lower levels of Dante's hell. Nothing natural, neither human nor animal, could have reproduced the tormented cry that was unleashed from her lips. She screamed again and for a brief moment, I could almost hear the sound of her sweet, gentle voice in the cascade of the horrific wale.

Even Krenkin appeared mesmerized by the display, turning his head to look longingly at his new queen, my blood forgotten for the moment. He emitted a low, sickly whine—a fanciful purring—as if trying to woo a mate.

For a long moment, Vera stared at us. Her head bobbing up and down above her long, skeletal neck. A strange balloon-like membrane under her chin puffed in and out, a response to his call.

"Vera," I choked on the words. Steely knives of pain slashed through my vocal cords as I spoke. "It's me. Jack."

She looked up at Krenkin. Then down to me and back up.

Then, she charged. I closed my eyes and prepared myself for death.

Why don't they just shoot me and get it over with?

The impact of Vera's violent assault nearly crushed me as her mass collided against Krenkin and then, the weight of the monstrosity resting on my chest was gone. I blinked. Opening my eyes. The savage forms of two unnatural creatures of science rolled across the floor in a deadly tangle. Claws ripped. Jaws snapped. And a geyser of blood and bile sprayed from the freshly torn armor of Krenkin.

34

Landers lifted his rifle and aimed.

Oh, now he wants to shoot!

"Scott, don't!" I coughed, a clot of blood spewing from my mouth. "It's Vera."

He looked at me briefly, before squinting through the crosshairs at the end of the barrel.

"Not anymore," he winced as the words slipped from his lips. "I've got to, Jack. Once she's finished with him, she'll turn on us."

"But you can't!" Nikki cried, jumping in front of Landers' rifle. "She's our friend."

"Nikki, please move away from the barrel of the gun," Scott whispered, peering over her left shoulder at the grappling monsters. "I really don't want to have to shoot you too."

"Um, yeah," Randy said, taking Nikki's wrist and pulling her gently out of harm's way. "I don't like it anymore than you do, but I'm pretty sure standing in front of his gun isn't the smartest way to stop him."

"But she could have killed us already, but didn't," she

explained, trying to wrench herself from Randy's grasp. "That's got to count for something."

Landers kept his aim fixed on the two titans battling furiously a few feet away. I watched...waiting, hoping and praying he'd do the right thing. After several excruciating seconds, he closed his eyes, let out a breath, and lowered his rifle.

I tried breathing myself, but only managed to cough up one of my lungs...or at least something that looked an awful lot like one.

The creatures' snarls and howls dragged me back to our dilemma. Slowly, I turned my head, unable to move the rest of my body, and watched the onslaught of the jenglot as they literally tore one another apart. Nikki slid over to me, cradling me in her arms.

"If we're not going to shoot them," Landers said, crouching close to me. "Then we need to get out of here while they're distracted. Randy, help me get him up."

Randy moved over to us, leaned forward and pulled my arm around his shoulder. Landers did the same and I soon found myself suspended between the two of them and hurtling for the laboratory door.

But I couldn't leave. Not yet.

"Vera..." I said, ignoring the pain. I looked behind us, at my friend, the monster...fighting the man that had committed the ultimate crime against her. A shudder wracked through me, threatening to bring me to despair. *She was a healer. A doctor, not a fighter or a mauler. It's just not right.*

Dad's words from the past suddenly rushed against the walls of my memory. *"God lets things happen, yes," he said. "But He never wanted it to be this way. It was Man, son. It was Sin. The sin of man is like a cancer, eating away at the vital and good things in life."*

"But doctors can operate on cancer. Cut it out."

"And God did just that," Dad smiled at me. He had the most comforting, fatherly smile. Without fail, it always washed away all

my fears. Sorrow. Until that day. *"But not in the way we might like. If God had just gone in and destroyed all sin, just cut it away, He would have had to use the scalpel on us. His children. But that would have defeated the whole purpose of Creation. He loved us. He didn't want to destroy us. So one day, He took all the cancer of sin in the world and put it into one man...Jesus. And He performed His holy operation on His Son instead."*

"But if God got rid of sin, then why do we still have to hurt?" I asked. *"Why does He still let bad things happen?"*

A trill scream exploded behind us, just as the doors slid open. We spun around to see an upright Krenkin plow a clawed foot against Vera's head, ripping her face with his hind talon. The larger beast loomed over her, roaring furiously before he plunged his hand down into her abdomen, ripping it open before my eyes.

"No!" I screamed, tearing away from Randy and Landers and stumbling back into the lab. Scott grabbed at my arm, but in a sudden rage fueled burst, I broke free and dashed to my fallen friend.

Without thinking, I crouched down, scooped up a grenade that had fallen out of my parka and ran towards the fracas.

"Oh crap," I heard Randy mumble, as the sounds of guns being brought up clattered behind me. "He's gone plum-stinking nuts."

I darted forward, pushing my legs as fast as I could and with a roar of my own, ran headlong into Krenkin driving him back a single step. The jenglot lashed at me, but I managed to side step, pulling the pin of the grenade. Its massive jaws snapped forward, grabbing for my head. My eyes focused. Everything stopped.

I stood just outside my body, watching. Detached. No longer in pain. No longer saddened. Numb.

I watched myself duck the creature's gaping maw, toss the grenade down its throat, and leap in slow motion to the right, just as another clawed hand slashed down. The jenglot stood up, straightening to its full nine foot height and let out a piercing bellow.

Then, he exploded. Chunks of chitin, charred flesh, and shards of bone rocketed around us, splattering against everything in their path. Globules of congealed blood showered to the floor, covering my tattered form. And then everything went black.

LATER, Nikki told me I was only unconscious about a minute. But it seemed like hours. During the blackout, I was back, once again, in my father's arms, crying uncontrollably over the loss of my brother.

"He lets bad things happen, son, for many reasons," he told me. *"It pains him. Believe me when I tell you that. But He has His reasons. I can't answer your questions completely. No one knows the answer and smarter men than I have asked since mankind first felt the pangs of death."*

I looked up at him as he wiped away a tear streaking down my cheek. Across my room, leaning against the frame of my door, was mom. I knew she was there before I ever saw her. She smelled of lilacs and cinnamon. A gentle, knowing smile crept up the side of her face while her mournful, bloodshot eyes leaked a steady flow of tears. Despite her own anguish, she nodded encouragement at me.

"But I can tell you one reason. There is one good reason God allows such things to happen to us," he said, putting his arm around me and pulling me close. *"It's to remind us of the thirst we have for Him. When things go wrong...when life is at its worst, it is then that we truly understand our need, our absolute dependence on Him. He created us that way. To hunger for Him. To thirst for His presence. It's primal. Programmed into us. And only during our darkest times, do we recognize the God-shaped drought each of us lives with...needing to be drenched with His love. Only His love is able to satisfy the spiritual dehydration that dries out our souls."*

We thirst for Him, I thought. *I thirst for Him. I need Him. Oh, dear Jesus, I need you! I can't do this alone. Not anymore.*

"And you'll never have to. Not anymore," I seemed to hear a voice say in the darkness. *"I'll always be with you, Jack."*

"JACK!"

I heard my name being called out again, only this time accompanied by a sharp ringing tone.

"Jack, wake up! Please!"

Oh, geeze. What the heck did I have to drink last night?

My brain pounded against the inside of my skull, struggling desperately to escape the confines of my thick head and get the heck out of there. I opened my eyes, but all was dark. I couldn't see a thing.

"Jack? He's awake," Nikki's voice. It seemed a long way off to me. 'Thank God, he's awake."

A low hiss whispered past my ear. I was being held. Strong arms. Solid. Must be Randy or Landers. I couldn't tell. Even with my sight still foggy, I felt the world spinning madly around me. The ringing in my ears wouldn't let up.

Something brushed through my hair. My vision began to clear and I found myself looking up at the chalk-white outline of Vera's jenglot face. She seemed serene, holding me in her arms, running her talons gently through my hair. For a brief moment, I imagined a smile across her lips.

"Jack, don't panic," Landers said. "We've got you covered."

"Scott, give it a rest," Nikki said, moving within my field of vision and kneeling down at my feet.

Vera tensed, growling softly at Nikki's approach. Then eased a bit, moving aside to let the missionary she'd developed a deep bond with take care of my pain wracked body.

Without a word, Nikki moved around, cradling my head as Vera backed away.

"No, wait!" I croaked. "Vera. Stop."

I looked over at Landers. Surprisingly, his gun was slung over his back. He and Randy moved forward, hauling me to my feet. Well, I wasn't actually sure I still had feet until I looked down and saw them.

Then I searched the room for Vera. She wasn't hard to miss. A trail of blood from several gaping wounds led my eyes straight towards her as she hobbled around the lab tables, bent down, and came up with a long, silver object.

Randy's thermos. It hadn't detonated like it was supposed to. We'd actually set two small explosive devices in it. One was intentionally obvious; hoping it would fool whatever demolitions experts examined it. The other was a little more devious, a small charge set in the confined tubing filled to the brim with ball bearings and Russian vodka. It was supposed to have been used as a distraction in case Witz mercenary team was late.

Slowly, tentatively, Vera strode towards us. Her hand outstretched, offering the thermos. I wasn't quite sure what she had in mind.

"That's a good idea," Landers mumbled. Apparently, he was smarter than me. "We need to blow the lab."

"Why?" Randy asked. "We'll just snatch the Queen and get out of here. The lab won't do anyone much good."

"We can't take the Queen back, Randy."

My friend stared at Scott before turning to me. If I could have spoken, I'd have argued out of principle, but I knew he was right. Despite the danger it posed to the villagers in the Malaysian valley, the Queen's existence posed an even greater threat to the unsuspecting masses throughout the world.

"What do you mean we can't take her back?" Nikki asked. "We promised. We gave our word to Shantili."

Landers eyed me warily. I closed my eyes and nodded my assent, praying that God would forgive me for the lives the jenglot would take when their blood craze ebbed.

"Because too many people know about the jenglot and Krenkin's experiments. People outside of ENIGMA who don't share the same scruples as me," he said. "In another few years there'd be another expedition, another lab. More human guinea pigs turned into blood thirsty monsters." He looked over at Vera with an apologetic shrug. If she understood the gesture, she made no sign.

"The only way to ensure that this never happens again is to destroy the Mother." He reached out and took the thermos from Vera's outstretched hand. He unscrewed the lid, reached his hand inside and pulled out a severed red wire. "It's what I thought. Their demo team disabled it before it went off. They were good."

He looked over at me again.

"It's your call," he said sternly. "You're in charge here."

I pointed a shaky finger at the other grenades lying on the floor. "Do it," I whispered. "Use them for more boom." Trying to form the words 'explosive power' wasn't something I could manage.

Without comment, Landers dashed over to the glass crate containing the hibernating remains of the jenglot Mother. As far as anyone knew, she was the only one of her species in existence. Where she came from...what she was...was still only vague speculations floating around in my head. After this, I would never find out the truth.

Scott fiddled with the wiring in the thermos, and reset the timing device tucked neatly at the bottom of the container. He then resealed it, screwing the lid tight, and set the three remaining grenades in a semi-circle on top of the glass tomb.

"Okay, it's done," Landers said, turning towards us. "We have five minutes to high-tail it out of here."

We moved towards the door again. I hung onto the shoulders of Randy and Landers as it slid open for us.

"Wait. Vera," I said, looking behind me. She stood there, in the center of the room, her clawed hand resting on the box containing the Queen. "Vera, come on."

She looked over at me, but didn't move. She didn't need to

speak for me to know what she was thinking. Crouching down, she lowered herself to the floor and curled up in a ball. A long, sad hiss whisking from her throat.

"Don't. Please don't," I said. "We can find a cure. Something."

Nikki moved over to me, putting a soft hand on my shoulder, tears welling from the corner of her eyes.

"Scott's right," she said to me. "That's not Vera anymore. She's already dead. She died the moment they injected her with that serum and she wants to rest. To ease the suffering she feels."

Tears rushed down my face. It wasn't manly, I know. It wasn't heroic or brave. But it was the only thing my crushed spirit could do at the moment. I knew Nikki was right. I owed it to Vera to let her go. The injuries she'd sustained in her fight with Krenkin were obviously mortal. But knowing something and accepting it are two entirely different things.

Vera looked up at me again with a silent nod. I knew exactly what she meant.

"I love you too, sis."

And I turned and let them lead me from the room.

35

We'd met up with Witz and what was left of his team topside and surveyed the damage. After some post-battle patch up work on the injured, my mercenary buddy fled the compound in all terrain vehicles he'd stolen from a nearby drug lord. His debt had definitely been cancelled as far as I was concerned. Of course, I knew before long, he'd be back in my pocket again—he really was a bad poker player.

Landers stayed behind when we left Siberia to clean up the mess Krenkin and his research had made. I still had major trust issues with him, but he'd proven himself pretty well in the end.

We soon started making our way back to the good old USA, but not before making a quick stop again in Malaysia. I'd gone back on my word. Not something I took lightly and let Shantili's people down. Sure they were bloodsucking mutant hybrids. Sure they'd tried killing me and my friends on a number of occasions. But now, having experienced the horror of Krenkin's experiment first hand and the indescribable suffering that went with it, I shared a certain understanding of them. If not a great deal more compassion.

Fortunately for the local villagers, most of the jenglot had been destroyed in the battle with Krenkin's men in the temple. The few surviving jenglot were not happy over the loss of their Queen and it took all my charm, and a few well placed shots in the air from the M4 rifle Randy had taken from Siberia, to convince them not to string us up like Christmas geese. But in the end, they saw it our way.

Nikki had said her goodbyes to the friends she'd made in Pingitti. She'd served the people well, but now, she said, it was time to move on. See what other things God had in store for her.

I guess you want to know about Nikki and me. I'm not sure what to say. Something was definitely different between us, though I couldn't put my finger on it to save my life. She was still the irritating, stubborn, and brash woman I'd first met in Pingitti, but I knew without a doubt that I cared a great deal for her. And though we never discussed it openly, she felt the same. Why spoil it by dissecting the relationship with words and labels, right?

And soon after, I found myself resting comfortably in the soft, leather seat cushions in the first class cabin of a transatlantic flight to Washington. Senator Stromwell had footed the bill, so who was I to argue. It was definitely much better accommodations than the junk pile we'd flown in upon our arrival to Malaysia, though I was still annoyed they'd forced Arnold to stay in the cargo hold of the plane. He was so sensitive about being kept in a cage.

"Are you okay?" Nikki asked, leaning up against me in our joined seat.

I opened my eyes, staring at the clean, beige ceiling of the cabin. Reaching up, I pulled the vent forward, feeling the cool, recycled air wash over my sunburned face.

"I don't know," I said. "Too early to tell."

"If it makes you feel any better...she asked Christ to forgive her. She trusted Him."

I sat up, gently pushing her away and stared.

Yeah, she trusted Him and look where it got her. But I knew the thought wasn't fair. I've seen a great many things in my life... creatures and beings that assure me there's so much more to life than the little time spent in the here and now. The things that happen to us—the pain we feel—are only temporal. There's so much more at stake than our immediate happiness.

"I'm glad," I said, closing my eyes again and leaning back in the chair. She followed close behind, her hand resting against my chest. The top of her head nestled just below my chin. "Nikki?"

"Yes, Jack?"

"Do you ever thirst for Him? For God?" I cracked one eye open.

She raised her head and faced me, an odd expression marking her face. "I suppose. Not nearly enough, I'm afraid. I think we all do really. I think He made us that way. But they say that by the time a person's mouth is dry and parched and literally aching for water, it's almost too late. They're already dehydrated and they didn't even know it. I think most of us are that way with God too."

I closed my eye again and mumbled something softly to her, but I couldn't tell you what it was. I was asleep before the words left my mouth.

THE CHAIR I sat in cut right into my back, its hard pine wood jutting in just along my spine. For a senator's office, it wasn't very comfortable. But then, that's what happens when you decorate it with Eighteenth Century antiques from the homes of some of America's Founding Fathers.

I looked over at the large, robust form of Stromwell, leaning back in his own, very comfortable looking office chair, a long stemmed pipe clenched tight in his teeth. He stroked Arnold's ear, as the dumb mutt lay curled in the man's large lap, kicking his hind feet in doggy bliss.

Traitor, I glared at my supposed faithful dog. His ears fell back on his head in remorse, but continued letting the senator scratch his most sacred of all petting spots.

Nikki sat primly in a chair next to him, the perfect picture of an obedient southern daughter. She gave me a knowing wink and smiled.

"Dr. Jackson," he said, his teeth shining under the bushy, Teddy Roosevelt mustache cascading liberally over his thick, pink lips. "I can't tell you how thankful I am you managed to bring Nikki back to me safe and sound. As agreed, five hundred thousand dollars has been wired to your account."

I nearly choked. "Five hundred? Sir, we agreed on three."

"I'm aware of that son, but you did such a great job, I thought you earned it."

I glanced at Nikki, then dropped my eyes. "No sir, I can't take it. As a matter of fact, I'm giving it all back to you."

"What? Why on earth would you want to do that?" he asked, pulling his wire rimmed glasses from his nose and leaning towards me.

I stared at both of them for several seconds, struggling with the best way to proceed. No matter how many ways I turned it over in my head, there was just no easy way to get around this.

"Nikki, I need to speak to your father alone for a minute."

Her eyes narrowed and her right brow arced, but she stood from her chair, kissed her father on the forehead and turned to the door without a word. I watched as she ambled from the room, closing the door behind her. Then I turned back to Stromwell.

"I'm going to be blunt with you Senator."

"I'd expect nothing less," he leaned back in his chair again and took a pull on his pipe.

"Good. Because I think you're as crooked as the Mississippi, Senator. This whole thing has stunk from the get go and I think you're behind it."

He narrowed his eyes and I knew where Nikki had inherited it from. He pulled his pipe from his mouth sat it on the ashtray and glared at me for a second. Then he laughed. I mean, it wasn't just a brief snort of a man whose nerves fluttered throughout his body. Nor was it the eerily poignant cackle of a crazy loon like Krenkin or Shantili. It was the warm, deep rooted, raucous laughter of a man genuinely amused without a trace of malice or pride. It was a rich, deep throated roar of mirth, shaking his stomach against the snug contours of his suit vest.

"That son, is most definitely blunt," he said between laughs. "I knew I liked you for a good reason."

His reaction was unsettling to say the least. I'd expected the practiced, slimy tactics of a seasoned spin doctor, skating through the issue like a snake in tall grass. I suspected anger, hurled threats and insults. But not this.

"And you think this because of ENIGMA?" he said, reining in his amusement.

I started, never expecting him to own up to any involvement with Landers' organization. Scott had sworn the senator's ignorance in the matter. He'd said Stromwell had been a mere pawn in his superiors' mandate to gain intelligence on the jenglot and Krenkin. But with the big man's question, I realized that either Landers had lied to me again or he hadn't known.

"Well, er, yeah," I fumbled for the words. "It makes sense. You set us on the chase for the jenglot with an ENIGMA agent posing as a career military man. The research I dug up on you revealed a long standing seat on the Senate's Scientific Advancement Committee. You spent a great deal of time in Russia as an attaché for the U.S. consulate in Moscow, giving you access to knowledge regarding Krenkin and his experiments."

"You seem to be well informed," he said, his warm smile widening. "And this is why you won't take my money?"

"I'm not finished yet," I growled. Shantili's words about Nikki's coincidental assignment came back to me. "And part of me thinks that you might have played a part in getting your daughter sent to Malaysia in the first place. It wouldn't take much to get the missionary organization sponsoring her to switch destinations. She told me herself that her first choice had been Afghanistan, but plans had been changed at the last minute."

"Now that," the big man stood up, slamming his fist against his desk. "I will not hold to. Yes, I do know about ENIGMA. I'm even one of the agency's charter members. But I'll draw the line when you accuse me of intentionally putting my little girl in danger. If you ask her, she'll tell you that I did everything I could to stop her from going over there."

"Well, you better think long and hard about who in the agency might not have had such qualms about Nikki's well being," I said, pulling a fresh cigar from my pocket and lighting it. I hadn't been in any life threatening danger, but at the moment, I just needed a good old fashioned smoke to calm the nerves. "Because someone switched her plane ticket at the perfect time. Think about it. I don't believe in coincidences, do you?"

Senator Stromwell stood silent, blinking at me. Then he lowered himself in his chair and pulled the pipe back into his mouth.

"You've got a point," he said finally. "I'll look into it."

"You do that," I said, standing to my feet and reaching out to shake his strong, meaty hand.

"You'll seriously not accept payment?"

I tried not to wince. A half million was a lot of research money. I was throwing away first class travel to easy street.

"I can't," I said. "I don't know where your money's been."

I moved towards the door and stopped, turning back to Stromwell. "But I do know what you could do if you felt compelled to thank me anyway. A scholarship fund," I said, Vera's sweet, caring face flashing through my mind's eye. She would definitely approve of that. "Specifically for abused, neglected, or abandoned girls seeking to better their lives by getting an education. That's what you can do."

Stromwell's grin stretched from ear to ear.

"A scholarship, eh?" he chuckled. "I like it. You're a good man, Dr. Jackson. An honest one. World needs more men like you to keep us political types on the up and up."

I didn't respond. I simply turned around and reached for the door knob.

"Dr. Jackson, wait," the senator said. "There's one more thing I'd like to offer."

I looked back at him and waited for him to speak, my hand clutching the knob.

"ENIGMA, Jack," he said, intentionally using my preferred name. "I'm talking about you becoming the project director of ENIGMA."

I WALKED out of Stromwell's office, seeing Nikki rise from the waiting room chair as I approached. She took my hand and we walked out of the antechamber and into the halls of the Capitol building.

"So what did you and daddy have to talk about?" she asked after several minutes of silence.

I pushed ahead, not taking my eyes away from the long hall we walked, the clip clop of Nikki's high heels echoing through the marble corridor. Arnold scurried across the floor, trying like crazy to keep his balance on the slick floors.

"Jack?"

I looked over at her pleading eyes, not stopping. And sighed.

"I confronted your old man on his involvement with ENIGMA," I said. "He confirmed it and offered me a job."

"What?"

"Oh, yeah. It seems that daddy dearest was one of the founding members. Holds a great deal of clout with them even now. He knew about Landers the whole time, although I have a feeling Scott didn't have a clue."

"So, he was behind the experiments? Vera?"

"He denies any knowledge of that," I scowled. "Says we were supposed to be going on a research mission only. Get you safe. Find out what the jenglot were. He claims he didn't know about ENIGMA's deal with Krenkin."

She stopped, holding onto my hand and wheeling me around.

"And do you believe him?"

I looked down at the floor, tracing the contrasting white and dark of the marble with my eyes.

"Jack, do you *believe* him?"

I looked up at her. "I'm not sure. I think he's telling the truth. He seemed awfully concerned about the whole thing, which is why he offered me a job."

"With ENIGMA?" She almost laughed as the word slipped from her mouth.

"Yeah. He thinks the agency would benefit from someone like me. Someone with the knowledge and skills I have, but also with integrity. He thinks I might be able to keep them straight."

"Did you take it?" she asked, blowing a single strand of hair from her eye.

"I told him where he could stick ENIGMA and his job," I said, grinning. "Then he told me I'd have an almost unlimited budget for my research, complete control of the projects chosen to investigate...the whole nine yards."

"And?" she asked, a wary smile spreading across her face.

"Told him I'd have to think about it."

"Good enough," she said, starting to walk towards the doors and pulling me along. "Okay, enough chit chat. I'm starving. Let's go get something to eat."

"All right," I said, pulling another cigar from my pocket as I stepped out onto the D.C. sidewalk. "But only somewhere that allows dogs."

EPILOGUE

The thin man wiped the rain from his thick glasses as he dashed across the street towards the two story brick house, resting peacefully on the sleepy *cul de sac* in the quaint Maryland suburb. The winter months had been cruel to the perfectly maintained lawn. Where once there had been lush, flower beds and cherry blossoming trees, there now stood nothing but muck-soaked weeds and withering branches.

The man moved up the lawn, practically leaping over the three steps to the covered porch. He shook out his umbrella and stomped the water from his leather shoes.

If anyone had been watching, they would have seen him cringe as a streak of lightning flashed dangerously close, raising the hairs on the back of his hands with electricity. Shaking, the man turned the knob of the front door and stepped inside.

The interior of the home was warm and inviting. A fire burned from under a hearth lined with family pictures of grandchildren and great grandchildren. One black and white photo of a nice looking man and his equally attractive bride sat dust free on a table in the foyer.

"Hello?" the man called out, pulling the drenched raincoat from his shoulders and hanging it on a rack next to the door. "Is there anyone here?"

"Just a minute," came the dry, crackly voice of an elderly female from somewhere in the house. A few seconds later, a matronly old woman skittered out from swinging doors that led to the kitchen. A great smile beaming across her face. "Oh, it's you. It's so nice to see you again, young man. He's been expecting you. Go on up the stairs, first door on the left past the bathroom."

The man nodded, returning her warm smile and dashed up the steps, two at a time. He couldn't stop his legs from shaking as he padded silently down the hall way, making his way towards the office of one of the most powerful, albeit shadowy, men in Washington. He stopped just short of the door, taking several short breaths.

"Stop your lollygagging and get in here," commanded a voice from inside.

The man opened the door and stepped into a plush office filled with the most unique collection of oddities he'd ever seen. An oddly malformed, humanoid skull with two large horns curling around each side, rested in a glass box on an end table next to a burgundy leather couch. The stuffed remains of a strange, leathery winged bird perched upon a petrified tree in the corner of the room. The young man found himself wishing he could spend days just inventorying the magnificent discoveries on display in the vast study. He had a feeling Jack would have a coronary if he ever saw the place.

The man looked across the room at the elderly geezer staring at him from behind a massive mahogany desk. The old man motioned for him to sit in the chair opposite the desk.

"Mr. Sanderson," the man addressed his elder. "It is most enjoyable to see you again."

"Enough with the pleasantries," Sanderson said, sticking an unfiltered cigarette between his lips and lighting it with a cough. "What's going on with Project NEPHILIM? The jenglot?"

The younger man felt a bulge moving up his throat, sweat glistening from his forehead. He wasn't looking forward to this discussion.

"Well, sir, I did as you asked and joined Jack's team..."

"That's not what I asked," Sanderson growled. "Tell me about the project."

"Um, well, it's kind of both good and bad news," he said.

Sanderson blew a stream of smoke above his head, inhaling it again before it dissipated completely.

"The bad news first," he said, closing his eyes and leaning back in his chair.

"Okay, the bad news. Well, we were correct in our assessment of Agent Landers. He disobeyed direct orders, betrayed Krenkin, and assisted Dr. Jackson and his team in destroying the jenglot Mother Queen."

Sanderson leaned forward, eyeing the younger man fidgeting nervously in his seat. "That was to be expected. Landers is an idealist. He's never seen eye to eye with me on anything. Additionally, ENIGMA isn't even one of my agencies. If it was, that sort of thing would never happen. What about the jenglot created by Krenkin?"

"All of them were either casualties or just disappeared from the compound. Even Jackson's Russian friend..." her name caught around the lump growing inside the man's throat, his own regret still fresh in his mind. "Vera Pietrova, didn't make it."

"So that's it then? All the money we've sunk into the jenglot program just sucked down the drain?"

"Well, sir..."

"Let's have it," Sanderson said, blowing a stream of smoke at the younger man.

"The mercenary, Kowskowitz, sir...he was able to procure a

sample of the Mother Queen's DNA from a cache in Krenkin's own sleeping quarters without Jack finding out," the man said awkwardly, pushing his glasses up higher on his nose. "As was our agreement with him."

"And we have the sample now?"

"Not exactly sir. Kowskowitz is trying to renegotiate. He's threatening to go to Jack with everything he knows."

"And the problem with that is?"

"He's asking for a ridiculous sum of money, sir. Three million to be exact."

"And if we don't pay him, he takes the DNA back to the cryptozoologist and tells him everything...especially about you."

"That pretty much sums things up, yes," the younger man said.

"Well, then, go ahead and pay the man what he's asking," Sanderson said with a grin. "There's too much at stake. The NEPHILIM experiments are too important to me. The jenglot research is vital to the project. Get the specimen at any cost."

The old man stood from his chair, walked over to a painting on the wall behind him and pulled it back, revealing a small safe. A few flicks of the wrist and the safe was opened, several stacks of currency raked into Sanderson's hand.

The younger man moved around the table, taking the money and securing it in an alligator skin briefcase resting against Sanderson's desk.

"The money really isn't important. It's the project. Its mission. Its secrecy. Those are what really matter. We can't have big mouthed mercenaries spouting out our secrets, can we? No. The money is unimportant," Sanderson said with a smile. "Besides, our friend Kowskowitz is a professional soldier. A great many dangers lurk on the battlefield."

The younger man gulped as he locked the briefcase and headed towards the office door.

"Oh, and Mr. Leeds?" Sanderson said.

Marc Leeds wheeled around to look at his boss. "Yes, sir?"

"Be sure to give my best to Dr. Jackson next time you see him."

Without a word, Marc turned back to the door and ran out of the house, heart thumping heavily against his chest.

CPSIA information can be obtained
at www.ICGtesting.com
Printed in the USA
LVHW041112301121
704812LV00008B/536

9 781088 014028